Lady ~~~~~~~~~~~~ grew very still; the color faded from her cheeks, and her smile drew itself into a frown. He watched her eyes go wide as the realization dawned on her, the pieces of the puzzle falling into place at last.

Somewhere in the trees above, birds twittered and flitted about; the edge of the Serpentine lapped quietly at their feet. The springtime afternoon marched onward as if today were but one of a string of simple, idle days, each the same as the last.

But for Harclay and Lady Violet, today was not quite so simple, nor so idle. It was suddenly complicated, mined with explosive truths and well-played deceptions and a most thrilling episode of a physical encounter. It was impossible; it was improbable.

And great God above, it thrilled Harclay to no end. He hadn't felt such excitement since he was a boy, allowed to accompany his father on the hunt for the first time. He would never forget the way the rifle had felt in his hands, the pounding of his heart as he took aim.

Granted, he'd ended up shooting the poor loader in the arse, a crime for which dear Papa had whipped him sense-less. But the thrill remained imprinted on Harclay's imagi-nation nonetheless, the same thrill he now experienced under the accusatory gaze of Lady Violet Rutledge.

She took a deep breath, all the while her blue-gray eyes never leaving his.

"It's you, isn't it?" she said, swallowing. "You're the thief who stole the French Blue!"

The Gentleman Jewel Thief

JESSICA PETERSON

B
BERKLEY SENSATION, NEW YORK

THE BERKLEY PUBLISHING GROUP
Published by the Penguin Group
Penguin Group (USA) LLC
375 Hudson Street, New York, New York 10014

USA • Canada • UK • Ireland • Australia • New Zealand • India • South Africa • China

penguin.com

A Penguin Random House Company

THE GENTLEMAN JEWEL THIEF

A Berkley Sensation Book / published by arrangement with the author

Berkley Sensation Books are published by The Berkley Publishing Group.
BERKLEY SENSATION® is a registered trademark of Penguin Group (USA) LLC.
The "B" design is a trademark of Penguin Group (USA) LLC.

For information, address: The Berkley Publishing Group,
a division of Penguin Group (USA) LLC,
375 Hudson Street, New York, New York 10014.

ISBN: 978-0-425-27207-7

PUBLISHING HISTORY
Berkley Sensation mass-market edition / July 2014

PRINTED IN THE UNITED STATES OF AMERICA

10 9 8 7 6 5 4 3 2 1

Cover art by Aleta Rafton.
Cover design by George Long.
Interior text design by Kelly Lipovich.

To Ben, for making my every dream come true.
You are one hunk of burnin' love.

Acknowledgments

I owe a lot of chocolate, and even more wine, to the following fabulous ladies and gentlemen who helped bring this work of fiction to life:

My agent, Alexandra Machinist, from whose incredible imagination the gentleman jewel thief first sprung. You are an inspiration, a rare talent, and an absolute joy to be around. When I grow up I want to be just like you.

Stefanie Lieberman, whose insight into the first drafts of this book saved it from being one hot mess. Your instincts are spot-on; gratitude for sharing your gifts with me.

My editor, Leis Pederson, who not only has the sexiest last name on the planet (ha!), but also took a chance on me and my gentleman jewel thief. You're the editor I've always dreamed of having. Your insight is immaculate, and you have a knack for picking the best lunch places in the city. Can't wait to do it again.

My copy editor, Sheila Moody, who should be canonized. Your attention to detail is nothing short of a marvel. Many, many thanks for your patience, your dedication, and your brilliant suggestions. I cannot express to you how much I appreciate the time you spent with Harclay and Violet.

My high school English teacher, Mr. Dailey, for encouraging the writer in me.

My family, especially my parents, who were endlessly patient with their awkward, weird, Mr. Darcy–obsessed teenage daughter. I'd like to think I turned out okay.

My friends, for loving me for who I am, and teaching me to do the same.

Steve McQueen and Pierce Brosnan, who provided badass inspiration for my (hopefully) badass hero. You are sexy; never change.

One

City of London, Fleet Street
Spring 1812

The evening's winnings in his pocket and a small, if indiscreet, smile on his lips, Lord William Townshend, tenth Earl of Harclay, strode into the bank. At once a gaggle of bespectacled Hope & Co. employees gathered at his elbow. One peeled back his coat while complimenting Harclay's cologne, even though he wasn't wearing any ("a vigorous choice, my lord, most vigorous!"); another took his hat and gloves and bowed, not once but three times, and appeared about to burst into sobs of gratitude.

Biting back a sigh, Harclay continued up the familiar wide staircase, polished with such enthusiasm as to make it impossible to climb without the aid of the sturdy balustrade. He admired the zeal of Mr. Hope's bankers, he really did. But to be greeted as if Harclay were Julius Caesar, triumphantly marching on Rome—it was a bit much, considering he came not to conquer Pompey, but to deposit a thousand or two.

And Mr. Hope—ah, he was an altogether different breed.

It was why Harclay had, upon his accession to the title some eight years before, chosen to transfer his not inconsiderable wealth to the then-unknown Hope & Co. For Mr. Hope possessed qualities Harclay was hard-pressed to find in his English set: Hope was foreign and exotic and infinitely odd, but more than that, he was possessed of a sort of magnetic brilliance that was at once off-putting and entirely hilarious. That Hope had, through wise investment, nearly doubled Harclay's fortune—well, the earl considered that quite secondary.

The doors to Hope's office were flung open to welcome him, and he strode into the cavernous room—more a museum, really, with a Japanese samurai suit of armor squatting in one corner and a passel of Persian rugs rolled up in another. Above Mr. Hope's enormous desk hung a monumental Botticelli, which, despite Harclay's admiration, was a bit indecent for a place of business, considering it depicted a breast-bearing goddess.

And then there was Mr. Hope: tall, broad, imposing in that strange way of his. He stood and, though Harclay waved him off, proffered a short but lyrical bow. Behind them the doors swung shut and Harclay let out a small sigh of relief.

"My dear Lord Harclay," Mr. Hope said. "To have braved such hellish weather to seek my company—why, after a brandy or two I'd blush! Speaking of . . . ?"

Hope raised an eyebrow to a stout pine sideboard crowded with crystal decanters winking seductively in the dull morning light.

"Good man, it's not yet noon."

Mr. Hope blinked. "Nonsense. In the north it's common knowledge a nip in the day keeps the doctor at bay. Please, do sit."

As Hope busied himself at the sideboard, Harclay folded his tall frame into a rather wide but rickety antique chair. It groaned ominously beneath his weight.

"I say, is this chair sound? I would hate to damage the"— he cleared his throat—"*lovely* piece."

Hope waved away his words, setting a heavy blue crystal snifter before him.

"Ah." Hope smiled, landing in his own chair, snifter pressed to his nose. "I daresay it will withstand its current burden, all things considered. It once belonged to Henry VIII—did you know he weighed over twenty stone at his death?"

"I did not," Harclay said, shifting his weight so that it rested not on the chair but on his own legs. "However did you manage to discover such a treasure?"

"That profligate prince regent of yours," Hope said. "Idiot fellow's so deep in debt he'd sell his own bollocks for a fair price. Whatever is left of them, anyway."

"Fair point," Harclay replied.

"No matter." Mr. Hope took a long, satisfied pull of brandy. "Assuming you have not come to discuss the prince's rather epic stupidity—in which case I am *most* happy to oblige you— how might I be of assistance this morning, Lord Harclay? A withdrawal, perhaps?"

Harclay shook his head. "Not this time. A deposit, actually, and a rather large one."

He placed his snifter on the desk. Reaching into his jacket pocket, he produced a stack of banknotes, each signed by its respective debtor and stamped with the credentials of various banks and agents.

Harclay watched in amusement as Hope struggled to smother his surprise. The banker coughed, pounding on his chest, and finally managed to wheeze a reply.

"Good God, my lord, did you ransack the royal treasury? Bankrupt the local gentry?" He lowered his voice to a whisper. "Not a duel, surely? Winner takes all? I hear blood wages are quite the thing."

Harclay laughed. For a brief moment he thought of his Manton dueling pistols, gleaming, gorgeous things that were his constant companions during a rather raucous youth. Alas, they had remained in their velvet-lined box for some time now, but Mr. Hope's toes would positively curl if he knew how often those guns had been Harclay's saving grace.

"No, no," Harclay said. "I'm afraid it's just a bit of luck I've come across at White's, games of chance and all that."

Mr. Hope scooped up the stack of notes and rifled through them. Harclay could tell the banker was biting his tongue to keep from exclaiming at the number of zeros on each note.

Hope clucked his tongue. "Tsk-tsk. Those gentlemen

friends of yours should know better than to gamble with *the* Lord Harclay. Hell, even I've been warned about you. Something of a legend you've become; they say your luck never runs out. That your stakes are impossibly high."

Harclay, legs aching, leaned as far back as Henry Tudor's priceless chair would allow without splintering into a dozen pieces. "My companions at last night's table were"—here that secret smile returned to his lips—"in a rather generous mood."

"Well"—Mr. Hope held up the stack of notes with a smile—"all the better for you, my lord, though your accounts are already robust, yes, *most* robust. Many gentlemen of—ah, your particular age and station have quite the opposite problem, I'm afraid."

"Indeed," Harclay replied. He was hardly surprised. For all their swagger and impeccable breeding, most of his friends were frightfully broke. Harclay pitied the poor fellows and helped when he could; nonetheless, there was no helping his set's near-complete lack of intelligence and savvy, and the temptation to best them time and time again proved far too enticing.

"Very well," Mr. Hope said. He clapped the long edge of the notes against his desk to gather them into a neat pile. "I shall see to this at once."

"Excellent," Harclay said and made to rise. "And it goes without saying—"

Mr. Hope pressed his thumbnail to his lips. "To the grave, Harclay. Can't have word of your companions' most sizable losses getting to the papers or, worse, to their wives."

"Gratitude, good sir, I do appreciate your discretion," Harclay replied. He was about to turn and exit the room when Mr. Hope held up his hand.

"And one more thing," the banker said. "I assume you have not received the invitation I sent, some days ago? Post is dreadful this time of year, what with all this rain washing out the roads, and I know a man of your stature would never be so rude as to send a tardy reply."

Harclay detected the slightest trace of irony in Mr. Hope's words and replied with no small measure of his own. "I abhor rudeness, Mr. Hope, above all things."

For a moment Mr. Hope studied Harclay, his dark eyes

twinkling, but the earl merely returned Hope's gaze with a measured amount of disinterest.

Of course Harclay had received the invitation, and, as he had done with all others from Mr. Hope, he had blatantly, rudely ignored it, as had many of his friends. The banker was rich beyond imagining, indeed, with the tastes and fine manners of a gentleman, but alas bore no title; the more rigid of Harclay's set zealously scorned Hope while harboring a secret envy of his fortune and freedom.

That Hope did not have the good luck to be born into a blue-blooded family mattered not a whit to Harclay. No, his reason for ignoring Hope's invitation was rather more mundane. Every year, on the first Friday of May, Hope hosted the most extravagant and hotly anticipated ball of the season. Hope, in usual form, attached to each ball a sufficiently ridiculous theme. Last year, the more adventurous of the *ton* arrived dressed as popes, assassins, and breast-bearing courtesans for "The Murderous Medici"; the year before, it had been "One Thousand and One Nights in the Emperor's *Hareem*," whatever that meant.

Harclay would rather forfeit his tongue, or even his manhood, than attend such a spectacle. The same tedious conversation with the same tedious debutantes; the crush of rooms and the smell of damp, drunken bodies; the spirited dances and inevitable swoons: all this glory, but raised to fever pitch by daringly cut costumes, cunningly crafted masks, and Hope's rather impressive cellar of cognacs and brandies.

No, Harclay mused, no, thank you indeed.

"I know you haven't attended many of my humble soirees in the past," Mr. Hope said, reading Harclay's thoughts. "But this year, I'm doing something a bit different."

"Oh?" Harclay said, with a longing glance toward the exit.

"Oh, yes," Mr. Hope replied, a sly grin on his lips. "Imagine it, if you will: the glory days of Versailles, when the Sun King, Louis XIV, ruled over the most splendid and sumptuous court the world has ever seen. The feasts, the silks, the pomp—*the jewels*."

A pulse of interest shot through Harclay so quickly he struggled to catch it before it showed up on his face. Jewels?

Now, this was something interesting—something different, new, unexpected.

"I'll let you in on a little secret," Mr. Hope said, lowering his voice. "After much searching, I do believe I've managed to locate one of the French crown jewels."

"The French crown jewels?" Harclay drawled in his best monotone. "Didn't they disappear ages ago, at the start of the Revolution?"

Mr. Hope smiled. "Don't play dumb with me, my lord, for you are as familiar with the tale as anyone else. We know a band of thieves broke into the royal treasury shortly after poor King Louis XVI and Queen Marie-Antoinette were arrested. The thieves, and the jewels, seemed to have vanished overnight. And now, nearly twenty years later, one of said gems has resurfaced."

"But how—"

Mr. Hope daringly waved his finger. "A gentleman does not kiss and tell."

Harclay furrowed his brow. "I believe that applies to something else entirely—"

"As I was saying," Hope said, nearly perspiring with excitement, "I've managed to purchase the *very same jewel* worn by the King of France!"

Harclay paused, trying in vain to contain his curiosity. "Which jewel, exactly? Surely not—"

"The French Blue? Yes, that's the one. It is the crown jewel of my collection, so to speak."

Harclay made a show of an enormous yawn, though it did nothing to still the rapid beating of his heart. The French Blue!—a treasure indeed. It was rumored to be the size of an apricot, and the most brilliant diamond ever discovered. Harclay had, of course, heard whisperings of the curse attached to the stone; but these only increased his interest. An enormous diamond, worn by kings and cursed by their royal blood?

Marvelous!

"I plan to display the jewel at the ball, Friday next. I've hired half the British army to guard them," Hope said with a smug scoff, "but it will make quite the splash, the jewel, don't you think? Oh, do make plans to attend, Lord Harclay. 'The

Jewel of the Sun King: An Evening at Versailles'—really, how could you resist?"

Harclay let out a well-practiced sigh of resignation. "Perhaps," he replied. "I've a busy season ahead, you see; I make no promises. And my valet, he's been unwell, and I can't very well attend in the nude . . ."

But Mr. Hope smiled beatifically at Harclay's excuses, knowing he had won over the reluctant earl; as if he knew he had been the first to pique Lord Harclay's interest in a very, very long time.

Two

Duchess Street, near Cavendish Square

Lady Violet Rutledge arrived at Mr. Thomas Hope's ball early, at the host's request. Indeed, a bit too early; upon entrance into Hope Mansion's soaring hall, she realized that she, Auntie George, and her cousin, Lady Sophia Blaise, were Mr. Hope's very first guests.

Together the three ladies gawked at the grandeur that surrounded them as they shed their spencers and accepted tiny coupes of champagne from a footman dressed in a towering powdered wig and white satin breeches. Hope had, as usual, taken the Versailles theme quite seriously: fragrant white lilies with blooms as large as dinner plates covered every available surface, and from some corner of the house Violet could hear an opera singer warming up a particularly piercing voice. Hope's parties were many things, thought Violet, but certainly never dull.

As she, Auntie, and Sophia climbed the grand staircase, Violet remembered with a small smile the previous year's ball. Dressed as a rather voluptuous Lucrezia Borgia, Violet had taken a near-fatal tumble down these very same steps, only to land in the outstretched arms of Pope Alexander VI—Mr. Hope had cunningly replicated the pontiff's crooked nose with bread dough and a pair of buttons.

Truth be told, Hope's infamous balls were a rare opportunity for Violet to steal away for a carefree evening of dancing and, if she were honest, shameless flirtation. The burdens of her everyday life—an ailing father, the viperish gossip surrounding her unmarried state—seemed to evaporate in the perfumed air of Mr. Hope's ballroom.

A shiver of excitement coursed up her spine as they entered the grand space, a trio of gilt chandeliers glowing dimly from above. Something was going to happen tonight, something exciting: she could *feel* it, a thrilling spark in the center of her chest.

Musicians were setting up in a corner; Violet noticed even they were in costume, complete with satin bows and hideous white makeup. A long table covered in sumptuous silk linens stood against a far wall of tall windows and was set with the contents of Mr. Hope's celebrated cellar of rare brown liquors.

"This is dangerous," Auntie George whispered. "The lighting, the music, the brandy—it's altogether too romantic. An ogre would look handsome in this light. Promise me you'll stay out of trouble. No, not you, Violet, it's too late for you. But Sophia . . ."

Auntie George turned pointedly to her daughter, eyes narrowed in warning.

"I promise," Sophia quickly replied. Perhaps a bit *too* quickly, for Auntie reached out and pinched her ear.

Sophia's cheeks flamed. The poor dear trembled with anxiety; it was her first season and she had yet to master the butterflies that inevitably filled her belly at every event. Violet reached out and took her hand, giving it a good squeeze. Sophia managed a small smile.

"You're the loveliest nymph this side of the Styx," Violet whispered, setting the sleeve of her water goddess costume to rights. What a nymph had to do with the Sun King and his jewels, Violet hadn't the slightest clue; but Sophia loved the idea, and Violet thought the gauze appropriately scandalous.

"I know I say this every night," Violet continued, head bent to Sophia's, "but you've nothing to fear. You are lovely and far wittier than anyone else in that ballroom. If you find you are frightened, just imagine whomever you're talking to is in the nude. That'll put a smile on your lips, make no mistake."

Sophia's shoulders relaxed as she let out a little scoff. "An old trick of yours, sweet cousin?"

"It works wonders; you'll see."

Sophia glanced over Violet's head. "Mr. Hope hired an awful lot of footmen. Do you think their pistols are part of the costume?"

Violet turned to see a phalanx of satin-clad, broad-shouldered men enter the ballroom. They did not look at all like footmen; they wore dark, inscrutable expressions, and a few were missing teeth. Beneath their shiny, ill-fitting waistcoats, Violet could indeed make out the imprint of pistols—and rather large ones at that.

"Dear me, I should hope not," Violet replied. "How eccentric, even for Mr. Hope."

At that very moment the man himself came into view, striding into the ballroom behind his pistol-wielding servants.

"Good heavens," Violet murmured.

Beside her, Auntie George let out a low whistle. "How extraordinary!"

Mr. Hope was coiffed and stuffed and powdered into a towering likeness of the Sun King, Louis XIV, complete with gilded staff and a long, curly black wig. He even sported a pair of red-heeled shoes fastened with diamond-encrusted bows. On his brow rested a gleaming coronet set with sapphires the size of grapes that, Violet mused, were very likely genuine.

"*Mademoiselles,*" Mr. Hope said, grimacing as his staff impaled his foot. "*Bienvenue à Versailles.* I was hoping you'd be the first to arrive."

"Mr. Hope," Violet said as Hope kissed her outstretched hand. "Your costume is nothing short of—er, epic. However do you manage to keep your neck straight with that wig on your head? It must weigh more than I do."

Hope swayed his head, the wig swaying along with it, and smiled. "Ghastly headache I've got, but it's worth it for the drama, don't you think?" He turned to Violet's cousin. "And Lady Sophia! You are a vision," he said, swallowing her whole with his dark eyes. He took her hand and pressed his lips to it, lingering a moment longer than was proper.

Sophia appeared happy, her face very pink, at his compliment. "Thank you, Mr. Hope," she said.

"A nymph, I presume? What a marvelous conceit. A goddess of the wood and of the hunt. The Sun King was a great hunter and would have delighted in such a creature. We go together, you and I."

By now, Hope was not only swallowing her cousin with his eyes but *devouring* her. Violet's narrowed gaze slid from Sophia to Hope and back again. It occurred to her that Sophia was not nervous; no, she was *excited*, thrumming not with dread but with anticipation.

Were she and Mr. Hope somehow acquainted, and not in the polite sense of the word? Though the tension between them was palpable, the very idea of them together was preposterous. Sophia was as quietly ambitious a debutante as any, and had set her sights on shackling a titled bachelor in possession of various crests and, hopefully, a castle. Violet couldn't blame her; having grown up in the tumult of genteel poverty, Sophia was wise to seek the stability, and profitability, of such a match.

Mr. Hope—well, Hope was a banker, a tradesman, and a foreigner besides; darkly handsome, too. He was, in short, everything that kept Auntie George awake at night; everything that should send a hopeful debutante like Sophia running for the proverbial hills.

And yet here they were, the banker and the debutante, blushing and flirting and smiling at each other, softly.

"Well"—Auntie George cleared her throat, looking anywhere but at the couple ogling each other—"what lovely decorations."

As if waking from a spell, Mr. Hope blinked and pressed one last kiss onto Sophia's hand. He rose with some reluctance, his satin costume rustling as he drew to his full height and motioned to one of his gap-toothed entourage.

"Surely you have been wondering why I selected tonight's theme, 'The Jewels of the Sun King,'" he began.

"I have," Violet replied, "and I wondered to which jewels the title referred, His Majesty's diamonds or his—"

"Genius!" Sophia said. "A genius theme, surely!"

He returned her compliment with a sheepish smile. "Why, thank you, Lady Sophia."

A beat of heated silence passed between them.

Again Auntie George cleared her throat. "Your theme, Mr. Hope?"

"Oh, yes!" he said. He turned to his guard-cum-courtier, who held out a box lacquered in black. Mr. Hope took the box in his hands and turned back to Lady Violet, his eyes dancing with excitement.

At once Violet's heart began to throb. Hope's box was the same size and shape of that which had held her mother's jewels, pearl necklaces and emerald brooches and bracelets of the finest jade beads. Over the years such priceless family treasures had been discreetly sold piece by piece, to cover the estate's mounting debts—debts she had only recently managed to pay off through her careful management of the family's investments. Violet was left with virtually nothing but her mother's simple gold wedding band, a tiny thing she now wore on a chain around her neck. It was her most treasured possession.

But here was Mr. Hope, proffering what was sure to be a jewel the size of a teacup. It made Violet dizzy, and not in a lovely, light-headed way.

"I have here in my hands a most precious jewel," Mr. Hope said gravely. "A priceless jewel, first worn by the great shahs of the Mughal court, and then by the kings of France. Louis the Sun King wore it pinned to a ribbon around his neck; Marie-Antoinette—yes, the *very one*!—is rumored to have smuggled it in her bodice on an ill-fated escape attempt from Paris."

Slowly, with great care, Mr. Hope unlatched the clasp on the box. Violet thought she might be sick with anticipation.

"Ladies," Mr. Hope continued, "I present to you *le bleu de France*, the French Blue."

Violet wished to remind Hope that she was perfectly capable of understanding French (though her powers of speech were quite dreadful), and that it would please her very much if he would stop flaunting his flawless command of the language; but as soon as her eyes landed on the glittering stone the breath left her body and she stood mute, transfixed.

For there, nestled in a puddle of fine velvet, was an enormous diamond, cut in an oblong circle roughly the size of a fig. It winked at once blue, then gray; Violet could even detect flashes of red and deep purple in its facets.

"My salts!" Auntie George cried. "Someone get my smelling salts!"

The diamond was beautiful, blindingly so. It was possessed of a gravity, a strange seduction, that made her want to reach out and touch it. To think King Louis XIV had once held this diamond in his royal fingertips! How dazzling he must have been, dressed in ermine and cloth of gold, the French Blue slung about his neck. To which ceremonies had he worn it? To which assemblies and balls and illicit, athletic couplings, conducted in the shadowy halls of Versailles, had the diamond been witness?

Really, the mind boggled.

"It's beautiful," Violet said breathily.

The banker positively beamed. "My pièce de résistance, as they say."

"Indeed," Violet replied, gaze transfixed on the jewel. "I've never seen anything quite like it. Even our own king, poor devil, doesn't have diamonds like this."

"It would be a great honor," Hope said, focusing his gaze on Violet, "if you, as one of my first clients and a dear friend, would do me the honor of displaying the French Blue to my guests and wear it about your neck this evening. I do believe it's the same shade of blue as your eyes."

Violet gaped at her host as if he'd just laid her flat on her back with a blow to the nose. Instinctively she fingered the gold band that hung from the chain about her neck. "I couldn't possibly," she said, eyes never leaving the gem. "Though it is lovely, the loveliest I've seen—"

Mr. Hope waved away her words. Another of his sinister men approached, bearing a second box. Mr. Hope opened it and produced a collar of exquisite diamonds, ropes of them dangling in various lengths from a single necklace.

The banker must have caught them staring, for he smiled and said, "On loan, from one of my—ah, associates. I thought it would be a perfect accompaniment to the French Blue."

No doubt by "associate," Hope meant some enormously

wealthy Italian duke or an equally foolish Romanov. Perhaps even the prince regent; Mr. Hope was possessed of a wide and influential circle of such "associates," with whom he traded priceless antiques, exotic African pelts, and extravagant jewelry worthy of a tsarina.

Violet watched as Mr. Hope effortlessly affixed the French Blue to the collar of diamonds as if he handled such treasures every day, perhaps over tea. He then turned to face her, the necklace strung about his fingers like the silken fibers of a spider's web.

"May I?" he said.

Violet gulped, tucking the ring into the folds of her costume. "You may indeed, Mr. Hope," she replied and turned away from him, patting her hair to ensure it remained coiffed close to her head.

She gasped when he slid the necklace about her throat. The diamonds felt cold against her skin, electrifyingly so; she shivered visibly and at once he drew back.

"Are you all right, Lady Violet?"

"Yes, quite. What a thrill to wear the Sun King's diamond, truly," she said and shivered again. For a moment she wondered if *this* was what it felt like to be Diane de Poitiers, that infamously decorated mistress of Henri II; or perhaps Catherine the Great, cloaked in diamonds on the throne of her Winter Palace.

Violet stiffened her spine, squared her shoulders. It was a thrill, an honor, to have a small piece of such exalted history hanging from her neck.

The jewel nested in the small, tender indentation between her collarbones. It was heavy, though not so cold now, having warmed to her flesh. If she moved her head just so, she could catch flashes of extravagant brilliance as the molten light of the ballroom reflected off its surface.

She turned to face her audience, and by their stunned faces concluded the diamond was, indeed, the same shade of blue-gray as her eyes.

"Well, then," she said, feeling suddenly light-headed. "More champagne?"

Three

"Remember, Avery, this very spot," Harclay said, pulling on his gloves. "I've the oddest premonition the evening shall end early."

"Very well, my lord." Avery shut the carriage door. "We shan't move, nary an inch."

"Good. Always such a crush, getting out of these things."

He took a deep, vigorous breath as he made his way up the front steps. It was a fine night, a very fine night indeed, a clear night sky above, and the spring air soft and cool against his skin. Harclay couldn't remember a finer night, not in all his days; for tonight he felt thrillingly, achingly alive. His every sense tingled; his blood coursed hot and ready through his veins. Since his meeting with Hope some days before, Harclay's mood had been effervescent, joyful even—and now, at last, the time had come.

With no little satisfaction he noted he'd arrived at just the right moment and in just the right costume: Hope's guests were just getting in their cups, and the mood was light, jovial, as if the heady anticipation of the night's event had not yet worn off. Like half of those in attendance, Harclay was vaguely attired as a French courtier, with powdered hair and the most enthusiastically patterned jacket his valet could find. Even with purple paisley swirling about his breast, Harclay was hardly distinguishable from the other unfortunately attired gentlemen in the room.

The stage, it seemed, was set.

A footman appeared out of the ether and passed him a goblet of what looked to be claret. Harclay sniffed it and to his surprise discovered it was brandy. Rascal, that Mr. Hope, disguising his liquors as wine; rascal, and genius.

Before ascending the heavily carpeted staircase to the ballroom, Harclay allowed himself a few breaths to savor the moment. Sipping his brandy—Mr. Hope's selection was always damnably good—Harclay allowed himself a moment to be lost in thought. He hated to steal from the man, truly, he did. Hope was an odd fellow, surely, but a good one, an intriguing one, and Harclay might think twice before robbing him if it weren't for the man's million-pound fortune.

The diamond—well, it was a drop in the bucket, really, and far too great a temptation for Harclay to resist. Besides, he'd return the gem to Hope in due time, once Harclay concocted a scheme as daring, as brilliantly ludicrous, as the one he was to set in motion tonight.

Making his way at last toward the ballroom, the earl found himself in a jolly enough mood to converse with a circle of pimpled debutantes and their perspiring mamas. Music floated through the hall, and in a nearby drawing room he caught a glimpse of a famous prima donna performing an aria. The crowd was growing, hundreds and hundreds of flushed faces, and Harclay followed it into the two-story ballroom, the roar of conversation echoing off its tall, coffered ceiling. With a secret smile he glanced at the trio of monumental windows that lined the back of the space, their ink-black panes reflecting the quiver of a thousand candles.

An audible hush trailed in his wake as those he passed began to recognize him. He caught a snippet or two that made him grin:

"The Earl of Harclay . . . they say he deflowered an entire village in Sicily. Yes, the nuns, too!"

"He's never lost a bet. Man won ten thousand off the Duke of Kent—twice!"

"It's said he wagered his palace up in Oxfordshire on a bet that a certain gentleman could not seduce a certain lady."

Harclay allowed himself a small chuckle. One of his favorite wagers, that, and now a legend at White's.

Sweeping his gaze over the crowd, his eyes caught on the gleaming baubles that hung from the ears and wrists and necks of several ladies, and the more discreet jewels that decorated gentlemen's waistcoats, their pocket watches. All these were nothing, he knew, absolutely nothing compared to the French Blue.

But the jewel was nowhere in sight. He managed to press his way to the refreshment table, where he exchanged his empty goblet of brandy-disguised-as-wine for a fresh one. Pulse thumping gloriously in anticipation, he surveyed the gathered guests over the rim of his glass. Dancing was about to begin, and out of the crowd came shouted requests for a cotillion, a reel.

Harclay dug his pocket watch out of his waistcoat. Nearly half past eleven; he didn't have much time now. He glanced about the ballroom, his gaze meandering through the hundreds of bewigged heads. Hope's hired guns lurked none too discreetly in corners and doorways; though dressed in full Sun King regalia, they were as conspicuous as foxes in a henhouse.

Harclay followed their gazes—there were so damn many of them! he thought with a thrill—until his own landed somewhere at the far end of the ballroom, close to the couples who were gathering to dance. At last his eyes settled on the bare shoulders of a single female.

The lady in question stood with her back to him. Licking his lips, Harclay couldn't help but notice what a lovely slope of back it was: pale, smooth skin that rounded softly over sinew and proud but feminine shoulders. There was something distinctly erotic about her naked flesh, something seductive about the way she held herself. His eyes followed the line of her spine up to her neck; the tiny hairs there cast gold in the light of the room, and he imagined touching her fine skin, first with his fingers, then his lips . . .

No, his blood roared, though it did nothing to quell the familiar tightening in his groin. *Absolutely not, you randy, rutting pig; now is not the time, nor this the place.*

It was imperative that he focus not on lovely shoulders and skin but on the task at hand. The time was drawing near, and he needed his wits about him; the theft required a series of actions as deliberate and intricate as the steps of a country dance, and it wouldn't do to be distracted by the charms of a lady, no matter how lovely her skin and shoulders.

But heavens, they were most lovely, delicious even; and when she turned suddenly to face him his breath caught in his throat, for to his dismay—or perhaps his delight; he couldn't quite tell—her front was even lovelier than her back.

The earl loved women, admired them, and was, for a short spell five years before, even addicted to them. It was no great secret he'd enjoyed the charms of famous actresses, royal highnesses, an American or two. But of late his desire had cooled somewhat, for reasons he couldn't quite comprehend. He hadn't taken a lover for some months now, which, as England's most notorious lothario, Harclay found rather depressing.

So it was at once unsettling, inconvenient, and wholly pleasurable to feel desire pulse through his veins once again at the sight of a beautiful woman.

His desire raced to fever pitch as Harclay's eyes traveled from the lady's round eyes to the enormous glittering jewel that rested just above an enticing slice of cleavage.

The French Blue.

How clever of Hope, thought Harclay, for the jewel appeared all the more alluring worn around this striking woman's neck. Her eyes, gray-blue and dark, glittered the same shade as the diamond and were just as lovely. For a moment he lost himself in those eyes, impenetrable pools full of laughter and mischief and was that a bit of naughtiness twinkling at the edges?

His body went up in flames, pounding with desire: desire for her, for the diamond. It was lust like he'd never known, and he felt damnably, deliciously like himself for the first time in ages.

Harclay vaguely recognized her as Lady Violet Rutledge, daughter of the Duke of Sommer and heiress to his meager fortune. If Harclay remembered correctly, this was to be her third season; at her age, she was nearly on the shelf and, he mused, likely lonely, frustrated in more ways than one, and ripe for the picking.

It was too easy, really. If he'd known Hope had chosen *her* to wear the diamond, Harclay wouldn't have hired all the gunmen, and certainly not the acrobats. Hell, with a few choice words, a discreet grope here and there, Harclay could have Lady Violet in his bed and the diamond in his safe by half past midnight.

Besides, after a few turns in the sheets, he could easily divert her thoughts from the theft to rather more unsavory things. After a few hours with her in his arms, he could surely make her forget the crime, the diamond, the chaos that was about to ensue.

Making his way toward her, the earl made no effort to suppress the achingly enormous smile that found its way to his lips.

Lady Violet was chatting companionably with Mr. Hope and his Turkish antiques merchant when she felt the prick of someone's gaze at the back of her neck. At first she ignored it—she was, after all, wearing the Sun King's fifty-carat diamond about her neck—but when the sensation did not abate, and instead began to pulse with heat, she turned at last to face it.

God in *heaven*, it was that cad William Townshend, Earl of Harclay. He was positively devouring her with his gaze. In principle she despised the man, as a lady of good breeding ought. But in his smug smile and overwhelming allure, Violet saw a challenge; in his eyes she recognized her own thirst for a thrill.

A fellow adventurer.

She couldn't resist.

Harclay smiled, that *devil*, showing rows of perfectly straight white teeth as he approached from across the ballroom. The crowd seemed to part as he strode forward, falling away from the earl's tall, broad figure. Despite Mr. Hope's Versailles theme, the earl was dressed exquisitely in the very latest of fashion, a nonpareil the likes of which Violet had never seen. He wore an emerald coat of so dark a hue it appeared blue, and then black, when he moved this way or that; his purple waistcoat and black breeches were made of the finest satin and were cut so close Violet could easily discern the earl's delectable physique.

His stiff white cravat, simply yet skillfully knotted, set off the square slant of his most perfect jawline. Swallowing the image of his person now that he was in full view, Violet's heart caught in her throat and for a moment stopped beating altogether. He was handsome, darkly, devastatingly so; and like every woman with two eyes and a pulse, she was positively thrilled by him.

Every set of eyes in the room followed the earl as he took Violet's hand and placed his lips on her fingers. He rose and smiled again. Violet drew her lips into the most lascivious grin she could manage, the area between her palm and first knuckle burning with the memory of his kiss.

He drew close, his breath warm on her neck, and whispered, "A most lovely costume, Lady Violet. A wood nymph, I presume?"

Lord Harclay was shameless, whispering in her ear like a drunken goat; despite the flutter of her pulse—a warning, a thrill—Violet was captivated. He was handsome, surely, but it was his confidence, his defiance of every rule and manner and courtesy, that drew her in as a moth to a flame.

Grinning ever so slightly, she flitted her gaze to his breeches and raised a single brow. "I daresay you're the expert in wood, Lord Harclay."

It was brazen, it was indiscreet, and God forbid anyone should have overheard her say it; poor Auntie would never recover. And yet the look on Lord Harclay's face—barely contained shock, his color high with pleasure—made saying it well worth the risk.

"I have that effect on gentlemen," she continued breezily. "The diamond doesn't hurt, either. A beautiful spectacle, wouldn't you say?" Violet splayed her fingers across her chest on either side of the diamond, her littlest fingers toying with the low neckline of her gown.

"Beautiful indeed," he replied, drawing even closer.

The top of Mr. Hope's enormous wig appeared over Lord Harclay's shoulder.

"Lady Violet!" Hope said. He fingered her elbow while

directing a look of consternation at Lord Harclay. "I trust you find your present company agreeable?"

Her eyes never leaving Lord Harclay's, Violet replied, "I know the gentleman finds my company very agreeable indeed."

"Most arousing, yes," Harclay said with a small smile, fingering her other elbow.

Hope drew back, brow creased. After a moment he cleared his throat. "The two of you are already acquainted, then—"

Harclay wrapped his fingers about her arm and pulled her from Hope's grasp. "You must excuse us, Hope, but Lady Violet is positively parched."

She bit her lip. "But I'm not thirsty."

He turned his head, eyes sparkling with laughter. "Oh, I do believe you are, Lady Violet. Though perhaps not for drink."

The earl's hand slid to grasp her own as he led her through the crowd. In her chest her heart skipped a beat as the warmth of his palm seeped through her satin glove. His grasp was gentle but firm; he moved through the crush of bodies with patient authority, nodding politely at acquaintances as he went.

At last they reached the refreshment table. She tried to drop his hand but he held fast. He pulled her very close to him, hiding their joined hands beneath the table.

For a moment they stood beside each other without speaking. Violet tried in vain to catch her breath; it didn't help that, beneath the table, her hand kept brushing Lord Harclay's leg. His flesh felt impossibly solid, unyielding to her touch. For a moment she wondered if the rest of him felt as hard, as warm, as strangely inviting.

"Would you like the punch?" he asked, nodding at the enormous cut-crystal bowl in the center of the table.

"I usually find punch rather weak for my taste," she replied, pleasure coursing through her at his start of surprise, "but Hope's concoction is as potent as brandy."

Lord Harclay reached for a coupe of punch and handed it to Violet, his dark eyes flashing as they met hers. "I've never met a lady with a taste for brandy," he said. "At least not one who admits to it."

"I've quite a few vices that might surprise you," she replied, leveling her gaze with his, "and I'm not afraid to admit to any of them."

He tugged on her hand, pulling her even closer. So close that their noses nearly grazed each other. It took every ounce of her control not to wince, pull away . . or dive in and discover just what, exactly, his lips felt like against her own.

"I'd very much like to discover the nature of said vices," he said, voice low, smooth, full of forbidden things.

"If only you were so lucky," she murmured in reply, pulse thrumming.

He took another coupe of punch from the table and held it between them. "A toast, then," he said, "to your vices, in the hope that I shall indeed be lucky enough to partake in them."

Violet clinked her glass against his and brought it to her lips. "And what about you, Lord Harclay? Rumor has it you've no small number of vices of your own."

His eyes flicked to the French Blue. "More than you could possibly imagine, Lady Violet," he said and took a long pull of his punch.

She watched him drink, the sinewy muscles of his neck working in time to his lips. The effect was hypnotic; so hypnotic that she failed to notice the gentleman, a boy, really, behind her, elbowing his way to the tables, until it was too late.

His sharp elbow found purchase just between her shoulder blades, pushing her into Lord Harclay's chest with a force that knocked her breathless. The coupe turned over in her hand, and punch spilled down the front of her gown.

"Make way, make way!" the man bellowed. "Can't you see the crush? Move along!"

Violet felt Lord Harclay grow stiff against her. She looked up to see his eyes darken with wrath as he turned toward the offender.

Oh, no. No, no, *no*. Even through the haze of desire that hung between their bodies, she could tell this wasn't going to end well.

She was right.

Harclay stuck out his foot just in time to trip the boy. He flew ass over heels to the floor in a whirl of blue coattails and fine French lace.

After a beat the boy scrambled to his feet, face wide with

shock as a rather impolite shout of incensed disbelief escaped his lips. He tugged the lace at his sleeves into place and huffed, smoothing the scant hairs of his sideburns.

"Apologize to the lady," Harclay said quietly. He cupped her shoulders and turned her to face the thin, pockmarked boy she now recognized as the Marquess of Tarrington's son and heir. The rotten stench of liquor and sweat rose from the boy like smoke from a cigar.

The boy sniffed his nose even higher. "She was in my way."

Behind her, Violet felt Lord Harclay suck in an impatient breath. *"Apologize* to the *lady,"* he repeated.

By now a small circle of spectators had formed about them, their faces open with glee at the unexpected treat of a public confrontation.

"Please," Violet said, turning to Lord Harclay, "it's nothing; let's get on—"

"Apologize," the earl said yet again, this time through gritted teeth, *"to the lady.* And if you don't, I swear to make a bloody mess of that ghastly thing you call your face."

The boy swallowed, face red with embarrassment, and lowered his nose. "I'm sorry," he spat out and turned away.

But Harclay would have none of it. He reached forward and none too gently grasped the boy by the shoulder, turning him to face Violet.

"Try it again," Harclay growled. "This time like you mean it."

The boy appeared as if he were about to weep. He bowed and, speaking loudly, said, "I apologize sincerely, my lady, for whatever grief I have caused you. I beg your forgiveness."

"Th-thank you," Violet stammered. Her gown felt sticky against her skin and unpleasantly damp. She must appear a fright.

"That will be all, Lord Casterleigh," Harclay said. "Now be off with you before I make good on my oath."

Without hesitation the boy scurried into the crowd. Lord Harclay turned to Violet, monogrammed handkerchief in one hand and a fresh coupe of punch in the other.

She took the handkerchief and went to work on her gown. The glittery gauze hid most of the stain, and what with the diamond about her neck, no one would pay much mind to her costume anyway.

Still, her cheeks flamed with mortification. Damned punch; she'd been so suave, so savvy in her flirtation with the earl, and then *this* had to happen.

"You missed a spot," Lord Harclay said, pointing to a stain just above her right breast.

Violet looked up from her ministrations to see him feasting on her person with his eyes. Incensed, she threw his handkerchief at his chest and took the coupe from his hand.

"I'm going to leave that spot, just to spite you"—she sipped at her punch—"so that your imagination might run riot with all the possibilities of removing it yourself. Perhaps with those lovely lips of yours; perhaps with some other, no less thrilling, methods."

Lord Harclay pulled back in mock horror. "You mean to torture me, don't you, Lady Violet?"

She finished the rest of her punch in a single gulp, licking her lips. "Indeed I do. And I shall relish every moment of it."

"Excellent," Harclay replied, taking the empty coupe from her and setting it on the table. He led her back into the crush. "A dance, then, to begin said torture?"

Four

Without waiting for Violet's reply, Lord Harclay turned toward the musicians. In a commanding baritone that belied his most indecent condition, he called for a waltz.

"A waltz?" Violet drew back. "But Hope won't have it! And neither will his guests. It's far too provocative, even for the likes of you and me."

But Harclay merely smiled. He dug a small satin pouch out of his waistcoat and tossed it across the ballroom. It landed with a satisfying *clank* in the outstretched palm of the gentleman playing first violin.

"A waltz, if you please!" Harclay called once more, and to Violet's great surprise the members of the orchestra took their seats and made to play.

A wave of disbelieving murmurs rolled through the room, but guests began to take their places—Violet could hardly believe so many members of polite society knew the dance, despite its reputation—and Mr. Hope appeared out of the ether, wig leaning precipitously off his head.

"I believe I've the pleasure of the first dance, Lady Violet?" he said, holding out his hand.

But Harclay stepped between them, his eyes, burning, on

her face. "You'll have to forgive me, Hope, but I'll take that pleasure for myself."

It wasn't a question, a polite "if you please"; no, Harclay's words were a command, delivered with quiet, savage equanimity. *I'll take that pleasure for myself.*

Mr. Hope stepped back, too startled to reply; and Violet—well, Violet fought to keep from smiling.

Harclay slid her arm into the crook of his own and led her to the middle of the floor. In the midst of a flurry of couples readying for the dance, he stopped and wound his way around Violet so he faced her. When he looked at her—damn him and those wicked, wicked eyes—she blushed and he smiled at her indiscretion. He stepped closer to her, eyes focused on her lips. His ardent attention made her feel suddenly, thrillingly alive.

Together they bowed. Harclay again stepped closer and put his hands on her: the right, firmly planted on the small of her back, and with the left he grasped her own, his fingers tangling with hers. Already currents of heat and blood coursed through her belly.

He breathed on her neck. She thought she might die.

The orchestra played the first notes of the waltz, and Harclay moved crisply, expertly, as if he'd been waltzing since he was in short pants. His eyes, dark, glittering in the light of the chandeliers above, never left hers. She felt the heat rise to her face and yet found it impossible to look away. Violet had never spent more than a fleeting moment this close to a man—a greeting, a polite kiss, a curtsy—but here was the Earl of Harclay, wealthy rake, ravager of virgins, with his arms wrapped around her, coaxing her breast closer and closer to his. So very, *very* close.

She followed his every step, every turn, and it wasn't long before she was blissfully floating in the quick *one-two-three* of the music, breathless, spellbound. With each turn the diamond tapped lightly against her chest, its flashes of fire reflecting in Harclay's eyes. And still his gaze never left hers; never once strayed to the mesmerizing jewel at her throat, a jewel worn by emperors and kings, a jewel for which most men would commit murder; never once strayed, even as she glanced at her feet to ensure they were still on the ground.

"Why a waltz?" she said, her words coming out in a breathy

hush that made her want to cringe. "You're sure to be shunned from every proper ball this season."

Harclay scoffed. "If only I were so lucky. I daresay I could run down Bond Street naked, shouting filth at the top of my lungs, and still the good members of the *ton* would welcome me with open arms. Those with eligible daughters, anyhow."

"But how many eligible daughters are left, really, that you haven't already despoiled?"

"Despoiled?" he said, smiling. "Now there's a word I haven't come across, not in some time."

"Indeed," Violet replied. "I imagine you've grown quite tired of 'pillage' and 'ravage,' what with having used them so often as you go about your daily business."

Harclay pulled her close to him, crushing her against his not inconsiderable flesh. He felt solid and warm against her, not at all like the steely, menacing predator she imagined him to be, and she let out a little sigh.

He pulled her closer, bending his neck so that his lips brushed against her ear. She arched against him, inadvertently deepening their embrace, and her blood screamed with—well, Violet didn't quite know what, except that she'd never felt anything so poignant in all her livelong life.

"I prefer 'pleasure,' myself," he murmured. "For as often as I pillage and ravage and take, pleasuring is what I most enjoy."

The music reached its crescendo, and Harclay spun Violet faster and faster, the room a glowing blur about them. Violet couldn't breathe, couldn't speak or hear or think; she could do nothing but return Harclay's searing gaze, her pulse throbbing in time to the memory of his words.

Pleasuring is what I most enjoy.

Heavens, what was one supposed to say to that?

"Yes, well," Violet said. "I'm afraid I shall not be among those lucky few whom you *pleasure* this evening. I rather prize my sanity—"

Harclay smiled, a knowing, sinister thing that made his lips appear all the more appetizing. "Sanity is overrated, and not nearly so good a time as sin and seduction."

Struggling to contain the impulse to wag her tongue at his most impertinent remark, she at last looked away in an attempt to gather her wits.

Thoughts tangled in an impossible knot, her gaze landed on the trio of tall windows that lined the wall above the refreshment table. Just who did this shameless Casanova think he was, saying such terrible—awful—wonderful things . . .

The crack and clatter of breaking glass shattered her reverie. She blinked and saw a handful of black-clad figures somersault gracefully through the windows and land soundlessly on the table. Somewhere in the back of Violet's mind, she registered that the intruders were most scrupulous in avoiding the glittering decanters that held Mr. Hope's priceless collection of brandy.

For a moment the ballroom went still, as if the guests were dumbstruck in disbelief; and then all hell broke loose. Screams, shouts, bodies tumbling over one another.

In the chaos, Violet nearly missed Mr. Hope's gap-toothed, costumed guards palming their guns and pointing them not at the bandits but at Hope's guests; one guard went so far as to press the barrel of his weapon against the Marquess of Kendal's forehead and shout at the poor man to stay put and shut his mouth.

What the devil? Hope's guards—Violet remembered with a shudder just how many of them there were—had turned against him? But how? Why?

Faces concealed by black kerchiefs, the intruders pulled sleek-looking pistols from their belts. They aimed at the ceiling and—*one, two, three*—they fired, the sound deafening as it echoed off the walls. People screamed and held their ears as they crouched low to the ground. Violet watched in horror as, one after the other, the bandits tucked their guns back into their belts and leapt high from the table onto the chandeliers. With herculean strength they climbed the massive fixtures arm by brass arm; and then, with knives they slid from their boots, the intruders began sawing at the silk cords that held the chandeliers aloft.

"My God," Violet whispered, pointing directly above their heads. "Look!"

Beside her, Harclay gesticulated wildly at the crowd with his arms. "Move! You're in harm's way! Get out, I say, get out from under the lights!"

Like a herd of stunned cattle, Hope's guests pushed and
shoved their way off the floor without a moment to spare.

The chandeliers fell through the air as if in slow motion.
Lord Harclay tugged Violet none too gently to the side, just as
the chandelier above them crashed to the floor, obliterating
the very spot they'd been standing on just a breath before. The
earth shook with the impact as the other enormous fixtures
followed suit. Their candles sputtered and died and the ballroom was plunged into darkness.

The screams quickly became unbearable, and terribly
frightening. Violet overheard guests praying—"Take me, sweet
Jesus, I'm ready!"—and a few men were weeping noisily, begging their wives to forgive them this transgression and that.

Violet realized with yet another shudder that the bandits
had fallen with the lights and were now roaming freely
through the ballroom, looking for God knew what.

She hadn't realized she was shaking until Harclay pulled
her against him, cradling her neck in his palm.

"It's all right," he whispered. "They shan't harm you, Lady
Violet. You have my word." She felt the hardened pad of his
thumb stroke the tender skin at the back of her neck; and
though she knew it was a mistake the moment she did it, she
leaned her head against his chest and allowed him to swallow
her in his arms.

"But how do you know?" she replied. "How do you know
they haven't come to finish the lot of us off?"

Amid the din she caught the slow, sure rumble of his
chuckle. "Lady Violet, I'm afraid you've read one too many
of those hideous novels of knights and duels and villains. You
must trust me, and keep close."

"Trust *you*?" she scoffed. "I may be in my cups, my lord,
but I—"

Harclay pressed his hand against her mouth. "Quiet," he
said and motioned toward the windows.

Pistols at the ready, the bandits silently surveyed the sea of
cowering heads before them. It struck Violet that they were
looking for someone, something. Were they here to kidnap
Mr. Hope or steal away with some heir or another? Had they
come to ransack Mr. Hope's personal vault, make off with

one of his many invaluable collections—Genghis Khan's swords, ancient Roman coinage, medieval Italian paintings?

No, no, that didn't make sense. Why rob Hope in the middle of a ball and risk being trampled and caught by the crowd?

Lost in her thoughts, Violet did not sense the pair of predators lurking at her elbow until it was too late.

They pounced on her with the violence of feral cats, clawing at her face, her throat, her gown. She cried out, a pitiful yell that was more a whimper of terror. Her heart went to her throat as she struggled uselessly against them, though she was no match for their strength. Tears gathered in her eyes, blurring the few shapes and movements she could discern in the darkness; her arms and legs burned with the effort of resisting her attackers. It wouldn't be long, she knew, before her body gave out and the bandits, damn them, would have their way . . .

Her attackers grunted, and for a moment their assault ceased. She blinked the tears from her eyes and saw Harclay looming over her, his right hand fisted in one bandit's hair while with his left he clasped the second bandit by the throat. He was breathing hard, a sheen of sweat glowing on his forehead in the blue-white light that streamed in from the windows.

With frightening force, Harclay threw one thief to the ground and with his free fist pummeled the other until he begged for mercy. The savory-sweet smell of blood filled the air.

After one last blow to the intruder's belly, Harclay straightened.

"Are you," he panted, "all right, Lady Violet?"

She took his proffered hand, and he pulled her upright so that she faced him. "Yes," she replied, smoothing her gown with trembling fingers. "I—I believe I'm intact. Just a bit shaken . . ."

And then, with a creeping, sickening certainty, it dawned on her.

The diamond.

Her hands shot to her throat. Where Mr. Hope's priceless French Blue diamond, of Mughal and Sun King fame, should have been, she felt only the clammy warmth of her skin, the scattershot scream of her own pulse.

"Oh, dear, the diamond," she managed, bile rising to her throat. "I'm afraid I'm going to be ill . . ."

Harclay lurched forward and held back loose strands of her hair as she retched into the dim shadows of the floor.

"The diamond," she gasped, voice rising with panic. "Lord Harclay, the diamond—it's gone!"

Five

Harclay pulled the monogrammed handkerchief from his sleeve, stained pink with punch, and for the second time that evening offered it to Lady Violet. He found her intriguing, even as she vomited on his shoes; the combination of tousled hair and disheveled dress drove him mad, *quite* mad, and if he wasn't careful his infamous wood would frighten the other guests, even in the dark.

"The thieves," he said, and, as if on cue, the masked bandits at his feet suddenly leapt to their own feet and made for the exit.

Violet took the handkerchief and dabbed at the corners of her mouth. "They've got it, the jewel!" She nearly cried.

"Stop them!" Harclay shouted, turning to face the crowd. "They are making off with the French Blue!"

The ballroom broke out in murmurs, but to Harclay's pleasure he noticed no one, save Mr. Hope, stood to stop them.

"Wait!" Hope cried, wig slipping from his head as he hurried after them. "You bastards, I'll have you hanged!"

At that moment a volley of pistol shots rang out—Harclay grinned at the recollection of just how simple it'd been to make Mr. Hope's guards his own—and panic surged anew from among the cowering crowd.

Guests pushed and shoved one another in a mad dash for the front door. Violet was violently thrust against Lord Harclay, shoe to shoulder, and he drew back ever so slightly so that she might not feel his—ah, his own jewel—hard against her skirts.

Harclay arched his neck and peered above the chaos, his gaze landing on a wildly gesticulating Hope.

"Hope!" he called. "Hope, what is it?"

"Get her out of here!" Hope shouted. "See that she's safe! The thieves could still be lurking about!"

Harclay very nearly smiled. All was going exactly, perfectly, to plan.

And then he looked down at Violet, who was, naturally, looking back up at him with those damnably alluring blue eyes, and he amended his statement.

All was going to plan, except for his rather inconvenient attraction to the woman from whom he'd just snatched an invaluable gem.

Details, he mused. Mere details.

Harclay roped his arm about her shoulders and began to push his way through the throng, but Lady Violet stood her ground.

"But my aunt," she panted, turning back to the crush. "And my cousin! Sophia, Sophia, where are you? Christ, Lord Harclay, I can't very well leave without them!"

He turned to her. "Such language!" he said with mock surprise. "You scandalize me, Lady Violet."

"Yes, well, I venture the occasion calls for it. I'm not leaving without my family!"

"Yes, yes, you are," Harclay replied. "I gave Hope my word. And God knows I could never forgive myself if I abandoned you and the thieves returned and stole that sanity you're so proud of. No, you are coming with me."

Before Violet could give voice to the inevitable protest, Harclay ducked and, wrapping his arms about her legs, threw her over his shoulder.

"I'll bite your—your behind I will!" she squeaked as he strode across the ballroom and into the hall.

"Help yourself," he replied as he made a brisk but elegant escape through the front door.

"Let's be off, then," Harclay said to Avery, ignoring the man's slack-jawed stare as the earl deposited Lady Violet neatly in his velvet-lined carriage.

Avery swallowed. "Very well. We heard the gunshots, and the crashes, but we didn't move, not one bit," he said, eyeing his master. "Everything in order?"

"Very much so, thank you," Harclay replied.

"Help me!" Lady Violet whined from inside the carriage. "He's trying to kidnap me, and the diamond, I've got to help them recover it . . ."

"Indeed, *very* much so. Home, please, and quickly," Harclay said, and he climbed into the carriage before Avery could ask any more questions.

"You cad!" Violet spat out as the carriage jolted into motion. "You can't just sling me over your shoulder like some barroom ladybird and take me from my family. They could be hurt, scared; I can't just leave them at the mercy of those thieves!"

Harclay smiled at the vehemence of her tone. Feisty, she was, and he liked it, though he could tell her nerves were in precarious condition. He turned to the seat beside him and with a small grunt removed the bottom cushion. There in the padded recess rested a few bottles of his favorite brandy.

"And the diamond!" she continued, smacking her palm against her forehead. "My God, I lost it! Poor Mr. Hope, I daresay he's out ten, twenty thousand pounds at least!"

"More than that," Harclay murmured and unstoppered the bottle with his teeth. The heady, rich scent of brandy swirled inside the carriage.

"I should've been more careful," Violet was saying. "I should have paid attention—no, I should've known wearing the diamond was a stupid idea and warned Mr. Hope against it. Oh, poor, poor Mr. Hope! What if this gets to the papers?"

"Oh, it'll get to the papers, all right," Harclay replied. He held out the bottle to Violet, who twisted her lips into a most delightful grimace.

She snatched the bottle from his outstretched hand. Bringing the bottle to her lips, she took one, two long gulps and with a little sigh sank deeper into her seat. Silence settled between them, the clap of the horses' hooves and the rattle of the carriage wheels against the cobblestones soothing, somehow, in that they were ordinary sounds, signs of life circling back to normal.

Even Harclay, hardened rake that he was, was having difficulty recovering from the evening's thrill. Despite his best efforts, his pulse refused to slow; indeed, it raced faster and faster the longer his eyes lingered on Lady Violet. Minx, that one, though he thought she looked quite lovely with punch-stained lips and wisps of hair forming a halo about her face.

He dug the nails of his right hand into his palm, and dug yet deeper.

You have just committed no small crime, he reminded himself. *You gambled all you are, and all that you own, on this theft. Now is not the time to wax poetic on the charms of a woman, no matter how lovely that particular woman may be.*

And still his thoughts spun in that general direction. Though he'd planned quite the spectacle for Mr. Hope and his guests, he hadn't intended the theft to be *quite* so operatic; and as he watched Violet tremble before him, he felt something strong and urgent slice through his chest.

Certainly not remorse, he reasoned. No, he did not regret stealing the diamond; the near ecstasy he felt at having executed, and escaped from, a rather brilliant crime made it well worth committing the theft. The Earl of Harclay had very few regrets, a fact upon which he prided himself; so why this sudden tenderness, this strange, unfamiliar ache at the sight of a woman in the throes of a veritable apoplectic attack?

After some moments spent silently swaying in time to the carriage, Harclay cleared his throat. "Better?" he asked.

Violet narrowed her eyes at him. "I suppose so, yes. Though of course Mr. Hope's diamond is still missing, and it's all my fault."

"Oh, heavens, girl, don't be ridiculous," he scoffed. He pried the bottle from her fingers, took a pull, swallowed with a satisfied sigh, and corked the bottle.

"But I'm not done—"

"Later, when we're back at the house. How could it possibly be your fault that a gang of strange men assaulted you at a ball and stole your necklace? Mr. Hope was foolish, yes, *quite*

foolish to let you wear it—I'll give you that. But you, dear
Lady Violet—the thieves wasted not a single thought on you,
until they saw the diamond around your neck."

Violet arched her brow. "You speak as if you were among
the thieves yourself, Lord Harclay."

Inside his chest his heart jumped, a rousing leap that had
him biting back a smile. She was more savvy than she let on,
this Lady Violet; and as he found himself leaning forward in
his seat, elbows on his knees so that he might be closer to her,
he realized for the first time just how precarious was his position. His admiration for this woman seemed to increase with
every moment he spent in her presence.

Perhaps it was best if he *did* take her home, drop her at her
father's front door, and be done with it.

But, he thought with a sly smile, that would be hardly
sporting of him; and not much fun besides. For he imagined
Lady Violet to be that rarest of creatures: a female capable of
very great fun indeed. Perhaps, beneath the stony layer of her
impertinence, her reputed abhorrence for men of all sizes and
stripes, there existed a creature of great wit, brilliant spirit,
and startling confidence.

Perhaps.

Ah, the hours of entertainment she could provide. In his
bed; on top of his desk, papers flying everywhere; in the
grand fountain at his palace in the country (a particular fan-
tasy of his); on the grass; on a settee in the smoking room; in
his carriage, the sounds of their union shocking those on the
street whom they passed . . .

"Lord Harclay!"

Her voice interrupted his thoughts, and he moved to cross
his legs in an attempt to hide his painful condition.

"Heavens, and here I was the one worried about holding
my liquor. Are you quite all right?" she said.

Again Harclay cleared his throat. "Yes, yes, of course. Just
working out where in my house you might stay the night most
comfortably."

"Spend the night!" she cried, the look of horror on her face
so extreme it made Harclay laugh. "But you can't be serious! I
may dance the waltz, Lord Harclay, and have a taste for stiff
punch, but I do have a care for my reputation. If it is discovered

I stayed unchaperoned at your house, I'll be ruined, and so will my family, my cousin Sophia—"

"No one will know. You have my word. You were with me when the theft occurred; Hope instructed me to get you out. You are under my care and protection now; it is my responsibility to keep you safe. And you won't be safe at your father's house."

"But my family," she repeated. "That's why I must get back to my family. My aunt will be frantic with worry, and my father—they are in danger—"

He held aloft the bottle in his hand. "I'll send word to your family straightaway, and send one of my men to keep watch. An irregular circumstance indeed, but what could one expect after a *most* irregular evening? Besides, I thought you said you wanted another drink."

To his great delight, this gave Lady Violet pause. After a moment, she huffed and made a great show of crossing her arms across her chest.

"If I can't be with my family, then I should be with Mr. Hope," she said, "trying to catch the thieves. I shan't rest until I do."

"Of course you won't," Harclay said. "But the thieves—whoever they may be—had a rather brilliant scheme in place, I'm afraid. For the time being they have disappeared, and no effort of ours tonight would go very far in finding them. Mr. Hope's house is likely to be a great mess, and us already in our cups." He looked to the bottle in his hand.

"No," he continued, "it is best we get a good night's rest and revisit the scene of the crime in the morning. I've found I can do most anything after a good breakfast and a strong cup of coffee.

"Besides, everyone in that ballroom was far too busy trying not to have their legs shot off to notice us leaving together. Given the circumstances, I hardly think it matters where you sleep tonight, as long as you escaped intact and unharmed."

She swallowed and looked out the carriage window, her hand splayed across her chest. "The diamond isn't the only jewelry the thieves stole," she said at last.

Harclay furrowed his brow. "Whatever are you talking about? I didn't see you wearing any other baubles."

She met his eyes. "I always wear my mother's wedding band on a chain about my neck. The chain must've tangled with the French Blue; it's gone. The thieves must have ripped it from my neck when they took Hope's diamond."

Harclay paused. "We'll get it back," he said slowly, not daring to meet her eyes. "We'll get your mother's ring back, Lady Violet, I swear it."

The carriage came to a slow but halting stop, nearly tossing Lady Violet into his lap (a near disaster, what with the jewel in his breeches). He pulled aside the curtain and looked out the window to see the towering facade of his house, the gas lamps on either side of the door flickering their welcome.

He'd done it. The French Blue was his, nestled safely if inelegantly within his undergarments, and no one had so much as seen him steal it, much less suspected him of the theft.

No one, that was, except Lady Violet Rutledge. She'd witnessed the crime, after all; and now that he'd been exposed to her considerable wit and cunning, he knew he would have to proceed carefully. For with the right clues—a careless word here, another there—she would doubtless unravel his scheme.

A challenge, he thought with a smile, and a gloriously unexpected one at that.

Six

Violet struggled to contain her surprise as she crossed the threshold into the Earl of Harclay's London house. A fashionable address, surely; the infamously opulent Harewood House occupied a prime location in the same square. And yet it was not at all what she expected. She'd envisioned a grotesquely large pile, draped in sensuous satin the color of rubies with a well-stocked liquor cabinet in every room: a bachelor's house, tailored to a life of wickedness and dissipation.

What greeted her, however, was not a nest of sin but a home of subdued, exquisite taste. It was obvious Harclay had taken pains to remain true to the house's historic character: hand-carved moldings decorated the walls, while tastefully worn black and white marble tiles covered the floor. Paintings of ancestors, their costumes extravagant but faces grim, lined a wide and simple stair.

There were no gaudy tapestries, no extra-wide beds or whores hiding in doorways (as far as she could tell, anyway). It was a gentleman's house, lovely and inviting; a fire burned merrily in the hearth, while a half dozen household staff greeted them with smiles. They were prudent enough to ignore the egregious breach of etiquette and propriety that Violet's presence presented, though she couldn't help but squirm under their curious gazes.

No one will know. You are under my care now; I will keep you safe.

Violet prayed Harclay kept his word.

"Lady Violet Rutledge is to be my guest this evening," Harclay said, handing off his hat and gloves to a footman. "I took her under my protection following a series of rather unfortunate events at Mr. Hope's ball. Please see to her every comfort. The back bedroom, I think, is where she'll be safest."

The maids bobbed their heads, and before Violet could so much as say good evening, they whisked her up the stairs and down a tall, shadowy hallway. They paused before a wide door and, opening it, allowed Violet to pass through. The room was dark at first but smelled of fresh air and clean linen.

She stood rather awkwardly to the side as one maid lit the candles while another worked to start a fire in the limestone fireplace. As the fire growled and crackled to life, a third maid let down Violet's hair.

"Shall I fetch more blankets, m'lady?" The maid frowned. "You're shaking like a leaf!"

Violet bit the inside of her cheek, willing her bones to be still. "No, thank you," she replied. "The fire will help."

The maid patted her shoulder. "No need to be frightened, m'lady; you're safe here. The earl looks after us all and sees that those under his roof are well cared for."

I'm sure the earl cares for the ladies writhing in his bed very well indeed, thought Violet wryly.

After Violet assured the maids, and assured them again, that she was most comfortable, they took their leave. She stood by the fireplace, blanket wrapped about her shoulders, and let out a long, slow breath. Her heart was racing; and as the silence settled in around her a small black sensation crawled out of her belly and invaded her limbs, her every thought.

Terror. Sheer, childish terror, like she hadn't felt since she was a child, running from the governess's swatting stick. She was positively immobilized by it and stood frozen by the fire, her gaze darting from this shadow to that, convinced each belonged to a bandit. Good God, she thought in panic, they'd found her, had followed Harclay's carriage, and now they would finish her off, carve her body into a hundred grotesque little pieces.

Where was that damned drink he'd promised her?

Violet nearly leapt into the fire at a brusque knock on the door. She swallowed hard and smoothed the long, loose waves of her hair from her forehead. Squaring her shoulders, she took the poker from the grate and made for the door. Surely the bandits, if they were to come at all, would come through the windows; it seemed to be their preferred method of entry.

Still, one could never be too careful. And though Violet had never heard of such a thing as a *polite* bandit, one who knocked on doors rather than breaking them down, she was frightened enough to believe they existed.

"Who is it?" she called softly.

"'Tis the butler, Avery," came a familiar voice. "Forgive the late hour, my lady, but I've a message for you."

Butler? But Avery had played the part of coachman not a half hour before, driving them from Hope's to Hanover Square. How very strange. Surely the earl could afford to hire a man for each position?

Violet cracked open the door and peered out into the hall. To her relief her eyes settled not on a bloodthirsty criminal but on the round, jolly face of Avery. He held aloft a silver tray, on which rested a neatly folded letter with her name scrawled in rather lovely script across the front.

"Thank you, Avery," she replied, opening the door wider.

As Violet took the letter in her free hand, Avery cleared his throat and rocked back on his heels. "Might I, ah," he began, "hold that for you, my lady?"

With his hairy brow he motioned to the poker in her hand.

"Oh, oh, dear me, it isn't what you think," she said and blushed so violently she feared, for a moment, an apoplectic attack.

"Very well, then. May I?" He took the poker and motioned to the grate.

While Avery returned the poker to its proper place, Violet opened the letter. Her hands trembled as she read it, though this wasn't fear; this was altogether too pleasant, a thrill.

I owe you a drink.
And there's that spot on your gown we must see to.
Follow Avery—he will bring you to me.

Violet's heart very nearly leapt from her chest; did he really mean to see to the spot? She looked down at her gown. There it was, a small lick of pink on the seam just above her right breast.

She took a deep breath, trying in vain to gather her wits.

A late-night letter, delivered by a trusted coachman-cum-butler; a command to join him in an illicit rendezvous involving brandy and perhaps—well, she dared not imagine.

Good God, it was the stuff of legend!

But Violet was not the kind of woman to swoon; indeed, she loathed those who did and wished most ardently they be exposed first as terrible actresses, and second as shameless attention-seekers.

No, Violet was better than that. And so she gathered the blanket and her wits about her, slid into her slippers, and without a word followed Avery into the dark unknown of Lord Harclay's house.

The rooms they passed were hidden by shadow and darkness, but Violet noticed a certain scent permeated the house—a scent she recognized from her waltz with Harclay earlier that evening. It had clung to his person as it now settled on every surface of his house. Lemon, and fresh laundry, and the slightest hints of leather and ancient musk.

It was *his* scent, unlike any other she'd known. There was something deeply personal about it, imbued with Harclay's history, his family, his past, and all he hoped for in the future. He carried the scent not as others carry cologne or perfume but as one would bear one's heritage, the pride he took in the love he bore his family.

Granted, Harclay didn't always deserve to wear such a grand scent. If only his exalted ancestors knew he'd shared that scent with half the females in London, left it lingering on the beds of the most sordid of establishments, they'd come back from the dead and remove his manhood, make no mistake.

At last Avery led her to a pair of slender doors. Soft light streamed from the crack between them, and Violet could make out the pound of footsteps, the tinkling of glassware, from within.

Avery opened the door and turned to her. "Madam," he said, and without another word he bowed and took his leave.

Violet stared into the room, her every sense achingly alive. A tingle of anticipation shot through the length of her.

This, she mused with a small smile, was dangerous.

She stepped through the open door with her head held high and as much grace as she could muster, what with her loose hair and a blanket wrapped about her shoulders.

"My lord," she said quietly, dropping into a curtsy.

"Lady Violet," he replied with a short bow. "Thank you for meeting me. I recognize my summons was most—unorthodox."

Violet's gaze rose along with her rise from the curtsy and fell on the shapely outline of Lord Harclay. She was forced to bite her lip against her surprise; he was in a shocking state of undress. He wore a white linen shirt undone at the throat, revealing a small swatch of taut, tanned chest. The shirt was tucked into a pair of tight buckskins that hugged his thighs so tightly she could see the shapely curve of his muscles beneath. He wore top boots—no wonder he'd made so much noise—and Violet felt the air leave her lungs as she drank him in, looking nothing like the gentleman she knew from the hours of her panic but rather like an unkempt, intrepid pirate, sun kissed and hardened, unafraid to pursue that which he desired.

At once an image flashed through Violet's mind: Harclay the pirate, pleasuring her on board his ship beneath the stars. He reared above her, kissing her neck savagely, a golden hoop dangling from one ear . . .

Oh, *God*.

"I say, are you unwell?" Harclay said. He stepped forward, head stooped as if in concern. "You look rather piqued."

Violet waved him off. "That drink you owe me, if you please, Lord Harclay."

Harclay grinned at her forwardness. "Very well. I've wine, brandy, even a bit of rag water—"

"Whatever you're having," Violet blurted out. "If you please."

"Of course. Please, sit," he replied, turning to the gleaming sideboard nestled into an alcove in the wall.

With no small effort, Violet tore her gaze from Lord Harclay's maddeningly perfect backside—really, it was egregiously lovely—and discovered Avery had led her to the drawing room. In the middle of the small space, a pair of sofas faced each other, and in the far corner, Violet made out gilt wingback chairs, flanked on either side by two small tables, each of which was topped by a silver candelabra. Two good-sized bookshelves, stuffed with dusty tomes, stood behind the tables.

It was decorated with the same impeccable, restrained taste as the hall and bedroom; Harclay's touch was everywhere, from the subdued mural of a country landscape on the walls to the faded but exquisite Axminster carpet beneath her feet.

Violet sat on the edge of a couch, arraying the blanket about her person so that Harclay might not so much as glimpse a finger. Better to wrap oneself up like a mummy, she reasoned, than hazard catching the earl's carnal attentions. From the sideboard came a muffled *pop*—what was he doing over there, anyway?—and Violet at last worked up the courage to break the silence.

"Do you think," she ventured, "that many people were hurt? I heard the gunshots, and the shouts, of course, but I couldn't tell if anyone had been harmed."

"As far as I could tell, no one was seriously injured," he said over his shoulder. "The thieves discharged their guns to scare us. If you recall, they aimed away from the crowd. Though I daresay Hope's ceiling is worse for the wear."

Harclay strode across the room to meet her, two fine crystal coupes—was that champagne?—in his hands. He passed one to Violet, and she stared at it as if he'd handed her a potato.

"Forgive me, Lord Harclay." Violet blinked. "Are we celebrating something?"

Harclay held out his glass. "To a successful evening."

"A successful evening!" Violet drew back. "But I don't understand—"

"We made it out alive, didn't we?" Harclay clinked his glass against her own. "Alive, unharmed, and with our thirst intact. A success indeed."

He threw back his champagne with all the vigor of a batsman at play. Violet brought hers to her lips with the intention of taking a ladylike sip. But as soon as the silky sweet liquid touched her tongue—it was good champagne, very, very good, and cold—she knew she was in trouble. She took one gulp, then another, the champagne smoothing her frayed nerves as it made its way through her limbs.

"Better," she said breathily when she'd drained the last drop from her coupe. "Much, much better."

Harclay raised his brow. "Another round, then."

Violet wiped her mouth with the back of her hand, her limbs suddenly loose, light. "No, thank you."

But the earl filled her coupe anyway, which she in true form finished straightaway.

He sat across from her, arm draped casually over the back of the sofa, and watched as she lapped at the last of the champagne. She felt her color rise under his scrutiny, and for a fleeting moment she met his gaze.

His dark eyes danced in the warm, low light of the fire; danced with something Violet found wholly unsettling. He appeared a wolfish predator, savoring the taste of the kill to come. Though he did not smile, the lay of his lips suggested he was amused by something, intrigued perhaps.

Violet looked away. He was terribly, awfully striking; and with the champagne taking captive her senses she found him unbearably so. Very carefully she placed her coupe on the table between them, a flag of surrender as if to say yes, Harclay, you won this round, but next time it won't be so easy.

"I am sorry you were ill-treated by the bandits," he said, his voice a low, rumbling purr. "I shall call my doctor in the morning, if you like."

Violet shook her head. "No, thank you, I'll be quite all right. A bit sore, a bruise here and there, nothing more. Though I'm afraid I shall require a doctor if I drink any more of your champagne. A dirty trick of yours, that."

"But it calmed your nerves, did it not? You were quite shaken, and with good reason. I daresay most females would suffer fits of hysteria for days after what happened to you this evening."

Heat rose in her chest, a boldness riled by the champagne that now coursed deliciously through her veins. The words bubbled to her lips before she could think to stop them.

"Indeed, Lord Harclay, you should know by now that I am not like 'most females.' If I were, I daresay you'd have dropped me at my father's doorstep and washed your hands of the thing," she said, shocked at the rising sharpness of her tongue but too far in to stop it. "Admit it. You have used the theft as an excuse to abduct me, to bring me unescorted to your home, so that you might seduce me."

For a moment she expected him to laugh; the words sounded ridiculous, even to a lady like herself who devoured several unsavory novels a week. But instead he leaned forward, closing the space between them.

"And what if I have, Lady Violet?"

His voice was calm, silken, barely above a murmur; shockingly intimate. Violet sucked in a breath at the rush of heat low in her belly.

"It's that damned stain you're after, isn't it?" she said with a smile.

His eyes traveled to the pink spot on her gown. Her nipples prickled to life beneath his gaze.

Slowly, deliberately, he reached forward and with an enormous hand covered her breast. She inhaled sharply, the breath catching in her throat as he bent his head and brought his lips to her flesh, just above the stain on her gown.

He pressed featherlight kisses onto her skin, small, heady things, his lips moving slowly over the rise of her bosom. The tenderness of his touch made the gesture all the more erotic; Violet found herself arching into his caress, her open mouth suddenly dry.

"I think," he said, nipping her breast with his teeth, "I've got it, that dreadful spot."

He raised his head and looked directly in her eyes, making no effort to hide his desire.

Lord Harclay leaned closer, closer, that peculiar, wonderful scent of his enveloping her; and then in a thrilling rush he dug his hand into her hair and pulled her to him, his thumb grazing her lips before he covered them with his own.

Violet was so taken aback that for a moment she entered a state of complete and utter paralysis, heart stalling in her chest. His kiss was urgent but gentle; his lips moved languorously, slowly, working to open her to him.

For a moment her eyes fluttered shut, and she allowed herself to imagine what it would be like if she gave in, allowed him to do what he wanted.

Again the image of Harclay-as-pirate flashed across her closed lids. This time he was peeling back her tattered chemise, flinging his tricorn hat across the deck in his urgency to have her, take her, pleasure her.

Pleasuring is what I most enjoy.

His breath was warm on her skin, and his mouth tasted sweet, the champagne lingering on his tongue. It was an altogether exquisite first kiss, not at all what Violet had imagined and yet so much better. Deliciously, dangerously good.

She had to stop. She couldn't forget her family, and this man—damn him—was making her forget not only her duty but her good sense, her wit, as well.

With a moan of frustration, she broke free. Her eyes snapped open; the look on Harclay's face was one of vague surprise and smug satisfaction.

No, she mused, *absolutely* not; he won the first round, but victory would be hers in the second.

Without thinking, she drew back and delivered a ringing blow to his cheek. He blinked, the skin pulsing red where she'd struck him, and to Violet's dismay his smug smile merely deepened.

"A strong arm you've got, Lady Violet. Do you box?"

"If the occasion calls for it, yes."

He surveyed her for several beats, a wicked gleam in his eye. "In my not inconsiderable experience, I've found that ladies who box are likely to be great gamblers as well."

Violet struggled to suppress the unwelcome smile that plied her lips at his joke. "While I regret my boxing days are behind me, I do like to gamble. I daresay I've a gift for it."

"Let us see, shall we?" Harclay said. He rose and disappeared into a darkened corner, only to emerge seconds later with a deck of cards in one hand and the uncorked bottle of champagne in the other.

She swallowed. She knew as well as Harclay that she couldn't resist the array of vices he now laid before her. Drink, dice, deeds done with hands and mouths and teeth. It was hell, it was heaven, and she wanted more of it.

"Tell me, Lady Violet," Harclay said, leaning across the table to refill her coupe, "do you play vingt-et-un?"

"I have, once or twice."

"Excellent."

"We shall require a banker."

"I'll play the banker." He offered her the deck; she cut it in the middle and passed it back to him. He shuffled the cards quickly, neatly, and set them on the table. "I propose a wager."

Now, *this* was interesting. She took the coupe in her hand and raised a brow. "Oh? And what, exactly, do you propose I wager?"

Harclay shuffled the cards smoothly between his hands. "Your virginity."

Violet nearly spit out her champagne and erupted into a fit of coughing. "My virginity?" She tried to laugh, a pitiful sound even to her ears. "What makes you think I'm still a virgin? I told you I'm a lady of many vices."

For a moment Harclay looked at her. She sensed him searching, digging past her swagger—and the champagne— for the truth that lay beneath it all.

"You're far too cunning a woman to dabble in *that* vice," he replied steadily. "For you know that such an act can lead to messy complications, among them marriage and children. No, you enjoy rather more simple vices, cards and liquor and the like. Perhaps you touch yourself every once in a while, just to see what the fuss is all about."

Here she blushed.

"Ah," he said with a smile. "Perhaps you touch yourself a good deal more than once in a while. I hope you've enjoyed what you've discovered. Of course, that doesn't change the fact that you've never lain with a man, not once. Though you often wonder what it would be like."

Violet looked away, biting her lip. "Speak plainly, Lord Harclay. What do you propose?"

"It's quite simple," he replied easily, as if he were discussing not her virginity but the weather. "If I win, I 'despoil' you, as you so cunningly put it. If you win—"

"One hundred," she blurted out. "If I win, you pay me one hundred pounds."

It was exquisitely stupid, of course, to wager that which she'd been taught to hold most dear. Perhaps it was the image of him half-naked at the sideboard, a pirate intent on pillage; perhaps it was the punch, the champagne, the night's disastrous events; or perhaps it was the kiss, good *God*, that kiss, that made her forget herself. Whatever it was, she spoke impulsively, without thinking, as if she were guided not by rational thought but by the heady, insistent pounding of her heart.

Besides, Harclay may have been a legendary gambler— she'd heard of his exploits long before she'd met him—but his prowess, and her wager, hardly mattered.

She was going to win.

What Harclay didn't know was that Violet was no novice herself; indeed, she thought with a small, prideful smile, she was good, better than good.

The best cheat this side of the Atlantic, make no mistake. She couldn't very well have kept the family afloat this long with just her luck, now, could she?

Seven

"One hundred?" Harclay said, setting out the cards before them on the table. "Let's make it one *thousand*, just to be fair. Surely your virtue is worth more than a shabby hundred."

He caught the flicker of surprise in her eyes. Dear girl, she was probably used to the sort of dull games played in the drawing rooms of dowagers and such; the sort of games played over tea and crumpets and polite gossip, the wager no more than a copper or two.

And here he was, intent on laying claim to her virginity over a game of casino. It was forward and rascally, even for him. Virgins held no particular draw for him; a messy business, that, accompanied, as far as he knew, by tearful, clinging hysterics that shriveled his lust more quickly than a swim in a Christmastide pond.

But the thrill from his well-executed theft had not yet subsided, and his blood hadn't felt so warm and alive for as long as he could remember. It could've been the champagne or the deliriously late hour, but he thought Lady Violet looked lovely. In the soft glow of the candles her cheeks flushed pink, her blue eyes danced as if to some maddeningly secret joke, and her hair!—glorious waves of it, pooling darkly about her shoulders and chest. It was all he could do not to reach across the table and touch it, bury his face in it.

Then there was the kiss. How her lips had seared his—his groin tightened at just the memory of it. Her mouth had been hot and slick, tasting sweetly of champagne, desire, possibility. They had moved in perfect harmony, he and she, heads bent at just such an angle, lips tugging languorously at just the right moment, as if it were the most natural thing in the world.

So lost was he in the memory of the kiss that he nearly missed Lady Violet clearing her throat and pronouncing herself the winner.

"What?" he blurted out, brow furrowed. On the table before her lay an impressive array of cards. He could tell at first glance that she had indeed won, and by a landslide at that; his pile was positively pitiful in comparison.

"But how?" he continued, at last meeting her eyes. They were narrowed mischievously, a grin perking at one side of those delicious lips.

"Twenty-one points, that's how. I say, my lord, for all your reputation I find you a most disappointing opponent. Surely you did not throw the game."

"No," he replied. "Certainly not." Rubbing his forehead with his first two fingers, he surveyed the cards in genuine bewilderment. He hadn't lost a game of casino since he'd been able to grow a beard. How the hell had she done it?

"You might make the note out to me, if you please, Lord Harclay. One thousand, no less," Violet said cheerily. She swept her hand over the cards and with startling skill gathered them into a neat pile. It was obvious she had done this before.

Harclay replied with a groan. By now his bollocks ached fiercely. He had fully expected to win, had even picked the carpet beneath her feet as their place of congress. But she had surprised him with her skill, that minx, for, contrary to his original opinion, she was no novice, a fact she'd hidden well until now.

A wicked, wicked trick she'd just played. Harclay hadn't had the wool pulled over his eyes in years—*years!*—and to be brought to his knees at last by Lady Violet Rutledge . . . It was humbling, wholly unexpected, and incredibly arousing.

He pulled a pillow onto his lap so that he might not embarrass himself any further. Clearing his throat, he said, "Another round. Double the stakes. You play banker this time."

Lady Violet scoffed. "Another round? After I've proven I can best you quite soundly?"

"Good God, woman, just deal the cards!" he nearly roared.

Though she obeyed without protest, she raised her brow as if to chastise him for the damned fool he was. But what with his entire body shimmering in anticipation, his manhood screaming for release, it was all he could think to do.

"Wait a moment." She paused. The blanket she clutched about her fell provocatively off her shoulder, revealing a tantalizing swath of sheer gown. "How am I to double my stakes? I've only one virtue to offer, after all."

Harclay smiled tightly. "I shall just have to take you twice, shan't I?"

He did not miss the pink of her cheeks burn red at his brazen suggestion.

This time he played carefully, thoughtfully, all the while keeping a close eye on Lady Violet. She played with concentrated gusto, cards flying through her fingers with the well-practiced skill of a seasoned player. Her gaze never left the deck, and more than once Harclay caught a curious movement of her lips, as if she were speaking to herself, or adding a sum aloud.

At last Lady Violet set down her hand. "I win," she said. "Twenty-one again, see?"

"For the love of all that's holy!" he exclaimed. He threw down his cards and fell back none too gently on the settee. "How do you do it?"

Again that tiny, maddening half smile. "Two thousand, if you please, though what sort of gentleman wagers so much on a few hands—you're certainly one of a kind, Lord Harclay."

For a long moment, he looked down at Lady Violet's face, his eyes following the contours of her features: down the angle of her nose, across the soft descent of her cheek, lingering a trifle longer than was proper at her lips. It gladdened him to see the weight of his scrutiny driving her color high and bright. He may have lost a game or two of cards; but the intrigue, the desire, that darkened Violet's eyes was well worth the loss.

"And you, dear girl," he murmured, "you are also one of a kind. Certainly luckier than anyone I've ever met."

Lady Violet smiled and looked down at her hands, busy shuffling the deck. "And *you*, dear sir," she replied, "must realize I am immune to such honeyed words for that very reason."

But beneath her haughty retort he sensed a sort of plea, as if her body, too, were drawn taut as a bowstring and begging for release.

The moment was ripe. He could smell the desire that rose from her skin, her hair, her breath, and before he knew what he was about, he was on his feet and reaching for her, blood roaring to life.

In a flash of sudden, violent movement, Harclay circled Lady Violet with his arm and pulled her to her toes against him, cupping her chin with his hardened hand, thumb holding her jaw in place. Her face was so close he felt the heat of her short, stunned breaths on his cheek. She pressed her hands against his chest in protest but he did not, could not, loosen his grip.

In her effort to push him away, Lady Violet lost hold of her blanket and it fell with a small sigh at her feet. She was left shivering in naught but her gauzy gown, a flimsy thing that exposed more skin than it covered.

Harclay felt her shaking and pulled her close against him. His erection prodded firmly, without shame, against her near-naked legs. The pressure, the feel of her warmth against his manhood, was at once delicious and maddeningly insufficient. He was reminded of his randy youth, when he'd wandered through life with a perpetually stiff member. How many poor women he'd rubbed against, looking for release; how dreadful it had been, for both him and the women!

He turned her away from him. Slowly, patiently, his fingers went to work at the satin buttons marching single file down her spine. He felt her tremble beneath his touch but she did not protest.

He reached the last button and, loosening it, allowed the gown to fall from Lady Violet's shoulders. It pooled around her feet in a sweet-scented tangle; she was left in her chemise.

Gently he raised her right arm, then her left; but when he tried to pull the chemise over her head, she shook her head.

Even a lady of vice has limits, he mused with a smile. He dropped the chemise back over her body.

Pressing a kiss into her shoulder, he turned her back around to face him.

Lady Violet stood very still against him. He could feel the prick of her hardened nipples pressing through his shirt. Her breasts pushed back against his chest, firm and insistent; from the feel of them they were generously sized, more than a handful each. Perfect, perfect, so goddamn *perfect*.

He nearly groaned as he imagined taking one breast, then the other, in his mouth, imagined her feminine curves filling his hands, her moans of surrender when he brought her to the brink with his touch . . .

He hovered above her, eyes wet with desire—a man completely transformed from the smooth, grinning devil of just a few moments before. She did not cower but rather stared at his naked passion in silent wonder, stunned by the force of his body, his desire.

"Why can't we both win?" he whispered in her ear. "Two thousand for you, and for me . . ."

Slowly, carefully, he slid his hand from her waist to her buttocks. Fisting the fine fabric of her chemise in his palm, he pulled the fabric up, up, with his fingers, baring first her ankle, then her calf, then a delicious, milky white thigh. Finally his fingers found purchase in the soft skin of her backside.

With the same care he slid his hand over her hip. She gasped as he cupped her sex in his palm, her curls soft and ticklish against his hardened skin.

"And for me, this," he said.

"Lord Harclay." She swallowed, voice hoarse. "You wouldn't, not after losing—"

"Oh, Lady Violet," he murmured, "I would indeed."

He slid his first two fingers deeper, so that they rested on either side of her sex. With great gentleness he opened her; she sucked in her breath but did not protest. With his second finger, he stroked the insides of her smooth, hot skin. Despite her fighting words, she was very aroused; slick and hot and pulsing. He stroked a little deeper, found the center of her sex, that small, delicious bead of flesh.

Lady Violet let out a breath. Her eyes flew wide, then fluttered shut altogether.

"Please, Harclay," she whispered, "please."

The words were more plea than command—what did she want? Please *yes*, please *no*? Perhaps, like all women, she wished for both.

When Harclay looked her in the eye he saw lust, and champagne, and desire and sex and fear. In her hands she'd fisted the fine fabric of his shirt, as if she clung to him for dear life itself.

"Please," Lady Violet repeated. Having a beat or two to compose herself, her voice was a bit steadier, her resolve stronger.

Gently he slipped a finger inside her, watching her face all the while. Instinctively she tightened around him, urging his finger deeper. She felt small, hard with desire, and deliciously wet.

Her eyes rolled back with pleasure as he began to move his fingers in tandem, one rolling the hood of her sex, the other deep inside her. Her hips circled against him, urging him to move faster, harder, and he obeyed. As she tightened further around him he slipped a second finger inside her.

Violet's eyes went wide but she did not protest. He stroked and he pulled and he touched until he thought he might explode himself. She wrapped her arms around his neck, her fingers digging into his hair, pulling it as she came closer and closer to her pleasure.

When it came he cried out with her, losing himself in the sensation of her pulsing hard and fast around his fingers. Her climax was violent and all consuming; she leaned against him, legs shaking, and he held her, waiting for the waves to subside.

His cock strained painfully against his breeches. How lovely it would feel to bury himself in her wetness, in that small, pulsing place that begged for him.

But, damn it all, he was a man of honor; and having just lost the wager, not once but twice, he couldn't possibly take her.

At least not now. Not like this.

Besides, delaying the pleasure would only increase it when—*if*—he ever did indulge in that particular vice with Lady Violet.

Not that it didn't bloody *hurt* to step away from her now.

At last Lady Violet opened her eyes; they were slick and sated and very blue.

Wordlessly, and with great regret, Harclay removed his fingers from her sex and let her chemise slide back down to her ankles. He loosened his grip and set her down on her feet, stepping back. Lady Violet stood still, unable to move or speak.

For some moments they stood beside each other, surveying a large painting of a woman in ornate court dress that hung above the fireplace. It took every ounce of his self-control not to take her in his arms, throw her on the settee, and have his way with her. How delicious she'd feel, still wet and willing, and, good *God*, those moans of pleasure—

"Ghastly portrait," she finally said. "All that lace and silk and still the old bag is as bracket faced as they come."

"That's my great-aunt Eugenia."

"You look nothing like her," Lady Violet said quickly and focused her gaze on her slippered feet.

Several beats of uncomfortable silence passed between them before he spoke.

"I hope you enjoyed"—Harclay gulped—"that as much as I did."

She did not look at him, but he could tell by the violent coloring of her cheeks that she had enjoyed it indeed.

"I'd like to brand you a cad, a shameless defiler with a thirst for one thing, and one thing only," she began softly, meeting his eyes at last. "But unlike the cad I'd thought you to be, you defended me before Lord Casterleigh. Why? Why'd you make that silly boy apologize? It wasn't necessary, you know."

Harclay stepped toward her. "Of course it was necessary. The idiot practically pushed you to the ground! No man should treat a woman with any measure of disrespect, big or small. Especially not a woman of mine."

His voice caught on that last word. Bloody hell, he hadn't meant to say it quite like that. But there it was; his face burned.

"Now it's my turn to apologize," he said softly, looking away. "I didn't mean—"

Violet smiled. "I know what you meant."

Laughter rumbled in his chest, but he did not reply. Silence settled between them, the slow, subtle cracking of the fire the only noise in the room.

Harclay cleared his throat. "I, ah, didn't . . . didn't hurt you, Lady Violet, did I?"

It was her turn to laugh. "No. Quite the opposite, actually. It's just—well, you're a bit of a sore loser, Lord Harclay. And after the way you played, I hardly believe you deserve to win."

"Aha," Harclay replied. "I can't say that I disagree."

He paused, gathering his thoughts. "But what about a consolation prize? A single question, which you must swear to answer truthfully."

Lady Violet pursed her lips, considering his request. "Very well, Lord Harclay. What is it that you'd like to know?"

It was bold of him to ask, very bold indeed, but he suddenly, urgently needed to know the answer. He told himself he asked on behalf of his own safety, so that he might avoid any mistake that would reveal him as the culprit of the theft.

But his racing pulse, and the ache in his chest, told a much different tale, one that Harclay was not entirely familiar with.

The words came out in a single, nearly unintelligible breath.

"What, exactly, is the nature of your acquaintance with Mr. Hope?"

Eight

Violet stared at Harclay as if a third ear had sprouted from the middle of his forehead. Of all the questions he could have asked, he'd chosen the one she absolutely, positively did not want to answer.

Not only was the earl terrifically handsome and, from what she could feel through her chemise, well-endowed, he was also savvy, clever in a way that was wholly unexpected for a man of his position. No doubt he was fluent in Greek and Latin and all that rubbish they taught at Eton and Cambridge. But he was fluent, too, in body language; he could read emotions, read a *person*, from a mere desultory glance or two.

He had, after all, pinned the very crux of her predicament after a single evening together and in a single, devastating question.

She met his eyes, hoping to find some clue as to why he asked, what answer he was looking for. But while Lord Harclay was a master at reading others, he was scrupulous in ensuring no one would return the favor. His features were carefully arranged in a vague expression that could have been boredom, polite interest, even distaste. It was the kind of expression he'd wear while listening to Great-Aunt Eugenia complain about her son-in-law's predilection for American whiskey, her husband's for Chinese opium.

What with her blood rioting, her legs and belly molten from his touch, Violet could hardly think. How could she possibly explain her dire circumstances to *him*, enormously wealthy, titled earl that he was? He would never understand. He'd judge her as a destitute fortune seeker intent on ensnaring the richest man she could find.

Which, maddeningly, couldn't have been further from the truth.

Violet took the first route that came to mind and pasted the most seductive smile she could manage on her lips.

"My dear, *dear* Lord Harclay," she purred. "Jealous, are we? Mr. Hope is a very handsome, very powerful man. Though I would hardly think a gentleman of your esteemed lineage would stoop to compete with a man of business."

The earl turned to her. His hands, she saw, were clasped tightly at the small of his back, as if he were restraining himself from reaching out to touch her.

"The only man with whom I compete is myself, Lady Violet, though I daresay Mr. Hope would make a most dangerous adversary."

He stepped forward, his face suddenly close to hers. He loomed above her—Violet's head barely grazed his chin—and in a low, steady voice said, "When you agreed to my request, you swore to answer truthfully. Out with it, dear girl; I'll not let you out of my sight until I have the hard facts."

Violet swallowed, trying her best to remain standing as the weakness in her knees suddenly returned.

There was no escaping this man. She'd just won two *thousand* pounds off him, and she did not doubt he would have what she owed him, whether she wanted to give it up or not.

With a sigh of resignation she turned back to the sofa. She sat quietly on its edge, bending to retrieve her blanket from the floor and wrapping it tightly about her shoulders. She turned her head so that she might not have to meet his eyes as she shared the awful truth.

"Best to start from the beginning, I suppose," she began. "My grandfather, the eighth Duke of Sommer, was a man of many interests. Art, architecture, antiques—our houses are stuffed with his treasures. Unfortunately, keeping his tenants fed was not among them. Like many of his neighbors, he hoarded the crops grown on his land, grain in particular, so that he might sell them at inflated prices.

"This, of course, led to the bread riots. In '95, and then again in '01, if memory serves. People were starving, but dear old Grandpapa made a fortune selling his grain to far-flung merchants. My father was appalled; in true British fashion they did not get on, he and Grandpapa. When my father inherited the title ten years ago, he reversed my grandfather's policies. He distributed his grain freely, so that people in our villages, and in London, might have something to eat."

Harclay offered a barely perceptible nod. "Very noble of him."

"Noble indeed," Violet replied, smoothing the blanket about her knees. "Though by the time I came out our family's fortune was all but gone, my father in his kindness having spent it. What little was left he invested in Mr. Hope's bank. My father is of the belief, you see, that the future lies not in land but in commerce."

"And you agree with your father, Lady Violet?"

She turned to look at him. He surveyed her dispassionately, though his eyes took on an intriguing sort of gleam. He was testing her, sounding out her honesty, her engagement with the truth.

"I do," she said. "Though, as you may have heard, my father has been . . . unwell for quite some time now. I'm afraid he may have invested our family's funds when he was not of sound mind."

"I see," Harclay said. "But surely you trust Mr. Hope to safeguard your investment. He's made me plenty of money."

"Of course I trust Mr. Hope! He has a brilliant mind for business and is a most interesting character besides. But for my father to have invested the bulk of our funds in Hope and Company stock—well, I don't need to tell you of the risk. Now that we own little more than a hundred or so shares, my family's inheritance, our fate, is inexorably tied to that of Mr. Hope himself."

Again Lord Harclay nodded, this time with slightly more

vigor. "I see indeed. That explains why you are concerned about the theft making the papers."

"If the public learns of the theft—why, who would trust Mr. Hope to keep his money safe if Hope himself was robbed, and in his own home? It would be a terrible blow to Mr. Hope and to his bank. The value of my shares would plummet, my inheritance all but gone—and with my father to look after . . ."

To her great horror, Violet could not finish. Her throat grew thick with tears; she hadn't realized just how terrified she was until this moment. She wanted to blame the champagne—*damn* Lord Harclay and that blasted bottle!— for she wasn't usually one to blubber; but she knew better. The reality of her predicament weighed crushingly on her shoulders, and it was all she could do not to burst into noisy, wet sobs.

She managed a glance at the earl and was surprised to see her own horror mirrored on his face. He quickly smoothed his features into his customary inscrutable expression, but she did not miss the darkness that flickered in his eyes.

Intriguing indeed. Was it possible the Earl of Harclay, that wildly wealthy rakehell, *sympathized* with her plight?

No, no, she reasoned, certainly not. It was probably as she feared: he thought she'd come to yoke him into matrimony, to pay down her debts with her fortune.

Violet straightened, cleared her throat. "So you see, Lord Harclay, my relationship with Mr. Hope is purely one of business. Of course we are well acquainted with one another, see-ing as our fortunes are so closely bound; we mingle socially, I pilfer his brandy when he's not looking, that sort of thing. But at the end of it we are business partners."

The earl appeared rather stricken and looked as if he were about to reach out and—what? Embrace her, take her by the shoulders and shake her, imploring her to get hold of her emotions?

Violet rose before he could so much as lay a finger on her person. At last Harclay turned to her. "If there's anything I can do to help, Lady Violet, anything at all, you need only ask."

She smiled. "Two thousand, if you please, and not a penny less."

"I shall have a note ready for you in the morning, at breakfast."

Her belly turned over, and turned again, the blood draining from her face. "Breakfast? But I've got to get back to my family—and I'm not one for mornings, really, especially not after a night like this one."

No, *no*, she couldn't very well show her worst self to this godlike creature, a creature who probably rose at dawn and loved nothing more than a long, hearty breakfast.

"Indeed. I usually rise at dawn, and I do so love a long, hearty breakfast. None of that tea and biscuits nonsense; I like coffee and meat—bacon and sausage—and perhaps even a pottage of oats and cinnamon. Yes, that's the ticket!"

Oh dear, oh dear, she thought in a panic, if he can read my thoughts, I'm really in trouble.

She tried to swallow her distress, though in all likelihood she appeared to the earl quite piqued.

"Well, then." He sighed and offered her his arm. "Shall I show you back to your room? I'll have the maids come to you early, so that you might have something to eat before you go."

Nine

The hall clock struck half past seven when Harclay strode into the cozy alcove of the breakfast room. It was a lovely little place, one of his favorite spots in all London, perhaps the world; shaped irregularly in a sort of octagon, the walls were covered simply in plum-colored silk, and a single large window looked out above an ivy-covered alley.

The familiar smells of frying meat and coffee greeted him as he crossed the threshold; the familiar paper, still steaming from Avery's iron, awaited him at the head of the table; and the familiar faces of Gregory and Mr. Kane, the footmen, were smiling at him, freshly scrubbed and well rested.

And yet, as he sat at his place and had the familiar white linen napkin placed in his lap, he felt not at all the familiar contentment he usually did at the start of the day. Indeed, he was seized by a *most* unfamiliar distraction and giddiness that, frankly, alarmed him.

After depositing Lady Violet at the door of the appropriate bedchamber—how he'd longed, quite violently, to bring her to his own and finish what he'd begun in the drawing room—he'd returned to his room and spent the rest of the night pacing before the fire.

Yes, the knowledge that the diamond was now in his possession still thrilled him. He was most satisfied with his performance and recalled with no small pleasure how alive he had felt during the theft, how brilliantly he'd executed his plan. The gap-toothed assassins were admittedly a self-indulgent addition to the scheme; but Harclay was only human, and a man after all. Such follies, rare as they were, had to be excused.

He *did* feel badly for placing Violet in so precarious a condition, what with her hundred shares of Hope & Co., and her future, hanging in the balance. It wasn't his intention to harm her, Hope, or his bank; after all, the lion's share of Harclay's fortune was deposited at Hope & Co., and he owned a goodly amount of stock himself. He'd return the French Blue when the time was right, before irrevocable damage was done. He would not see Violet hurt, not by him, not by anyone; she was far too marvelous a gambler, and dashedly beautiful besides.

Ah, Violet: he recalled her smiling wildly in his arms as he whirled her about the ballroom; what a vision she was standing before the drawing room fire, in naught but loose hair and chemise; her coquettish smile, half-hidden behind the bedchamber door as she waved him good night . . .

"Sir?" Mr. Kane was saying. "Shall I bring you a small plate to tide you over until the ladies arrive?"

Harclay blinked and for a moment stared at Kane as if seeing the man for the first time.

"Er, indeed, that would be splendid," he replied. His response came out gruffer than he'd intended. Apparently, and to his great distress, it annoyed him that Kane had interrupted his Lady Violet reverie.

His fist came down on the table. "Damn that woman!"

The china clattered; his coffee sloshed out of its cup.

Harclay did not realize he had spoken the words aloud until Kane poked out his head and peered curiously at his master.

"Ahem. Are you quite well, my lord?"

Carefully, without meeting Harclay's eyes, Mr. Kane set his cup back to rights on its saucer.

"Not at all, Mr. Kane," Harclay replied with a sigh. "Not at all."

From the hall came the tinkling sounds of female laughter. At once both men straightened. Harclay took the paper in his hands and snapped it open, lest he be caught waiting slack-jawed for their arrival.

As was her habit—poor dear was as clumsy as a drunkard—his elder sister, the Dowager Countess of Berry, tripped into the room. It was all he could do not to roll his eyes; even as she approached thirty, Caroline seemed unable to remain upright for more than two minutes at a time. Luckily her lack of grace did little to diminish her beauty, at least in Harclay's eyes. She had their mother's dark features and pale, unblemished skin. Her penchant for sweeping, dramatic hairstyles lent her a Continental air, as if she were a creature of Marie-Antoinette's court.

Then again, Marie-Antoinette—famous teetotaler that she was—would hardly countenance a lady who always appeared to be *well* in her cups.

He held his breath as Lady Violet entered. To his relief—or perhaps his dismay; he couldn't quite tell—she was dressed smartly in one of Caroline's morning gowns. It was a virginal sort of thing, pale muslin with a high neck and a matching pink ribbon tied around the bust.

Apart from the slight blush that stained the apples of her cheeks, her color appeared healthy. Though she couldn't have slept more than a handful of hours—it was well past three when they'd gone to bed—she looked fresh, eyes bright.

Above the top of his paper he caught her gaze. Apprehension flashed across her eyes, very blue in the bright light from the window; and there was something else, a flicker of laughter, perhaps, and he wondered if the champagne hadn't quite worn off yet.

"Ladies," he said, folding the paper and rising to his feet. "Lovely of you to join me, and at so early an hour. I trust you have made each other's acquaintance?"

"Indeed," Caroline replied, brow raised as if to say, *Acquainted indeed, but it's the real story I'm after.*

She turned to Lady Violet and took her hands. "The maids informed me of Lady Violet's presence this morning, and I went straightaway to see her. Poor dear told me about the tragic events at Mr. Hope's ball. To think, a thief made off with the French Blue in the midst of a crowded ballroom! I wonder how he did it."

"Well"—Harclay cleared his throat—"hardly worth thinking about, seeing as it's over and done. We must focus our energies on helping Mr. Hope capture the perpetrators, so that the diamond might yet be found."

"Hear, hear," Caroline replied. She took her customary seat at his right. Lady Violet sank demurely into the chair at his left.

"I daresay missing Mr. Hope's ball was a brilliant stroke of luck," his sister continued. "But oh, how I longed to attend!"

Lady Violet stirred sugar and cream into her coffee and set the spoon with a small *ping* on the saucer. "Are you not yet out of mourning, Lady Caroline?"

"Only just," she replied with a small sigh. "But my dearest, darling little brother insisted Mr. Hope's ball was *not* the place for my—what did you call it?—oh, yes, my 'reemergence' into society."

"Oh?" Lady Violet arched a brow as her gaze shot to Harclay. "Wanted to keep all the fun for himself, did he?"

"Hardly," he said gruffly and once again snapped open the paper in protest.

His reasons weren't entirely ignoble. Of *course* he wanted to keep all the fun for himself—but he also wanted to keep his sister far from harm. What if, God forbid, she had been assaulted by the thieves or, worse, ogled by one of Hope's unscrupulous foreign friends?

Besides, Caroline would have doubtless managed to make a bloody mess out of all those costumed courtiers—their wigs and long dresses and canes were hideously ripe for her kind of disaster.

"Any mention of the incident in today's paper?" Lady Violet asked. Her tone was casual, nonchalant, but by the way she avoided his gaze he could tell she was eager to know.

"Let us see," Harclay replied. He glanced quickly over the headlines, the news, and the society pages.

Nothing. To his very great relief, and doubtless to Lady Violet's, too, there was no mention of Mr. Hope's ball nor the theft of the French Blue.

"We have more time yet, Lady Violet," he said with a smile. "No doubt Mr. Hope had a hand in it; he's got friends at all the papers. Probably paid a pretty penny to buy us time, so that we might find the diamond before the story is out. In any case, I imagine he desires to be the hero, cunning and powerful enough to track down and destroy his enemies. As it stands now—well, the hero he is not."

Lady Violet let out a long, slow breath and seemed to settle more comfortably in her chair. "We shall have to get to work, and straightaway. The thieves could very well be on their way to St. Petersburg for all we know. It won't do to give them a head start."

"Masked bandits, a cursed diamond—it all makes for a delicious mystery, does it not?" Caroline clasped her hands at her chest. In her excitement she managed to elbow poor Mr. Kane, who was at that very moment filling her plate with fragrant little sausages.

With a groan Harclay watched as the tureen fell from Kane's hands and landed with an enormous clatter on the floor.

Not yet eight o'clock, and already the day was proving a trying one.

"Don't be silly, Caroline. I hardly think it appropriate for you to be involved in this mess, seeing as you're perfectly capable of making your own here at home."

Caroline straightened from helping Mr. Kane retrieve the sausages from the carpet. "I became involved the moment the two of you walked into this house, having barely escaped with your lives. I shan't miss the fun this time, *Lord* Harclay, despite your most selfish efforts to hoard it for yourself."

"Hear, hear," Lady Violet replied and offered Harclay a most wicked smile between bites of bacon.

Harclay resisted the temptation to gather the paper into a ball and hurl it at his guest. Rather, he folded it, running the crease between his thumb and forefinger with great vigor, and was about to place it on the table when Avery appeared at the threshold.

Harclay took one look at the man and knew something was afoot.

The ladies, sensing trouble, dropped their silverware and looked first to Avery, then to Harclay.

"Yes, Avery?"

"Forgive me, my lord, I've rather urgent news from Mr. Hope. One of his men waits now in the front hall. It seems they have caught the thieves and are keeping them at Mr.

Hope's house for questioning. Mr. Hope also asks after the Lady Violet Rutledge."

Harclay's pulse quickened, and he bit back a grin. Events were proceeding just as he'd planned: Hope and his men moved down a path that led them away from the diamond.

And, of course, away from Harclay.

Lady Violet was on her feet and at his side before he could reply.

"Bring round the carriage, Avery, and make quick work of it. We haven't a moment to spare, nary a moment!" she said.

Avery gaped at Lady Violet, then turned to Harclay.

Harclay sighed, unable to keep the ends of his mouth from twitching upward. "Very well, Avery. We leave at once."

Avery bowed and, with one last look of bewilderment at Lady Violet, moved crisply from the room.

"You've quite the cheek, and so early in the morning," Harclay murmured as they made their way through the house, Caroline stumbling a few steps behind.

She turned her head, and for a fleeting moment their eyes met. "I daresay it will be my cheek that leads us to the men who did this, and to the diamond."

Again that same rousing beat of his pulse. "Yes," he replied. "I daresay it will."

Ten

Violet was surprised to see Cousin Sophia and Auntie George seated in Mr. Hope's exquisitely curated drawing room. She was, however, positively *shocked* to see Sophia still sporting her gauzy costume from the previous night. The dark smudges beneath Auntie's eyes told Violet that Sophia had indeed spent the night doing something wholly, unforgivably scandalous.

The moment they turned their gazes to meet her own, Sophia and Auntie dove forward and crushed her in their arms.

"You naughty girl, we were so worried!"

"The shots! I thought you'd been killed!"

"I say, whose dress are you wearing?"

"Oh," Auntie said, eyes fluttering as she placed a hand on her chest. "Oh, how relieved I am you are unscathed and in good spirits. We received Lord Harclay's note. Handsome fellow, isn't he?" Her eyes peeked over Violet's shoulder.

"But don't you think," she continued, lowering her voice, "don't you *dare* think it excuses your behavior! Running off into the night *with a known rakeshame*! Why, even just saying the words makes my chest palpitate, yes, *palpitate*! As God is my witness, the two of you will be the end of me!"

"You must not blame Lady Violet," came a voice from behind. "I take full responsibility for the unfortunate events of last night."

Violet turned—what an odd thing for him to say, as if he'd been responsible for the theft of the jewel and all the trouble that ensued—and nearly bumped noses with Lord Harclay. His knee brushed against the middle of her thigh, and for a moment she was transported back to his drawing room. Her blood leapt at the memory of his hands on her skin, the taste of his kiss as he opened her with his lips . . .

"Dear Lady Wallace," Harclay drawled as he bent to press those same lips to Auntie's gloved fingers. "On my honor, I shall take great pains to ensure your niece's reputation does not suffer on account of my actions. I may have become . . . overly excited in the heat of the moment."

Indeed, Violet recalled him pressing that excitement against her skirts as he kissed her senseless in his drawing room.

"Thank you, thank you very much," Auntie stuttered as she looked Harclay up and down and back again.

Violet bit back a smile. Even Auntie George, in all her matronly exasperation, was not immune to Harclay's wickedly effortless charm, his indecent good looks.

"So you understand, Aunt Georgiana, that Lord Harclay's intentions were most honorable," Violet added. "Besides, the Dowager Countess of Berry, his sister, is currently residing at his house and was a most rigorous chaperone."

Auntie George opened her mouth to reply, but at that moment Mr. Hope strode purposefully into the room. At his heels limped an enormously muscled man with a wide, square face, marred only by a black eye patch that covered his left eye.

"Harclay! Lady Violet! Thank God you've come. Please, sit, sit, we haven't the time for niceties."

Violet did not miss Mr. Hope exchanging a glance, and a small, secret sort of smile, with Cousin Sophia as they took their places.

Violet arranged herself on a sofa between Sophia and Lady Caroline, who perched awkwardly on the edge of the cushion like an oversized parrot.

"First things first," Hope said, drawing up before the small crowd. "We have managed to apprehend a band of men whom we suspect were involved in last night's theft. We're keeping them down in the scullery for the time being; my men brought them in at dawn and have been questioning them since."

"Who are they?" Violet asked, wondering if by "we," Hope was referring to himself and Sophia. "How do you know they're connected to the crime?"

To Violet's surprise, Mr. Hope's color rose, and he cleared his throat not once but twice.

An unfamiliar voice, low, rumbling like thunder, broke the silence. "We found them at a whorehouse in Cheapside," the one-eyed man said. "Fistfuls of guineas, black clothes strewn about the place. One of them wagged his tongue to a lady friend and told her all about the crime. She went to the madam, and the madam, naturally, went to Mr. Hope."

"Naturally," Violet quipped. Really, the longer she knew Hope, the more interesting he became. She didn't take him for the type to visit houses of ill repute; but then again, he was acquainted with virtually every figure of import in London. Madams of such houses, she supposed, were very important figures indeed when one considered the appetites of that lesser sex, *man*.

After a good pat on Auntie's shoulder—she was on the verge of a swoon—Lady Violet turned back to the gruff stranger.

"And who, good sir, might you be?"

"Ah, yes, forgive me!" Mr. Hope rocked back on his heels. "Allow me to introduce Mr. Henry Beaton Lake, a . . . Well, I don't quite know what you are these days. An old friend? Anyway. He's generously offered his services in solving this little puzzle of ours."

Violet detected a trace of irony in Hope's words. "Services?" she replied, narrowing her eyes at Mr. Lake. "What sort of services, exactly?"

Mr. Lake returned her gaze levelly, his one green eye blazing. "The sort that is not to be discussed among polite company, my lady."

Mr. Hope groaned.

"How marvelously mysterious!" Lady Caroline exclaimed. In her excitement she very nearly pitched off the sofa. Mr.

Lake lurched forward—my, thought Violet, he moves rather quickly for one with a limp—and snatched Caroline by the elbows.

The room exclaimed all at once; Auntie George blanched and began flapping both hands at her face in an attempt to fan herself.

"Oh, how clumsy of me," Caroline continued as she righted herself on the cushion. "Marvelous, no, that's not at all what I meant. About your limp, or your eye, of course, nothing marvelous about that, but I imagine you're quite the adventurer—"

Lord Harclay cleared his throat. "Thank you, Caroline, I'm sure Mr. Lake knows what you meant."

He turned to Mr. Lake. "I'm afraid your eye patch is giving the ladies all sorts of delicious ideas. Best to let them rest their eager imaginations. In the meantime we shall interview these scoundrels and, with any luck, be done with this sordid business."

The gentlemen, knowing their window of opportunity was short indeed, scurried from the room as if it contained not four ladies of breeding but a pride of pacing lionesses.

But Violet would not be excluded from the hunt for the thieves. Not only did she have her inheritance, her family's livelihood, to consider; she felt responsible for the diamond's disappearance. She had been wearing it, after all, when it was stolen. Snatched from her neck, as easily as if she were naught but a helpless child. She should've paid better attention, should've tucked it into her stays the moment the brigands crashed through the ballroom windows.

No, she would not allow others to fix her mistakes for her. She was possessed of enough faith in her own cunning to believe she was capable of tracking down the French Blue. She had managed to keep the family intact and well cared for these past three years—no small feat, considering the enormous sums it took to keep Auntie fed and Sophia dressed. Surely, if she could manage that, she could find the diamond and secure their future.

Besides, Violet had to admit Lord Harclay's involvement in the hunt played no small part in her enthusiasm for it. It would certainly lift her spirits to lay eyes on his glorious person in the trying days ahead.

And so, before the other ladies even opened their mouths in protest, Violet was on her feet and bounding for the door. She slid through the narrow gap just in time, the door swinging shut at her back and catapulting her into the gallery.

She hurried after the men, catching up at last with Lord Harclay. His long legs afforded him a laughably enormous stride. Violet had to trot to keep pace.

"Are you sure you want to see this?" Harclay said without looking at her. "I did not refer to this business as sordid in jest."

"Don't be ridiculous," Violet panted. "I've known sordid business plenty enough, having lived with Auntie George and Cousin Sophia my whole life."

She thought she saw the flash of his teeth, a smile perhaps; but as quickly as it appeared it was gone.

They made their way to the basement of the house. Mr. Hope's kitchen, a cavernous space covered in gleaming white tile, was already bustling with the day's business. As she passed by, Violet breathed in the familiar scents of rosemary and butter, mingled with savory, spicy odors she did not recognize.

Mr. Hope led them to a small room at the back of the house. As they approached, Sophia could hear men's voices, several of them all talking at once.

Pausing before the door, Mr. Hope turned to them. "No use employing the authorities, seeing as how the Bow Street Runners have been hideously underfunded these past few years. I've brought in my own security force, the same I use at the bank to guard our assets. They're good, the best money can buy."

As if on cue, the door opened and a crisply dressed man, clutching a clay pipe between his teeth, emerged. He met eyes with Mr. Hope and shook his head.

"Nothing yet," he said. "But we could use more coffee, if you please, Mr. Hope."

Over the man's shoulder, Violet peeked into the room. The supposed thieves sat about an oblong table, their hands cuffed to the chair spindles. Mr. Hope's men were seated on the opposite side of the table. Smoke rose from their pipes—apparently Mr. Hope hired only men with chimneys for lungs—while empty cups crowded before them on the table around a porcelain pot.

The bandits appeared wretched. Their faces, a ruddy, purple-red like moldy radishes, were swollen with drink and exhaustion. Whatever they felt—remorse, anger—it weighed upon them heavily,

Their rumpled sleeves were pushed up to their elbows. She noted with a spark of interest that their forearms were heavily muscled, extraordinarily so. Thick, corded veins ran the length of their arms and webbed about the backs of their hands.

Whatever their profession—Violet deduced it wasn't thievery, for who built muscles like that picking pockets?—they were obviously fellows who enjoyed sport.

"Let me talk to them," Violet said, reaching for the door. "I've got an idea."

She was about to cross the threshold when Lord Harclay grasped her none too gently about the arm. "You can't possibly be serious, going in there unescorted to face those men. It isn't safe."

Violet looked down at his hand, the fingers wrapped tightly about her flesh. She tried her best to ignore the heat that pulsed through her body at his touch.

"I'm quite serious," she replied. "If you'd just allow me a few minutes with them—"

"Absolutely not," Harclay said. "If any of those men so much as lays a finger on you, I shall have to avenge your honor, and God knows this house has witnessed enough gunplay to last a lifetime. No, if you go in there, I am going with you."

Violet opened her mouth to protest—she could avenge her own damn honor—but one glance at the stone-set gleam in his eye, and she thought better of it.

"Very well," she replied, straightening her skirts. "But don't think for a moment I'll allow you to take charge, Lord Harclay."

With a roll of his eyes he reached for the door and held it ajar as she whisked past. "Oh, believe me, Lady Violet, I wouldn't dream of it."

The late-afternoon sun streamed through the shutters of Harclay's study, glinting off the brandy that lay untouched in its heavy crystal glass on his desk. He'd been sitting here for hours now, the day quickly descending into dusk, in an attempt to discern without much luck how in *hell* that bloody woman had done it.

The pounding in his skull, still thick from the previous night's champagne and almost complete lack of sleep, did nothing to help him parse the details of Lady Violet's interview.

With a scoff he recalled how she had sidled up to the bandits, how she'd paced most provocatively about the room, the only sound the soft *whoosh* of her skirts as she bandied them about her hips. Clever girl, she did not forget, not for a moment, that the thieves had been found bare-assed in a whorehouse and very likely had not had the chance to finish their business. The sight of a woman, she knew, was sure to capture their imagination.

Violet had used this knowledge to brilliant effect. Not only had she coaxed the thieves to talk; she'd coaxed them into talking about the details she was after. To Harclay's great pleasure, the bandits had revealed exactly what he'd wanted them to: everything . . . and nothing.

The way the bandits—and Mr. Hope's security force—had looked at Lady Violet drove Harclay mad, even now. It was all he could do not to wrap her in his arms and remove her from their openly ravenous gazes. The thought of sharing any part of her with any of these men made his blood run hot; he'd stood protectively at her side throughout the entire interview, brooding in what he hoped appeared to be threatening silence.

Pointing to the bandits' hands and arms, Violet had correctly deduced that the thieves were part of a traveling circus, acrobats in town for nightly exhibitions in Vauxhall Gardens. In barely decipherable cockney they'd told their story: how they'd been approached one evening a week before by a strange-looking fellow with bad teeth and a fake beard (how, Harclay wondered, did they know the beard was false but miss the awful wooden dentures?). How the man had offered each of them fifty pounds—twenty-five right then, the other half after the crime had been committed—to make a mess of Mr. Hope's ball.

"But what of the diamond? What instructions did the man give you about stealing Mr. Hope's diamond?" she'd asked.

The acrobats responded with blank stares.

"We ain't bover wif no diamond," one of them said. "Man make no mention ov it, just paid us to make a right nice racket."

Violet met Harclay's gaze above the heads of those gathered about the table, eyes narrowed in concentration. He could see the silent calculations taking place in that lovely head of hers, the effort to put together the scant pieces of this puzzle.

"And what of the other twenty-five pounds the man owes you? Have you received it yet?"

"Nah," replied the man. "Seein' as we been caught, we ain't expectin' to see the rest. Though that ain't exactly fair, now, is it?"

Harclay had not had the chance to discuss the findings with Lady Violet. Mr. Lake, that one-eyed ginger—really, Hope was possessed of a most bizarre acquaintance—had immediately cornered her after the interview. To Harclay's dismay the two of them had disappeared down the hall, heads bent in conversation.

Even now his chest flared with something unpleasant, something hard, at the memory of Violet's arm looped through Lake's. Just what did she tell him, and he her? Did they deduce, correctly, that these red-faced scalawags had nothing to do with the diamond?

Had Violet, with that cunning, scheming mind of hers, somehow concluded that Harclay himself was the thief?

He jumped to his feet, unable to bear the speculation a moment longer. The light from the window burned gold, and felt warm on his skin; checking his pocket watch, Harclay saw it was quarter to five. If he hurried, he could make it to Lady Violet's house just in time to escort her on a stroll through Hyde Park. The fashionable hour, that golden stretch between five and six in the afternoon, was fast approaching.

It was admittedly a bit late for a call and, seeing as he'd never called on Lady Violet or her family before, a somewhat minor breach of propriety for him to appear on her doorstep.

Harclay smiled. Never mind minor breaches; he'd devoured Violet whole, had put his hands on her body and brought her to exquisite pleasure. She didn't seem to mind then; she probably wouldn't mind now.

As Avery helped him into his jacket in the front hall, Harclay assured himself that he called on Lady Violet for strictly practical purposes. He needed to know what she was thinking, how far she was coming in solving the crime.

Yes, he concluded, a short stroll would surely accomplish that. And then he'd take his leave, be on his way, perhaps stop at White's for a nip and a refreshingly female-free meal.

But the lightness of his step, and the irrepressible smile on his lips—"I see your health is restored, my lord," Avery said with a grin—told a much different story.

Harclay was about to exit through the front door when Lady Caroline skidded into the hall. She stood before him with arms akimbo, trying her damnedest to arrange her features into a scowl of consternation.

"And where, dear brother, do you think you're going?"

It was all he could do not to groan aloud. "If you must know, dear sister, I am going to call on Lady Violet. I feel rather terribly for her, what with the missing diamond and all that. It's only proper I see to the condition of her nerves."

Caroline surveyed him through narrowed eyes. "The *condition* of her *nerves*? I don't believe you for a moment. But if you allow me to accompany you, I promise not to pursue the matter any further."

Harclay sighed. These women—all women—would be the death of him, the death of all mankind.

A female-free dinner at White's was a refreshing prospect indeed.

Eleven

Taking yet another turn about the room, Violet clasped her hands behind her back. "I cannot make sense of it, Mr. Lake," she said. "Why were those men hired, if not to steal the diamond? Why waste hundreds of pounds on acrobats, just to have them shoot up Mr. Hope's ceiling?"

Her thoughts throbbed in her head, racing and tangling and tripping over one another to form a rather impossible knot. Somewhere in the back of her mind she sensed her exhaustion, the ache of her knees, and the roil of her belly as the last of Lord Harclay's champagne worked its way through her body.

Damn the man to hell, she had better things to think of than his kiss, the vision of him in buckskins and billowing sleeves before the fire. But despite her best efforts to focus on the task at hand—finding the French Blue's thief—time and time again her thoughts returned to the Earl of Harclay, especially as the afternoon wore on and her patience wore thin.

"Did the acrobats mention anything else? Anything at all?" Mr. Lake asked.

Violet had convinced Hope and Mr. Lake to decamp to her family's house so that she might change clothes. They were in

Violet's study—well, her father's study, really, but she'd repurposed it the previous year after the duke grew too ill to use it—and Mr. Lake was seated across the large desk in one of two round-backed chairs. His stiff leg was stretched out before him, and every so often he would reach down and with a wince squeeze the muscle above his knee.

He was a handsome fellow, Violet thought, despite his wounds; even his eye patch made him appear mysterious, debonair. He was careful in his dress, and in his grooming: his thick queue of strawberry blond hair was tied with a narrow green ribbon that matched the color of his eye.

She'd certainly heard of him. Mr. Lake came from an old, well-respected family, but as the third—or was it the fourth?—son, he was forced to seek a life outside the family manor. Despite his lack of fortune he'd managed to purchase a commission in His Majesty's army; beyond that, she knew nothing. Violet suspected the details of his employment were intentionally scarce.

"Wait," Violet said, suddenly coming to a halt. "What if that man—the one in the wig, who hired the acrobats—what if he was using them to create a distraction? As a way to create chaos, so the crowd was too occupied by the gunshots and the sudden darkness to notice him snatching the diamond from around my neck?"

Mr. Lake clapped his hands. "I think you're on to something, Lady Violet. Now it makes sense, if the thief indeed employed a Trojan horse–type strategem. Distract Mr. Hope's guests with acrobats hurtling through the windows, shooting their pistols, and dousing the lights, so that the thief could attack and steal the jewel unimpeded and under cover of darkness."

Violet nodded, slowly. "Clever. Yes, very clever indeed. Still, you must admit it was reckless of the thief to steal a priceless diamond in the midst of the season's grandest ball. He snatched the French Blue, and managed to escape with it, in plain sight of nearly five hundred people. *Five hundred.* And as far as we can tell, no one saw a thing."

"It doesn't help our case that nearly everyone in that ballroom—guests, orchestra, staff—was in costume," Mr. Lake said. "What if the thief was not among the acrobats or the gun-wielding guards at all, but among the guests? Dressed like everyone else in the guise of a courtier or king? That way he could move virtually unnoticed through the crowd."

Violet nodded. "It is certainly possible. But Mr. Hope is so well liked, and well respected, by his guests. What motive would drive someone to steal from his benevolent host?"

Mr. Lake held up his hand. "Let's go over this one more time. Tell me everything you remember, from the time you arrived at the ball to the moment of your departure."

Violet fell heavily onto the wide leather chair opposite Mr. Lake—this was to be the third time she told her tale—and began talking. She told him of her arrival with Auntie George and Cousin Sophia, of Mr. Hope placing the French Blue about her neck.

And then she told him about Lord Harclay. She remembered with startling clarity the way he looked when he approached her from across the ballroom, and the feel of his hands on her body as he led her through the waltz. How in the darkness he pulled her against him and whispered, *You must trust me, and keep close*, in her ear; how he pummeled the intruders, then slung her over his shoulder as if she weighed no more than a parasol.

"Interesting," Mr. Lake said, interrupting her reverie.

Violet looked away, so that he might not see her blush. "What's so interesting this time around?"

"It seems you were accompanied by Lord Harclay—*only* Lord Harclay—the entire evening. Are the two of you in any way connected? Courting, perhaps?" Mr. Lake said.

Violet admired the man's blunt manner—it would go a long ways, she knew, in the search for Mr. Hope's diamond— but at this moment it was all she could do not to reach across the table and box his ears.

"Absolutely not! He merely asked for a dance, and I couldn't very well refuse the Earl of Harclay. It just so happened we were at each other's side when the acrobats crashed through the windows."

"And he was at your side when the diamond was stolen?"

Violet shrank back into the chair, thinking. "Yes," she replied, the realization dawning on her. "Yes, I suppose he was. Almost as soon as the men attacked me, he was batting them away. He must've been right there beside me."

Mr. Lake steepled his fingers. "But Harclay says he saw nothing?"

"Well, he hasn't said as much; but I assume if he did see the thief in action, surely he would have said something to me or, better yet, tried to catch him. Besides, he was too busy pummeling my assailants to have paid much attention. And then there was the darkness—I could hardly see my own feet."

Mr. Lake nodded, furrowing his brows. "I shall have to talk with him. Perhaps he has some insight, some small piece of information, that we have overlooked."

"Perhaps," Violet replied. She rose to her feet and resumed her slow, steady steps around the room.

The clock sounded five strikes from the mantel, and Violet yawned as if on cue.

"Well," she said, "we've come quite far today, though not far enough. At the very least we have a better idea of who our thief might be. Someone with the skill and confidence to work alone; someone with the cheek to steal a fifty-carat stone in front of five hundred people; someone with funds enough to squander hundreds of pounds on mere distractions; someone, perhaps, who was at Mr. Hope's ball *before* the acrobats incited chaos."

Violet tapped a finger against her chin. "But who could that someone possibly be?"

There was a slight rap at the door, and Violet turned to see William Townshend, Earl of Harclay, standing in the threshold with his hat in his hands.

The weather was particularly pleasant, the late-springtime sun shining with such ardor that most of the ladies strolling in Hyde Park had traded their long pelisses for more stylish cropped spencer jackets.

Harclay thought Lady Violet looked particularly fetching in hers, a lavender concoction of muslin and lace that, though it covered her bosom well enough, somehow drew attention to that part of her he so admired. It was difficult not to stare as they made their way through the park, already crowded with members of the fashionable set taking a leisurely stroll before the evening's more rousing events. For a moment Harclay wondered which of those events Lady Violet would attend, if any. He wouldn't mind another waltz with her in his arms, though in all likelihood he'd have to travel to Vienna to find one; his countrymen the English were such terrible prudes.

"Your sister and Mr. Lake certainly get along," Lady Violet said, glancing over her shoulder.

"It appears so," Harclay replied, craning his neck. Caroline and Mr. Lake strolled a few steps behind, her gloved hand resting firmly on the man's forearm. They'd been inseparable since Mr. Lake, despite his injuries, very nearly carried Caroline down Lady Violet's front steps to keep her from taking a tumble.

"It must please you to see your sister happy after all those months of mourning. Poor dear, I can't imagine losing one's husband, and at so young an age."

"She is very dear to me indeed, though heaven knows she owes me a fortune. The surgeon alone cost me a hundred this year. Do you know she's broken five bones—nose included—and is missing three teeth?"

This made Lady Violet laugh, a little sound that made his heart swell. "Do you know, Lord Harclay, that *you* owe *me* two thousand pounds? You said you'd have it ready at breakfast. Surely you know debts of honor must be paid straightaway."

"Perhaps"—he arched a brow—"I prefer to be in your debt, my lady. That way I have an excuse to enjoy your presence for an indefinite period of time, for I know you shall pursue me until you have what you're after."

For several beats Lady Violet surveyed him in silence. Harclay could tell by the gleam in her eye that he'd set the wheel of her thoughts in motion. To his delight, he found her endlessly clever. He'd meant his comment to give her pause. It wouldn't be long, he knew, before she pinned him as the thief.

At last they came upon the Serpentine River, that glorious man-made stretch of green-blue water that divided Hyde Park neatly in two. Paddleboats dotted its molten surface, carrying ladies with parasols and their outstretched beaus. The noise from Rotten Row opposite the water carried over, the shouts of dandies loud and clear as they trolled about in precariously bright-colored phaetons.

It was London in springtime, a spectacle Harclay had

experienced every year throughout his nearly three decades of existence. But today the experience was different; with Lady Violet's arm looped through his own, the tableau of Hyde Park that stretched before them suddenly took on new significance. The sun was brighter; the water, clearer and more invigorating; the people friendlier; and the smells—well, for the first time the scent of freshly shorn grass overpowered that of horse manure.

"But what if I tire of your ploy?" she said at last. She fixed her gaze on the river, holding her gloved hand to her brow to block out the sun. "I could put that two thousand to good use, you know."

"Then perhaps I shall have to double down," he replied.

"*Again?* Four thousand! Why ever would you do such a thing? I imagine these sorts of sums are rather ruinous after a while."

He let out a long, low whistle. "Only ruinous when I deal with you, Lady Violet. You see, when I gamble, I usually win. As to why I propose doubling down—well, I'm afraid the only answer I have for you is because *I can.*"

"Because you can," she scoffed. "Of course."

Harclay shrugged. "What other reason is there?"

Lady Violet turned to face him. She stepped closer, as if by getting a better look she might better understand him, peculiar creature that he was. Harclay was at once startled and terribly aroused by her proximity. Her perfume—tuberose, pepper— tickled his nose and made his blood riot in his veins. By the way her eyes darted about his face, he could tell she was looking for something, some clue that she had missed.

Oh, she was getting close. Very, very close indeed.

"And you think you can win?" she said.

He smiled, inched his face closer to hers. "I know I can."

"Awfully confident, aren't you? And such cheek, thinking you might have a chance after I beat you soundly, not once but *twice*! Though I suppose to you, it's only money."

"Only money indeed."

Lady Violet's gaze landed on his lips. "Only money," she repeated. "*Only money.*"

She suddenly grew very still; the color faded from her cheeks, and her smile drew itself into a frown. He watched

her eyes go wide as the realization dawned on her, the pieces
of the puzzle falling into place at last.

What was it she'd been saying when he walked into the
study?

*The thief is someone with the skill and confidence to work
alone, with the cheek to steal a fifty-carat stone in front of
five hundred people. Someone with funds enough to squander hundreds of pounds on mere distractions.*

*Someone who arrived at Mr. Hope's ball before the acro-
bats arrived.*

Sounded like Harclay, all right, though by now Lady Violet knew he typically dealt not in hundreds, but in thousands
of pounds.

Somewhere in the trees above, birds twittered and flitted
about them; the edge of the Serpentine lapped quietly at their
feet. The springtime afternoon marched onward as if today
were but one of a string of simple, idle days, each the same as
the last.

But for Harclay and Lady Violet, today was not quite so
simple, nor so idle. It was suddenly complicated, mined with
explosive truths and well-played deceptions and a most thrilling episode of a physical encounter. It was impossible; it was
improbable.

And great God above, it thrilled Harclay to no end. He
hadn't felt such excitement since he was a boy, allowed to
accompany his father on the hunt for the first time. He would
never forget the way the rifle had felt in his hands, the pounding of his heart as he took aim.

Granted, he'd ended up shooting the poor loader in the
arse, a crime for which dear Papa had whipped him senseless.
But the thrill remained imprinted on Harclay's imagination
nonetheless, the same thrill he now experienced under the
accusatory gaze of Lady Violet Rutledge.

She took a deep breath, all the while her blue-gray eyes
never leaving his.

"It's you, isn't it?" she said, swallowing. "You're the thief
who stole the French Blue!"

Twelve

Violet couldn't tell if the fire that rose in her chest signaled pleasure or pain. For some moments, Lord Harclay stood quietly before her, dark eyes betraying nothing save a devilish sort of glimmer. What was he thinking, she wondered, and why does he not deny the accusation as rubbish, fiction, a tale conjured by her overeager imagination?

But she knew the earl would do no such thing. His was a far too subtle mind to ever admit guilt, for he felt none; no, from that dark glimmer in his gaze she could tell he felt nothing but the satisfaction of a job well executed, and pride.

Pride in his skill and—dared she even think it?—pride in her savvy, her ability to sniff him out before anyone else aired the slightest suspicion. Doubtless Lord Harclay, being the extremely marriageable sort he was, what with his title and fortune and good looks, was used to women of the simpering type. Women with nary a thought in their pretty heads except how to snare him in the mousetrap of matrimony.

And Violet certainly wasn't interested in that. The men in her life—her father, Mr. Hope—were trouble enough, and she'd be positively birdbrained to invite this member of the male species to join the fray.

Though, much to her chagrin, she had, admittedly, been unable to think of much else these past twenty-four hours. Lord Harclay taking possession of her for the evening's first dance; Harclay as pirate; a fuzzy Harclay pouring her yet another glass of champagne. That was how she'd come to the sudden realization of his guilt, putting together all of Harclay's many pieces to form a startling, *thieving* whole.

He had, after all, offered a toast to "a successful evening" the night before. Successful indeed—he had managed to thieve a priceless gem before the eyes of five hundred people.

Perhaps in the back of her mind Violet had known all along. It was obvious the man was quite reckless in his search for a thrill. Not only had he risked his reputation on a single dance—really, who called for a waltz before a crowd of hundreds of London's finest?—he also had wagered *one thousand pounds* on a single game of casino. Not even the prince regent, that wastrel and debt-ridden drunk, gambled with such large sums.

And then there was her memory of the theft itself; he had, after all, been at her side when it occurred. How easy it was for him, in the midst of her tussle with the supposed thieves, to quietly snatch the French Blue from around her neck, and no one the wiser.

As the words fell from her tongue—*I suppose to you, it's only money*—the truth suddenly, thrillingly crystallized. The only man in all the world with enough cheek, and enough cash, to orchestrate the theft of King Louis XIV's priceless blue diamond in the middle of the season's most well-attended ball was, without a doubt, Lord William Townshend, Earl of Harclay.

It was all she could do not to spring in the air with shouts of "Aha!" and "I knew it!"—unseemly behavior, surely, during the fashionable hour at Hyde Park.

The earl's lips drew into a wickedly dazzling smile. "I am most flattered by your accusation, Lady Violet. Most flattered indeed, for whoever perpetrated this crime was a man of no small wit."

"I can have you arrested," she stammered, heart knocking about her ribs. "Locked away in Newgate, with all the other thieves."

He took a step closer—much closer than he should—and held up his hands. "I would gladly be your prisoner, if you'll have me."

Again the fire in her chest rose. "I'd whip you senseless."

Harclay's smile widened. "*Mm.* I like the sound of that."

"Oh, do be serious!"

"You'll need evidence," he said, his face mere inches from her own, "and clues, lots of clues. For surely this master thief of whom you speak has stashed away the diamond in some well-hidden safe box; wouldn't you agree?"

Bastard, Violet thought, he's dodging me, refusing to set his wager one way or the other.

Well, she sniffed, two can play this game.

Gritting her teeth, Violet shoved her finger into his chest and leaned in. Her lips hovering just above his—she could tell by the spark of surprise in his eyes that he was expecting a kiss—she purred, "I know you did this, Harclay, and I'm going to prove it, whether you admit to the theft or not."

"I hope this means I'll be seeing more of you, Lady Violet, preferably at my house in Grosvenor Square. D'you think people will wag their tongues at late-night visits if they are of an investigative nature?"

"Yes, if it's the sort of investigating you're talking about," she replied tartly. "Tell me, why did you do it?"

His eyes flashed; his smile broadened. "Don't disappoint me now, not after we've come so far. What a silly question; you know why," he murmured.

For a moment her eyes betrayed her and slipped to his lips. A familiar wave of heat coursed through her limbs. Damn him; he may have been a thief and a liar, but he was a delicious thief, and a *very* handsome liar.

"You can expect plenty of late-night visits from me," she managed, "but not of the sort you're expecting."

Laughter rumbled in his chest. His lips parted, and he was about to speak—or kiss her; Violet couldn't quite tell—when a high-pitched howl sounded behind them.

Violet turned just in time to see Lady Caroline cartwheel into the Serpentine, a look of horror crossing her face before she fell into the water with a heavy, ominous *splash!*

"My God!" Violet cried. At once she and Lord Harclay

darted for the water, but Mr. Lake—an appropriate surname, Violet thought wryly, considering the circumstances—had already leapt, boots and all, into the river.

"Stay here." Lord Harclay held out his arm. "You'll sink like a stone in all those skirts."

The earl leapt into the fray. Violet watched with her heart in her throat. Harclay wasn't joking when he accused Lady Caroline of lacking coordination; poor dear was thrashing about in the water, sinking faster and faster until all Violet could see was her hands, waving wildly just above the surface of the river.

At last they emerged, Lady Caroline slung between Lord Harclay and Mr. Lake as they pulled her from the water. Soaked to the bone, they laid Caroline gingerly on the shore, where she coughed up copious amounts of water in between her moaned apologies.

By now a crowd, mouths gaping, had gathered to witness the spectacle. But Mr. Lake, it seemed, cared not a whit, for he fell to his knees beside Caroline and scooped her in his arms. He helped her to a sitting position and gently patted her back, coaxing out what was left of the water.

"There, there," he practically cooed. "There, there, Lady Caroline, it's quite all right."

Violet wondered vaguely what the one-eyed man had said or done to Caroline that sent her flying into the river. But whatever it was, she appeared to have forgiven him; for she clung to Mr. Lake as if for dear life itself, embracing him with egregious vigor.

"I swear to you," Lady Caroline was saying, "I swear to you, I shan't tell a soul, nary a soul!"

Lord Harclay met Violet's eyes over Caroline's head. "Pray, Lady Violet, can you translate?"

Violet merely shrugged. It was obvious Caroline and Mr. Lake were lost in the moment, in each other. Quite touching, actually, to watch the two of them moon over each other like lovestruck players in a Shakespeare comedy.

And then there was Cousin Sophia, who was at this very moment in the company of the season's most eligible bachelor—the Marquess of Worceshire, or was it Weddington?—in her father's drawing room back home. Violet found him adorably dull, but Sophia seemed to like him well enough, and he *did* come with that castle her cousin so desperately desired.

A certain ache panged inside Violet's chest, right where her heart should be. She recognized it at once as the kind of silly, ill-fated longing that doomed said Shakespeare players to poison-induced deaths. Not at all Violet's style; but oh, how lovely to be in the early throes of blossoming affection, the giddiness and excitement . . .

"Lady Violet," Harclay said, his words an exhausted sigh. He abandoned Romeo and Juliet and was making his way toward Violet, water dripping from his soggy person. His clothes were indecently plastered against his body, revealing an altogether Michelangelo-esque physique. Broad, rounded shoulders swept into forearms of rippled muscle and sinew; a taut chest narrowed to a slim waist, his hips accentuated by hard slices of bone.

It was all she could do not to lick her lips and whistle in appreciation.

But it was his smile, a sheepish sort of thing, that really captured her attention. "Lady Violet," he said again and burst out laughing as he motioned to his sopping clothes. "Surely your thief is far too elegant a person to ever be caught swimming in the Serpentine, and at the fashionable hour! Bloody freezing, it is."

He looked down and she followed his gaze to the front of his breeches; and without fully understanding the joke—did cold water somehow adversely affect his *excitement*?—she began laughing, too, and at once she felt giddy, and excited in more ways than one.

The laughter caught in her throat.

Giddy and *excited*?

Oh no. Absolutely *not.*

She couldn't be falling for this thieving, practically naked man dripping before her, the tatters of his shirt a reminder of the warm, inviting flesh that hid beneath. They were adversaries, enemies, the proverbial cat and mouse.

Violet couldn't be falling for Lord Harclay.

Most certainly, emphatically *not.*

*   *   *

"Y ou may cut the acrobats free," Violet said as she paced before the crackling fire. "For I've reason to believe I've found our thief."

Hope handed his hat to a waiting footman. "Who is he? And why isn't he here, damn it?"

Violet exchanged a glance with Mr. Lake. They were in Hope's study, its walnut-paneled walls gleaming in the low light of the oil lamps. While she paced before the fire, Lake sat wrapped in a woolen blanket, his wet, disheveled hair plastered to the sides of his face.

Lake nodded at the sideboard. "Pour us a drink, Hope."

"I don't want a drink."

"Yes, you do."

With a sigh Hope retreated to the sideboard. "What the devil happened to you? You look like you fell—well, like you fell into a lake."

"Very funny." Lake scowled and took the glass from Hope. "As a matter of fact, it was the Serpentine."

Violet fought the smile that rose to her lips at the memory of Lake hurtling into the water after his Juliet. "And at the fashionable hour, too. Poor Lady Caroline—I don't know if she'll ever recover!"

"Lady Caroline?" Hope furrowed his brow. "Lord Harclay's sister?"

"She was chaperoning Lord Harclay and I as we took our turn about Hyde Park this afternoon," Violet said. "Halfway through our stroll, Mr. Lake mysteriously appeared from behind a tree, and next thing I knew Lady Caroline was careening into the Serpentine. The two of them get on splendidly. If I didn't know any better, I would think they were very old friends indeed."

Lake blushed; Hope eyed him wearily. "You forget, Lady Violet, that Mr. Lake doesn't *have* any friends. Especially friends of the female variety."

"My friends are none of your business," Lake bit back. "Lady Caroline had the misfortune to fall into the river; I jumped in after her. No one was harmed. End of story."

Violet could tell Hope was trying not to laugh. "I am sorry

to have missed this stroll of yours. Apparently it was quite eventful. You didn't find our thief, too, in the midst of all your adventures?"

Violet met Lake's gaze before turning to Hope. She took a deep breath, steeling herself against the onslaught that was to come. "Actually . . . "

"You did?" Hope wrinkled his brow. "You *did.*"

"I did indeed. You see, Mr. Hope, I've good reason to believe that the Earl of Harclay stole your diamond."

Mr. Hope sputtered on his whiskey, a great honking noise. "Really, Lady Violet, now is not the time to jest. Why, Harclay is not only an *earl*, and one of the most powerful peers at that; he is also one of my largest and most faithful clients. Tread carefully."

Violet swallowed hard and resumed her pacing. "I would not dare make such an accusation if I wasn't convinced it were true. Just as you would not dare forget my inheritance is invested in Hope and Company stock. I understand, Mr. Hope, how much you have at stake; I, too, risk everything in this."

Hope looked as if he were about to cry, or perhaps erupt into a fit of rage. Violet could only hope for the former.

"But how? And, more importantly, why? I know for a fact the man's got more money than all the pharaohs of Egypt. *Combined.*"

"It makes perfect sense," Violet replied. "Only a man of Lord Harclay's hubris is bold and brash enough to thieve a diamond in the midst of a ball. Don't you see? The man is desperate for a thrill. Look at how he gambles, wagering small fortunes on this trifle and that. It's only money to him; he's got plenty of it, and is willing to spend thousands in the pursuit of excitement."

Violet sidled up to Hope at the sideboard. "Harclay is rich, he is clever, and he is bored. A more potent combination for a crime such as this does not exist."

Even as she said the words, Violet's heart took off at a gallop. Tread carefully indeed. With Harclay now in play, each of them stood to lose just about everything: Hope, his bank; Violet, her family, her fortune, her pride.

Never mind the fact that Harclay was a very rich, very powerful enemy. There would be no second chances.

"I pray you're wrong, Lady Violet," Hope said, finishing off his whiskey. "But if Lord Harclay is indeed our man, we need to find out where he's hiding the diamond. And we mustn't forget the diamond collar; I borrowed it from a . . . friend, who misses it very much."

Lake nodded. "There's no negotiating with a man who wants for nothing. If what you're saying is true, Lady Violet, the only way to get back the French Blue is to take it. I can canvass his house; and Hope, you might search his records for any mention of a recent acquisition . . ."

"No," Violet said suddenly, impulsively. "I'll do it."

"Are you sure that's wise?" Hope turned to her. "You just said you've got quite a bit at stake here."

"I said I'll do it. Lord Harclay and I—" Violet looked away, hoping to hide the heat that rose to her cheeks. "Trust me. I've a much better chance of finding the French Blue than either of you."

Hope cleared his throat. "Are you and the earl . . . fond of each other?"

"No."

"Very well." Lake rose from his chair, shouldering off the blanket. "Don't say we didn't warn you, Lady Violet. The earl is a dangerous man, and you could very well be harmed, or worse, while on the hunt for the jewel."

Violet met Hope's eyes. "I'm the one who lost the French Blue. And I'm the one who's going to get it back."

Thirteen

The study was a muddle of loose paper, scrolls, and over-turned pots of ink. Drawers gaped open, and a bookshelf on the far wall appeared to have been ransacked.

Avery poked his head into the room, too frightened, it seemed, to step foot into the fray.

"Yes?" Harclay said, voice edged with impatience. He was on hands and knees on the carpet beside his desk, peering beneath a behemoth of an armoire.

Avery cleared his throat. "Might I be of some assistance, my lord?"

"I'm looking for my stationery," Harclay said, turning back to the armoire. "I've decided to host some guests for dinner, but I cannot find the proper paper on which to pen the invites."

Without looking, Harclay could sense Avery gaping, his mouth opening and closing noiselessly. Poor man didn't know where to begin: the guests for dinner—Harclay hadn't hosted a soul in two seasons—or the stationery, which the earl hadn't touched for a spell longer than that.

"A bold move," Avery said, eyes gleaming with amusement,

"drawing your enemies close, very close indeed. Are you sure it is wise, so soon after—well, after the event?"

Harclay sighed. His butler, who also happened to be his most trusted and wily associate, was right; but what choice did the earl have? He had to begin the chase anew.

Reading his master's thoughts as readily as if they were scrawled across his forehead, Avery offered a curt nod and crossed the room to stand before the dreaded armoire. "I do believe the stationery is in here, my lord."

Harclay rose to his feet, ducking just in time to avoid the armoire door as it swung open.

"Here you are, sir, fresh as the day they were engraved," Avery said, placing a thick stack of heavy, clean-edged paper in his hands.

Harclay sighed. "Never thought it would come to this, me penning handwritten invitations to *dinner*," he said.

"Marvelous, isn't it? I will begin the preparations straightaway. Any requests for the menu?"

Harclay heaved the paper onto the last available corner of his desk. "Champagne, I suppose."

Again Avery cleared his throat. "And the food?"

"Oh, the usual—a side of beef, turtle soup, that sort of thing. Perhaps an Italian ice cream from Gunter's; I'm partial to the chocolate myself."

The butler had to restrain himself from clapping with delight. "Excellent choices, my lord. I'll see to it."

Avery turned and practically skipped out of the study, leaving Harclay alone with his quill and a pile of dusty stationery.

It had been three days since the affair of Hope's diamond; and for reasons Harclay did not entirely understand, he was disappointed Lady Violet had not yet called on him, or at the very least tried to arrest him.

Perhaps, clever girl, she was waiting for him to make the first move. She knew full well the chase thrilled him just as much as the crime itself. He would hardly allow himself to be ignored, especially by the woman intent on hunting him down.

With a swipe of his forearm, Harclay cleared the desk and settled down to pen his invitations. Being foremost in his mind, Lady Violet's invitation was the first he decided to write.

Dearest Lady Violet—

Yes, yes, that would do. He smiled as he imagined her rolling her eyes at "dearest"—while she would claim to hate it (and him), some small part of her would wonder if his greeting was indeed sincere.

Dearest Lady Violet—

I find myself in an insufferable position: not only have I not quite finished seducing you, but I also owe you a great deal of money. Please join me for dinner tomorrow evening at half past eight. Bring your aunt Georgiana and Lady Sophia; others of our mutual acquaintance shall join us.

I shall be serving both the brandy and the champagne that you so liberally enjoyed. Perhaps after we again indulge, we may settle our accounts?

Yours, H

Oh, that is bold, very bold indeed, he thought with a smirk. It was the sort of invitation Lady Violet was powerless to refuse. Not only did he promise her money; he quite cleverly, if he said so himself, intimated that he would give her more than that. A kiss, a touch, another move or two in a game they both so clearly enjoyed—really, how could she resist?

Though Lord Harclay's invitation had very nearly sent her into a fit of fury, it was, of course, far too tempting for Violet to resist. She spent the better part of the day selecting her outfit for the dinner, deciding at last on a cream ball gown of heavy silk that was overlaid with a gauzy three-quarter dress of pale pink.

Violet stood before the mirror in her dressing room, surveying her appearance as her lady's maid helped her into elbow-length silk gloves. Fitzhugh, who'd been Violet's lady's maid for as long as she could remember, had wrapped her thick plait around her head, pinning it at the temples. She'd then artfully tucked a few large, pink rose blossoms into the plait, "to match your color."

"Goodness, dear," Fitzhugh tsked. "Are you warm? You look flushed."

She hadn't realized how nervous—excited?—she was to see Lord Harclay until it was time to leave. Violet stood at the threshold of her house, shaking with anticipation. Outside, a lovely spring evening beckoned; Auntie George's shabby town coach waited on the lane.

Cousin Sophia stuck her head out the coach door. "Well, aren't you coming, Violet? We're going to be late!"

"Trust me, Mr. Hope always arrives at a fashionably tardy hour at these sorts of engagements," Violet called from the house. "You won't miss a minute of his company, I promise."

Sophia made a great show of sticking out her tongue and fell back in her seat.

Violet turned to her father, who in a rare moment of clarity had come downstairs to bid her farewell.

"Oh, to be young again," he said with a smile. "I remember the excitement of those wild nights. It is perhaps one's finest hour; I do so hope you treasure it, and enjoy yourself as much as you are able."

Violet squeezed his hands, not daring to ponder what, exactly, he spoke of when he mentioned "wild nights."

"I shall certainly try, Papa," she replied.

"You shouldn't have to try very hard, my dear. Yours is a rare beauty. Surely this Harclay fellow intends to propose."

Violet nearly choked. "Heavens, no, I'm afraid I shan't be that lucky lady. Besides, I've got you to look after. You're all the company I need."

"Pish," her father said. "I'm a loopy old mess. Don't waste your time on ornery old men like me! Go after Harclay, make him yours."

I'll go after him, all right, she thought. She pecked Papa on his cheek, the skin as tremulous and fine beneath her lips as tissue. "Good night, Papa. I shall see you at breakfast, and then perhaps a stroll in the afternoon?"

"Capital!" he replied, offering her a salute in parting.

With a sigh that did nothing to relieve her nerves, Violet stepped out into the night.

As soon as Avery cleared his throat at the door, Harclay was on his feet. He hardly heard the butler intoning introductions; his attention was focused solely on Lady Violet.

She looked ravishing; to his dismay—or perhaps his delight; he couldn't tell—she appeared even more beautiful than he remembered. In true Violet fashion, she wore a daringly cut gown that displayed her curves to their fullest advantage. He swallowed audibly at the sight of plump half-moons of breast that appeared ready to bare themselves at any moment.

Her hair was dressed in a shiny braid circlet that sat on her head as a crown. Roses, fully bloomed, were tucked about her ears. Their fragrance was fresh and potent—just like Violet.

She smiled at him. Desire—sudden, wild—bloomed low in his belly. He sucked in a breath, hoping to calm his blood lest he frighten his guests with the wood of which Lady Violet was so fond.

Damn her, he thought, she has come to toy with me, tease me.

And damn her again, it's *working*.

"Ladies," he drawled with a bow, placing a kiss first on the hand of Aunt Georgiana before turning his attention to Lady Sophia's.

He drew up at last before Lady Violet. Her eyes, glittering an alluring shade of indigo in the light of the candles, met his. Without willing it, a smile rose to his lips.

"And Lady Violet," he said. "I thought you'd never come."

Aunt Georgiana let out a panicked breath and dabbed at her forehead with a lace-edged kerchief. "Your invitation was *most* unexpected, Lord Harclay. But lovely! Certainly lovely, and your home is just—well, it's rather exquisite, isn't it?"

She turned to survey the drawing room, doubtless with no little suspicion. It was obvious that Lady Violet had shared her hunch with everyone gathered here tonight that Harclay had stolen the French Blue. He'd noticed it the moment Hope and Mr. Lake arrived. There was an edge to their greeting;

their eyes took on a sort of calculating glimmer, as if sizing up Harclay and his home as potential evidence.

Though Hope wasn't entirely convinced, at least in Harclay's mind. Members of the *ton* simply did not behave in such a manner, stealing diamonds and whatnot from their esteemed neighbors. No doubt Hope was having difficulty believing Harclay was capable of such a crime. The earl had time yet before Hope tightened the noose and forced his hand.

It was, really, making for a most thrilling chase.

"Forgive me," Aunt Georgiana was saying, her eyes on Sophia as she moved toward Mr. Hope. "I must see to my daughter before she and Mr. Hope run off to Siam. The way they look at each other . . . "

Aunt Georgiana darted off, allowing Violet and Harclay a moment alone. Lady Violet leaned toward him, one of her roses brushing his nose as she whispered, "Missed me, have you? I knew you couldn't stay away long, but three days! You must be desperate."

"Perhaps," he murmured in reply. "Though I venture it's not the sort of *desperate* of which you speak."

She drew back, and he noticed with delight that her cheeks burned pink.

"As I've said before," he continued, "you are welcome to visit my home anytime, Lady Violet. Anytime at all, especially at night, and without chaperone."

Daringly, she tilted her neck and bit her lip. "You forget you lost that bet, my lord."

"Perhaps," he replied, licking his lips, "perhaps I can convince you to oblige me, despite that fact."

She scoffed, a warm, throaty sound. "You're not used to being the loser, are you, Lord Harclay? The world doesn't work that way. The piper must be paid; debts must be settled. Your exalted position does not excuse you from paying up."

"Paying up?" He smiled. "If I didn't know any better, I'd say you were an inveterate gambler. Tell me, what's your secret?"

Lady Violet returned his smile. "Not before you tell me yours."

"Why, dearest girl," he replied, "I haven't a clue what you're talking about. Might I get you something to drink? Perhaps that champagne of which you are so fond?"

"Yes, thank you, that would be lovely," she said, daggers in her eyes.

Harclay turned to flag one of the footmen and was pleased to see from the corner of his eye Lady Violet snap open her fan and wave it before her flushed face.

He handed a coupe to her and took one for himself. "To what I hope will be yet another successful evening," he said, holding up his glass for a toast.

"I'm afraid my success and your own are rather at odds," she said and clinked her glass to his. "For me, a successful evening would entail proving you're a rotten thief, and retrieving Hope's diamond; and success for you would mean hopelessly despoiling me. And we both know *that's* not going to happen."

"Oh, Lady Violet, by now you should know better than to doubt my prowess. And besides, I never meant to despoil you; if you remember, I prefer—"

"Pleasuring," she said in a clipped voice, not daring to meet his eyes. "Yes, I remember."

By now her fan was working double time, the fine hairs at her temple dancing in the breeze.

Brilliant, he thought, absolutely *brilliant*. Not ten minutes into our conversation and already I'm making her sweat.

The dinner gong sounded a bellowing bass, and once again Avery appeared at the door.

"Ladies and gentlemen"—he clicked his heels together—"dinner is served."

The ladies stood; the gentlemen finished the last of their champagne. Lady Violet turned to Harclay and dropped into what some would consider an insultingly low curtsy. "Make no mistake, my lord," she purred, "I *will* catch you. On my honor, I will see that justice is done."

Impulsively he reached out and thumbed her chin, tilting her face closer to his. "Well, then," he replied, "let the chase begin."

Fourteen

———— ✦ ————

O n the well-muscled arm of Mr. Lake, Violet made her
way into Lord Harclay's dining room. Though she was
hardly surprised by the room's style and elegance, it left her
breathless nonetheless. The high ceiling was covered in antique
mirrors, reflecting paneled walls lacquered a mellow shade of
black. The doors and windows were trimmed with gold-leaf
molding; two enormous gilt chandeliers hung from golden
chains, crystals sending darts of glitter and flash about the
room. A fire crackled merrily from a raspberry-hued marble
hearth, fending off what little was left of the spring chill.

Two towering candelabras, silver engraved with the Harclay family crest, were set on the long table. Dozens of tiny
wineglasses, each destined, no doubt, for a sampling of the
earl's impressive cellar, winked beside gilt-edged china.

A half dozen bewigged footmen waited behind the upholstered dining chairs. From the side gallery came a familiar
pop, and Avery appeared bearing a bottle of champagne on a
silver tray.

Harclay took his place at the head of the table, his sister, as
the highest-ranking lady, to his right. Across the table his

eyes met Violet's, and it dawned on her quite suddenly that she was to be seated to his left. At once her heart, so recently recovered from the episode in the earl's drawing room, began to pound and heat rose to her face.

She took her place at Harclay's side with all the steely reserve she could muster and waited until the other guests were situated before taking her seat. Cousin Sophia sat beside Mr. Hope, their heads together in suspiciously quiet conversation; Lady Caroline sat at Mr. Lake's side, his one eye gleaming with mischief.

Really, thought Violet, it was akin to a circus. She wouldn't be surprised if, God *forbid*, Harclay's hired acrobats-cum-assassins suddenly appeared and began swinging from the chandeliers.

Violet was vaguely aware of the polite murmur of conversation that filled the room; the scent of roast meat and rising bread wafting in from the kitchens; Auntie George discreetly kicking Cousin Sophia under the table. But the presence of Lord Harclay, mere inches from her elbow, was wholly distracting. Her every sense was alive with the mere thought of him. It was impossible to breathe, much less use her powers of deduction. How was she ever going to seek out the French Blue in such a state?

The first course was served, delectable turtle soup paired with the crisp champagne. Violet gulped the golden-hued liquid as if this were her last evening on earth.

"More wine, Lady Violet?" Avery asked, proffering the decanter. "Or would you prefer something else?"

From the other side of the table, Auntie George was clearing her throat in a rather obvious warning; but Violet, nerves singing, paid her no heed.

"More wine, yes, thank you," she said, and as soon as her glass was again full she brought it to her lips.

But before she tasted so much as a drop, fingers warm and hard wrapped around her own and brought the glass back to the table.

"Pace yourself, Lady Violet," Harclay said, "for I do believe this evening shall prove a late one."

Violet's blood jumped at the growl in his voice. She didn't dare meet his eyes; rather, she glanced about the table and was pleased to note her fellow diners were far too involved in their own games of seduction to pay much heed to her own. Except Auntie George, of course, whose high, feathered headdress trembled with rage.

His fingers lingered a beat more than was necessary, scorching her skin with their touch. When he moved to withdraw, he traced small rivers of fire from her knuckles to the very tips of her fingers, the move slow, enticing, arousing.

Violet swallowed. "Not if I have my way. Your house may be overlarge, Lord Harclay, but surely a clever fellow such as yourself would hide a diamond in only a small number of secure locations. Sock drawer, safe, lily pond. I daresay I'll sniff it out and have you in chains well before midnight."

Lord Harclay chuckled. "But might we enjoy dinner first? I saw to the menu myself. 'Twould be a shame to be dragged away from the beef, and in irons."

Despite herself, Violet felt a grin tugging the ends of her mouth upward. "Very well. I suppose it's within your rights to enjoy meat one last time. I wonder what sort of porridge they serve at Newgate."

"I daresay some of the best in the city," Harclay replied cheerfully and stuffed his mouth with a well-sauced chunk of fish.

The wine was good; no, it was better than that, the best Violet had ever tasted. And heavens, there was a lot of it. More champagne for the fish course, and a smoky bordeaux so dark it appeared as ink in the glass for the meat; a burgundy, this one sweet and tasting of cherries; and finally, as Avery brought out the cigars, a fruity white from the Loire Valley.

Though Mr. Hope and his allies dined with the man they suspected of stealing their livelihoods, they laughed and carried on as if they had not a care in the world. As the meal progressed, and the wine was poured, and poured again, the mood was no longer somber but, to Violet's chagrin, quite celebratory.

It was obvious her fellow guests were far too enamored of Lord Harclay, or at least his cellar, to take her accusation seriously. That they did not trust her judgment irked Violet. She was no novice in the world of cheats, thieves, and degenerate gamblers; but it appeared she would have to prove herself nonetheless.

At last Lady Caroline stood and announced the ladies'

retirement to the drawing room. Across the table Violet caught Mr. Hope's gaze.

This much wine will excuse any behavior, she urged him through her eyes. *Prod Harclay, see what information you can gather.*

Mr. Hope seemed to understand, for he nodded and placed a cigar gamely between his teeth.

Violet was not the only guest a shade past tipsy; as she followed the ladies out of the dining room, Lady Caroline walked as if she had adopted Mr. Lake's limp, while Cousin Sophia fell into the table. The pitcher of lemonade they *should* have drunk crashed to the floor, sending the footmen into a tizzy. Poor Avery appeared ready to burst into tears.

"Oh, dear, how terribly embarrassing," Sophia whispered, smoothing back her hair.

Violet looped her arm through her cousin's and led her into the hall. "Don't worry," she replied, patting her hand. "We're all foxed, no shame in admitting it."

They followed Lady Caroline through the house, the halls blazing with the light of dozens of chandeliers, sconces, and candelabras. Violet's heart sank at the scope and scale of the place; while it wasn't palatial, it was whatever came just before that. How foolish of her to think Harclay would hide the diamond in his sock drawer; there were literally thousands of nooks and crannies and hidden moldings in which he could keep the French Blue.

Even with the help of a hundred of Hope's men, it would be akin to finding the proverbial needle in the haystack.

Still, she couldn't give up, not this early in the chase. There had to be a way of forcing Harclay's hand, of discovering the diamond's location. And she was going to be the one to do it, come hell or high water.

Lady Caroline led them to a different drawing room, this one with walls upholstered in emerald green velvet. A new-fashioned billiards table sat in the center of the room, surrounded by clusters of leather chairs and twill sofas. A well-stocked sideboard beckoned from one wall, and it was all Violet could do not to sidle up and ransack its contents.

Cousin Sophia and Auntie George were sequestered on a sofa, Auntie George waving a finger before Sophia's face in apparent consternation. Lady Caroline took advantage of the rare moment of privacy and turned to Violet.

"Come, Violet, let us take a turn about the room," she said and held out her hand.

"Dinner was lovely," Violet said. She tried not to wince when Caroline trampled her foot.

"Lovely indeed. William hasn't hosted company at this house for years. No one could convince him to dust off the old family china—no one, that is, until you came along. He dances a waltz with you at Hope's ball and suddenly all is aflutter! My brother, bless his black soul, doesn't hand out compliments often; but oh, Lady Violet, you must realize dinner was his way of complimenting your charms, and your beauty."

Inside her chest Violet's heart skipped a beat. Trying her damnedest to ignore the strange sensation, she scoffed a reply. "I hardly think Lord Harclay invited me to dinner so that he might compliment me. It's—well, it's a bit of a strange situation, really, between the two of us."

"Strange, yes!" Caroline smiled. "I haven't seen my brother look at anyone the way he looks at you. I saw the way you two gaped at one another at the table. You were blushing so violently I was worried you might swoon."

Violet straightened. "I do not swoon, Lady Caroline, and I am quite proud of that fact. And besides, I am hardly the only woman he has *looked* at. I daresay he's *looked* at half the women in London."

"Oh, he's looked, all right," Lady Caroline said. "But not the way he looks at you."

"He's not looking at me for the reason you think," Violet replied.

Caroline waved away her words. "Oh, that little thing, about you accusing him of stealing Hope's diamond? It will pass, as those sorts of things usually do."

Violet halted, nearly sending Lady Caroline headfirst into a polished credenza.

"You know about that?" Violet gaped. By now her blood was thrumming; she felt the familiar trickle of perspiration along the boning of her stays.

"I do. You forget, Lady Violet, how quickly word travels in London this time of year. Of course, I hope to convince you that the only thing William ever stole is perhaps a biscuit from Cook's tin."

"I regret that I disagree," Violet said slowly, and they resumed their stroll. "I do so hate to trouble you, Lady Caroline—"

"It's no trouble as long as at the end of it you make an honorable man of him. Honestly, this libertine business has gone on long enough."

"But the diamond," Violet choked out. "It is imperative we recover the diamond—"

"The diamond, yes, no doubt in my mind you'll recover it. You're a clever girl, Lady Violet; clever and confident. A combination, it seems, my brother is unable to resist.

"And though I trust you know how to handle such a delicate matter," Caroline continued with a confidential pat on Violet's hand, "you must proceed with caution. William can be quite the cad, but he does care for his family and friends— cares for them quite deeply. As deeply, I believe, as you care for your own family."

But before Lady Caroline could finish that tantalizing tidbit, the man himself strode into the room. It could've been the wine taking captive Violet's senses or it could've been Caroline's confession or the memory of his hand grazing hers at the table, but God above Harclay cut a dashing figure. He was laughing at something Mr. Hope had just murmured in his ear; Harclay's teeth flashed, revealing lips stained purple from wine.

And oh, the very thought of how delicious he would taste after that excellent bordeaux—Violet forced the thought from her head. *Remember,* she chided herself, *your family, and your fortune, rest on proving this man a thief and a criminal.*

The men trailed masculine scents of cigar smoke and brandy into the room behind them. Eyeing the billiards table, Mr. Lake challenged the ladies to a game. Caroline disappeared from Violet's side in a tumble of ungainly movement, while Cousin Sophia all too eagerly accepted a billiards cue from Mr. Hope.

Violet sighed. So much for Hope's probing; the only information he seemed to have culled from his audience with Harclay was the difference in taste between a Canadian whiskey and an American one.

"And you, Lady Violet?" came a familiar voice. "Are you as skilled at billiards as you are at cards?"

Violet turned to face Lord Harclay. His dark eyes were trained on her person in an illicit fashion, as if he knew what she looked like under all the layers of her clothes.

Which, of course, he didn't; though he certainly knew what she *felt* like.

"Billiards is hardly an appropriate pastime for proper English ladies like myself," she replied smoothly. "Though from the well-worn appearance of your table and cues, I venture you are quite the master."

"Master, no," he said, rocking back on his heels. "But I am good enough to teach you how it's done. Come, I'll let you play with my stick."

Violet sighed, rolling her eyes. "Even I know it's called a cue. You're just trying to make me blush."

Harclay drew to her side, his enormous hand splayed lightly on the small of her back. His wine-stained lips at her ear, he whispered, "I hate to inform you, Lady Violet, but it seems to be working."

"You flatter yourself. It's the wine, my lord, and not your ill-mannered remarks that have made me flush," she said. Gently pressing her fingertips to her cheek, she could feel the scalding heat of her skin. Goodness, she was probably the color of a tomato.

Harclay tucked her arm into his side and led her toward the billiards table. From a waiting footman—really, did the earl employ the whole of Christendom?—Harclay took a sleek cue inlaid with black and white ivory checkers and handed it to Violet.

"Ladies first," he said and nodded across the table. Both Lady Caroline and Sophia were practicing awkwardly with their cues.

Violet looked upon the cue with no little distaste. "How do I even hold it?"

"I thought you'd never ask," Harclay replied with a grin. He stepped toward her, his peculiar, heady scent enveloping her in a cloud of heat, and held up his hands.

"Now, Lady Violet, I'm going to have to touch you—"

An enormous clatter, followed by several cries of terror, interrupted Violet's reverie. Just as she was imagining the delicious feel of his hands all over her body—surely billiards was a pastime of great physical contact?—Lady Caroline managed to launch a cue ball off the table. With sickening accuracy it flew across the room and slammed—*thwack!*—into Auntie George's forehead.

It was like something out of a comedy: Auntie George flew heels over head backward, revealing a mountain of lace petticoats as her chair catapulted over. She was left sprawled on her back with legs in the air, the ball rolling harmlessly off to the side.

"Oh, dear," Violet breathed. Before she could so much as blink, Lord Harclay was on his knees at Auntie George's side. He held up her head and was calling for water, smelling salts, anything that might revive her.

"And brandy!" he said to the footmen. "Make haste, make haste! We haven't a moment to spare."

Violet blinked, just to be sure she wasn't imagining the scene before her. Was Auntie George really sprawled out on Harclay's priceless Axminster carpet? And was Harclay actually performing a selfless act and *helping* her?

It was hardly to be believed.

Violet fell to her knees beside Harclay, and together they cooed and prodded and patted until Auntie George came back to life. Dazed—the wound was sure to bruise—she was otherwise unharmed.

"I do *so* apologize, Lord Harclay," Auntie George said, tears streaming down her face, "I'm terribly embarrassed, I swear to you I don't usually put on such a frightful display."

Harclay smiled down at her, and with his giant calloused thumb gently pushed the tears from Auntie's cheeks. His tenderness, his patience was at odds with everything Violet knew about the earl. But he *had* come to her rescue at Hope's ball, defending her against that rude, pimply boy who'd doused her with punch. A waste of good brandy, that; it would've been a disaster besides, if Harclay hadn't made it right.

Violet watched as the earl brushed an errant curl from Auntie George's brow. Who was this man? Was he a rascal, a gentleman jewel thief out to ruin the livelihoods of hundreds, of thousands of people? Or was he a kindhearted fellow who flattered old widows and loved nothing so much as his family, his friends, a decent turtle soup?

"No need to apologize, Lady Georgiana," Harclay practically purred. "Might we make up a room for you here? I hardly think it wise to subject you to the rigors of travel."

Auntie George managed to sit upright; her eyes rolled a bit in their sockets, but she appeared otherwise recovered. At once her gaze fell on Sophia, arm in arm with a certain Mr. Hope; and Auntie shook her head. "Lord Harclay, that is most kind of you, most kind indeed, but I would hate to put you out. No, I believe I'll be quite all right, if you'll just help me to my carriage. Come, Sophia, it's time to leave."

Brushing off the other gentlemen, Lord Harclay lifted Auntie George in his arms and made for the front door. As Violet followed them through the hall, she heard Auntie's tinkling laughter and caught Harclay smiling down at her as if she were not a plump, dazed dowager but a debutante in the flower of her youth.

Avery, who by now was as white as a sheet and making profuse apologies, opened the front door. The nighttime air, heavy and a bit chilly, sauntered into the house. Violet stood at the threshold and shivered. A sudden, puzzling desire to stay overwhelmed her. Outside, the night smelled of rain and a sleepless evening ahead. Harclay's house was so warm and bright, and she hadn't made any progress at all in seeking out Hope's diamond.

The other guests were being helped into their coats and hats and gloves; it seemed Auntie George's accident signaled the end of the evening.

Violet's heart sank. But it was too soon! Too early! There was work to be done . . .

Of course, Harclay's presence, and his promise to *touch* her, had nothing to do with her desire to stay. Absolutely, positively *nothing* at all.

At least that was what she told herself.

Violet climbed into the carriage and waved good-bye to Harclay as he strode up the steps and into the house. In the seat across from her, Auntie George was already laid out and snoring.

Her gaze shifting from Auntie George to Harclay's house and back again, Violet made up her mind. With her chaperone knocked out cold, she had the rare opportunity to search the earl's house without Auntie's well-intentioned, but extremely irritating, interference.

Holding a hand to her lips, Violet caught Sophia's gaze.

"You wouldn't dare!" Sophia hissed, reading the intention so clearly written in Violet's eyes. "And if you go, I want to come with you."

Violet shook her head. "Next time, Sophia, I promise! I'll be home before dawn."

Before Sophia could protest any further, Violet slipped from the carriage. It groaned ominously beneath her weight; she cringed—surely Harclay couldn't hear that from the house, could he?—but continued forward. The coachman looked down and was about to speak, but Violet again shook her head and motioned for him to carry on.

She turned to face the house. Behind her the carriage wheels creaked as they made their way down the lane; and then—

Silence. Lovely, portentous silence.

Heart drumming in her chest, she wrapped her coat more snugly about her breast and slipped to the back of the house. Gravel crunched beneath her feet; fearful of making noise, she attempted to move off the drive but ended up tangled in a rather tremendous hedge of ivy.

It grew dark the farther she moved from the street. Using solely her sense of smell—for horses, as much as she admired them, were malodorous creatures—Violet managed to locate the stables.

A good place to start, she reasoned, though the diamond wasn't very likely to be hidden there. No matter; she was happy to turn over every pillow, turn out every room and closet and alcove, if it meant finding the French Blue.

Closing the door quietly behind her, Violet stepped into the stables and cast off her hood. A single lantern illuminated the space; from the looks of it, the stable hands had just finished their nightly cleanup and were off to bed.

The stables were, as she expected, immaculately clean. The familiar smells of hay and horseflesh filled her nostrils; somewhere a horse snuffed, while another moved lazily about in its stall.

She took the lantern and held it high as she made her way through the space. The very idea of her trespassing thrilled her; her heart was beating with such solid intent, she could hardly breathe.

And to think—she could be getting that much closer to the diamond! Violet's footsteps quickened. She glanced this way and that, crouching to examine a feed basket, a barrel of apples, and a particularly lovely saddle fashioned of Spanish leather. She turned up nothing, but the excitement of the chase was intoxicating. The more she looked, the more determined she became.

Violet stood and was about to search an alcove when a voice—*that* voice, his voice—sounded over her shoulder.

"Aren't you glad I told you to refrain from imbibing too much wine, Lady Violet?" Lord Harclay said. "Otherwise you'd be far too drunk to search my property for the French Blue."

Violet spun around, lantern swinging in her outstretched hand. The earl leaned against the wall, one leg draped casually over the other, his arms crossed about his chest. He was grinning—a saucy, knowing grin—and his dark eyes danced in the low light.

Her blood jumped. She wasn't in her cups, not nearly, but Violet had enjoyed just enough wine to make her head feel pleasantly fuzzy. She hadn't considered what she would do were she to be caught.

She ignored the thought that she'd *hoped* to be caught by Harclay; that she *wanted* to be caught, and taught a lesson or two by this shameless rakehell.

Violet opened her mouth, then closed it when she could think of nothing to say. Harclay stood quietly before her, waiting for her reply.

Rain, soft at first, tapped on the roof above. All at once the tapping became thunderous and heavy, signaling a downpour.

Still Violet's tongue was as stone in her mouth.

Her pulse was loud in her ears, and it suddenly grew very hot in the room; so hot she could not bear it.

Violet dropped the lantern with a solid *thwunk*. She turned and ran.

Fifteen

H arclay dashed through the door after her. Rain pummeled his face and shoulders; a few steps and he was soaked through to his undergarments. The water, enormous, chill drops, practically sizzled when it met his skin; he was burning, had been alive with desire since the moment Violet swept into his drawing room.

And what luck, to find her snooping about his property alone. Dear girl couldn't resist—but resist him, or the pull of the diamond, he couldn't tell.

No matter her reasons, she was here, trailing the scent of roses in her wake. And he wasn't about to let her escape.

Lady Violet, however, was quick on her feet. She tore across the drive, her slippers finding purchase in the gravel. He cursed as he skidded after her in his ridiculous beribboned dress shoes. Damnable pumps, he swore never to wear them again; they pinched his toes besides.

"Violet!" he called after her, the rain nearly drowning out the sound of his voice. "Lady Violet, wait!"

He at last was able to snag the sleeve of her dress. Wrapping his fingers around her arm, he tugged her none too gently to a stop and whirled her around to face him.

"Heavens, girl, I'm not going to hurt you!" he panted.

Violet's eyes flashed with something he didn't recognize—not anger, no, but something akin to it. Lust, perhaps, mixed with no small measure of hate.

Whatever it was, it thrilled him to no end.

"Despite what the others may think," she spat out, shaking off his touch, "I know you are guilty, Harclay, and I intend to prove it with hard evidence. How else am I to find the diamond if I don't actually *look* for it?"

Rivulets of rain coursed down her hair, already plastered to her head, and soaked her thin pelisse. The silk gown she wore underneath was beyond ruin. He felt a pang of guilt for driving her out into the rain; he'd already been witness to the ruin of her nymph costume. The dear would have no clothes left after he was through with her.

"Here," he said, and he tugged his arms free of his jacket. He wrapped it around her shoulders—little good it would do now, but still—and nodded to the house. "Let's go inside and talk about this. I'll have Avery bring up some tea."

But she stood her ground. "It's not in the stables, is it? The diamond. Damn you, Harclay, you interrupted my search! It wasn't as thorough as I would've liked."

"No, it's not in the stables," he said teasingly and took a step closer. He could see she was shivering. "Come, Violet, let's get you inside before you take a chill. Though your aunt may throttle *you*, I'll not have her displeased with me."

With a little huff she followed him toward the house. Harclay wondered how he was going to control himself with Violet's clothes painted against her body like a second skin. It was going to be a terrible, delicious, enthralling struggle.

"You and Auntie George seem to have made fast friends," she said. "How brazen you are with your charms, flirting with defenseless women young and old. You're shameless."

"For God's sake, she'd just been hit in the head with a billiards cue."

"That sound was awful, wasn't it?" Violet replied. "Made my stomach turn. I do hope she'll recover."

Harclay lifted the latch on the kitchen door and held it open for Violet. "I'm afraid she'll have a rather frightful headache in the morning, but from the look of it she'll be on her feet in a day or two. Cold compresses will help, as will strong coffee. You must send me word of her recovery."

Lady Violet stepped inside the dim hallway, shaking off her sleeves. Harclay took the collar of his jacket in his hands, and as he removed it from Violet's shoulders she turned to face him.

He drew a breath of surprise; she was practically in his arms.

And practically naked. Her face was turned upward toward his own; she surveyed him with those damnably beautiful eyes, the lashes casting long shadows on the pale slope of her cheeks.

"Why do you care so much about Auntie George?" she asked.

He felt himself go red about the ears. "I know you think I'm a scalawag, Violet, but I do have feelings. Especially for those who happen to be my guests—and are related to a rather clever lady with whom I am newly acquainted."

Violet's eyes softened about the corners. He thought he could detect a smile trying to break free at the ends of her mouth; but before he could be sure, she was overtaken by a rather violent shudder.

"It-t-t's quite c-c-cold in here, Lord Harc-clay," she said.

Without thinking—for it was quite the natural thing to do, what with her enticing proximity—he took her in his arms and pressed her against his chest. At once her shivering came to a halt; he could feel the warmth of his skin seeping into her own. Slowly, very slowly, she melted against him, pressing her ear to the flat of his breastbone.

"Do I make you nervous?" she murmured, the smile finally reaching her lips. "Your heart is r-r-racing."

"*Nervous* isn't quite the word, Lady Violet," he replied.

She laughed. "Ah, yes, I can tell that w-w-wood of yours is alive and well."

"Can't be helped," Harclay said with a shrug. "If you would only indulge me—"

"I t-t-told you before, my lord, you lost that b-bet. And I'm still waiting on my p-prize, besides."

"Ah, yes, that," he said. Again Violet shivered against him; he ran his hands up and down the length of her arms, gently, patiently. Beneath the wet layers of her clothes he felt the goose pimples rise on her skin; but she did not protest against his touch. She lifted her head from his chest and looked up at him expectantly.

Good God, she was lovely, her blue-gray eyes enormous, lips stained an indecent shade of red from the wine. He swallowed, willing himself to remain still, not to thrust her up against the wall and take her right here in the kitchen galley.

"How did you f-find me, out in the stables?" she breathed.

Harclay scoffed, lowering his head so that his lips hovered just above her mouth. "For all your cunning, you made a rather epic racket. And don't think I would let you out of my sight, not even for a moment; I saw you slip from your aunt's carriage, and heard it, too! Must be ancient, that coach, for it creaked most fiercely when you jumped."

"Ancient indeed," she was saying, but her eyes were trained on his lips, "like riding on a haywagon . . ."

He couldn't bear it. Something about the warmth of her body against his, those striking, intelligent eyes, and—Christ!—those just-bitten lips. He felt as if he were under a spell, his movements governed by the heady pounding of his heart.

Bending his neck, he pressed his lips gently against Violet's mouth. At once the memory of their first kiss took captive his thoughts. It had been thrilling, that kiss, but this one was better, their lips already acquainted and far more eager. Hers were possessed of the same brilliant cleverness as her mind; they moved slowly, thoughtfully, over his own, innocent but sure.

He cupped her face in his hands, grazing the curve of her chin with his thumb. She let out a small moan, opening her mouth to him, and the slick warmth of her nearly drove him wild. It was all he could do not to devour her, not to ravage her lips with his own.

Harclay felt her begin to shiver, and he pulled her closer, closer, and yet she still trembled. His self-control virtually in shreds, he commandeered what little was left and pulled away.

They were both breathing hard, the force of the kiss leaving them silent for several beats.

"A bath," he panted. "You need a hot bath before you take ill."

She shook her head, a dazed look in her eyes. "I'll be a-a-all right—"

He wrapped her in his arm and led her to the kitchen, an enormous space that glittered with copper pots and smelled pleasantly of cinnamon and baking bread. A few kitchen maids were still washing the china from dinner in the trough-like sink across the room.

"Stoke the fire," Harclay called to them, "and have hot water brought up to my chambers for a bath. Quickly, if you please!"

Before Lady Violet could protest, Harclay swung her up the narrow stairs and into the candlelit haven of his bedroom.

Violet was never one for theatrics—it was shameful, really, the displays put on by debutantes these days—but by the time they reached Lord Harclay's chambers she was shaking so hard her teeth chattered like a pair of foxed matrons at the season's first ball.

She'd been soaked through by the rain, yes, but truth be told it was the earl's kiss that had set off the fireworks in her heart, her belly. The way his lips moved over her own, pulling, feeling, had sent tingles of desire pulsing through her limbs—tingles that, to her great embarrassment, now turned into tremendous, uncontrollable shudders.

From the corner of her eye, Violet caught Avery and a footman setting a gleaming copper tub before the fireplace, where a freshly tended fire crackled pleasantly and warmed the room.

"Avery, bring up the water when it's ready," Harclay murmured, his eyes never leaving Violet's face.

The butler bowed. "I took the liberty of warming a few blankets by the fire, my lord. They're on the bed, should you require them."

With a short, polite bow that belied the complete and utter impropriety of the situation, Avery left the room.

At once Harclay's hands were on her body, tearing at her pelisse and gown and stays with a quiet savageness that brought heat back into her body.

"E-eager, are you, m-m-my lord?" Violet managed a tremulous smile. "How sh-sh-shameless of you to take ad-advantage of my c-c-condition."

"Don't be silly," he replied, helping her to shrug off half her clothes in one swift movement. "The faster we get these wet clothes off you, the faster I can get you warm."

She wondered how, exactly, he was planning to do that. Was the bath a mere decoy for more sinister methods? She glanced at the bed—a massive but elegant affair of lacquered mahogany and white linen—and wondered if he meant to warm her *there*.

"D-d-do you bring all your wom-wom-women up here?" she asked.

Now he was tugging at her stays, ravaging the sturdy lacing with his enormous callused hands. His fingers brushed against the bare skin of her back; they felt deliciously hot and sure.

"Never," he replied steadily. "I'm rather territorial about my bedchamber. And my bed, I'm afraid. I consider it a bit of a sanctuary, a place of rest and reflection. Women, though I admire them, are not conducive to such things."

He turned her away from him as he continued working on her laces.

"So y-y-you prefer the f-f-floor?"

Though she couldn't see his face, she could sense his smile. "Among other places, yes," he said.

Her gown fell with an unceremonious *squish* at her feet. For the second time in a single week—really, this man was an expert at cornering her half-naked—she stood before him in naught but a chemise and stockings.

Violet turned away from the flames, away from Harclay. The heat of the fire raised careless curls of steam from the fine muslin at her shoulders. And still she shook, the chill—or was it the anticipation?—causing her skin to break out in waves of goose bumps.

"This has to come off, too," he said quietly, running a finger along the edge of her chemise at her neck.

She swallowed. His touch felt lovely; the loveliest sensation she'd yet to experience in her twenty-two years.

"All r-right."

Harclay gathered the chemise at her hips and lifted it

gently over her head. She stepped out of her stockings, tossing them into the darkness.

And then she was as naked as the day she was born. Instinctively, Violet wrapped her arms about her breasts; she grew very still, the chill all but gone from her body.

Behind her, she heard Lord Harclay suck in his breath and sensed him draw close.

"You"—he murmured—"are very beautiful, Violet."

She felt him place a single finger on the last knob of her back, just where her buttocks met her tailbone; with that same finger he traced a line of fire up the length of her spine. The tide of sensation, every part of her alive, was overwhelming.

Her eyes fluttered shut as he wrapped his fingers around her neck and pulled her mouth to his. She felt powerless against the onslaught, boneless and full of longing. The chill of the room was agony; the heat of the earl's touch, paradise.

Harclay was right. While Violet loved to gamble, to drink brandy and curse like a sailor, she did not dare indulge in carnal sins. She'd read of the act in novels, of course, in French pamphlets, and in the faces of married friends; and yet none of it had prepared her for *this*—this kind of heaven and hell, the inescapable desire to do things she'd never done with a man who robbed her of her fortune, and her fortitude.

She shivered; with one last tug at her bottom lip, Harclay pulled away. Violet blinked and he was back, wrapping her tightly in a cashmere blanket. He turned her to face him and tugged the blanket even tighter about her shoulders. At once the warmth of the cashmere seeped into her skin, and she shuddered one last time before relaxing into the cocoon of Harclay's arms.

Violet watched him through her lashes; though his features were carefully arranged into an inscrutable whole, his eyes were wet and dancing. She could feel him, *him*, even through the thick blanket, prodding against her legs.

"Life must prove most uncomfortable, what with that—that *thing* in your pants."

Laughter rumbled through his chest. "You've no idea, Lady Violet. Though I pride myself on my ability to control such urges while in public, it seems I am unable to resist you, especially in private."

There came a knock on the door. Harclay quickly tucked Violet behind him, and she peeked over his shoulder to see Avery and several footmen bearing great, steaming pots into the room. Two at a time they emptied the pots into the tub. At once the scents of lavender and rosemary filled the chamber.

"And the candles, don't forget those," Harclay said.

Avery bowed. "Of course not, my lord."

Several more footmen entered the chamber, carrying what appeared to be every available candle in the house. They placed the candles about the tub, creating a forest of flickering flames that cast a glow on the steam rising from the scalding hot bathwater.

Violet's skin prickled in anticipation; if Harclay didn't throw her on the bed and have his way with her first, this bath was going to feel lovely indeed.

The footmen disappeared, shutting the door quietly behind them. Silence settled heavy and expectant between Violet and the earl.

At last he cleared his throat.

"A book to read, perhaps, while you bathe?" Harclay said.

Violet blinked. "Yes," she replied. "Please."

Harclay turned and disappeared into the darkness; she heard a door open, a door shut quietly. Violet stood beside the tub, breathing in the lavender scent of the water in an attempt to calm her nerves. Surely it was better to bring a book into the bath rather than the earl himself.

Several moments passed without any sign of Harclay's return. The water beckoned, cooling by the moment.

"My lord?" Violet called out into the room, unable to see beyond the steam that rose from the tub.

No answer. She waited a beat. Silence.

Where the devil did he go? She looked at the water, hot, inviting, and fragrant, and shrugged her shoulders. For the hundredth time that day, she damned Harclay to hell and slipped out of the blanket. She sucked in her breath, the chill night air raising goose bumps on her skin, and slipped into the tub, careful not to douse the candles with splashes of water.

She nearly moaned as the heat of the water enveloped her limbs and loosened her muscles, and she was half-asleep with pleasure when a sudden squeak, a chair leg sliding across the wooden floor, jarred her to life. Her eyes flew open to rest on Harclay staring down at her.

"I beg your pardon!" she cried. She crossed her arms about her torso, covering what she could. By the gleam in his dark eyes she could tell she was failing, and quite miserably at that.

She grew still in the tub, paralyzed by the pleasant sensation of her blood quickening pace inside her skin. Heat bloomed in her chest, rushing the tips of her breasts to solid points that broke the surface of the water. She was embarrassed by her body's blatant invitation, but despite herself she thrust her breasts higher, exposing both orbs of wet, slippery pale skin to the chill air.

Harclay dropped the book to the floor and approached slowly, accepting the invitation with his eyes. He circled the tub once, twice, three times, the sound of his shoes against the floor mimicking the riot of her heart. She recognized the look on his face—the intensity of his eyes, the forbidding tightness of his lips—it was the struggle to control himself revealed. Above the steam that danced on the surface of the water she could tell he burned, as did she, though she dared not bat an eyelash, afraid to scare him away. Tonight she could not blame her desire on the heat of excitement that followed a lucky hand; tonight there was not a thrilling crime to fault for her lack of self-restraint. Tonight it was just the two of them, and she wanted him badly, more than she had wanted him under the spell of that night's revelry.

He skimmed the water with his fingers, releasing a curling waft of lavender into the air. She shivered as he shrugged out of his coat and lowered himself onto his knees beside the tub. His fingers reached deeper into the water, dancing on the skin of her thigh, and he glanced at her from under his eyelashes. She blinked, parted her lips.

Yes.

The ends of his mouth turned upward in a small grin, confidence restored, and his fingers continued to dance higher, higher, and she jumped when he touched her. They both laughed and he leaned forward, his chest and belly flush against her own, and he crushed his lips against her throat. His deep, thunderous kisses sent her flying; she held fast to either side of the copper tub, her desire igniting her body so quickly she feared she might burst skyward in a flash of flame.

She sat upright and pulled his head toward her own. She pressed her lips against his, using her teeth to pry open his mouth. The force of the kiss knocked her backward and she fell into the steaming water. Still their lips tugged and pulled and caressed. She placed a hand on either side of his face and pulled him underwater with her, and for several seconds she reveled in the weightlessness of their embrace.

"Well, well, my dear," Harclay panted when he came up for air. "It seems your strength has been restored."

"Perhaps," she replied. It was impossible to take her eyes from his lips; below the water, his fingers worked to open her, caress her, and she felt her control slipping away.

His strokes were gentle and confident, brushing again and again that part of her that was most sensitive. She thought she might cry out from the pleasure of it, a building pressure that screamed for release.

"Please, oh, please let me go," she whispered as her head fell back with a *thump* on the ledge of the tub.

Harclay smiled. "Not yet, Violet, but soon," he murmured and brought his lips back down on hers.

Just when her desire reached fever pitch, Harclay withdrew his dancing fingers.

"What?" she panted. "No, please, don't stop . . ."

Harclay lifted her from the tub, one arm beneath her shoulder, the other supporting her knees. As small rivers of bathwater ran down her limbs, she shivered and looped her arms around his neck, never breaking the kiss.

He set Violet gently down upon his bed. The linens felt warm and inviting against her naked back. She pulled him down with her and for a moment they lay against each other, breathing hard. The weight of him on top of her left her breathless; she liked the feel of him, the reminder of his enormity, the enormity of his desire for her.

He grasped the back of her head and pulled her toward him, running his tongue along her jaw. She cried out; he moaned. As he moved over her the feather mattress tickled the backs of her arms; the warmth of the sheets quickly dried her skin.

His hands moved over the clean smoothness of her body, stopping to linger at her breasts and then between her legs.

And then his head dipped lower, lower, his lips trailing over her skin as he went, biting here, savoring there. She dug her hands into his hair, fingering its silken strands, and watched, heart pounding, as his mouth moved over one hip, then the other.

With one hand he cupped the back of her thigh, just below her buttocks, and pulled her legs apart. She opened her mouth to protest, but watching him settle between her thighs, her hands tangled in the dark gleaming mass of his hair, sent her desire soaring.

What comes next? she thought wildly. *What can possibly come next?*

Harclay rolled Violet's nipple between his thumb and forefinger, teasing it to a hard, tight point; his other hand moved from her thigh to her belly, splayed palm down to hold her in place.

Violet lifted her head. The earl grinned—a wicked thing— and his head disappeared between her legs.

At the first stroke of his tongue on her sex, Violet's eyes flew wide; she tugged at his hair, her pleasure growing with each caress, each kiss, each knowing, lingering touch.

He kissed her, again and again, over and over, his tongue moving quietly, expertly, over the tip of her womanhood—the center of all this lovely, breathless sensation. She should be embarrassed; she could feel herself grow wet, very wet, see her slickness on his lips when he half smiled over the mound of her sex. But oh, *oh*, there wasn't room inside her for embarrassment. Not when she felt like *this*, wanton and needful and captivated. Captivated by him, by the way he made her feel.

Violet's hips rolled against him, begging for more, for less. She watched as his head dipped, rose, dipped again, his hands working in time to his lips, his tongue. She watched him cup her breast, her flesh hardening beneath his callused palm. His other hand moved from her belly to her groin, holding her just where her leg met her sex; his thumb held back her folds as he moved over and in her with his tongue.

He pinched her nipple, hard, between his fingers; a bolt of searing pleasure shot through her.

"Please," she moaned. "Please, Harclay, don't stop."

She was arching over the bed now, her fingers tearing at Harclay's hair as if she might float away. Need and pleasure fought to take captive her body; she furrowed her brow in an attempt to calm the surge of sensation in her belly.

Again that bolt of pleasure, this time stronger, harder.

Violet saw stars as her climax pounded against every sense, every limb, every thought. She bit her lip but the cry came anyway. Seeing Harclay nestled in the cradle of her legs only made the sensation pulse brighter, pulse again, and again, and again.

Her heart felt as if it might explode from her chest as the spasms of insistent, heady pleasure between her legs slowly subsided.

Harclay wasn't kidding when he said he enjoyed *pleasuring*.

He rose from between her legs, pressing wet kisses onto her belly, beneath each of her breasts.

When at last he collapsed on the bed beside her, a satisfied smile on his lips, he kissed her mouth. She tasted herself on his lips, the salty tang of her desire. She drew back, embarrassed.

"Oh no," he said, and pulled her back to him. "You taste so sweet, Violet. So very sweet."

He was still clothed, though she could feel the heat of his skin seeping into her own through his wet shirt. He made no move to deepen their embrace, nor to push her any further down this dangerous and delicious path.

Her heart sank.

"No more," Violet said, her words more question than command.

Harclay shook his head and smiled. "No more." His lips feathered across her forehead. "Quite enough excitement for one night, wouldn't you say? Besides, if I don't stop now I'm afraid I shall ravage you, and quite soundly. And you know how I feel about ravaging."

He wrapped an arm about her shoulders and pulled her to him. Resting her head against his chest, she felt his cock straining against her legs.

"What about you?" she asked.

Rubbing his eyes, he gritted his teeth and let out a long, low breath. "I beg you, Lady Violet, do not tempt me."

His usual slick irony was gone. Violet could tell he was in pain, the kind of sweet, terrible pain she'd experienced just before—well, just before she lost all sense of place and time and self.

Violet sighed, fingering the fine linen of Harclay's shirt. "I suppose you win this time."

Again the rumble of laughter in his chest. "Yes, I suppose I do. No small feat, considering my opponent," he replied and pressed a lingering kiss onto her lips.

Sixteen

Avery gaped at Harclay as the earl strode into the break-fast room at quarter to eleven.

"Forgive me, my lord," he said, hurrying to help his master into his chair, "but we were worried you'd died in your sleep! I've managed to keep the kippers warm, sir, but I'm afraid we'll have to make you a fresh pot of coffee."

"Thank you, Avery. I'm going to need it this morning." He groaned as he settled rather uncomfortably into his customary spot. His nether regions still ached from the previous night's encounter with Lady Violet. Good thing he'd taken her home hours before; at this rate, his desire for her would've eventually killed him. Just thinking of her sent spasms of pleasure, and of grief, through his groin; he still tasted her on his lips. He hadn't felt such poignantly unfulfilled lust in— why, as long as he could remember. The Earl of Harclay, a Casanova of no little renown throughout Great Britain and the Continent, never denied himself when it came to women. So why the *hell* had he held back when Violet was warm and willing in his arms?

He kept telling himself that he was merely tired, that he hadn't wanted to deal with the mess that came with deflowering a virgin. For a virgin she certainly was, though her words, and her confidence, would lead one to think otherwise.

But, God save him, he knew in his little black heart none of that was true. Some small twinge, not altogether unpleasant, in the very center of his being hinted that such reasons had nothing to do with his strange behavior. Nothing at all.

Harclay pushed these thoughts from his mind and focused on the cup of steaming, fragrant coffee Avery set before him. Surely coffee would heal him of the night's desire; and if not coffee, then brandy would do the trick. He'd try anything to chase away the image of Lady Violet's face as she looked up at him in the kitchen galley; and then there was that moment, that heady, wild moment, when he was nestled between her legs, and she arched against his mouth . . .

"The paper, sir," Avery was saying.

Harclay nearly jumped as the butler placed the news before him.

Avery continued speaking as he busied himself at the sideboard. "Thought you might be interested in that story there on the front page. Looks like the papers finally caught wind of our little adventure."

Harclay grew very, very still. Coffee in hand, he glanced down at the paper. Sure enough, the headline screamed RARE JEWEL SNATCHED AT BANKING SCION'S BALL.

Despite the dire news—would Hope do something so drastic as to freeze Harclay's accounts until he confessed?—the earl found himself grinning.

"And so the plot thickens," he murmured and finished his coffee.

At exactly eight o'clock that evening, Harclay and his sister, Caroline, slipped into their supper box. The first show, a bawdy comedy, was just beginning. Harclay let out a low whistle of appreciation at the view. He'd rented this same box at Vauxhall Gardens for nigh on seven years now; not only did it afford the viewer a panorama of the stage, and of the lovely spring evening in the distance, but one could also take in the far more interesting sights of the other supper boxes. There was the prince regent's just off to the right, always bustling with the dregs of the *ton*. To the left stood one of the larger boxes, where the Dowager Baroness Blankenship entertained a steady stream of nubile young men. And a bit farther than that was Mr. Hope's box, in true Hope fashion decorated with strange-looking statues brought all the way from India.

Just as Harclay hoped, the banker's box was full of familiar faces. There was Lady Sophia, already tipsy on Vauxhall's infamous arrack punch; Lady Georgiana, her wounded forehead hidden behind an enormous headdress; and Mr. Hope, of course, smiling beatifically as if to convince the world that nothing, not even the theft of his prize jewel, could ruin his mood.

And then Harclay's heart dropped to his knees when his gaze fell at last on Lady Violet Rutledge. Jealousy flared hot and unbidden in his belly as he watched her laugh at something Mr. Lake was saying. She looked especially beautiful in a gown of light blue gauze, the low neckline trimmed alluringly with French lace; though there was a weariness about her eyes that Harclay found worrisome.

"Might I call up Mr. Lake?" Caroline said, interrupting his reverie. "I see him over there, in Hope's box. Perhaps our two parties might join together."

Harclay cleared his throat and took a long, deep draft of his arrack punch. Damn if the stuff couldn't fell a steer; it eased the pounding of his heart ever so slightly, just enough for him to regain control of his faculties.

"Let's wait until after we eat," Harclay replied. "I've ordered up the ham, your favorite."

Caroline leaned back from the table and grinned. "You and Violet playing your games again?"

Harclay arched a brow. "Games?"

"Oh, heavens, William, no use feigning ignorance. Did you really think we wouldn't notice?"

But before he could ask to whom she referred, exactly, when she said "we," a phalanx of waiters arrived bearing trays of fragrant food.

They ate in relative silence, the sounds of the players, and of the crowd, floating into their box on a warm breeze that hinted at summer. Though the comedy was a lewd one,

Harclay was hard-pressed to participate in the laughter of the crowd. It was impossible to tear his eyes from Hope's box.

What was Lady Violet eating? With whom was she speaking? What was she thinking—could she be thinking of him, of the near-violent passion that had sparked between them the night before? Or was she thinking of Hope, and her inheritance, wondering how she could press the earl to give up the diamond?

As soon as the first entertainment was ended, Harclay stood abruptly and handed his empty punch glass to a waiter. "Come, Caroline, let's us be the visitors for a change, shall we?"

Quick as lightning, Caroline was on her feet. She took his arm and tore him from their box. Harclay would've wondered at her enthusiasm were he not consumed by his own.

Heart drumming in his chest—even for him it seemed a bit cheeky to show himself, the chief suspect, in Hope's box—he held open the red velvet drapes for his sister to walk through. The tinkling of crystal and the exuberant laughter of those well on their way to getting good and foxed filled his ears as he stepped into Mr. Thomas Hope's lair.

All eyes turned to Harclay and the laughter died down, replaced by an uncomfortable silence the earl tried his best to ignore. Across the box he met eyes with Lady Violet. Color appeared on her cheeks as he nodded his greeting. Her eyes were a stormy shade of gray in the light of Vauxhall's hanging lanterns.

She looked angry . . . and interested . . . and aroused. A combination that, on anyone else, would appear frightful but on Violet—it was lovely, so much so that he felt his mouth grow dry, his groin tightening ominously.

"Lord Harclay," Hope said, standing. "Welcome. Please, do take a seat."

He motioned to an overstuffed chair wedged between his and Lake's. Though Violet was sequestered on the other side of the box with the ladies, she could doubtless hear whatever passed between the men. With one last longing glance in her direction, Harclay sat and accepted a glass of punch from a hovering waiter.

"I saw the news this morning, Hope," the earl began, clearing his throat. "It goes without saying that I still offer my unconditional cooperation in recovering the diamond, should you require it."

Hope raised a brow. Harclay could tell the man was weighing his words. It was obvious he wasn't entirely convinced the earl had stolen the French Blue, but his eyes gleamed with suspicion nonetheless.

"Thank you, my lord," Hope said. "We are managing the search quite well on our own. Mr. Lake here is chasing some interesting leads, and I have no doubt we shall hunt down this scoundrel, and find the diamond, in no time at all."

"Scoundrel indeed," Harclay replied, smacking his lips as he sipped the punch. "Speaking of, Mr. Lake, I'd appreciate it if you didn't look at my sister as if you wanted to eat her."

Both Mr. Lake and Caroline looked up from staring into each other's eyes. Mr. Lake opened his mouth and appeared ready to apologize when Caroline interrupted him.

"And here's the pot calling the kettle black!" she nearly cried, leaping to her feet. "You look at Lady Violet in much the same way. Though I must confess, at moments like these I wonder she does not turn up her nose at the beastly brute you can be. Mr. Lake may look at me however he likes, William, and I'll not have you opining on the subject in public."

"It is a compliment, Harclay, for I find your sister most lovely," Mr. Lake growled. He tugged gently on her hand in a futile attempt to coax her back into her seat.

"Lord Harclay," Violet said loudly from across the box. "Would you join me? It appears the second show is about to begin."

She stood and gestured to the front of the box, where a high balustrade bordered the edge of the stage. The invitation seemed to fulfill its intended purpose: Caroline and Mr. Lake quietly settled into their chairs, while Mr. Hope turned to Lady Sophia with a smile.

With a sigh of resignation—Caroline was ungainly, yes, and the eldest child, but she *was* his sister, damn it, and that meant he had an obligation to protect her from men and their sinister machinations—the earl rose and offered his arm to Violet.

"How foolish of you to make a scene, tonight of all nights," Violet murmured when they reached the balustrade. "Surely you know we cannot afford to have further scandal attached to Mr. Hope and his friends. Not after today's news."

"Give it a few days," Harclay replied. "In a week no one will remember that headline. What with the war in Spain and Prinny's follies—"

Lady Violet glared at him. "You insult me with such nonsense, my lord. Just today, dozens of Hope's clients closed their accounts or moved the bulk of their money elsewhere. His losses number in the tens of thousands of pounds."

"My accounts at Hope and Company should more than make up for that," Harclay replied. "And I swear to you, my money isn't going anywhere."

"Except that two thousand, of course. That belongs in *my* account."

"Of course." Harclay grinned. "Though I'm afraid I shall require you to collect your winnings at my home. At your earliest convenience, if you please; I'm afraid your stockings and pelisse look rather out of place in my wardrobe."

Color rose to Violet's cheeks, but the dear girl would not be thwarted. "You wouldn't know it by looking at him, my lord, but Mr. Hope is enraged. He may be an eccentric, but above all else he is a brilliant businessman. He will have his vengeance."

Harclay swallowed, hard, and gave his cravat a small but decidedly vicious tug. What he would give for a stiff pour of that arrack punch . . .

Truth be told, he hadn't given the consequences of the theft much thought when he'd snatched the French Blue from Violet's breast. It was merely a game, a game the earl played rather well; a game that kept him occupied, his senses sharp. He never meant to hurt anyone. He'd always planned on returning the jewel besides—in, of course, as ingenious a way as he'd thieved it in the first place.

Still. That did nothing to soothe the tightness in his throat. *Remorse.* Violet, her hundred shares of Hope & Co. stock, her family . . .

Harclay tugged at this cravat again. He'd just have to devise a new plot to return the diamond, and then all would be well. Yes, a plot; a plot that perhaps gave Violet the vindication that she was seeking, that assured the safety of her family's wealth.

A plot that proved to the world she was the clever, determined, wholly irresistible woman he knew her to be.

"Yes, well." Harclay cleared his throat. "Only time will tell."

"And how much time do you think you'll serve at Newgate, Lord Harclay, once I prove your guilt?"

Harclay patted Violet's shoulder. "It's going to be much more difficult to pay you the two thousand I owe you from jail, Violet."

Violet squared her shoulders; he could tell she bit back a smile. "I think you'll find a way, my lord."

Looking down at her face, alive with mischief and not a little of that dreadful arrack punch, Harclay sensed his heart quicken. Without thinking he drew her close, very close, so that he loomed over her. His body pulsed with desire. Her smile faded and she parted her lips, her protest no more than a short, hot breath.

"Might I expect the pleasure of your company again tonight, Lady Violet? You've still the house to search, after all. May take you days, weeks even. Might as well get a head start."

"Best watch your back," she said, motioning over Harclay's shoulder. "For our old friends the acrobats are looking at you, and they've murder in their eyes. Perhaps they've pinned you as the cunning thief you are. Don't you owe them money?"

Harclay suddenly turned, his heart skipping a beat as his eyes fell on the stage. For there stood *the* acrobats, the very same ones he'd hired to create all that ruckus at Hope's ball. Though they waved at the crowd, their gold-trimmed costumes glimmering in the stage lights, they directed their dark gazes at the earl. The hair at the back of his neck bristled as he returned the favor.

Clear as day he saw the recognition in their eyes. They knew he was the masked man who'd hired them those weeks ago.

But how? When Harclay had confronted them in Mr. Hope's kitchen, they hadn't a clue who he was. Someone must have tipped them off; someone who knew Harclay still owed the thieves quite a bit of money.

"Bloody hell," Harclay cursed under his breath. The chase was proving to be an interesting one, certainly; now he would be pursued by not only Lady Violet and Mr. Hope but these villainous little bastards, too.

Ah, well. He'd just pay them the rest of what he owed and be done with it. A trip to that squalid little tavern in Cheapside tonight, and the earl could begin plotting the French Blue's return.

Still. Something about the way the acrobats were looking at him—glaring, really—felt wrong.

He turned to Violet. "It wasn't you, was it? Who told these men that I was the one who hired them?"

"No." She shook her head. "Though I do wish I could take credit. A brilliant move, wouldn't you say?"

"Perhaps," Harclay replied, returning his gaze to the stage.

Seventeen

— ✦ —

The streets of Cheapside were quiet, eerily so. A lone figure, wrapped tightly in a misshapen cloak, trudged past. The smell that rose from the mud was nothing short of biblical.

Harclay turned down a narrow alley, his horse nickering as they probed deeper into squalor. Above, misshapen tenements hovered over the street and blocked out the clouds that hung low in the nighttime sky.

A rat—or was it a dog?—scurried across the alley and through a hole in the wall of a wattle-and-daub house up ahead. A rough wooden sign hung from the rafter, emblazoned with the image of a mouse dangling from the jaws of a black cat.

Harclay reined in at the familiar sight of the Cat and Mouse. He dismounted, his boots sinking to the ankle in a particularly pungent puddle.

At least I don't have to wear that ridiculous beard, he reasoned, now that the acrobats knew who he was. And the wooden dentures he'd donned to recruit the acrobats that first time around had made speaking without a whistling lisp most difficult.

Perhaps it wasn't so bad someone had sold Harclay out to

THE GENTLEMAN JEWEL THIEF 133

the acrobats; it certainly saved the earl no small amount of trouble today.

The Cat and Mouse was typical of most public taverns, if not slightly more filthy and certainly smellier. It consisted of one large, low-ceilinged room, its round wooden tables scattered around a soot-blackened hearth. Even at this hour, the place bustled with the usual crowd: prostitutes, and the men who paid for their services. The air was dark, lit only by fat tallow candles, and reeked of unwashed bodies, tobacco, and stale ale.

Not long ago, Harclay would've relished a retreat to a tavern, albeit one slightly more upscale than this. But today he had no time for such frivolity; he waved off an approaching barmaid with a monumentally large, swinging bosom, and made for the back of the tavern.

There, seated around a corner table with their backs to the wall, sat four smallish men. They were hunched over their mugs, eyes gleaming mischievously as they watched Harclay approach.

Without much ado, the earl tossed a small but weighty satchel onto the table with a satisfying *clink*. Like vultures pouncing on a carcass, two of the acrobats dug greedily into its contents, while the third raised his head in greeting.

"Milord," he said with a black-toothed smile. "Mighty kind ov ya to join us. Take a seat, if ya please."

"Who told you?" Harclay asked, ignoring the man's invitation. "Who told you I was the one who hired you?"

The acrobat's smile widened. "Can't be givin' away all our secrets, milord," he replied, and turned to his accomplices. "How much ye got, lads?"

"Seventy-five pounds, even," Harclay said. "I counted it myself."

"Seventy-five!" the man scoffed. "A most meager sum indeed, what wiv all the bover we been through. Wouldn't you agree, lads?"

The two acrobats looked up from their pile of guineas and grunted their agreement.

"That's what I owe you," Harclay replied steadily. "And that's what you'll get. Not another copper."

"We ain't shook no hands." The acrobat grinned. "And we ain't signed no papers. Now that we knows where ya live . . ."

Harclay's blood jumped. He placed his hands on the table, leaning forward until he nearly butted heads with the scalawag. "You threaten me again, or so much as show your face on my street, and I'll kill you. Understood?"

The acrobat leaned back, his rabbitlike eyes glittering. "Understood, *milord.*"

Harclay stepped out into the night, pulling his cloak closer about his shoulders. It had begun to rain, though only a scant drizzle made it past the upper stories above, hanging over the lane.

He tried to shake off the feeling of unease knotted in his belly. Those blackguards were nothing more than greedy drunks. He'd paid them the seventy-five they'd agreed to; they wouldn't dare come after an earl, and a wealthy, well-connected one at that.

The earl let out a sigh, relieved to be done with the thing, and urged his horse into a gallop. Harclay rode like the devil through the darkened streets, his eyes blurring as they picked up the pace. He didn't know why he rode to Violet's, or how he even got there; but he did not stop until he drew up in the mews behind her house.

Violet closed the door and fell back against it, relieved to finally be alone in the sanctuary of her bedchamber. Behind her closed eyes the week's heady scenes played out. Her waltz with Lord Harclay—she remembered everything about it; she shivered at the memory of his hand on the small of her back, his lips on her ear. And then there were the caresses in his drawing room, and his slow, patient kisses— kisses he'd pressed on every slope and corner of her body— last night on his bed.

Piece by piece she took off her clothes, the feel of the fabric sensuous against her skin, until she was naked. Tonight she especially loved the feel of her body. It reminded her of Lord Harclay, his eagerness to touch her, and the way she felt when he did; the small, quiet scrape of his hands moving on her skin, the goose bumps, the pounding of their hearts against each other.

And that blasted diamond—she was getting close, if not to

the French Blue, then to Harclay's confession. He'd acted strangely tonight, tugging her about Mr. Hope's supper box in a furor she didn't quite understand. Perhaps, at last, he was coming apart at the seams; perhaps the guilt was gnawing him into an admission of his sins.

She climbed into bed, sliding beneath the sheets. As she turned to blow out the candle, she heard a soft tap against the window across the room. She froze.

"Who's there?" she whispered, wrapping the sheets tightly around her torso.

Speak of the devil, she thought with a smile, and he doth appear. Lord Harclay climbed through the window and landed none too elegantly on his feet. She could hear the patter of rain through the open window; he was soaking wet. Somewhere along the way he'd lost his coat and was dressed simply in a white cotton shirt, now sheer, and black breeches.

The pirate—ah, he was alive and well.

"Climbing through a window," she whispered. "Really? You must be blinded by your lust for me."

"Ah, humble as a saint, you are," he murmured, tugging his legs free of their muddy boots. "Besides, I doubt I'm the only one in this room 'blinded,' as you say, by my baser needs."

As if on cue, Violet smacked her lips in appreciation as Harclay drew up before her, his clothes plastered against his enormous frame. "Tell me, my lord, why have you come?"

He crawled on top of her, straddling her with his knees. "Why, Lady Violet, I mean to pleasure you, of course. If I am not mistaken, you seemed to have enjoyed my . . . attentions last night."

Droplets fell from his curls onto her face. One landed in her eye and she laughed. He smiled and shook out his hair, then leaned in to kiss her wet skin.

"But how," she panted, "did you manage to climb up so high?"

Laughter rumbled in the earl's chest. "I've got a strong back," he said, trailing kisses along her jaw.

Her blood quickened as his lips moved over her throat, down to her collarbones; the sheet fell away. He moved to her breasts, his kisses rallying her body awake. She propped herself up on her elbows, pressing herself against him, and with trembling fingers he traced the outline of her hips. She breathed, kept breathing, unable to express the terrifyingly delicious effect of his hands on her body. He moved his mouth over one breast, then the other, up to her throat, her jawbone. He took her lower lip between his teeth, pulling, antagonizing the heat low in her belly.

"Wait," Violet said, holding her hand up to his chest. "Wait. Tell me truthfully—why did you come?"

Lord Harclay paused, holding her gaze. A beat of silence passed.

Violet's heart went wild in her chest. It was wrong of her to bait him like this, but she needed to know—needed him to *tell* her why he'd pulled her aside in Hope's supper box, why he'd risked his life climbing through her third-story window in the middle of the night.

How could he care for her when he was attempting to rob her of her future? Like her affection for him, it didn't make sense.

"Damn you," Violet said in a clipped voice, throwing the blankets aside and turning as if to rise from the bed. "You haven't answered a single question I've asked you—"

"I needed to make sure you were here. Safe," he said. For a moment he paused his indecently thrilling assault on her person and looked into her eyes. His were dark, flashing with desire, but there was something else, something new. Was it fear?

There was a sudden tussle at the door. Violet froze; it was a miracle the whole of London couldn't hear the blood pulsing in her ears. Harclay fell to the bed beside her, pulling his wet shirt off over his head and slinging it across the room.

Violet cuffed his shoulder and held her finger to her lips. "You know if we're caught we'll be forced to do terrible things!" she hissed.

He raised a brow. "Terrible things?"

"Marry."

She was surprised when, rather than some witty riposte, Lord Harclay met her words with steady silence; and was surprised again when she felt a pang of regret. It was obvious his silence meant he did not wish to be caught—and thus be forced to marry her—didn't it?

She stiffened her spine. She certainly had no intention to be wedded, either, especially to a beastly rakehell like him.

Still. His silence irked her.

"My lady?" came a voice at the door. "Is everything all right? I heard a noise and thought to check on you."

"Yes, Fitzhugh, I am well. Nothing more than a . . . strange dream," Violet replied. "You may go back to bed."

Violet and Lord Harclay listened with bated breath as the sound of the maid's footsteps faded down the hall. Silence settled between them; Violet was aware of the slow rise and fall of Harclay's bare chest beside her on the bed.

She turned to him, propping herself up on an elbow. She made no effort to hide her nakedness; though she'd known the earl no more than a week, they were the both of them beyond silly things like clothes.

Harclay's eyes trailed from her eyes to her lips to her breasts. His gaze was like a caress. Her skin ignited as if it were his fingers doing the work; and yet he made no move to touch her.

"God, you're lovely," he said hoarsely. "If this is the state in which you sleep every night, I should climb through your window more often."

Violet smiled. "I daresay Fitzhugh will grow suspicious of all the strange dreams I'm having."

"You could always come visit me, at my house. I so enjoyed last night's interlude," he replied, pressing a kiss onto her neck. "You'd have the opportunity to snoop about my rooms, besides."

She looked away, trying her damnedest to ignore the pounding of her pulse as his lips trailed lower, lower. "I'm afraid this is all rather dangerous, even for us. A diamond is one thing, Harclay; being forced to wed, quite another."

He took her nipple in his mouth for one last kiss. She gasped aloud as heat sliced between her legs.

"Dangerous enough that you wish me to stop?" he murmured, his lips hovering a hairbreadth from her breast.

She nodded rather more vigorously than she intended. "Yes," she said, clearing her throat. "I'm safe, see? No use prolonging your stay. Fitzhugh or, God forbid, my father is sure to hear us if we continue—"

"If that is your wish," he said with a sigh, "then I shall take my leave. As long as you remember what you promised me— if you see anything, *hear* anything strange, you'll send for me."

Violet watched as he stood and struggled into his sopping wet shirt. "What aren't you telling me?" she said quietly. "If you were in your right mind—assuming you are even *possessed* of such a thing—you wouldn't care a whit about my safety. Surely you recall I mean to ruin you?"

"I vaguely remember something of the sort," he said, furrowing his brow in mock confusion. He pulled on his boots and turned to her, leaning over her on the bed. "Despite that fact, dear girl, I am far too involved in this intrigue between us to ever feign indifference. Whether you'll have me or not, I do care." He pecked her lips with his own and made to leave.

"Do be careful, Lord Harclay, for should you fall and break your neck, the diamond will be lost to us forever," she replied tartly, ignoring the softness of his words. "And if what you say is true, then you won't risk my future happiness by climbing through my window again."

But he did, the next night, and the night after that; every night for nearly a week, he climbed through her window and into her bed. And though he merely teased her—their *affaire* progressed no further than his expert touch would allow— Violet found she very much looked forward to their candlelit conversations, if one could call their rather more carnal encounters such a thing.

She told herself her enthusiasm was nothing more than a desire to seek out the diamond, to uncover whatever it was he was hiding from her. But her heart, the way it pounded at the sound of Lord Harclay prying open the window at half past midnight, called her bluff. And even she, consummate cheat that she was, couldn't work her way around that truth.

The note arrived one week to the day after Harclay stared down the acrobats at Vauxhall Gardens.

He was walking home after a particularly frustrating— titillating—midnight visit with Lady Violet, his thoughts lost in a haze of desire. Though his mind was plenty occupied with memories of her body, the delicious scents of clean water and perfume that rose from her skin, again and again his thoughts returned to her words on that first night he'd climbed through her window.

Violet had warned him to silence and said something about being found out and forced to marry. She'd caught him entirely off guard with that hateful word, a word he'd banished from his vocabulary altogether the moment he came of age.

Harclay had stared into the darkness without replying to Lady Violet. He knew she had little, if any, desire to marry at all; doubtless she'd wanted to bite her tongue after speaking of such an odious subject. Hence, he reasoned, her silence.

But *his* silence—well, the comment had struck him as violently as a blow to the belly. For to his great shock, he hadn't been mortified, scared stiff, by her mention of *marriage*. Rather, it lay lightly on the current of his thoughts, as it still did now, days after the fact.

For years he hadn't thought of marrying anyone, much less a woman intent on branding him a thief. Not until that moment, when the words fell hushed and expectant from Violet's lips, languorous and swollen from his attentions.

And yet the very idea that her words *didn't* irk him was terrifying indeed. What did it mean? Why did he not recoil in horror, as any man in his right mind should? Marriage was where good men went to die; marriage meant responsibility and fidelity and the screaming hysterics of babies . . .

So why did the idea of marrying Lady Violet, quick-witted beauty though she was, not frighten him to his very toes?

Virtually paralyzed by this strange machination of his mind, Harclay had lain very still, his tongue like stone in his mouth. Good thing her body was there to distract him—her breasts were far too perfect to ignore—and the evening proceeded as if nothing were amiss.

In his usual manner, Harclay walked the four blocks from Violet's town house to his own, the gas lamps casting his shadow in sinister shapes about the cobblestone streets. Last he'd checked it was quarter to two in the morning; beyond the lamps the darkness was complete, oppressive.

The earl headed toward the back of his house, silent and dark save for a few windows high up; his rooms, kept warm and lit by the indomitable Avery.

As Harclay approached the door—the very same one through which he'd ushered Lady Violet, sopping wet and chilled to the bone, just days before—a flutter of white caught his eye, there on the stoop. At first it appeared to be a wounded bird, perhaps, or a feather missed by the cook, but on closer inspection Harclay discovered it was a page of newspaper, folded clumsily so that it was no bigger than his pocket watch.

He bent down to pick it up. As his fingers smoothed the surface of the paper, he felt a pulse of fear, cold and hard, race up his spine.

Harclay raised his hand to knock on the door, but Avery opened it before he had the chance.

"My lord," he said and then, his eyes alighting on his master's pale features, exclaimed, "is everything all right?"

Stepping inside, Harclay turned to Avery and nodded at the candle he held in his hand. "The light, if you please."

Harclay began unfolding the small package, taking care not to tear the delicate paper. From the look of it, the newspaper was from that morning: a few headlines detailing the latest Spanish cities captured by Wellington, another article about Mr. Hope's missing diamond.

His hands shaking with impatience, Harclay at last opened the page. Inside, scrawled in enormous, barely legible script, was a note. The ink was bold and black and splattered across the headlines.

Wee require unother 75 poownds
Tomoroww Noon at the Cat and mowse
cheepsyde
We no were She lives

Rage pounded hard, loud, through Harclay's veins. Those greedy, conniving bastards; he should've known they'd come for more money, should've guessed they'd come for Violet.

He crumpled the note in his hand. How foolish he had been to visit Lady Violet these past nights; likely those damned acrobats followed him right to her window. The thought of those black-toothed bastards kidnapping her, putting their filthy hands all over her lovely skin . . .

He cursed so loudly, so fluidly, that poor Avery jumped back, the candle trembling in his hand.

"Did you see anyone?" Harclay growled between clenched teeth. "You must've been waiting for me, down here in the kitchens. Did you see anyone deliver this note?"

Avery shook his head. "I poked about outside, my lord, perhaps an hour ago. I didn't see a soul. Nor did I see the note—it must have arrived just before you."

Harclay let out a long, hot breath. At least he knew Lady Violet was safe—for now.

Running a hand through his hair, Harclay turned to Avery. "Speak of this to no one. Hire extra men to keep watch at Lady Violet's—discreetly, of course, as I do not wish to alarm her or her family."

"Of course." Avery nodded.

"And tell our footmen to carry guns and keep an eye on my sister," Harclay said. "No one comes in or out of this house without my permission. Is that understood?"

"Very well, my lord, I shall see to it," Avery said.

"And have the house turned out tomorrow. Every room, every cranny and fireplace and corner, cleaned and put back together again. You are to report anything out of the ordinary to me."

"Yes, my lord," the butler replied. After a beat, he cleared his throat, and Harclay noticed him shifting his weight from one foot to the other.

"Well?" Harclay said, raising a brow. "Come, now, Avery, out with it."

"Begging your pardon, Lord Harclay, but you shan't protect anyone if you don't get some sleep. You'll need your wits about you these next few days. Your strength, too."

"Very well," Harclay replied, though he knew there would be no rest for him tonight, not until he untangled Violet from his plot. "To bed, to bed. But I shall break my fast at the usual hour, Avery. Have my sister up as well. We have an important call to make, first thing."

Eighteen

The morning sun, pale and warm, flooded Violet's chamber as Fitzhugh pulled back the drapes. Violet opened one eye and discerned at once that the hour was early, too early for one such as she who'd been up half the night kissing a rain-soaked rake in her bed.

"I am sorry to disturb you, my lady," Fitzhugh said, as if reading Violet's thoughts, "but you have callers."

Violet turned away from the light, digging her naked arms beneath the pillow. "Tell them I am not feeling well. Wretchedly early for a call, isn't it?"

Violet heard the quiet splash of fresh water as Fitzhugh filled the washbasin. "Pardon my boldness, milady, but I don't think there's anything wretched about these callers. One in particular."

"Who is it?" Violet moaned.

But Fitzhugh was intent on playing coy. "They are waiting downstairs in the drawing room. With his grace the duke. Your *father*."

Violet leapt from her bed as if it were aflame. "But you know very well Papa can't accept callers! He isn't even allowed downstairs—last time, he managed to set half my books on fire—"

"I'm afraid your callers insisted," Fitzhugh replied, decorously ignoring Violet's complete and utter nudity.

Strains of laughter wafted up the stairwell into Violet's chamber. Her belly turned over at the sound; she recognized that laugh, that deep, rumbling voice.

"What should you like to wear? Perhaps the persimmon?" Fitzhugh asked. She opened the door to Violet's dressing room and began fussing with her mistress's meager collection of gowns.

"The one brought over by the milliner last week," Violet replied. "The French silk promenade gown, with the tassels."

Fitzhugh paused. "A bit fancy for the morning, milady. Shows quite a lot of skin."

Oh, the earl's seen much more skin than that, Violet thought. She shivered with anticipation as she sat at her vanity and began tugging a brush through her curls, mangled from sleep.

After what seemed an eternity, Violet swept into the drawing room with all the elegance she could muster at so early an hour. Her eyes alighted on the merry scene before her and it was all she could do not to gape in wonder.

For there, seated before a pleasant fire with delicate cups of tea in their hands, sat the Earl of Harclay, his sister, Lady Caroline, and Violet's father, the Duke of Sommer. All of them wore great smiles and high color, as if they'd just shared a particularly humorous jest. Violet's heart skipped a beat. She hadn't seen her father laugh, or appear so happy, since he'd fallen ill some years ago.

"Violet! At last!" the duke said, rising to peck her on the cheek. And then, lowering his voice just enough so that everyone in the room could still hear, "Capital chap, the earl, with bollocks and brains both. I knew he'd taken a liking to you. I approve, I say, and most heartily!"

Across the room, Violet met eyes with Harclay. He was looking at her intently, his dark gaze smoldering with laughter and just a hint of heat. Her plan to chastise him, to bring him to account for calling at such an ungodly hour, faded as she felt a smile tug at the corners of her mouth. It seemed the earl's good humor was contagious.

"William," Lady Caroline was saying, cuffing his shoulder, "you should take your own advice and stop ogling Violet as if you'd like to eat her. And in her father's own drawing room! The shame of it."

But in true fashion, the earl would not be thwarted. He leapt to his feet and crossed the room in two enormous, impatient strides. The breath left her body as he bowed and drew up before her; desire crackled palpably in the tiny space between their bodies.

"Lady Violet," he murmured, a wicked grin on his lips, "it has been far too long."

"Yes," she replied, swallowing. "An eternity."

An eternity indeed—all of six hours.

Her father clapped the earl on the back. "Lord Harclay has requested the honor of your presence this morning, my dear Violet. Was it a drive you mentioned, my lord, or a dance? Though I'm afraid we haven't any musicians."

"Let us save the dance for later. This evening, perhaps, if the lady will have me," Harclay replied smoothly and turned to Violet. "I was hoping you'd accompany me on a drive this morning. My sister shall join us as chaperone, of course, seeing as your aunt Georgiana is, by all reports, still suffering the aftereffects of that unfortunate billiards incident."

"Poor woman." Violet's father shook his head. "Looks like a gargoyle, she does, ready to sprout horns from that bump on her head."

Violet cleared her throat and looped her arm through the earl's. "A drive would be lovely, thank you," she said and tugged him none too gently toward the door.

"Godspeed!" Lord Rutledge called after them. "And don't hurry back. 'Tis far too lovely a day, and Violet too lovely a girl, to be stuck inside with an old man like me!"

Violet did not notice Lord Harclay's unease until they were settled beside each other in his gleaming phaeton. It was an enormously elegant and dangerous-looking affair, the vehicle lacquered black and trimmed in Harclay's signature shade of blue. It was drawn by a matching pair of Andalusians, hides polished to such a sheen they rivaled the earl's Hoby top boots. She checked her bonnet, discreetly, digging the pins closer against her scalp; an infamous whip, Harclay had a reputation to protect. Doubtless he would drive like the devil, even with a lady beside him.

As the earl took the reins in his hands, he looked over one shoulder, then the other, scanning the street. His foot tapped impatiently against the floorboard; against the smooth skin of his jaw his muscles twitched.

His display of anxiety was unnerving; Violet had grown accustomed to his smooth-talking ease. He was a man who seldom, if ever, allowed his feathers to be ruffled, who was unceasingly calm and collected and wicked.

"You might as well tell me what it is that's bothering you," she said. "I'll find out one way or another."

The earl's smile was tight and brief. "Let us hope you do not, Lady Violet."

Beyond that, he offered no explanation. Urging the horses into motion with a low, expert whistle, Harclay led the phaeton into the lane, Lady Caroline following closely behind in the Townshend family coach.

Violet squared her shoulders and looked out over the side of the phaeton, resolved to remain undistracted by the brooding, magnetic presence beside her. She would have an answer to her question, whether he liked it or not. But every now and again her gaze would find its way to him, her pulse quickening at the very sight of his hands, his fingers, those *eyes*.

The muscles in his shoulders and arms strained against his coat as he directed the horses this way and that; the smooth skin along his cheekbones and brow gleamed in the strengthening sun. Gritting her teeth, she sat on her hands, lest they of their own volition reach out and grope the man in ways they shouldn't.

"I'm taking you to my house," he said. "I'm having it turned out today, and I thought it a perfect opportunity for you to continue your snooping."

"You mock me," she sniffed. "What did you do with it? Ship it off to Russia or some such nonsense? Bury it at your country house? Sink it into a Scottish loch? Hope's diamond can't possibly be in your bedchamber if you're allowing me to search it."

"Perhaps." He shrugged. "Perhaps not. But I am enjoying our little game far too much to let the trail go cold, as they say. I hardly think I could bear it if you abandoned me for another suspect."

"If we weren't in public, I'd throttle you. And besides, I shall never consider another suspect; I know you are my man," Violet replied, turning away in a huff. "I say, is that Mr. Lake in the carriage with your sister?"

Harclay's head swiveled in that direction. Sure enough, they could see the outline of Mr. Lake's enormous, hulking figure through the coach windows. It appeared he was leaning toward Lady Caroline, doing something with his hands.

Violet bit back a smile as Harclay cursed.

"Christ have mercy, my sister shall be the end of me. And that devil—how I despise him! If she ends up with child, I'll have his head."

"Pish! And what of your sister's happiness? Even a fool can see the affection that grows between them."

"Caroline's contentment means the world to me," he growled, "but there's something about Lake I don't like. He isn't who he says he is; he keeps secrets. I can see it in his eyes. I fear he shall do no more than steal her heart and break it."

Violet sighed. She did not dare give voice to her own fear that Harclay was doing the very same to *her* heart.

As soon as Harclay reined in the horses before his house, he leapt from the phaeton and wordlessly reached for Violet. Clutching her waist in his hands, he lifted her from the vehicle as if she weighed no more than a feather and set her on her feet.

It was obvious he was in a rage, for without thinking he clasped her hand within his and stalked toward the coach. Even through the fine kidskin of her glove, she could feel the warmth of his callused flesh sinking into her own. A wave of energy coursed through her, goose pimples pricking to life on her arms and legs.

Waving off the groomsmen, Lord Harclay yanked open the coach door. Violet gasped in surprise as her eyes fell on the empty seat beside Lady Caroline.

"Where is he?" Harclay hissed. "I know he was in the carriage with you, Caroline, so where did he go?"

Caroline tucked an errant curl behind one ear and, as if she hadn't heard her brother speak at all, made her way out of the coach. Instinctively, Harclay reached out with his free hand and caught her just in time before she tripped on her dress and fell face-first into the drive.

"Well?" he insisted warningly.

Lady Caroline sniffed. "I don't know what you're talking about, William, but I do wish you'd stop harassing me so. How Lady Violet can tolerate your moods, I have nary a clue."

She turned to Violet and tugged her from the earl's grasp. "Come, my dear, I understand my dear brother would like you to have a tour of the house. It would be my pleasure."

Her arm looped through Lady Caroline's, Violet found herself climbing the great steps of Harclay's London house, Avery beaming from the front door. She felt a pang of regret—would the earl not accompany them?—and looked over her shoulder, her gaze finding his. His jaw was set; his eyes blazed. He appeared a wolf, tense with vigor just before setting out for the hunt.

"I shall return shortly," he said, as if reading her thoughts. "I've an errand to see to in the city. Promise me you'll stay."

Violet furrowed her brow. This didn't make much sense; why did he bring her to his house, only to leave to run a mysterious errand?

But the way he looked at her, that strange, hard gleam in his eyes, made her swallow her reservations. "Of course," she said. And then, impulsively: "Take care, my lord."

Harclay bowed and disappeared around the house.

Nineteen

The welcome Harclay received at Hope & Co. was mark-edly cooler than that which he'd enjoyed just a few weeks before. Bank employees turned from him, not as if he were a triumphant Caesar but rather a Medusa come to turn them all to stone, snakes roiling from his head.

Harclay brushed past them, his mood grim. He didn't have time for the usual Hope & Co. theatrics; he needed seventy-five pounds, and quick, lest those conniving acrobats get their hands on Violet.

His pace quickened at the thought. The rage he felt toward those cads, toward himself, was nothing short of murderous. He could not bear the fact that it was his own carelessness, his lust-fueled stupidity, that put Violet directly in harm's way.

He would not see her hurt. No matter the consequences, the blood that would be spilt; the earl would see her safe and happy, her life, her family, her fortune secure.

Harclay prayed Hope would allow him this one last with-drawal; he prayed his accounts were not yet frozen. The earl had contemplated returning Hope's diamond—for that would solve everything, wouldn't it?—but the banker was a wily fel-low, and a consummate businessman besides. Even if Harclay did return the jewel to him, Hope was just as liable to have him arrested as he was to shower him with thanks. After all, returning the diamond was tantamount to an admission of guilt.

No, it was too much of a risk; if he was arrested, thrown in jail, who would protect Violet from the acrobats? They would come after her, whether or not the earl returned the French Blue to its rightful owner. Besides, he had bigger plans for Hope's gem, plans that involved Violet, his favorite carriage, and a very good bottle of Scotch.

He was about to mount the stairs, railing clasped firmly in his hand, when a hugely tall man stepped in his path.

"Excuse me, my lord," the man said. "Mr. Hope is not accepting calls this afternoon. If you would but leave your card, I shall—"

Harclay shoved the man unceremoniously to the side, and continued up the stairs. "Hope will see me," he growled.

"My lord!" the man called out, racing up the steps after him. "My lord, you musn't!"

But he was no match for Harclay, who barged through the closed doors of Mr. Hope's office just as his man, breathless with exertion, reached the top step.

Mr. Hope stood behind his desk in naught but his waistcoat, leaning on his hands above an enormous stack of newspapers. He raised his head, surprise flashing in his dark eyes as they fell upon the earl.

"I need to make a withdrawal," Harclay said without ceremony. "And quickly."

Mr. Hope rose to his full height, surveying Harclay from across the room. The earl could tell he hadn't slept in days; heavy, dark circles ringed his eyes, and though his face was carefully composed into a mask of indifference, Harclay saw strain in the furrow of his brow.

"I assume you've seen the papers?" Hope asked.

"I don't have time for this," Harclay replied. "I don't mean to be rude, Hope, but time is of the essence—"

"Eight days," Hope interrupted. "I've been in the headlines for eight days straight. Each headline worse than the last; by now all of London must think me a brainless buffoon. Never mind the success of my business before the French Blue incident. Now I am being judged on one bloody night of theatrics; a drop in the proverbial bucket, as they say. And my business—it has suffered greatly, Harclay. Greatly indeed."

Harclay bit back his impatience. "I understand your frustration, Hope."

Hope shook his head, his voice even, deadly calm. "I don't think you do. You see, when Lady Violet came to me with her little theory about you being the thief, I very nearly dismissed her out of hand. Why would Lord Harclay do such a thing, I thought, and to me of all people? I've guarded his investment, shown him generous returns.

"But we've no other suspects, you see. And as I've watched my clients vanish, scared off by my seeming incompetence; as I've watched the value of my company plummet—well, I need someone to blame. And I'm afraid that someone is you."

The earl froze as the meaning of Hope's words dawned on him. "Please, Hope, listen to me. I'll give you anything, anything at all, but it is imperative that I make this withdrawal, or Vio—"

Hope held up his hand. "No," he said simply, and turned back to his papers.

"No?" Harclay replied, voice rising with panic. "What do you mean, *no*? I've well over a hundred thousand at this bank, and I demand access to those funds!"

"I've locked your accounts until the French Blue is returned to me. You'll not see a bloody penny before, mark my words. And if you did not steal my diamond yourself, as you claim, then this shall certainly prove motivation for you to help us find the man who did."

Harclay stared at Mr. Hope, speechless. Rage and fear, helplessness and panic, choked him. He'd never felt this way; he was used to being immaculately aloof, handsomely amused. How the *hell* had he come so far, changed so much?

In a single rapid beat of his heart, the answer came.

Violet.

What would those bastards do to Lady Violet, now that he couldn't pay? How would they kidnap her? What if they harmed—or, worse, *killed* her on account of his playing this all wrong?

"Goddamn it, Hope!" Harclay shouted. "I need that money.

Seventy-five pounds, and I swear I shan't ask for more until the diamond is found. I'm in trouble, and so is Lady—"

"That's your problem," Hope replied savagely, color flooding his cheeks as he again rose to face the earl. "Now get out of my bank before I summon my men."

Harclay thrust his face into Hope's. "If you do this, you'll have blood on your hands."

"Mr. Robbins!" Hope called, and the large man from the stairs appeared at Harclay's side. "Please escort Lord Harclay out of the building. No need to make a scene. Unless, of course, he resists."

Harclay thrust his finger into Hope's chest. "You'll regret this, I swear it. I'll make you regret this."

The earl was yanked from behind, and Mr. Robbins tugged him down the stairs and through the bank. Harclay saw naught but red; now he knew how King Louis, poor bastard, felt as he was dragged through the streets of Paris to greet *madame guillotine.*

Once they were outside, Harclay shrugged off the man's grip and swung onto his horse. Without a backward glance he tore out into the street. He needed to get to Violet, and quickly. His time was up; the acrobats would be after her, if they weren't already.

A rm in arm with Lady Caroline, Violet trailed through the house's endless number of chambers, each larger and lovelier than the last. There were the bachelor's quarters on the third floor, outfitted with secret staircases and copious amounts of leather; the music room, complete with a pianoforte salvaged from Versailles; even the halls were studies in elegance, trimmed in painted paneling, the ceilings wild with heavenly frescoes.

While rounding a corner, Violet managed to peek into Harclay's personal chambers. A score of maids were busy changing the linen, the snap of sweet-smelling sheets filling the air as they floated on the springtime breeze. Violet recalled with a little shiver the feel of those same sheets against her bare skin. How different the room appeared in the light of day; how very much the same.

She was tempted to slip into his dressing room, snoop about his sock drawer—really, how foolish of her to think he'd hide Hope's diamond *there* of all places—but Violet knew Harclay's chamber was sacred to him. To her, too, having christened it with her cries of passion, the blazing desire that moved through her on that very same bed.

It would be wrong to defile his sanctuary by ransacking it in her search for the French Blue—wrong, and callous. But there had been more headlines about the theft, more news of investors big and small pulling their money from Hope's bank; all week she'd watched the price of her shares steadily decline. If she didn't find the diamond, and soon, she faced the very real possibility of poverty.

The thought terrified her, it did; and yet as she made her way through the earl's achingly lovely town house, her mind wandered again and again to Lord Harclay. That peculiarly pleasant scent of his was everywhere; his passion and ardor and respect apparent in each priceless antique, in the smiles of his staff and the pleasant glow emanating from his sister.

For a moment she allowed herself to fantasize about being a part of all this loveliness. To share such a life with such a man; to see him, and live with him, in these rooms, every day for the rest of her life—

She gasped at the strange, dull pain that sliced through her heart.

"Goodness, my dear, are you all right?" Lady Caroline asked, brow furrowed. "You look flushed."

Violet landed unceremoniously in the nearest seat. "Yes, yes, I am—I am just fine, thank you. This heat! It seems summer has arrived early."

"Indeed it has," Caroline said, taking a seat in the chair beside her. A knowing smile curved about her lips. "You're worried you'll never find it, aren't you?"

Violet drew back, shocked. "I—I don't understand," she stammered.

"Love," her hostess replied, blinking. "You're worried you'll never find love."

Letting out a relieved laugh, Violet shook her head. "I'm afraid I've other things to worry about, Lady Caroline."

"Well," she replied, looking away and smoothing her skirts,

"I am. I'm worried I'll never find love. The good kind, anyway."

Violet allowed a long moment to pass before speaking. "Your husband—did you not love him?"

"I thought I did," Caroline replied. "Indeed, when we were married, I was overwhelmed by my affection for him. But when I—I lost a baby, you see," She paused and shook her head. "We were both mad with grief. My husband especially. He haunts me still."

Violet reached for her hand. "And now you fear his ghost shall chase off whatever happiness is meant to come your way."

"In a manner of speaking, yes," Caroline replied. "And that is why I now must beg your forgiveness and excuse myself. I've—something to see to."

For a moment she eyed Violet, waiting for her to respond.

"Your secret is safe with me," Violet assured her, taking Lady Caroline's hand in her own. "Lord Harclay shan't know of it. You have my word."

"Thank you, Violet, I am grateful for your discretion." Caroline rose to her feet. "Are you sure you'll manage on your own? You have free rein of the house. I imagine my brother shall be returning shortly. He'll have my head when he discovers I've left you."

"Nonsense," Violet replied. "Now off with you, Lady Caroline. It won't do to keep Mr. Lake waiting."

Caroline smiled, a sheepish sort of thing. In an ungainly swirl of purple and blue silk, she took her leave.

At last, Violet was alone. *In Lord Harclay's house.* The diamond, if she could find it, was hers for the taking.

She hesitated. Ten paces to her right, a handmaid emerged from Lord Harclay's chambers, shutting the door soundly behind her and disappearing down the hall.

Silently Violet stood, and as if in a dream she walked slowly toward the door. Her thoughts rioted; inside her chest she felt that same, searing pain from moments before.

She steeled herself against the sensation. Now was her chance; she would likely never have this opportunity again. And with Harclay due home any moment . . .

With one last glance over her shoulder, she took the heavy knob in her hand and turned it. She cringed as the door creaked open. Quickly she slid inside the room and closed the door behind her.

It was warm in Harclay's bedchamber, despite the breeze that blew in from the open windows. The afternoon sun was high and bright, shimmering off the blue silk bedclothes; the scents of clean linen and lemon furniture polish tickled her nostrils.

The chamber, so intimate and shadowy the night of her failed stable snoop, was suddenly overwhelming. She must have overlooked the amount of furniture it contained. Heavens, there appeared to be dozens, hundreds, of drawers and bookshelves and curios—all possible locations in which the diamond could be hidden.

Best begin with that damned sock drawer, she rationalized, if for no other reason than that it was as good a place as any to start.

Violet tiptoed through a far door into the adjoining dressing room. Polished cherry cabinets lined every wall; leave it to Lord Harclay to have not one sock drawer but twenty.

She reached out and gently opened a large, heavy drawer. Peeking inside, she found it was filled with neat stacks of blindingly white neckcloths.

Well, she thought with a smile, the earl certainly keeps his valet busy. This drawer alone could outfit an entire army of well-dressed dandies.

Carefully she picked through the starched fabric—if ironing were art, these neckcloths would be masterpieces—but found nothing.

She closed the drawer and moved on to another, and then another, digging through each one, running her fingers along the wood's smooth, gleaming edges. There was something particularly intimate about touching Harclay's cravats, his breeches, the carefully pressed linen shirts stacked neatly on a shelf; as if by touching the fine fabric of his shirts she might better understand the feel of his bones, his warmth.

His scent was everywhere, the lovely smell of his skin rising from the silks and satins as she fingered them. A wave of longing washed over her. It had been all of three hours since they'd parted; it might as well have been an eternity. These clothes, lifeless and yet very much alive with the memory of

Harclay's flesh and shape, were a poignant reminder of his absence.

Violet shut the drawer, drew a long breath through her nose.

The diamond. *Remember the diamond.*

Squaring her shoulders, she resumed her assault on Harclay's wardrobe. At last she found it: the sock drawer of which she'd been enamored since the night Hope's diamond was stolen.

With renewed vigor, she tore through its contents: a seemingly endless array of silk stockings, each a fashionable shade of black or white. They felt as fine as water against her skin as she dug deeper into the drawer.

Violet couldn't tell if it was disappointment or relief that caused her heart to flutter as she dug yet deeper and came up empty-handed.

But the diamond had to be here—she'd pinpointed this spot from the moment she'd called Harclay out as the gentleman jewel thief he was.

The middle two fingers of her right hand brushed up against something solid. Her heart suddenly, jarringly, stilled as she wrapped her palm around an object roughly the size and shape of a walnut. It was swathed in a heavy silk stocking, so she couldn't be sure—and what was that beside it, another sock, perhaps, this one filled with something weighty, irregularly shaped—

She jumped at the loud *thwack* of the chamber door as it slammed shut. The object, whatever it was, fell from her hand as she wheeled about.

Her heart, still dumbfounded and motionless, rose to her throat as her eyes fell on the man before her.

Twenty

"Lord Harclay!" Violet exclaimed, her hand going to her throat. "You gave me quite a fright!"

One look at him and she knew something was afoot. He appeared distraught; the morning's unease had grown, it seemed, to full-blown terror. His hair was askew and his face ashen. Mud caked his boots to the ankle, and there was a wild look in his eye that hadn't been there before.

"Heavens, what happened—"

But before she could finish, Harclay crossed the room in three enormous strides and, taking her face in his hands, brought his mouth down to hers. The kiss was urgent, savage, unlike any other they had shared. She felt herself yielding to him, her arms circling his neck as she dug her hands into his hair.

At last he pulled away, tugging her bottom lip one last time between his teeth. They were breathless, their chests working against each other as they gasped for air. A stray beam of sunlight passed across the back of Harclay's head, surrounding him in a halo of gold. She stood, transfixed, as illuminated dust motes floated lazily about him.

Harclay held her close against him. She laid her ear to his chest and heard the frantic beating of his heart. It was all so overwhelming; how unlike him to show such emotion, to handle her so roughly and then press her close against him as if he would suffocate without her.

"What's wrong?" she said, her voice muffled against his chest. "Tell me, Harclay, please."

He looked down at her, and she could tell he was weighing his words, wondering how much he should share. He shook his head, a shadow of a smile crossing his lips. "Tell me, Lady Violet, do you have plans for this evening?"

"Plans?" She blinked. Out of all the things he could've said, she wasn't expecting that. "Almack's, of course. By the grace of God we managed to secure a voucher for Cousin Sophia, dear girl, and now she is most eager to attend."

Harclay groaned. "Ah, yes, I'd forgotten today is Wednesday. How I *loathe* Almack's—ghastly company and no liquor. It's paramount to torture. Alas, it seems I have no choice in the matter."

"I don't recall asking you to escort me."

The humor left his eyes as he looked down at her. "From this moment forward, Lady Violet, I shan't leave your side."

She surveyed him, her pulse quickening. "You can't do this."

"Do what?"

"You can't come running into my arms, kissing me like—well, like *that*—and expect me to believe that nothing is wrong. What sort of trouble are you in, Lord Harclay?"

A beat passed between them before he spoke, his voice low and strained. "I do not wish to share this burden with you, Violet; you must trust that I am able to bear it alone. But know this: I shall keep you safe, no matter the cost. You've nothing to fear, I swear it."

"I've plenty to fear, if that's the only explanation you'll give me."

He pressed a kiss to her forehead and looked past her to his disheveled drawers. "Have any luck this afternoon? I see you've been at my dressing room."

Violet hesitated, remembering the promising objects she'd discovered in his sock drawer. She couldn't very well speak to him of it; by the time she was able to retrieve them, whatever they proved to be, he'd have moved it to a more secure location.

In all likelihood, the objects she'd discovered were not

jewels anyway but snuffboxes, perhaps a misplaced pair of cuff links. Even the Earl of Harclay wasn't bold enough to hide a priceless gem in his sock drawer.

Was he?

"No luck at all, I'm afraid," she said at last, mustering the most charming smile she could manage. "Your wardrobe proved a formidable opponent. Just how many waistcoats do you own?"

"Far too many." Harclay sighed. "My valet is a most enthusiastic shopper; I don't have the heart to turn away any of his designs. Most of them end up in his wardrobe, anyway. The arrangement seems to suit us both."

"Very generous of you," Violet replied, narrowing her eyes as she surveyed the man before her. In bright flashes of memory, she recalled the way he'd defended her at Hope's ball, his tenderness toward Auntie George, his rapport with her father. Was it possible that Harclay, beastly thief, gambler extraordinaire, libertine, was a man of decency, of goodness?

"Well!" he said, and to her chagrin, he loosened his grip on her face and stepped away. "Quite enough poking about for one day, don't you think? Best we get you home in time to change. I'm afraid we'll need a bit of time before Almack's to get good and foxed."

"Foxed at Almack's?" Violet raised a brow. "How daring, even for you."

Tugging the bodice of her ball gown a smidge lower, and then lower again, Violet surveyed her appearance in the mirror and moaned in frustration.

"This one won't do, either," she said and turned her back to Fitzhugh so that she might undo the gown's buttons.

"But you've tried on every dress you own!" Fitzhugh waved to the tangle of colored silks and satins that covered Violet's bed. "There's naught to be done; the one you've got on is most lovely. And the *earl* will like it just fine."

"The earl?" Violet said, whirling to face Fitzhugh. "But how did you—"

She shrugged her shoulders, smiling. "He's only been waiting in the drawing room downstairs for nigh on two hours. Are you certain he doesn't mean to make an offer?"

Violet scoffed. "If he does, I shall take it as a sign of the apocalypse. Lord Harclay would rather suffer a fiery death than take a wife."

"Ah," Fitzhugh replied. "No wonder you like him. A rake, the kind of man one could never possess. Makes for a thrilling chase, does it not?"

Violet shook her head. "No. No, *like* is far too mild a word, Fitzhugh."

The maid coaxed Violet into the cushioned seat before the mirror and went to work on her mistress's hair.

"The earl's had his men here all day, you know," Fitzhugh said, words garbled by the pins she held in her teeth.

Violet's heart skipped a beat. "His men? Whatever do you mean?"

"At least a dozen of them, standing guard at the doors. Your father was in a right tizzy 'bout it, he was. The earl sent a note apologizing, but there's been talk of nothing else among the servants downstairs."

Violet swallowed the sudden tightness in her throat. Something was amiss—why else would Lord Harclay have her house under his watch? Did he fear for her life? Her father's, her family's? Or did he mean to do them harm himself?

She shook that last thought from her head. They were on opposing sides, she and the earl, but surely he would never so much as wish her harm, much less perpetrate it himself. She had become acquainted with him well enough—very well indeed—to know he enjoyed her company and her caresses besides.

"Tell me, Fitzhugh," Violet said carefully, "have you noticed anything strange recently? Any visitors? Gossip among the staff?"

"Nothing I can think of, my lady. Nothing except the Earl of Harclay's frequent calls, of course. Had one of the kitchen maids in a full swoon this morning, he did. I'm afraid the entire female staff is liable to fight you for him."

Violet bit back a smile. "He's not *that* handsome."

Fitzhugh pushed one last pin into place. "Oh, yes, he is, mistress, no use playing that game. Now off with you," she said with a wink. "If the apocalypse is nigh, you haven't much time together, have you?"

* * *

The four fingers of brandy Harclay drank with Lady Violet's father had done nothing to assuage his nerves. His every sense was alive as he disembarked from his coach, sweeping his gaze over the dreary facade of Almack's. The sight of his men, scattered incognito about the street, only made his limbs hum with tension.

He knew—in the pit of his stomach he *knew*—the acrobats would make their attempt tonight. And the earl would do everything in his power to stop them. No one but Harclay would have the pleasure of handling Lady Violet's person this evening.

She took his outstretched hand and descended from the carriage, followed by the Lady Sophia and Aunt Georgiana. Violet looked so lovely in her pale lavender gown it made his chest hurt.

Other members of the *ton*, swathed in pearlescent silks and sharply cut coats and peacock feathers as tall as a horse, lined up along King Street, filing slowly through Almack's door.

Harclay ignored their stares, tucking Violet's arm through his as they bypassed the line. He slid the doorkeeper, Mr. Willis, a guinea—discreetly, of course—and together with his small party made his way into the assembly rooms.

As they mounted the narrow, creaking stair—really, Harclay hadn't a clue why his friends practically fell over themselves about this place—Violet turned to him. Her voice was low and urgent.

"Your men were guarding my house today," she said. "I want to know why."

"I'd say my men are the least of your problems," he replied as they mounted the last step. He nodded in the direction of a gaggle of patronesses who were shamelessly ogling Harclay and Violet. "It appears we've made quite the scene, and it's not yet nine o'clock."

Violet tugged him to a halt and faced him. "Please," she pleaded. "Let me help you. Tell me, Harclay, what's wrong—"

"Oh, what luck, the dancing's begun!" He pulled her closer. "Shall we?"

The ballroom was crowded with the cream of London

society, and with narrowed eyes Harclay scanned the sea of faces before him. His gaze darted to each of the four corners, to the large, double-height windows on one wall, and to the orchestra balcony that lined the other. Nothing suspicious, as far as he could see.

But the noise—it was nothing short of deafening, what with the shouted conversations of nearly one thousand people—concerned him. It was the perfect cover; those diminutive beasts could slip in and out of the crowd, and commit a heinous crime, with no one the wiser. Even if Violet had time to scream, the sound would be lost in the tide of music and voices and the pounding feet of dancers.

The lighting, too, was dim at best. Even with the blazing light of three enormous chandeliers above, the ballroom was a maze of shadows.

Harclay tightened his grip on Lady Violet. In the middle of the room, dancers were arranging themselves into lines for a cotillion. He very nearly groaned; it was going to be difficult indeed to keep an eye on Violet in the midst of its intricate, spirited steps.

He turned to her and bowed over her hand, hoping she did not see the look of chagrin on his face. "May I have this dance, Lady Violet?"

She smiled. His heart skipped a beat.

"You may indeed, my lord," she replied. "It is a long dance, this one, and I intend to badger you for answers throughout its entirety."

"Splendid," he said. "And it goes without saying, my dear, we shall be partners for the remainder of the evening."

He was surprised when she threw her head back and laughed. "That is hardly wise, considering your rather epic aversion to marriage. You know what everyone will think if we spend all night dancing together."

"I don't care what they think." He kept his voice even, measured, though his insides were anything but. "I won't share you with anyone, least of all these fools. You'll dance with me, or not at all."

Joining the line of female dancers, Violet whirled to face him. "Very well," she said, eyes flashing. "Just remember when we're forced to marry, it's all your fault."

"Oh, come now," he said. "You'd at the very least be pleased with yourself for shackling a shameless rake like me, a man no other woman could bring to account."

She rolled her eyes. "A dubious honor, surely."

The music began and so did the dance. Though he could hardly enjoy himself, knowing that a band of acrobats intended to kidnap the woman before him, he couldn't help but notice Violet's exquisite grace and poise as she moved through the steps. She danced as an angel, floating through the sequence as if on air.

Above the din, she met his eyes and grinned. All the breath left his body, as if he'd been socked square in the belly; her eyes appeared very blue and happy.

And if it weren't for the worry he bore, he had no doubt he would feel very much the same.

He could see her color rising; from his ardent attention, or the exertion of the dance, he could not tell.

The music came to a rousing, spirited conclusion. Harclay returned Lady Violet's grin and dipped his head to bow.

He heard the ballroom erupt into polite applause as he straightened, his gaze returning directly to Violet.

Only she wasn't there before him, where she'd been standing just half a heartbeat before.

Pulse surging with terror, he frantically looked this way and that, pushing aside bodies as he searched for Violet's dark curls, her blue-gray eyes.

Nothing.

She was gone.

Twenty-one

———— ✦ ————

It all happened so quickly, Violet could hardly piece together the events that led her to this moment: disheveled and shouting obscenities in the back of a foul-smelling hack.

She'd felt a tap at her shoulder just as she was making to curtsy before Lord Harclay. She turned and met eyes with a smallish man, bad teeth and all that, whom she recognized straightaway as one of the acrobats hired to help the earl steal Mr. Hope's diamond. Her eyes went wide with surprise—she remembered wondering how he'd snuck into Almack's, what with the formidable Mr. Willis guarding the door—and then four pairs of small, callused hands closed around her limbs.

Violet could hardly think, much less protest, as they pulled her through the crowd, raucous from dance, to a hidden side door. No one so much as glanced her way; she was just another body, jostling for air in a crowded ballroom.

The acrobats pushed her roughly down a dark, narrow set of steps. By now she realized she was in trouble and started to yell, to scream. One of the men pressed his palm to her mouth and twisted her hands behind her back.

White-hot panic seared through her as they tossed her into the hired hackney.

And now here she was, being bound and gagged with lengths of greasy flax linen. She tried kicking the men, biting them, flailing her arms about; but they merely held her against the seat until both her legs and arms were tied.

"Right, then, missy," one of them said, his smile rotten. "What shall we do with ye?"

The hack began to move. Violet screamed with all her strength, tears springing to her eyes, but the sound was muffled by the gag they'd tied around her head.

Shouts sounded outside the carriage. Violet thought she recognized one voice and turned her head to look out the back window.

Her heart went to her throat as she watched Lord Harclay gunning after the carriage, arms thrusting at his sides as he ran toward her. His face was a mask of intensity, his eyes black with rage.

Despite his enormous stride, the hack managed to pull away from him. It veered dangerously into the street before breaking into an all-out jostle.

Violet caught one last glimpse of Lord Harclay before he was lost to the night. He'd been gritting his teeth against the pain of his exertion when he threw up his hands and shouted her name. She could hardly hear it over the pounding of the horses' hooves, and of her own heart, but she could see his lips form the word, a strangled cry that promised vengeance.

Now she understood—Harclay's strange behavior, his men at her house. She understood why he would not answer her questions, though that did not make her want to strangle him any less.

Someone had betrayed him to the acrobats, told them it had been the Earl of Harclay who'd hired them to create a scene at Hope's ball. The acrobats, being greedy, scavenging scalawags, went after him for the money he owed them. Believing Violet to be his paramour—which, she thought indignantly, she most certainly was *not*—they must have threatened to kidnap her if he did not pay.

Here she paused. But why *didn't* Harclay pay them? Seventy-five pounds was a great deal of money to her, but to the earl it was akin to spare change. She knew he would never

intentionally put her in harm's way. All he had to do was go to
the bank—

The bank.

Of course!

Mr. Hope must have frozen Lord Harclay's accounts. The
earl wouldn't be able to touch a penny until Mr. Hope allowed
him to do so.

She imagined Harclay's rage when Hope delivered the
blow. He must've felt helpless and embarrassed and terrifyingly, thrillingly, angry.

Violet wasn't sure if it was satisfaction that now bloomed
in her chest—satisfaction that Hope had at last espoused her
theory of Harclay's guilt—or fear. Fear for Harclay, fear for
herself.

Turning back to the carriage, she surveyed her assailants. It
was obvious they were anxious, though they appeared to relax
the farther they drove from Almack's. She did not allow herself
to ponder what, exactly, they had in store for her; rather, she
kept her thoughts trained on Harclay and the valiant rescue he
was sure to orchestrate if these bastards didn't slit her throat
first.

The ride seemed to last an eternity. She watched through
the hack windows as the elegant, well-kept streets of St.
James's became the poorly lit alleys of Cheapside. She could
hear the entreaties of lightskirts, calling out from doorways
and taverns to passing men; the stench was beyond words.

At last one of the acrobats pounded the roof of the hackney, signaling a stop. Violet swallowed, hard, and steeled herself against whatever was to come next.

"We'll take this off ya," one of the acrobats said, unwind-
ing the lengths of cloth that bound her mouth and limbs, "but
if ye so much as squeak, it's goin' back on, ye hear me?"

Violet sniffed her reply; she worried if she spoke, her
voice would wobble pitifully with fear, with rage.

The coach door opened and the four little men leapt out
into the street. They glanced over their shoulders and, content
that no one was about, pulled Violet down to join them.

A raucous roar sounded from across the lane. The hack
pulled away, revealing a low, squat tavern, its rough wooden

door virtually surrounded by prostitutes of every shape and size. Above their heads swung a barely legible sign: THE CAT AND MOUSE.

Violet bit her lip against the revulsion that rose in her throat.

The roar grew more raucous as the acrobats tugged Violet toward the tavern's entrance. Even from here she could smell the gin, hear the fistfights, see the leers of unwashed men.

She hesitated at the threshold, and the women there pounced on her at once.

"Ah, fancy lady ye got here, lads! She'll fetch a nice price inside!"

"It's a lady!" one of them drawled. "Yer high and mighty ways won't do ye much good here."

Another approached and took hold of Violet's earbob. "I say, is them real pearls?"

With a rather savage tug, the woman plucked both bobs from Violet's ears and cackled with glee.

"Leave her be, eh?" one of the acrobats snapped as he pushed Violet over the threshold into the tavern.

"I would appreciate it, *sir*," she growled, "if you didn't handle me so roughly. I know how to walk."

She followed their leader to the back of the tavern. A scarred oak table emerged from the dark of the corner. There, burying his face in a woman's rather enormous breasts, sat a dull-faced drunkard.

The acrobats shooed them away and motioned for Violet to sit in the drunkard's vacated chair, her back to the wall.

Again panic spread its wings in her chest. She was all but invisible in that chair, even from the tavern's entrance. These men could do anything they wanted to her and no one the wiser.

"Well, then," the acrobat said, nodding at the chair, "I'll make ye sit if ye won't do it on yer own."

With a huff of indignation, Violet did as she was bid. The chair was hard and uncomfortably warm from its previous occupants.

The four acrobats sat, forming a protective barrier between Violet and the tavern. At once a barmaid appeared with mugs of steaming cider, which she placed before each man with a wink.

Violet cleared her throat. What could better quell her panic than a draft of strong cider? Besides, she reasoned, it would buy her time to think, and perhaps devise a plan of escape.

"I would like a drink," she said in the most officious tone she could manage. "A strong one."

The barmaid cocked a brow and looked to the men at the table, who in turn looked at one another in bewilderment, as if she'd requested not a drink but a go with one of the ladies outside.

"Ye got the money to pay fer that?" one of them said at last.

Violet sniffed. "Add it to Lord Harclay's tab. I hardly think one mug of cider much matters, given the sum he owes you."

"That's just the thing," he replied, leaning over the table. "The lord ain't paid us yet."

"Well," Violet said, trying another tack, "you have my life as security. Surely I am worth at least one little mug of cider."

Despite himself, the acrobat returned her suggestive smile. Only when one of his fellow thieves nudged him in the ribs did the smile fade.

"Right, then," he said, "a mug of cider for the lady. But only one! And make it quick, would ye?"

Violet batted her eyes at the man in gratitude, and though it was dark she could see him blush.

Excellent. These men, like most, were dimwits and lechers, and drunks besides; after a few mugs they would be well in their cups and more interested in the company of loose females than Violet.

That would be her opportunity for escape. She only had to wait an hour, maybe two, and then she could slowly edge away from the table and dart out of the tavern when they weren't looking. And then—

And then what? She didn't know her way around Cheapside; hell, she didn't know where she was to begin with. God knew what dangers awaited her in the street outside.

That was if she even *made* it outside. What if someone—an acrobat or one of his cronies—detained her before she could make her escape? Would they hurt her, touch her, *kill* her even?

Her cider arrived, and the acrobats watched as Violet took a long, desperate pull.

"Easy there, lass," one of them murmured. "Didn't know the ladies drank cider, and like *that*."

Violet shook the anxious thoughts from her head. Tonight of all nights she could not, *would* not, break. She'd made it through twenty-two years without so much as a crack; and she would make it through another twenty-two, no matter the intentions of these bastards.

She let out a rather long, theatrical sigh of satisfaction as she brought the mug down on the table with a *clap*.

"I daresay, sir," she replied, wiping her mouth with the back of her hand, "there's quite a bit about me that might surprise you. By chance, do any of you carry a deck of cards? I'm in the mood to play."

Twenty-two

"Unhitch the horses," Harclay barked, tugging at the reins that held his pair of perfectly matched Andalusians.

"But my lord!" Avery said, mouth agape. "We haven't a saddle! How are you to ride?"

"To hell with the saddle," Harclay replied, turning to his groomsmen. "Come on now, lads, put your back into it! We haven't the time!"

"Shall I retrieve your pistol, my lord?" Avery asked, nodding toward the Harclay town coach.

The earl flashed open his jacket in response, revealing two pistols tucked into the waistband of his breeches.

They were drawn up before Almack's, surrounded by Harclay's squad of gunmen and armed footmen. Avery was overseeing the entire production; through the haze of his fury, Harclay recognized the butler showed great grace, all things considered. Who else would remember to stock the family town coach with an extra bottle of brandy *and* a handful of pistols?

At last the horses were let free. Harclay waved away the assistance of the grooms and swung up onto the horse's bare back. It was more uncomfortable than he could have ever imagined; but the image of Lady Violet, eyes wide with shock and terror as she watched him run after her, was powerful enough to make him forget himself entirely.

"Give my apologies to the Ladies Georgiana and Sophia. Tell them I shall return Violet, unharmed, by morning," Harclay said, looking down at Avery. "Otherwise, tell no one what has occurred here. God forbid this gets to the papers and harms Hope any further."

"Very well, my lord," the butler replied. "Godspeed, sir, and good luck."

Harclay took off, urging the horse faster and faster through the lamp-lit streets. At last his investment in horseflesh paid off: the Andalusian was indeed so swift and sure that Harclay was forced to hang on to the horse's mane for dear life.

When he reached his town house, he swung off the horse and shouted for a stable hand to saddle him. As fast as Harclay's legs would take him, he bounded into the house and up the stairs, giving quite a fright to a young handmaid on the way.

He tore into his bedchamber, pristine from his staff's ministrations, and flung open the door to the dressing room. In the darkness he reached for the sock drawer—by now he'd memorized its location by heart—and pulled it open.

He dug about a bit before he fingered the French Blue's distinctive shape. Pulling it from its nest of silk stockings, he held it up to the light of the fire in his bedchamber.

It was lovely, casting a rainbow of glittering confetti about the room. In this light it appeared a shade past blue, with hints of gray. The color, exactly, of Lady Violet's eyes.

Pain pulsed black and heavy in his chest. How close she'd come earlier that day to finding the diamond; really, how did she know to look in his sock drawer?

He shook his head, a smile rising unbidden to his lips. She was brash and bold, wily and clever. Though he'd assured Lady Violet he would never marry—and he never would, he assured himself, not *ever*—he wouldn't mind spending the remainder of his days in the company of a woman like her.

But tonight the earl didn't have time for such thoughts. He had nothing short of a herculean task before him. Without sufficient cash, Harclay was going to have to bargain for Lady Violet's life with Hope's diamond.

It was magnificent enough to catch the acrobats' attention, more magnificent than a horse or some silver flatware from the Harclay family vault. He didn't have time for any of that besides; already, too many minutes had passed since Violet had disappeared down King Street. Rage flooded his veins at the thought of her bound and gagged, being taunted and tortured in some filthy, dismal corner of the city.

He tucked the diamond into his jacket pocket and ran.

Though she'd been unceremoniously abducted and dragged to this filthy, dismal corner of the city, Violet had to admit she thoroughly enjoyed taunting and torturing her captors by besting them in round after round of cards.

For nigh on two hours now they'd been at it: games of casino, vingt-et-un, and faro, among others the acrobats called by less savory names. And time and time again, Violet managed to win, amassing a small pile of coppers from which the acrobats would steal when their luck ran out.

With each round of cards came also a fresh round of cider. Violet quietly ignored hers while her captors drank more greedily the longer their losing streak continued. They were sloppy players to begin with; when drunk, they were dismal.

It was, really, far too great a temptation for Violet to resist. Cheating had never been so easy, and besides, her winning seemed to distract the acrobats from the fact that they had *kidnapped* her and she was theirs to do with as they pleased.

Around them, the sounds of the tavern intensified as the night grew darker; Violet supposed it was well past midnight by now. For a fleeting moment she thought of Harclay, and inside her chest her heart skipped a beat. She wondered if he would come for her—how could he negotiate with her kidnappers without access to any of his funds? Surely these men had no interest in anything other than cash.

One of the acrobats made a strange, slurring sound, and suddenly his head hit the table with a low, dull *thwack*. Violet jumped back in surprise.

"Get up, ye fool," said another and soundly slapped the man's forehead. But it appeared the man was out cold. The acrobats exchanged glances across the table, but after a beat returned to their cards. One of them cursed; another emptied his mug and shouted a jumble of gibberish that Violet assumed was a call for another round.

Now was Violet's chance. If she could just get past their table and into the press of bodies that now crowded the tavern, she would be free. The acrobats could never catch her, not in this crush.

Slowly she began edging her chair away from the table, careful that it did not so much as squeak as she moved. She turned ever so slightly, her legs together on one side of the chair, and faced the tavern. Placing her feet on the floor, she gritted her teeth and willed her limbs to move.

Pulse pounding—what would they do to her, if she were caught?—she rose to her feet and leapt into the crowd.

That single moment felt like an eternity; the anticipation was nothing short of awful. Violet landed not on her feet but on a bear of a man about to take his first sip from a full mug of cider. The cider went flying through the air, spattering everyone, while the man cursed and took a blind swing with an ax-sized fist.

Violet watched in horror as his fist hurtled toward her face. She couldn't move, nary an inch with so many bodies surrounding her; and so she scrunched tight her eyes and waited for the inevitable explosion of pain.

But that explosion never came. She felt herself suddenly jerked backward, rough hands on her shoulders and arms and waist. Her eyes flew open to land on the three remaining acrobats, faces swollen with drink and ire.

"Tie the bitch back up!" one of them shouted.

Violet's belly turned over at the violent edge in the acrobat's voice, the malice in his eyes. Oh God, she'd misjudged them: fools they were, certainly, but dangerous fools, drunk fools, and now they were angry. It was akin to swatting a bees' nest, and she had a feeling she would come to regret cheating these men.

They pushed her back into her chair and she let out a cry of pain as they pulled her arms roughly behind her. One of the men bound her hands so tightly she could feel the linen rubbing a burn into her skin. Another leered into her face, his foul breath roiling her insides. She recognized the gleam in his eye: desire, the drunk, violent kind.

"I like ye better tied up, now, lass," he murmured and moved closer, as if to kiss her.

Violet swallowed the panic that rose in her throat. She gathered every ounce of courage she could muster and, drawing back, she spit right into the man's eye.

"Bloody hell!" he cried and fell backward.

The other two acrobats turned to her, disbelief mingling with rage on their faces. Violet's triumphant grin was short-lived, for one of them lifted his hand and unceremoniously brought it down, hard, on her cheek.

She felt the blow with her entire being. For a moment the world around her went black, and she tasted blood—her lip, likely; her ears were ringing, an ominous, high-pitched sound.

Don't swoon, she warned, gritting her teeth. *You never swoon, remember?*

Though if there ever was a time to do such a thing, now would be it.

The world slowly came back to her, hazy and smelly and terrible. The pain was rivaled only by her fear. Whatever was going to happen next, she wasn't going to like it.

The acrobat—the same one in whose eye she'd spat—was still looking at her, his face close; and in the dimness, she could tell he was unbuttoning his breeches, while a second man was getting to work at her skirts.

She closed her eyes against the prick of tears swallowing the terror that tightened her throat.

There was a tremendous noise, a clap of thunder that Violet felt in her bones. Something sticky and hot splattered across her exposed skin; she heard the acrobat cry out, a gurgling, sinking sound.

Her eyes flew open.

For there in the middle of the tavern stood the Earl of Harclay, a smoking pistol in his outstretched hand. Even in the shadowy dimness, Violet could make out his face, handsome and dark with rage.

At her feet lay the slain acrobat, the hole in his chest pulsing plum-colored blood all over her slippers.

Harclay met her eyes across the room. His flashed with focus, with fury. For a moment they slipped to her bleeding lip, and she could see them flare dangerously. She sure as hell wouldn't want to be on the wrong end of his pistol.

Violet hadn't realized the tavern had grown as silent as a tomb until Lord Harclay spoke.

"Untie her," he growled at the two conscious acrobats beside her. "Do as I say and perhaps I won't put a bullet between your eyes."

But the men would not be cowed. They drew weapons from their jackets and pointed them steadily at the earl.

"We want what ye owe us," one acrobat replied, and he moved his arm so that his gun pointed not at Harclay but at Violet. "And perhaps I won't put a bullet between *her* eyes."

Harclay did not hesitate. He dropped the gun and held his hands up in surrender. As he lifted his arms, Violet saw the gleam of a second pistol tucked into his breeches. She widened her eyes at him in warning, and at once he lowered his arms. The pistol remained hidden beneath his waistcoat.

"I don't have the money," Harclay said, "but if you'll allow me, I'd like to show you something even better."

The acrobat wrinkled his nose. "What's better than money?"

Slowly, his gaze never leaving the armed men, Harclay dug two fingers into the pocket of his jacket and produced a small, shining object that appeared inky dark in the light of the tavern.

Violet's breath left her body. *The French Blue.*

The French Blue!

And Harclay was about to trade it for her life.

"Diamonds," Harclay replied. "This is the largest diamond yet discovered on earth, gentlemen. It belonged to the kings of France."

The acrobat held out his hand. "How can I be sure it's real?"

Harclay handed over the diamond. "Touch it and you'll see."

Violet watched as the acrobat held Hope's diamond up to the light. Lust, pure and potent, slowly widened in his eyes, as if the jewel were casting a spell upon him.

She felt it, too: the diamond's strange pull, her desire for it pounding against her rib cage. If the diamond ended up with these drunken acrobats, it would be lost forever; pawned, sold overseas, buried. Hope would be ruined; her own inheritance, gone.

No. Violet could not—*would* not—allow these bastards the pleasure.

She met eyes with Harclay. He nodded imperceptibly, reading her thoughts.

"I assure you, the diamond is genuine. All fifty carats," Violet said and struggled against the chair. "Now untie me!"

The acrobats exchanged grunts; while the one continued to survey the diamond, the other lowered his gun and loosened Violet's hands.

Taking advantage of the diamond's spell, Violet quick as lightning jerked her knee against the acrobat's nose. He fell to the floor and she made a grab for his gun, but his partner was too quick. He took her by the hair and wheeled her to face Harclay, holding his pistol to her head.

"Don't come any closer," he warned, "or I'm liable to shoot that bullet we been talkin' of."

Still holding one hand up in surrender, Harclay slowly extended his right arm, as if to reach for Violet.

The acrobat tugged her closer against him, giving her hair a good, hard tug. Violet gritted her teeth at the sudden sharp pain. Bastard would pay for that, she swore silently, and pay dearly.

"Easy, there," Harclay said, reaching farther. "You've got the diamond—should fetch you much more than seventy-five pounds, surely. Now give me the girl. That was our deal, remember?"

Violet sensed the acrobat hesitate. With the gallons of cider he'd consumed, he was a bit slow on his feet. She could feel him thinking through the proposition, the wheels of his mind turning with no little resistance.

And so she took her chance. Meeting Harclay's eyes one last time, she suddenly ducked, ramming her elbow into the acrobat's belly. He shouted, an animal sound, and Violet heard his gun clatter to the floor.

In the space of a single heartbeat, Violet reached out and tore the pistol from Harclay's waistband. She whirled around to point the gun at the acrobat, who was still crouched over from her blow.

Clicking back the safety, she thrust the pistol against his skull.

"Hand over the diamond," she said, surprised by the deadly calm of her voice. "Hand it over or I swear to God I'll kill you."

The man looked up at her, eyes narrowed with hate; and when he did not respond, she shoved the barrel of the gun even harder against his head.

She sensed Harclay hovering behind her. It felt so good to feel him again, the familiar heat of his body pressed against hers, that her eyes almost fluttered shut with the pleasure.

But then the acrobat was spitting blood, coughing, and he held out his hand and opened his fingers. There in his filthy palm glittered the French Blue, glinting gray and silver in the low light.

Violet stood, transfixed. After everything—the ball, the theft, her search, and Hope's futile efforts to find the blasted jewel—there it was. It seemed surreal, as if she were in a dream.

An arm—Harclay's arm—shot out from behind her and was about to reach for the diamond when out of the shadows came the sound of a pistol being cocked. Harclay grasped Violet by the waist and pulled her to the floor just in time to duck out of the line of fire. The bullet whizzed above their heads, and Violet's pistol hit the ground with a heartrending *crack*.

Violet righted herself, only to see the fourth acrobat—the one who'd passed out face-first on the table some time ago—emerge from the darkness, gun held in his hand.

The man holding the diamond disappeared behind his partner. Violet was about to make a dash for him when Harclay pulled at her from behind. She dug her heels into the floor, refusing to be dragged away.

"The diamond!" she cried. "We can't just leave it!"

His hands on her were strong and firm, and despite her best efforts, she found herself being taken farther from the acrobats.

She was shouting now, pummeling him with her fists. "Harclay! Let me down!"

"If we stay we'll be killed," he replied steadily. "Come now, Violet, don't make me throw you over my shoulder again."

"But the French Blue—my shares! And Hope—"

He whirled her around to face him, crushing her against him. "Leave it. I won't lose you. *Can't* lose you. I could stand to lose the diamond; but you—to me your life is without price. None of this matters, has any meaning whatsoever to me, if you are gone."

The earl was very close to her now, lips hovering over hers. With her heart in her throat, the gun at her back, she had no choice; she nodded her assent, her chest filling not with the shame of her loss but something else—something lovely, and light, something that felt out of place here in the midst of all this danger.

Harclay swept her out of the tavern and into the night. He lifted her onto his horse and circled her with his arms as he swung up behind her.

Twenty-three

———— ✦ ————

Only when Harclay had Violet wrapped safely in his arms, the two of them ensconced in darkness as they rode back toward Mayfair—only then did the floodgates of his relief open.

He relaxed against her, reveling in the weight of her body against his. And though she tried to resist, she slowly, very slowly, melted against him; and from his chest his heart took flight, soaring toward the sky with a lightness he'd never known before.

Forget that damned diamond. This—whatever this was— it was so very much better.

Above their heads, a thousand stars burned white and blue. The air was warm and soft, a summer night after a seemingly eternal spring chill. Harclay breathed deeply, content, and smiled when Violet did the same.

He wanted to take her back to his house, and make love to her thoroughly in the warmth of his bed. He wanted that more than he'd ever wanted anything. But her family would be worried; he could only imagine Auntie George's reaction when she was told Violet had been kidnapped by a band of scala-wag acrobats.

And so he took her back to her father's house, where even at this hour the lights were blazing. Harclay felt Violet stiffen as they pulled to a stop before the front steps.

She turned her head to face him. For a moment they said nothing, eyes trained on each other's lips, breasts heaving with the effort to catch suddenly lost breath.

Violet ran her tongue along her swollen bottom lip—damn those blackguards, he would go back and finish what he'd started—and he felt a now-familiar tightening in his groin as he watched, transfixed.

"If it weren't for you, Lord Harclay—"

"William," he replied. "I am William to you. I think we know each other well enough by now, don't you?"

She tried to suppress her grin and failed. "If it weren't for you, *William*, I wouldn't be in this mess."

When he opened his mouth to protest, she placed a hand on his chest to silence him. Her voice was low, barely above a whisper, when she said, "And if it weren't for you, I wouldn't be on this thrilling little adventure of ours."

He thumbed her chin and lightly ran a knuckle over her bruised lip. "Kidnappings and pistols and bloody lips are hardly thrilling."

"When compared to my usual turn at Almack's on Wednesday evenings, I daresay such things *are* a thrill. At least to me."

She looked down at her fingers, tangled in his lapel, and then she looked up at him, her eyes shining in the light of the streetlamps.

It felt as though his heart had swollen to ten times its size in his chest. She was so damn lovely.

Violet let out a sigh as she turned her head toward the house. "But I suppose one eventually must return to one's life. They'll be worried, my family."

"Of course," Harclay replied and slid to the ground. He reached up, his hands circling her waist, and helped her down beside him.

For a moment the two of them hesitated, his hands remaining on her body. His own was screaming in response; screaming with desire, the desire to possess her, take her home with him so that he might not have to let her go.

"Thank you," she said. "For saving me. Even though it was your fault I was kidnapped in the first place. Will you miss it?"

"The diamond?" he replied. "I didn't think twice about bargaining away the bloody thing, not with your life in the mix. I always thought it belonged around your neck, anyway, and your neck alone. Nothing—no one—makes it look lovelier than you, with those eyes of yours."

Violet tilted her lips toward him at that and began to rise on her toes as if to kiss him, but just then the front door of the house burst open and Auntie George's cries of relief filled the air.

Violet made to pull away from him, but he clasped her hand in his own and brought it to his lips. "Good night, Violet."

She looked back at him, her smile wide. "Good night, William."

Despite Violet's kind wish for a good night, Harclay found himself restless—surprising, when one considered he'd managed to get Violet kidnapped, and then save her again, all in the space of a single evening. His limbs ached for action, refused to stay still.

Hands clasped at the small of his back, he paced before the fire in his bedchamber, trying his damnedest not to look at the inviting mass of his bed. For when he thought of his bed he thought of Violet sprawled out naked upon it, and it was all he could do not to run out the door and into the street like a lunatic to find her.

The girl had just been *kidnapped*, for God's sake. Poor dear was probably traumatized, and already asleep, her maid having tended her wounds. Surely she wasn't awake in her room, thinking of him, of their adventures, as she'd called them. Surely not.

And yet—and yet *he* couldn't help thinking of *her*. His pulse was racing; his thoughts, a jumbled, lustful tangle as he recalled with startling clarity the image of her, whirling to face him, her fingers wrapping around his pistol . . .

He smiled at that—and then he groaned. If *only*.

Violet had been so self-assured then, so full of energy and life and resolve; and for the first time in an age he'd felt that same sense of purpose. As if he'd been placed on this earth solely to protect her, be with her, entwine his life with hers.

He shook the thought from his head. It was a dangerous thought, that one; it smacked of commitment, which of course meant marriage—

"Damn it all!" he cried out suddenly and reached for his coat.

He had to see her.

Avery, bless the man, must've read his master's mind; for he was waiting by the back door with a taper in one hand and two fingers of brandy in the other. Without a word he passed the brandy to Harclay, who took it with a nod of gratitude.

"Don't wait up for me, Avery," Harclay said, wincing as he downed the brandy in a single gulp.

The butler bowed his assent. "Very well. I shall leave the fire lit in the kitchen and the door unlocked."

"You're too damned thoughtful for your own good. Thank you, good man."

"You are most welcome, my lord." Avery smiled. "And best of luck."

I'm going to need it, Harclay thought as he swept out into the night. *This woman, this clever, passionate, damnable woman, is going to be the end of me.*

He went by foot. The streets were empty and quiet and full of shadows; and so, when he saw an approaching figure, he thought it nothing more than a trick of the gas lamps, perhaps, or a tree bending to the breeze. But as it approached, Harclay began to recognize that shape, those shoulders and the lovely, lithe neck.

The same neck and shoulders that had first caught his eye at Hope's ball those few weeks ago.

Harclay started into a run. What was she doing, alone on the street and at this time of night?

She came into his arms, hard; against his breast her heart pounded, strong and willing; and light rose through his body from his legs up to his chest and lips. Of their own volition his hands found her face and he covered her mouth with his.

The kiss was savage and sweet all at once; he felt dizzy, as if the earth were shifting beneath his feet.

He took her hand and led her back to his house.

Twenty-four

—— ✦ ——

Violet felt the pounding of her heart pulse through her entire being as Harclay shoved open the door with his shoulder. The impatient static between them was palpable; she felt drawn as tight as a bowstring, her body screaming for release.

It had been foolish of her to sneak out in the middle of the night; even more foolish to make a dash for the cavernous house that belonged to Lord Harclay—*William*. But she couldn't sleep, couldn't do anything except think of him, his words as he'd swept her out of the tavern.

None of this matters, has any meaning whatsoever to me, if you are gone.

It dawned on her then that she felt the same. What had started innocently—well, not *innocently*, but simply enough—as a game of cat and mouse had suddenly become something more.

There was Hope's diamond to consider, of course, and the stock she held in his company. It was no small thing, and even now it made her head hurt to think of it. And though the thought of living without the security the stock afforded her family was terrifying, the idea of living without Lord Harclay—his mad-

dening cockiness, his foolish thieving, his savage protective-
ness, and, good God, those lips—filled her with an inexplicable
sadness.

Violet had meant to catch the earl, trap him in his own
game and ruin him for what he'd done to her and to Mr. Hope.
And though she hadn't entirely lost her way, she'd been
unquestionably sidetracked—and now here she was, being
led by William into his house in the middle of the night, her
pulse racing with anticipation. She had no foolish notions
about his intentions . . . and certainly none about her own.

She'd come to be ravished—no, *pleasured*, as the earl had
so eloquently put it—diamond be damned.

William led her over the threshold—she smiled wryly at
that—and with a small kick closed the door behind them. At
once the house's scent filled her lungs, and she felt a longing
so powerful it left her breathless. She clung tighter to Harclay,
and he in turn pressed her more firmly against him.

They came upon the kitchen, a fire glowing in the hearth
and a single candle flame waving from the heavy plank table
in the center of the room. Heat bloomed in Violet's belly at
the sight; how reminiscent it was of the night she'd spent in
Harclay's bath before the fire, his fingers all over and in and
around her—

William made as if for the stairs to his bedchamber, but
Violet tugged on his coat. "Wait," she whispered.

He drew her against him, coaxing her into the kitchen
until the backs of her thighs rested against the table. Her hair
pooled around her shoulders and face; she looked up at him to
find a man transformed. His dark eyes were liquid, wild; he
bent his neck, his lips hovering over hers before he kissed her,
gently, deeply. His tongue moved along the inside of her lips,
opening her to him, and he took, and kept taking, until they
were both breathless from the assault.

William dropped his hands from her face, and Violet
moaned at the loss of his touch. With his one free arm, he
cleared the table, glasses and china and candlesticks shatter-
ing to the floor, and through the clank and clatter she could
feel his desire quicken pace. He reached for her and lifted her
in his arms, laying her down on the table. She struggled to
find his lips, and when she did, she parted them with her

tongue. He kissed her back with great concentration, moving inside her mouth, savoring every slope, every sinew.

He moved over her and she gathered him between her legs, cradling his waist with her knees. She pulled him toward her, pressing her body against his. The crushing weight of him shocked her, delighted her, and the kiss became frantic, messy. He took her leg in his hand and pushed back her skirts, running his fingers up her thigh. His touch sent waves of heat through her belly and chest. His thumb crawled up the inside of her leg, edging closer, closer. His lips moved over her jaw and down her throat, sending her pulse racing, and she arched her back, pressing more tightly against him. Her hands clutched the back of his neck and shoulders possessively, marveling at the strength and breadth of his frame as his hardened muscles tightened beneath her fingers.

He kissed her throat, brushing his lips against the blood that pulsed just beneath her skin. "Heaven help me," Violet whispered, pulling his hair with her fingers.

"Are you all right?" He stopped to look at her, brushing his nose against hers.

His eyes were wide with desire, with fear, and inside her chest she felt her heart skip a beat. Somewhere in the back of her mind she felt her control slip, her body hot and liquid and dangerous. An ache, at once warm and painful, settled into the hollow in her belly.

Good *God*, he was good; better than that.

"Yes," she said breathily. "Yes, please don't stop, William."

And so he resumed his assault on her senses. He reared up over her, terrifying, hellishly handsome; and taking her pelisse in both his hands, he tore it off her. The fabric made a terrific rending noise as William pulled it from her body, revealing the thin muslin gown beneath.

He sucked in his breath at the sight of her breasts, straining against the gown's neckline as she tried, and failed, to catch her own. They met eyes for a beat; and then he was tearing at the fabric, his fingers working feverishly to gain access to her flesh.

Her gown came loose at the seams, and again that ripping noise that further stoked the pressure building between her legs. She threw her head back, allowing him to do as he pleased, and watched as their shadows moved over and through each other on the ceiling.

At last—my God, my *God*, at last—his fingers brushed against her bare skin. William clawed his way through the gown, tossing it to the ground. He tore at her stays, and she breathed a sigh of relief as they loosened and fell to the floor.

All that was left between her and the earl was her chemise. He slithered down toward her feet and grasped the fine linen with both hands. Meeting her eyes above the slope of her body with a sinister smile, he ripped the chemise down the middle.

Swaths of her skin were revealed, burnished gold by the light of the fire. The air felt cool and poignant against her skin, and with a wave of pleasantly painful sensation, her breasts hardened to fine dark points.

His eyes swept the length of her; she could see his Adam's apple working as he swallowed, hard, in appreciation.

"Violet," he began, and he raked a trembling hand through his hair. "You are so lovely."

In response, she reached for his lapels and pulled him toward her, pressed her mouth to his. Her bruised lip began to bleed and throb but it only served to stoke her desire. Her fingers tangled in his cravat, trying to tug it loose, but he wrapped his hand around her wrist, pulling her away from him.

"But I want to see you—"

"Not yet," he growled. "We must tend to you first."

He gathered both her wrists in a single hand and wrenched her arms above her head. He stifled her cry with a ravenous, violent kiss.

"Do you trust me?" he whispered, staring down at her from above.

She smiled slyly at that. "I don't very well have a choice, do I?"

Beginning at her lips, he traced his mouth down her neck, across her collarbones. Wave after wave of goose bumps rose on her skin; and when he took one nipple, then the other, between his teeth, she had to grit her own to keep from crying out.

Heat sliced between her legs over and over and over again as he kissed and touched and teased. Her body began writhing against him, seeking release in his solid weight; how heavenly it felt with him pressed to her, to be surrounded by his strength and self-assurance.

Just when she thought she might be drowned in the cresting wave within her, William kissed her hip bone, then moved to her thighs, drawing closer and closer—

Yes.

"God, yes," she said on an inhale, digging her hands into his hair as he pressed his lips against her . . . *her*.

He shoved her legs apart and bent his neck lower, his tongue moving over and around and in her. He splayed the fingers of his right hand over the triangle of dark curls and with his thumb began stroking that small bead of flesh that was the very center of all this sensation.

He was, she was learning, very good at this.

Violet was blinded by it—his lips and tongue working on her in tandem with his finger, the pleasure of it so enormous it almost hurt.

He moved expertly, increasing the pressure and pace of his caresses in time to her rising desire. His mouth felt light and warm against her, stoking her higher and higher until she was crying out, begging for him to let her go.

She couldn't stand it any longer; the pressure was too great, the pain searing and hot and terrible—

Her climax came in an explosion of light and sound, a pounding that wracked every corner of her body, left her gasping for air. She fell and fell and kept falling, waiting for the sensation to subside as she cried out his name.

When at last she opened her eyes, she saw William watching her from his perch between her legs, a strange gleam in his eye.

"I understand why," she panted, trying to catch her breath, "you so enjoy pleasuring. You're damnably good at it."

One side of his mouth kicked up at her compliment. Slowly he rose to his knees and began untying his cravat. "Oh, I'm not through with you yet, Violet."

"Again?" she said in disbelief. "But how—I don't think I am able to bear it—"

He shook his head, that sly smile deepening. "Oh, I think you very able, darling."

Her pulse, sluggish from the earl's previous attentions, leapt at the endearment.

Darling.

Warmth, a different, but no less heady, kind, washed over her. She'd never thought about being anyone's darling; but now that she was William's, she felt very glad. What a thing to have missed all these years. What a gift, a joy, a wonder.

She started at the unexpected prick of tears. Violet was never one to weep, much less at a moment like *this*. What was there to cry about in the Earl of Harclay's arms?

Right here, right now at this very moment, her world was whole and perfect. She'd never felt anything like it, this loveliness, this completeness. Nothing to fight and no one to protect. Just her, and William, and their wildly beating hearts between them.

A tear slid from the corner of her eye down her temple. Above her, she sensed the earl hesitate.

"Really, Violet, I hate to ask again. But are you sure you're all right?" he said, his voice suddenly soft.

Blinking furiously to keep further tears from falling—this was too good to stop now; she wanted everything he could give her—she replied, "I'm fine. Better than that."

"You don't look fine."

She swallowed and tried to smile, her eyes falling on his hands, which were poised above the last button on his waistcoat. Best to change the subject, she reasoned, get him away from this dangerous line of questioning.

"Why the hell are you stopping?" She nodded at his hands. "Please, keep going!"

A beat of silence passed as he surveyed her. She could tell he wasn't entirely convinced that she was all right, but after a few moments, his smile returned, and he unbuttoned the waistcoat and flung it aside.

He stepped off the table to stand on the floor. She watched as he pulled his shirt over his head, revealing bare shoulders and chest, and let out a little laugh of disbelief.

He was beautiful, every sloping muscle and taut plane of flesh a study in perfection. His arms were thickly corded; his hands, enormous and capable; and then he was unbuttoning

his breeches, sliding them along with his smalls down his jut-
ting hips.

His cock leapt free, rigid, brash, the skin smooth and glis-
tening. Though she'd felt his hardness through her gown, she
hadn't quite expected *this*.

Despite her trepidation, her body leapt to the challenge.
Again she felt the heat rising from low in her belly. She swallowed, fear and curiosity coursing through her in equal
amounts, and met his eyes.

He slid a hand up the length of her, from her thigh across
her belly and breast to her face and lips.

And then the earl was again on the table, rearing over her
in a cloud of muscle and shadow. Against her he felt warm,
and welcome, and entirely too lovely to possibly exist in this
life.

When he kissed her, his lips were no longer violent but soft
and pleading, and through them she felt the breadth of his
affection for her, the desire he felt in his every limb.

Her body rose to meet his, and he pressed against her, his
lips moving from her lips to her jaw to her throat. She closed
her eyes at the pleasure that spiked through her, the bitter-
sweet sensation of his teeth scraping her flesh.

His mouth again moved to one breast, then the other, and
she cried out; her hips rose against his, pressing against him in
a search for more sensation, more contact, more *everything*.

They fell back to the table, his bulk suddenly between her
legs. He used his weight to pry them farther apart, supporting
himself on elbows placed on either side of Violet's head.

He caught her gaze. The question was there in his dark
eyes; anticipation thrummed between them, his sweat mingling with hers on the plane of her belly.

She returned his gaze, pleading *yes, yes, please yes*.

He settled further against the flesh between her legs; she
felt his cock nudging against her. He took her right hand and
guided it down toward her groin.

"Here," he said, his voice rough, strained. "Feel me. Feel us."

William covered her hand with his own and guided it
down, *down*, and with knowing fingers wrapped hers around
his hardness. She gasped in surprise and, curious, ran her
hand the length of him.

He sucked in a pained breath, wincing.

"Did I hurt you?" she asked.

He laughed and shook his head. "Quite the opposite."

She felt herself blush at the compliment. His fingers tightened around hers; she could tell he was struggling to hold back.

"Feel me go inside you, darling," he whispered into her ear. He used his thumb and forefinger to part her folds, and with his hand he guided himself farther against—*into*—her.

Her eyes went wider as she felt the first bit of pressure, her thumb and pinky now pressed firmly against her own slick flesh. Instinctively she squeezed her hand, and he hesitated, pulled back.

"No," she said and used her hand to guide him back against her. "No, I want more, all of you, William."

With his hand he pressed even harder against her. She felt herself open to him, the folds of her parting to admit him.

He continued to press, and press, his hand wrapped so tightly around her own she thought her fingers might break. The pressure mounted and it was her turn to wince—he was hardly inside her and already she felt herself straining to fit him.

"Heaven above, it's small in there," he groaned. "Relax, dearest, that's it, just relax—"

With a grunt he sank farther into her—*much* farther—and she gasped, all the while wanting more, and more still.

"Keep going," she panted. "Please, William, keep going."

And then with no small force he thrust into her, leaving her hand tangled in the triangle of his hair wedged just above hers. He took that hand in his own, weaving his fingers into hers as he watched her face, his dark eyes clouded, flashing with something like pain.

For a beat he remained very still, allowing her to adjust to the feeling of him. It wasn't nearly as painful as she'd imagined it to be; and as her discomfort subsided, pleasure bloomed in its place, rising through the whole of her all the way to her lips, which curved of their own volition into a smile.

"Ah, there it is," Harclay said, his voice low, rumbling in his chest. He pressed his lips to the corner of her grin, a gentle caress.

"It can't be helped," she said softly in reply. "This feels so—so very lovely."

He slowly, very slowly, began moving against her, in and out, *in* and out, thrusting with a bit more vigor each time. All the while he held her eyes captive with his own. They were liquid with intensity, watching her response to his body, his movements.

Again that same heat rising within her, at once unbearable and very sweet. Her hips bucked against his, seeking to drive him deeper, heighten what was already a heady sensation.

As if on cue, William reached down and ran his thumb across the very tip of her flesh, just above the juncture where they came together. At his touch fire flooded her being. Coupled with the pressure of him inside her, the sensation was beyond poignant, an urge she could not resist.

Violet pressed against him harder as his thumb moved more quickly over and over her, curling, teasing, stoking the pressure within her until she could hardly breathe.

She bit her lip and closed her eyes and held on for dear life. Sensing her mounting frustration, William covered her mouth with his and kissed her, his tongue gliding along the insides of her swollen lips. Taking, taking.

He moved over her ardently now, his belly sliding against hers. The friction, it was too much; it was not enough.

His mouth was moving across her jaw down to her throat; she arched, the sensation white-hot as he pounded into her one last time.

Violet felt him go still, gritting his teeth, and cry out just as she was lost to her own pleasure. It was excruciating; it was exquisite. Her heart was thudding in her chest, her legs curling against his flanks as if to lessen the rending blow of her climax.

Her entire body pulsed in time to the sensation between her legs, a wave that slowly receded. She was left breathless and damp with sweat beneath him. When she opened her eyes she found William staring down at her, his own wide and open and vulnerable.

"What is it?" she whispered. She tried to shift beneath him but he held her fast with the weight of his body.

He looked at her for a long moment, breathing hard. She could see his thoughts, frantic and new, flitting across his eyes, and she reached up to stroke his face.

"Marry me," he said.

Her heart skidded to a stop.

Twenty-five

———— ✦ ————

The words were soft, velvet, more entreaty than question or command. That was not at all what she had expected him to say—certainly not now, not *ever*.

This was the Earl of Harclay, his body still tangled in her own, the ravager of whole villages of Sicilian nuns and all that. Until this moment Violet assumed William would rather burst into flame than be leg-shackled to a self-proclaimed spinster like herself.

"Why?" she asked. "If you believe you are obliged to marry me after—well, after *this*, then you needn't bother—"

"I'm asking you to marry me because I want to, Violet," he replied steadily. "I know by now the both of us hardly have a care for propriety. That's got nothing to do with my proposal. Well, very little, at least."

"Very little?"

His fingers trailed to her belly.

"Oh," she said, suddenly understanding. "Oh yes, I'd quite forgotten about that."

With a wince he slid out of her. His seed followed, a warm stream that made her cheeks burn. His hand trailed from her belly to her sex; he cupped her, gently, his middle finger gliding between her folds. She felt a bit sore, a bit raw; even so, she rose to his touch.

"A dangerous detail to overlook, Violet. Even now I feel my seed inside you. We shall make beautiful babies, you and I."

Violet scoffed, despite the happy softening of her heart, her limbs. *Beautiful babies.* She'd never thought much about children. Not until now, anyway. Not until she realized she could be making one with William.

"Besides, *this*, as you call it"—he swept his eyes over their joined bodies—"is bloody perfection. I want you, Violet. I want you to stay with me this night and all the nights after that. I want to marry you, I want you to become my family, I want to make children with you. I want you with me every minute of every day. Losing you to those beastly acrobats . . ." He paused, anger flashing in his eyes. "Well, let us say I was not a happy man. I'll never be without you again."

Her blood coursed warm and singing through her limbs, setting her heart fluttering at the loveliness of his words. A now-familiar ache—a longing, something beautiful—settled over her breastbone as she considered his proposal. She knew, she *knew* in her bones this feeling between them was heavenly, something she dared not name.

For love had no place in her life. She'd never thought much of it, or marriage. Her lot lay with her family: who would care for her father, for Auntie George and Sophia? Who would look after their estates and their accounts, who would balance the ledger each week, if Violet were to leave them to start life anew as someone's wife?

For years now she had considered herself as good as a spinster. With all her responsibilities, she wasn't available to wed; and for years now, she'd contented herself with visions of an independent future, one in which she took no husband but enjoyed the ability to say what she wanted to say, and do what she wanted to do, without a care for what others thought. She had her inheritance, and a house in London; a very good library and Fitzhugh. Ingredients she'd always thought would make for a long, happy life.

So why did it hurt—dear God, it *hurt*—to look up at him

and say, "But you and I are on opposite sides, William. The two of us becoming husband and wife—it's impossible. Not only are we both repulsed by the very idea of marriage—"

"For a long time, Violet, I believed I *was* repulsed by marriage. The thought of marrying anyone I knew, all the debutantes and the family friends and fortune seekers, seemed nothing short of a death sentence. I didn't understand why anyone would do it. And then—"

Violet couldn't help herself. "And then?"

He grinned, a lopsided thing. "And then I met you."

The words, and all they meant, hung between them. Violet swallowed and looked away, tears burning the back of her throat. She suddenly felt very heavy, a terrible, hard sensation in her belly. How she longed to give in, to say yes, and have Harclay all to herself for the rest of her life; make all those beautiful babies.

But the habit to think first of her family, and of the hard work she'd put in keeping them safe and happy, was not so easily undone. She *had* to think of her estate, and of Hope's diamond; she had to prove to Hope, to everyone, that she was capable of taking care of herself, and of her family. That she was cleverer than all the dandies and earls whom she'd passed up in lieu of Papa, Sophia, Auntie George. That no gentleman, no matter how handsome or capable or thrillingly brilliant in the bedchamber (or kitchen), was worth sacrificing her family, and her freedom, for.

"No," she said softly, her voice tight. "Thank you, William, for the lovely proposal. But I cannot marry you."

Violet turned her eyes back to see Harclay's smile fade.

"Tonight," he said, "tonight I saw your boldness, and your bravery, in play. I'd never seen anything like it. I saw the fire that burns in you and I am drawn to it, Violet. I cannot stay away. Please don't ask me to stay away."

"You forget I've a family to look after. And a diamond to recover. I shan't be thwarted by—by your pretty words."

"Ah," he replied, a savage edge to his tone. "So this isn't even about me. It's about your damned pride."

Violet attempted to free herself from Harclay's embrace, but he held her fast, pressing her against the table with the weight of his body.

"Please, let me go," she panted. "I can't breathe."

"Now you know how I feel."

And suddenly his mouth was on hers, his lips tearing at her savagely. She tasted blood but she didn't care; tears blurred her vision and she closed her eyes, losing herself once more to the poignant loveliness of his touch. With his fingers he parted her sex, and entered her slowly; and then he was again moving, thrusting, against her. It felt very much the same and yet different this time around; there was an intensity about Harclay's movements, a desperation that hadn't been there before.

Her climax came, swift, devastating, and left her shaking beneath William. He gritted his teeth against his own release; and when he was done, he pressed his forehead against hers, his breath hot on her cheek.

"Open your eyes." His voice was jagged, edged with pain. "And look at me."

But Violet couldn't. Tears snaked out of the corners of her eyes and trailed down her temples into her hair. They were unwelcome, hot and sticky against her skin.

"I'm sorry," she whispered, shaking her head.

"Violet," he said, the single word strained, as if he were suddenly sapped of will. He rolled to her side and gathered her in his arms, pressing her flesh against the warmth of his own. With his thumbs he drew away her tears.

She breathed deeply, surrounding herself with his scent, the scent of their lovemaking, as if she would memorize it. A wave of misery inundated her at the thought that this could—*would*—be the last time she'd be in William's arms. She ran her hands up and down the length of his forearms, his shoulders, reveling in his shapely strength and the muscles that rippled invitingly beneath her touch.

At last, when her bones had gone numb from being pressed against the hard table, she untangled herself from his arms and wiped her eyes with the heel of her hand.

"I suppose I should be going," she said, glancing about the floor for her clothes. They were everywhere—well, what was left of them—in shredded strips of linen, silk, muslin.

Harclay spun off the table onto his feet. "What if I refuse to give you any clothes? I've ripped yours to shreds. Would you stay with me then? Or do you despise me so much you'd rather walk home naked?"

"I don't despise you," she replied quietly. "Not in the least, William. It's just—"

"It's just imperative we don't get caught," he said with a sigh, running a hand through his dark hair. "Of course. I'll run upstairs for some clothes, and then I shall escort you back home."

Violet swallowed, hard. "Thank you."

He turned back to her suddenly, his eyes flashing. She swallowed him whole with her gaze—really, the man was handsome clothed, but naked he was nothing short of *wicked*—and failed. She watched his cock harden beneath her gaze and, heat rising to her cheeks, wondered at his stamina.

"I shall escort you back home," he repeated. Climbing into his breeches, he winced as he buttoned up his erection. "But I'm going to fight for you, Violet. No matter what you say, or whatever your reasons for refusing me, I will fight to make you mine."

Violet looked away. "You know I cannot have you, William."

He stepped toward her, and without willing it she drew a breath of anticipation. Smiling, he replied, "We'll see about that," and disappeared up the stairs.

Harclay helped Violet first into stockings and chemise, then stays, gown, slippers. He'd stolen it all from Caroline's closet some days before in the hopeful anticipation of just such an event; though he never, not for all the world, would've guessed it would be this good, that she would be this sensual, this willing; that he would be moved to his very core by her touch.

Even now, as his fingers trailed across her skin, fastening, buttoning, tying, he was wild with desire. It was all he could do not to rip off her clothes once more and throw her back on the table. How he longed to possess her all night, to take her up to his bed and keep her awake until the sun rose, her refusal be damned.

He felt as if he were a man possessed. What else could explain his ardent proposal, his vow to fight for the woman standing before him? Just hours earlier he'd sworn off marriage, as he'd done now for almost a decade. The sudden change didn't make sense, and it was terrifying besides.

And what bigger fool was there than one who fraternized with the enemy? Violet had set out to ensnare him, and unbeknownst to her she had succeeded. Hell, he'd only realized it himself mere hours before. He'd been falling for her all along; for her confidence, her humor, her complete and utter disregard for rules and propriety and the opinions of others; he'd fallen for her cursing and her cleverness and her beauty, for her body and her refreshingly forward enjoyment of his own.

Now he belonged to her, body and soul, heart and mind. He'd never felt so sure of something in all his livelong life. There was no going back, no time for regrets. Harclay would make her his, whether she willed it or not. He'd seen the flash of pain that crossed her eyes when she'd refused him; he'd wiped away the tears of remorse that fell freely down her lovely face. And he'd felt that remorse, and that pain, as his own. He couldn't stand to see her cry. He would make things right, he would, and then she would agree to be his. She had to. He didn't know what he would do if she refused him again.

Fastening the last button at the nape of Violet's neck, Harclay placed his hands on her shoulders and pressed a lingering kiss onto the flesh there. He felt her shudder against him.

"I'll find the diamond," he whispered in her ear. "And then I will come for you, Violet."

She shook her head, smiling, eyes trained on her feet. "Not if I find it first."

"Ah," he replied and kissed her just below her ear, "so the game is not yet finished."

"Hardly. I don't think either of us is able to resist the challenge. We enjoy playing too much, don't you agree?"

"Perhaps," he said and kissed her once more before bundling her in a pelisse and turning her to face him.

"Are you going to be all right?" he asked.

Violet replied with a watery smile. "Let's be off, then."

Looping her arm through his own, he led her down the kitchen galley and out the back door. The night was at its darkest and a bit chilly; Violet shivered, and when he pulled her closer to him she did not protest.

They were making their way around the side of the house, through the garden, when Harclay heard a male-sounding grunt, followed by an unceremonious shuffling in the bushes.

He pulled Violet to a stop behind a statue; and when she looked at him with wide eyes, he held a finger to his lips. Peering beyond the statue, Harclay watched as Mr. Lake emerged from the bushes onto the drive, plucking leaves from his jacket.

Lake tilted his head to look up at the house. "Good night, my lovely," he whispered.

Harclay followed the man's gaze up the side of the house, coming to a halt at Caroline's window.

Caroline's window. Of course.

His pulse flared with anger. Lake had bloody cheek, sneaking into Harclay's house in the middle of the night to do God knew what with Caroline. Somewhere in the back of his mind, a voice reminded him that he, too, was guilty of pursuing illicit rendezvous.

But that was beside the point, he told himself. And not at all the same. Violet—well, she was *Violet.* And Caroline was *Caroline.* Obviously two very different scenarios!

"Good night!" Caroline purred. Harclay gritted his teeth at the silkiness of her voice—he recognized satisfaction there, and exhaustion, too. Whatever Mr. Lake had done, he had done it thoroughly.

It was enough to send the earl into a fit of fury.

Beside him, Violet was tugging at his arm. "Wait, William, don't—"

But he was beyond words. He swung out into the drive, gravel skidding from his enormous, livid stride, and before Mr. Lake knew what he was about, Harclay walked right up to him and drove his fist into the man's cheek.

Caroline's scream filled Harclay's ears as he watched Mr. Lake stumble backward, nearly losing his balance before regaining his footing.

The earl had forgotten just how big Mr. Lake was; though he was crippled, the man practically had muscles sprouting from his ears, and was half a head taller than himself.

He pushed the thought from his head as Mr. Lake stood before him, holding his cheek.

"Mr. Lake," Harclay said dryly. "Imagine finding you here,

and at this hour! What an unexpected surprise. To what do we owe the honor?"

"I daresay my intentions are better than your own," Mr. Lake spat out. He nodded at Violet, who suddenly appeared at Harclay's elbow.

The earl tucked her behind him and held her there with his arm. "You haven't a clue what my intentions are, Lake. My affairs are my own," he hissed. "You trespass on my property. You harass my sister, despoil her under cover of darkness, while she is under my protection. Tell us, what other secrets have you been keeping?"

Mr. Lake gritted his teeth and took a menacing step toward Harclay. Behind him, Violet let out a little cry of fright, and Mr. Lake drew up, his face mere inches from the earl's.

"Stop it!" Caroline called from her window. "Stop it this moment or I'll—I'll jump from this window, I will!"

"I'd catch you if you did," Mr. Lake replied, his eyes never leaving Harclay's. "Though I daresay your brother might shoot me in the back before I could reach you."

"I would do it gladly, if it meant getting rid of you," Harclay growled.

"Not if I do away with *you* first, you rotten, cowardly thief," Mr. Lake said. "I am getting close, very close indeed, to recovering Hope's diamond and incriminating you as the crook who stole it. The jewel is, through a bit of deft maneuvering, within my grasp. It won't be long now before you are locked away in jail, your title forfeit, your fortune gone."

A cold, clammy spider of foreboding crawled up Harclay's spine. *Through deft maneuvering the jewel is within his grasp.*

Of course. Why hadn't the earl seen Mr. Lake's guilt sooner? The realization washed over him with heady force, the blood marching madly in his ears.

"You," he spat out. "*You* were the one who informed those damned acrobats that I was the man who hired them. It's all your doing—the ransom note, Hope turning me away at the bank, and"—Harclay swallowed, hardly able to finish—"and Violet's kidnapping. It was all *you*."

Mr. Lake thrust his face toward the earl's, nearly head-butting him. "It was the only move I had to make, and so I made it. I never meant for Violet to be involved; on my honor,

I would never, *never* place her in harm's way. Though I cannot say you didn't deserve it. Plundering Lady Violet, ruining her fortune and her family. You didn't expect to get away with it, did you?"

Harclay bit his lip against the white-hot wrath that exploded in his chest. He'd never felt such wild emotion. All he could think of was Violet and the terror he'd seen on her face through the hackney window as the acrobats made off with her.

His fury was beyond dangerous. His hands curled into fists at his sides, he knew they would fly into motion at any moment, not stopping until Mr. Lake was a bloody, pulpy mess, not stopping until Violet's suffering was avenged.

When he spoke, Harclay's voice trembled with quiet rage. "Today, at dawn," he said. "Farrow Field, just outside the city. I'm sure you know it well. Choose your second. I shall bring the surgeon."

His words elicited a gasp of surprise from Violet, but before she could protest, Mr. Lake stepped back and bowed.

"I accept your challenge," he replied. "And make no mistake, Harclay, I don't mean to aim wide."

Harclay smiled. "I would be insulted if you did."

He heard movement behind him, and out of the corner of his eye he saw Violet dashing between himself and Lake. Caroline skidded through the kitchen door and was hot on Violet's heels, coming to a halt at her side.

The two ladies surveyed their respective gentlemen, eyes gleaming.

"Idiots, the two of you!" Violet cried. "What good will a duel do, except to wound or kill you both?"

Caroline glared at her brother. "If you hurt him, Harclay, you'll be as good as dead to me," she said, her voice deadly calm. "Do you understand? I'll disown you, shame you, throw you to the wolves."

Harclay glared back. "He isn't worth your affection, Caroline. He's no better than a dog."

"How would you know?" she snapped in response. "You don't understand the first thing about him! And now you're off to kill each other. Don't you have a thought for my happiness? For Violet's?"

Caroline motioned to the lady in question. "The two of

you will destroy us all through this duel of yours. I beg you, both of you. Cry off."

But the earl would not be swayed. "Cry off? When the black-guard compromised you, and nearly had Violet raped, nearly had her killed? I think not."

Harclay turned to Mr. Lake, rage blurring his vision. "I shall see you at dawn."

In one swift, violent motion, he pulled Violet to his side and made for the lane in front of the house.

Violet looked over her shoulder. "I'm sorry!" she called out. "We shall remedy this, Caroline, I swear it!"

Twenty-six

———— ❖ ————

In the sanctuary of her bedchamber, Violet waited for the darkness to fade into dawn. Despite her protests, Harclay had refused her request to accompany him and instead had locked her in her own house, admonishing her to "get some rest."

Like hell she would! She wanted to laugh at the absurdity of it. Rest, after making love to William, discussing their beautiful babies together? Rest, after witnessing the earl challenge Lake to a duel?

She'd never seen William so angry, so brutally emotional; his fury had frightened her. The thought of losing him to Mr. Lake's pistol was terrifying. Violet couldn't allow the duel to go on—couldn't allow Harclay to die protecting her honor.

What little was left of it, anyway.

Doubtless Mr. Lake was a crack shot. Heavens, the man had survived years in Spain under Wellington; surely his skill with firearms was nothing to scoff at.

It was all so hideously wrong and hardheaded. It took a special kind of idiot to willingly stare down the barrel of a gun in a freezing field at dawn. Honestly! It was a wonder any men were left in the world at all, what with their propensity for brandy and insults and pistols.

And yet her heart ached at the thought of doing nothing, of leaving William at Mr. Lake's mercy. Damn the man to hell, she had to save him from himself. But how? Locked in her father's house, she couldn't very well run breathless onto Farrow Field, begging the men to lower their weapons. She didn't even know where Farrow Field *was*, though through the years she'd heard whispers of it. The gentleman's choice spot for a duel; many men had lost their lives there or had been grievously wounded. It was certainly no place for polite females.

Violet almost laughed out loud.

She certainly wasn't polite; if she had been, none of them would be in this mess in the first place. No, she knew herself to be something altogether different. A gambler, a cheat, a singular spirit with little care for what others thought or did.

And it dawned on her that William, the Earl of Harclay, was very much the same.

They both cursed and drank and danced the waltz; they kissed hard and laughed harder and never refused a surprise midnight visit.

Whether Violet despised or adored him for their likeness, she knew in that moment she could not allow him to be shot in the chest on her account. Surely William knew her well enough by now to know she wouldn't let him go without a fight.

She turned to the window, heat rising to her cheeks at the memory of Harclay falling through it. The darkness was muted somewhat by the first gray strokes of dawn's approach. There wasn't much time left; she had to take action, and quickly.

Harclay falling through the window.

Violet remembered him laughing at her wonder. *I've got a strong back* he'd said.

"Of course!" she cried aloud, hand flying to her forehead. "Fitzhugh! Fitzhugh, please, we must hurry!"

"The terms," Avery panted as he at last reached Harclay after running across the field, "are as follows: twenty paces and, of course, the salute. Only at the drop of my handkerchief may you shoot."

With trembling hands, Avery accepted Harclay's dueling pistol to check it one last time.

"Nervous, are you?" Harclay asked with a wry smile.

"No, sir," Avery replied curtly. "Just a bit rusty is all. I've been laboring all these years under the impression that you'd fought your last duel quite some time ago, when you nearly lost a leg to that thin gentleman with the tiny head."

"Ah, yes, my duel with Lord Araby," Harclay scoffed. "Imbecile was killed not thirty minutes after, at his second duel that morning. Ah, the days of our youth. How foolish we were."

"Were?" he scoffed, shaking his head.

Before Harclay could reply, Avery placed the gleaming Manton dueling pistol in his master's grasp and motioned him onto the field.

Only as the earl strode through the grass, the morning air clammy against his skin, did the reality of his position sink in. He'd fought tens of duels, and he'd managed to survive mostly unscathed. So why did this duel, *this* fight, feel so different?

He glanced across the field at Mr. Lake, his enormous frame looming in the half-light of dawn. Not only was Lake possessed of the same size and skill as Harclay—it would be the first time the earl had faced such a formidable opponent— but never before had Harclay fought to *protect* a woman's honor.

And Violet was not just any woman. She was *his* woman, the maddening, lovely woman who had managed to capture his attention and his imagination and now his heart.

Before, Harclay was always the one doing the insulting. How many times he'd been called to account by offended fathers, brothers, uncles, husbands—well, suffice it to say it was not an insignificant number.

But now—now Harclay was the offended party; *he* was the offended lover who would risk his life on behalf of the woman for whom he cared. Cared for very much.

So much it scared him.

The earl glanced up at the sky. The last of the stars were fading out to gray; the horizon burned pink and yellow with the approaching sun. It was going to be a fine summer day, warm and bright. He wondered how Violet would fill the hours; would she think of him, of all they'd shared last night?

Just thinking of her face, beautiful and clever, sent a shock of pain through him. He must've gasped aloud, for suddenly the surgeon appeared at his side. Only after Harclay's adamant assurances that yes, yes, he was quite all right, did the man once again turn his back and disappear to the edge of the field.

Squaring his shoulders, he held up his head and met Mr. Lake's fiery gaze. Rage, hot and wild and blinding, filled Harclay once again. He understood why all those men he'd dueled against had put their lives on the line, though such duels were usually resolved before any shots were fired; at this moment, Harclay would do anything, kill a man or set fire to the world, so that Violet's suffering might be avenged.

The deadly silence that settled between Harclay and Mr. Lake was pierced by Avery's voice, instructing them to meet at the center of the field. Lake's steps were sure, his limp all but gone. Harclay covered the distance in a handful of long, angry strides before coming face-to-face with Mr. Lake.

"Lord Harclay," Lake said and made his salute.

Harclay nodded and returned the favor. His opponent's one green eye gleamed in the morning light, hard and inscrutable. Lake's fair skin was mottled red about the cheeks, lending him a ruddy, healthy air. For a moment Harclay thought of Caroline, and though he was about to kill the man, he understood why Mr. Lake appealed to her. How unlike her old goat of a husband he was: strong, intimidating, determined.

Which explained, of course, why Harclay had caught him sneaking out of Caroline's room in the middle of the night.

"I am sorry to have offended you," Mr. Lake said, his voice even. "But I love your sister. I care only for her happiness, her honor, and if I live I have every intention of making her my wife."

"Caroline deserves better, and you know it," Harclay replied savagely. "I do not accept your apology. Avery! We turn at your command."

Avery stepped forward, as if to separate the two gentlemen; he glanced uneasily from one to the other. He opened his mouth as if to speak—Harclay could see the words in the man's eyes, *Are you sure you want to do this, all things considered?*—but the earl cleared his throat in warning.

"Very well," Avery said, defeated. "Ready!"

Together Harclay and Mr. Lake both turned on their heels so that their backs were pressed against each other, guns held skyward at the crooks of their shoulders.

"Count paces!" Avery called.

The earl stepped forward, silently counting his paces as he stalked across the field. *One, two, three, four.*

Twenty paces was nothing to scoff at; Mr. Lake must have been nearly as expert a marksman as Harclay to agree to such a distance. If Lake meant to shoot him right between the eyes, there was a very good chance that he would do it. Harclay knew this duel would end only in blood.

Eleven, twelve.

The dew from the grass beaded on the toes of his boots. It reminded him of the way droplets of rain had run down Violet's face and neck that night he'd caught her in his stables. Though he wondered what had possessed her to begin her search there of all places, he couldn't deny he was glad she had; for she appeared heavenly in the rain, dress sticking to her skin in all the right places.

The thought of never seeing her again, never peeling off her clothes and having her to himself, settled black and heavy over his chest.

Sixteen, seventeen, eighteen.

Harclay struggled to breathe. From the corner of his eye, he saw the surgeon and his assistants turning away from the field, averting their gazes.

Around him the world was quiet, save for the soft shifting of grass beneath his boots; but in his ears his heart marched loudly, a plea to stop, to end this silly exercise.

He did not stop.

Nineteen, twenty.

Harclay whirled to face his opponent, the movement swift and calm, his thoughts an unbearable cacophony. He raised his arm and stared down the polished barrel of his gun, only to meet eyes with Mr. Lake across the field.

Gulping back the rising tide of foreboding that rose in his throat, Harclay released the safety on his pistol.

Avery approached, holding a handkerchief high above his head.

With one last, weary look at his master, he let the handkerchief fall from his fingers.

Harclay did not hear Violet's cries until it was too late.

Twenty-seven

— ❖ —

Violet tore across the field, ignoring Fitzhugh's panted warnings and Caroline's admonishments not to leave her behind.

"Stop!" Violet cried, holding up both her arms. "For the love of God, *stop*!"

William was standing on one end of the field with his back wedged toward her. His stance was purposeful, authoritative, as if he'd done this a hundred times before; legs wide apart, shoulders squared, his arm thrust forward with the pistol held fast in his hand. She could see the billowy white linen of his shirt peeking through the cuff of his jacket—the same shirt he'd tugged over his head just hours before, after giving her the most intensely pleasurable night of her life.

Violet quickened her steps. She watched in horror as Avery approached the field and raised a bright white handkerchief above his head.

"No!" she shouted. "No, no!"

This can't be happening, she thought wildly as she pumped her arms and legs with all the strength she could muster. *Please let this be a nightmare, some trick of the imagination, for if Harclay dies, if Mr. Lake dies, it will be my fault.*

She was coming upon Avery now. Behind her, the surgeon had seen her and was chasing after her, motioning wildly for her to stop. But she couldn't; she had come this far, and the momentum of her body, and of her determination, would carry her over the threshold.

Her insides lurched as Avery let go of the handkerchief; she nearly slammed into him half a heartbeat later, and narrowly missed him only to cross directly into the line of fire.

She realized she was a perfect target for the gentlemen's dueling pistols only after the shots went off. It all happened so quickly, in the space of a single breath, that she hardly understood what was occurring.

"Please!" she was crying, her hands still in the air. She turned her head to face Harclay, just in time to watch him fire his weapon. For a split second his face was concealed by a cloud of gun smoke; and then his brows went up in surprise, his dark eyes wide with terror as his gaze fell upon her.

William opened his mouth—he was shouting, she could tell from the tears that gathered in the corners of his eyes—but she could not hear it. There was a rushing, violent sound just off to her right, so loud it was deafening.

White-hot pain sliced through her ribs as the bullet dug into her flesh. For a moment her vision went black. She couldn't breathe, couldn't move, and she felt her knees buckling and the weight of her body carrying her down, down, *my God, am I dying, have I already died?*

When she came to, Harclay was cradling her in his arms. He held her against him, one hand on the nape of her neck, the other on the small of her back. He was shouting something she couldn't quite make out; but when he turned his attention back to her, she saw tears spilling from his eyes. And suddenly she was afraid.

She opened her mouth, willing her tongue to move, but no words came out. Instead she tasted blood and felt it spilling out onto her lips. Her body began to shake uncontrollably; the world went dim at the edges of her vision.

The surgeon and his men were upon her then, tearing at her gown.

"Is she going to be all right?" Harclay asked. He took his hands off her body only when Mr. Lake appeared and pulled him away from her.

Violet watched as William rose and dug a trembling hand
through his hair. "Is she going to live?" he cried, making no
effort to wipe away the tears that fell freely down his face. He
dug his fists into his hips and began to pace before her.

It was becoming difficult to breathe. Again she tried to
speak, and this time only a single word came out.

"William," she said. Her voice sounded strange and far
away.

He fell on his knees beside her, cradling her face in his enormous hands. The surgeon was calling for laudanum, for wine,
and for something else that sounded suspiciously like *saw*.

"Violet," William said. "Violet, I am sorry. I am sorry."

He felt her trembling and leaned closer. "It's going to be
all right," he murmured, kissing her lips. "I promise, Violet, I
will make everything all right."

The pain throbbed to enormous proportions; at her back
the grass felt unbearably prickly and wet. The surgeon was
swirling something dark in a small vial; he passed it to William, and he held it to Violet's mouth.

"This will help you feel better," he said.

It was all she could do to open her lips and with a grimace
swallow the foul-tasting potion. The liquid was like sweet fire
in her veins; at once the pain eased, and her heart slowed its
frantic pace.

"Thank you," she whispered.

Again the world began to dim. The surgeon was digging
into her; she could vaguely feel the sensation of his cold metal
instrument scraping against her bones. The sound was nause-
ating, and for a moment she wished for death, for a release
from this visceral, bloody struggle.

William's face hovered above her. Stray beams of the rising sun gleamed through the leaves on either side of his head.
They felt lovely and warm on her clammy skin. She was cold,
very cold, and terrified.

Terrified that this would be her last morning. Her last
breath. The last time she would ever see William. Ever feel
his hands on her.

She turned to him. "Hold my hand, please," she said.

He clasped both her hands in his and held on, tightly.
Though tears still fell down his cheeks, his eyes had taken on

a familiar, determined gleam. Just looking at them made her feel better, made her feel safe.

Violet wanted to keep that feeling in her heart forever.

Her thoughts were fading, as was her pulse. She was freezing.

She was filled with regret, with loathing and grief and tenderness, devotion and affection. Looking into William's eyes, she felt all these things. Tears slid from the corners of her eyes, across her temples, and into her hair.

"I hate you," she whispered. "William, I love you."

The dimness closed in, her eyes fluttering shut. There was one last searing, torturous spasm of pain, and then, nothing.

"Might I have a tray brought up, Harclay?" Violet's father asked. "It's been two days and you've had nary a single bite to eat. Though you've very nearly drunk dry my entire cellar."

He bent over the earl, brow furrowed anxiously. Harclay couldn't help but smile at the man; though he was still in nightcap and slippers, his concern was touching.

"No, thank you, your grace," Harclay murmured, waving his empty snifter. "Though if you've another drop to spare, I'd be much obliged. I can always send for my own, if you'd like."

The Duke of Sommer, and the chair onto which he collapsed, groaned in unison. "Nonsense. I'm sure we can dig up something. Though your household is most concerned, Harclay, *most* concerned. Your man Avery refuses to leave my kitchen, and he's been sleeping on a cot in the downstairs hall. Why don't you go home, get some rest?"

Harclay motioned to the unimposing door across from them. "Because Lady Violet needs me. I'm not moving from this spot until she is on her feet and feeling better."

Sommer patted Harclay's knee with a knobby, veined hand. "When she is well, you'll be lucky if she doesn't return the favor and shoot *you* in the ribs."

The earl scoffed. "I wouldn't blame her if she did." He paused. "I know I've said it a hundred times, but I'll say it a hundred more—"

"Yes, yes, you're very sorry and feel terribly about the accident," Sommer said, waving away his words. "You can say all you want to me. It only matters what my daughter thinks, whether or not she'll accept your apology. I'll pray for you, poor man."

"Thank you, your grace. I believe I'll need all the help I can get," Harclay replied.

Again Rutledge patted his knee. "I know it's difficult to fathom, what with all the bloody commotion of the past few days, but before Violet was—harmed, I'd never seen her so happy. So full of life, of purpose. I believe she'd been lost for quite some time, convinced she had to care for me, for the family." He motioned to the house around them. "She is frightened for me, what would happen if no one were left to see to me, to see to all this. But my dear sister Georgie and I, we are stronger than we appear, and more clever. Though none are so clever as Violet."

"She is indeed clever, your daughter. Most intelligent woman I've ever met," Harclay said, swallowing the moon of sadness that rose in his throat. "Far too intelligent for a man like me."

"Pish!" Rutledge said. "It's a well-known fact that all men are idiots. Women—ah, women have always been the wiser sex, though it pains us to admit it. We aren't worthy of the ground upon which they walk. But we try our damnedest, don't we?" He winked.

Violet's father made to rise, and with Harclay's help he lurched to his feet. "Violet will come around," he continued with a knowing smile. "You are a good man, if a bit impulsive. I know that you will love my family as you love my daughter. As you will love the family the two of you shall make together."

Again Harclay swallowed, hard. "Thank you," he said, voice husky with the threat of tears. "I hope you're right."

"Of course I'm right!" Rutledge replied. "Now, let me go find some of that brandy you're after. Perhaps I'll join you in a finger or four."

"Capital," Harclay said, guiding the elder man toward the stair. Auntie George appeared, ringlets trembling at the sight of the earl—she wasn't about to forgive him as readily as Lord Rutledge—and helped her brother down the steps.

Harclay fell heavily back into his chair, wiping away a tear before it could fall from the corner of his eye. He didn't blame Auntie George; he felt unworthy of life, of each breath he took. *He* should be the one suffering behind that closed door; *he* should have been shot. Not Violet. She deserved none of this.

The earl had hardly moved from this spot since the surgeon and his men had brought her here to recover—or to die—following the accident at Farrow Field. He couldn't eat, couldn't sleep. Even the herculean amount of alcohol he consumed did nothing to dull the crushing guilt that plagued him day and night.

Caroline refused to speak to him, though Mr. Lake visited Harclay and Violet often, bearing bottles of brandy. He appeared just as disheveled and distraught as the earl, and after apologizing a thousand times, he cursed himself a fool and vowed to do everything he could to ensure Violet's recovery.

Though, by the surgeon's last report some hours before, Harclay knew she was not doing as well as he'd hoped. She'd had a fever for three days now, and during that time she hadn't opened her eyes once, nor so much as muttered a single word.

It was enough to break Harclay's heart. He thought he might die from regret, from the remorse he felt on account of his arrogance. He should've listened to Violet and his sister when they'd warned him not to duel Mr. Lake. It was a stupid, selfish thing to have done. And now he faced the prospect of living the rest of his life bearing the weight of that regret and remorse, of living without Violet at his side.

To make matters worse, Violet had fallen unconscious before he could tell her what he'd been carrying in his heart for weeks now, though only recently had he had the courage to admit it.

I love you, he'd said, just as her hand went limp in his own. *Violet, I love you. I've loved you since, from the crush, you turned to face me at Hope's ball. You were the most beautiful woman I'd ever seen. I love you, I love you, I love you.*

The door opened in front of him. Harclay leapt to his feet as Lady Sophia emerged, carrying in her arms a basin filled with bloody water. He met her eyes. She shook her head and looked away.

"May I see her?" he whispered.

"Yes," Sophia replied. "But you musn't stay long. Surgeon's orders, she is to rest."

Harclay nodded his gratitude. "Of course. And if you should require anything, anything at all—"

"Just your prayers, Lord Harclay."

Again he sensed the prick of tears behind his eyes. Hell, his whole face hurt from all the crying he'd done these past few weeks.

Lady Sophia placed a hand on his arm. "It's all right. She will be happy to know you were with her. Go in."

Taking the doorknob in his hand, Harclay took a deep, shaking breath. He opened the door and stepped into Violet's bedchamber.

He tried to focus on the happy, sensually charged hours they'd shared in this room, the look on her face when he'd clumsily climbed through the window that first time, her smile and the light in her eyes.

But it was impossible to think of such joyful things when faced with the scene before him.

Violet was laid out upon her bed, the sheets drawn up to her waist. Her entire torso was wrapped in snowy white linen bandages—freshly changed, it appeared, by Cousin Sophia. A splotch of blood in the center of Violet's right rib cage seeped through the bandages, slowly spreading into a bruise-like pool of red, rust, and purple.

She was very pale. Paler than the previous day. Her dark hair, slick with sweat, was held tight against her head in a long braid that snaked over her shoulder. She breathed in short, shallow breaths, her chest hardly rising with the motion.

It hurt his heart just to look at her. A fresh wave of sorrow inundated him as he kneeled beside the bed. He took her hand in his own and brought his lips to her fingers, closing his eyes. Her skin felt hot and sticky.

"I'm so very sorry," he whispered for the thousandth time that week. "Violet, I am sorry."

His eyes snapped open at the small sound of rustling bedclothes.

Heart in his throat, he watched as Violet's eyes fluttered open. She turned her head on the pillow to face him.

For a long moment he was unable to speak. He looked into her eyes, bloodshot and bright with fever, and his pulse leapt in relief.

"Violet?" He swallowed. "Violet, can you hear me?"

In his ears the silence of the room grew deafening as he waited for her reply.

She did not speak; rather, she tilted her chin and raised her lips in the barest shadow of a smile.

But it was a *smile*. And suddenly she looked once again like the Violet he knew and loved, full of fire and mirth and wit.

That one smile very nearly bowled him over.

He ran his thumb over the top of her hand and made to talk to her for as long as she was able to listen.

Harclay spoke of their courtship, the moment they met, and the first waltz they danced together. He remembered with a laugh her cutting remark about his wood, and Caroline cartwheeling into the Serpentine with Mr. Lake. He told her how annoyed he'd been when she won those games of casino, annoyed and fascinated by her skill.

But most of all, he assured her he never meant their game to play out like *this*. He assured her over and over that he would take it all back, the thrill and the chase and the sneaking around, if it meant sparing her this fate.

"I am a fool, a selfish fool," he said. "But I suppose if I weren't, I wouldn't be a fool for you, Violet."

By then her eyes had been closed for some time, though Harclay would've liked to believe the faint smile still graced her lips.

Twenty-eight

— ❖ —

Two weeks later

Violet woke up slowly, her eyes fluttering, and fluttering again, before she was finally able to open them.

With her first waking breath a great wave of pain washed over her. She gritted her teeth against it, eyes burning with tears.

Looking down at her body, she saw her chest and ribs were bound with fresh bandages. There didn't ever seem to be any gore, thank God, or Violet knew she would've finally swooned for the first time in her twenty-two years.

In a rush of violent memory, Violet recalled that her first swoon had already occurred—after she'd been shot in the belly by William Townshend, Earl of Harclay, during a duel on Farrow Field.

She blinked back the tears. It had been like this for days now; she'd wake up, happily ignorant of everything but the warm summer air and the scent of rosewater that rose from the bedclothes, and then—

Then she'd remember. She'd remember leaping from a downstairs window into Fitzhugh's waiting arms—neither of them had made it through that exercise unscathed—and collecting Lady Caroline from Harclay's house.

Violet would remember the sudden, searing pain in her side, and Harclay's tears falling hot and fast on her face as he hovered above her.

I hate you, she'd told him. *I love you.*

Violet swallowed. She hadn't even known she felt such a thing for him until that moment when, delirious with pain, she realized she was frightened to face whatever came next *without him.*

Try as she might, she could not remember William's response, or if he said anything at all. After that moment, the world was black, her memory filled with feverish imaginings, one long, haunting nightmare.

Across her bedchamber, the curtains danced and billowed in the breeze. From the slanting amber light, Violet could tell it was evening, and a lovely one at that.

She sighed—*hell,* that hurt!—and tried to shift upright in bed. Her every limb ached; even her breasts felt sore. She looked down. Had they *always* been so big, so full? Perhaps they were merely swollen from the fever.

"Hello?" she tried calling. Her voice cracked and felt strange in her throat, as if she hadn't used it in ages.

Swallowing, she tried again. "Hello!"

This time it worked, for, half a heartbeat later, William stumbled through the door, followed closely by her father, Auntie George, and a passel of men she took to be surgeons.

Her heart leapt painfully at the sight of Harclay. He appeared nothing short of tragic, face bruised and gaunt, eyes bloodshot. Sporting a full, dark beard and greasy hair, he was wearing only a loose linen shirt and buckskins.

Though he was thinner than she remembered, he nonetheless appeared the pirate she had come to know and love. She sucked in her breath at the quickening of her pulse, pounding against her injured ribs. It was excruciating, but she could not tear her gaze from him. She'd told Cousin Sophia to keep him out of her room; at last he'd slipped past her guard.

She would be lying if she said she wasn't glad to see him.

"Violet!" he exclaimed breathily, falling to his knees at her bedside. "I'm very happy to see you."

She arched a brow in reply. "I don't know who looks worse for the wear, William, you or me."

Laughing, that deep, rumbling sound in his chest, he took her hand and trailed kisses along each of her fingers. She gasped—in pain, in pleasure, a bit of both—and Auntie George peeked over his shoulder, clucking her tongue.

"Gently, now, go gently, if you please, Lord Harclay," she said, though her tear-filled smile belied the command.

Violet nodded and smiled and assured everyone that yes, she was in pain, and yes, she could breathe. Her father kissed both her cheeks and smiled; Auntie George blew none too quietly into her handkerchief. The surgeon sidled up to the opposite end of the bed and took her pulse, felt her forehead. He nodded.

"The fever has broken," he said. "No small miracle, considering I dug a bullet out from between your shattered ribs. I'm afraid the pain may continue for week or two yet; but you should be on your feet in a few days, maybe less."

"Thank you," Violet said, her eyes never leaving Harclay's. "Would you allow us a moment?"

The surgeon cleared his throat. "Actually, I was hoping to have a moment with you myself. There's something I would like to discuss with you—privately, if I might—"

Violet waved him off. "Later, thank you," she said.

He looked from Violet to William and back again; with a sigh, he turned and, following Lord Rutledge and Auntie George, left the room.

The door closed behind them with an authoritative *clap*. And then Violet was alone with William, her heart swollen near to bursting in her chest.

He moved to speak, but she placed her fingers against his lips, preferring instead to savor him with her eyes. For several long minutes she gazed at him, and he gazed back, his black eyes ringed with gray-blue circles.

Circles the same shade as Hope's diamond.

The realization was like a blow to the belly. Violet had

completely forgotten about that blasted jewel and all the pain that came with it. She swallowed against the tightness in her throat. Her exquisite joy at seeing William mingled with a livid sadness: sadness on account of her position, her duty to secure the French Blue and ensure her family's security.

God *damn* Harclay. Why'd he have to be such a fool and steal the diamond in the first place? This was all *his* fault, *his* doing.

From the look of him, he hadn't left her side since he'd shot her. And though her heart swelled with gratitude and something else—something deeper—that also meant he hadn't gone out in search of the missing diamond.

Which meant, of course, that it was still within her grasp if Mr. Lake had not found it first.

William must have sensed the sudden shift in her mood, for he squeezed her hand. She looked away, gritting her teeth in an effort to control the panic and pain that coursed through her entire being.

"Violet," he said quietly. "Darling, look at me."

"Please don't call me that," she whispered, choking on the words as she said them.

Cupping her chin in his hand, he pulled her to face him. "I do not know where to begin—I might apologize forever, if I could."

She looked down for a moment, willing her tears to remain in her eyes. They did not. She sniffed and again met his eyes.

"I'm sorry." His voice was gruff. He cleared his throat and tried again.

"I'm sorry about shooting you, for fighting that duel. I'm sorry for even challenging Lake in the first place. I am sorry for putting you in the middle of my—my foolish escapades. I am sorry you were kidnapped—even now, Violet, it kills me to think of you bound and taunted by those beastly creatures. I am sorry about jeopardizing your family's future, and your happiness. I am sorry about hurting you. You must know I never meant any of it.

"But—" He finally took a breath. "But I will never—*never*—be sorry that I met you. I am not sorry that we met and fell in love. And I hope you aren't, either."

Violet sucked in her breath. She could hardly bear it. How she longed to give in, to admit her love for him and her desire to be with him, always.

But she couldn't. *Wouldn't*. She still had to prove herself; she still had too much to lose.

"William, you've hurt me so badly—I told you not to fight—"

"Don't you think I know that?" he said, tugging a hand through his dark hair. "Violet, I *shot* you, for God's sake! I deserve to be shot myself. The guilt, it's been so terrible I can't tell you how many times—how often I've thought about selling my soul to the devil, so that you might be spared. I'd give anything"—he stopped, voice cracking—"anything to take back what happened to you."

Violet steeled herself against his words, stoking her anger so that it might overcome the pity she felt for him, the love.

"Would you give back the diamond?" she asked.

He blinked, the expression on his face as shocked and saddened as if she'd just shot *him* in the ribs.

"Yes," he said. "From the beginning I planned to give it back. To you, to Hope. I didn't come here to discuss the French Blue, but if you desire it—"

"What else is there to discuss?" she replied. "That's what this is all about, isn't it?"

"No, it's not," William ground out. "You know that's not what we're about at all. I love you—"

"What good is love if I lose this house, my inheritance, my family?" she snapped. A hardness, black and raw, spread over her chest into her throat. It felt awful to say these things to him, but she'd already come this far; she couldn't turn back now.

"Don't do this, Violet, I'm begging you," he said. "I'll get the diamond back, make sure the world knows it is once again safely in Mr. Hope's possession. His business will recover, and your family's fortune will be secured. And then we'll be married, perhaps in the parish on my estate—"

"William," Violet cut in, shaking her head. "This game we play. It can't go on forever—not when it's become so dangerous. Once I find the diamond—and I *will* find it—you and I, we won't fit together the way we do now. You live for the chase. I live for the thrill. You think we'll feel the same about each other once it's done?"

She watched the indignation shade his eyes a darker shade of black.

"Once upon a time I was that man," he said steadily, "but don't you dare accuse me of thinking you nothing more than a *chase*. It's an insult to your intelligence, for one thing, and a blatant falsehood besides."

Violet swallowed for what felt like the hundredth time and looked away. He was right, of course. She didn't know why she was saying the things she did; but the poisoned words kept falling from her lips, the blackness spreading through her limbs, surrounding her heart.

Again Harclay cupped her chin in his hand and turned her head to face him. "I know you are a woman with little patience for fools. And so I am asking you one last time," he said. "Violet, please marry me. For heaven's sake, make an honorable man of me."

"I already told—"

"I love you," he continued. "I stayed by your side for weeks now. I hope to stay forever. This is the last time, Violet. The last time I'll stand before you and ask you to be my wife. I shan't ask again."

The smooth violence of his words assured her that no, he *wouldn't* ask again. This was her chance. Her only chance.

And before she could think, *Wait, what is it I really feel?* she blurted out, "No. No, William, I thank you for your concern, but it's—us, we—it's just not possible."

The earl pushed away from the bed, rising to his feet, and ran a hand through his hair. Breathing a deep, frustrated breath, he turned back to her.

"Fine. But you can't say I didn't try, Violet. You can't say I didn't attempt to make this right."

Violet struggled to hide her rising panic. "My side hurts," she said. "I need to rest."

Biting the inside of his lip, William surveyed her for several beats. A fresh pulse of pain sliced through her at the sight of his watery eyes.

"Good-bye, Violet," he said at last, his voice tight.

She cleared her throat. "Good-bye, William."

He turned and without a backward glance stalked from the room.

The tears came hot and fast now, blotting out the world around her. For all her bravado, her anger toward William, she'd never felt such a sense of terrible remorse in all her life. She wept; and no matter what her father said, no matter the wine Cousin Sophia brought up, nothing could console her.

When she'd cried herself into a virtual stupor, Violet was at last faced with the surgeon. He slipped quietly into her room after Sophia had left and for several minutes busied himself at Violet's escritoire.

He turned and handed her a small vial of dark liquid. When she raised her brows, he said, "Laudanum, mixed with a bit of wine. It will help with the pain."

"Nerves, too, I hope," she replied and managed a small smile.

The liquid tasted foul but she drank it anyway.

"There is something you wanted to discuss?"

"Oh, yes," the surgeon said. He grasped his hands behind him and rocked back on his heels, as if gathering strength for the coming revelation.

"Well?" Violet said. "Please, sir, you've nothing to fear. After having been *shot in the ribs*, I hardly think whatever news you have shall upset me."

"Perhaps," the man said, clearing his throat. "Perhaps not."

Violet's eyes went wide. Her pulse quickened. "What?" she asked. "What is it?"

Twenty-nine

---·❖·---

The Earl of Harclay returned to a house turned inside out. During his absence, the entire residence had been ransacked. In his study, musty, crinkled paper was everywhere, an overturned inkpot leaked onto his chair and carpet, and drawers were tossed about, books and bills askew. Avery claimed the staff was drugged; he found them snoring in a heap in the basement. Doubtless that rogue Mr. Lake had something to do with this.

Harclay hardly noticed the mess. Stalking through the front door, Avery jogging closely behind at his heels, Harclay tossed his jacket and hat aside.

He ignored Avery's gasp of terrified surprise at the condition of the house and headed for his study.

"Send up hot water for a bath," Harclay growled over his shoulder. "Make sure it's scalding."

Battering aside the study door, Harclay made a beeline for the gleaming liquor cabinet. Praise God, whoever his visitors had been, they'd left his collection of brandy intact.

In a swift, brutal movement, he lopped off the round crystal topper from a decanter and poured himself a full glass. He downed its entire contents in a single, desperate gulp.

He threw his head back, eyes closed, and waited for the liquor to make its way into his blood. He felt sore and starved in every corner of his being. His clothes were dirty and wrinkled; his beard unshaven and untrimmed. He needed a good scrubbing, and a good, long, slobbery drunk, the kind that erased one's memory, at least for a little while.

But no matter how much brandy he drank—in a matter of minutes, he finished the entire decanter—he couldn't forget Violet. Her wound, her face, her heartless, scathing refusal.

Elbows on the top of the cabinet, Harclay sank against it. His knees felt rubbery, his head full of hate and regret and sadness. He was a mess, no two ways about it, and he hadn't a clue how in hell to go about fixing the tangle in which he found himself.

What a fool he was, to believe she'd rethink her refusal after he put a bullet between her ribs. What an idiot he'd been, to ask her to marry him *again* after she responded that first time with an unequivocal *no, no, no.*

What sort of masochist was he besides? It seemed he could not get enough of Violet, no matter her unkind words, her work against him.

He'd turned into just the sort of idiot he loathed: sick with love, positively *sick* with it. His life was in shambles, and over a single woman, a single heartbeat, a single presence he could not seem to get enough of.

Not a month past, he would have thought such a thing impossible.

Harclay turned back to his study, and as if for the first time allowed the chaos of his surroundings to sink in. As if his day wasn't terrible enough—now *this*.

At once he knew it was the work of Hope's men, including Mr. Lake. Harclay saw the cripple's pity for him in the sparing of the brandy and of the Harclay seal, which stood upright exactly where the earl had left it four—or was it five?—weeks ago.

Everything else was a disaster. Drawers turned out, furniture left open and askew; it appeared as if someone had enjoyed a deliciously athletic midnight rendezvous in the room.

Harclay stood before the gaping windows, allowing the evening breeze to wash over him and cool his skin. He understood the assault for what it was: a threat.

He had to find the diamond, and soon, or they would all drown in this quagmire together—the earl, Mr. Hope, Caroline and Lake, Lord Rutledge and Violet and all their dependents.

And no matter her feelings for him, Harclay couldn't bear the thought of hurting Violet. He would find the diamond, if only to keep her safe. He would find the diamond for her sake, and hers alone.

Sighing, he ran a hand through his hair. The brandy had at last dulled the edges of his consciousness, leaving in its wake a pleasant, half-asleep murmur in his veins. His murderous mood was all but forgotten, and for the first time in what felt like an eternity, he was able to think.

By now the diamond could be anywhere—Prussia, the prince regent's jewel drawer, Putney. Doubtless those grasping acrobats had sold the French Blue off by now. But to whom? For how much?

Harclay recalled with a pang of annoyance that he was as good as broke until Hope allowed him access to his accounts. He had little cash available at the house; perhaps a guinea or two, nothing that would even come close to being enough to buy back the jewel.

There was the family silver, of course, Harclay's horse-flesh, and all the priceless antiques his grandfather had brought back from the Continent two generations before.

But what would a wily pawnbroker, or a slick master jeweler, possibly want with a Medici portrait?

It was hopeless.

Curses he didn't even know existed bubbled from his lips as he pounded up the stairs. To his very great relief, Avery had managed not only to find the copper tub in the midst of all this ruin but also to fill it to the brim with steaming water. The bath was in its usual place, drawn up before the fire; beside it stood a fresh decanter of brandy and a heavy crystal snifter.

Harclay grinned. At least he still had Avery.

The earl spent an hour, then another, sunk up to his chin in the bath. What had once been his favorite place to think had become a nightmare. Every time he thought he was getting somewhere with this plan or that, he would recall Violet bathing in this very same tub. How lovely she'd looked, like a mermaid, with her dark hair fanned out in the water around her. How he'd tasted her, right there on the bed, her slickness on his lips. Pressing that slickness onto her mouth.

Brandy, and more brandy, and more brandy still.

It did nothing to erase the image of her naked curves, her swollen lips, and the smile he'd left on them when he was done.

There was only one thing he could do.

"Avery!" he called. "Avery, bring the razor. I shall need a shave. I'm going to White's."

In all the world, there was no better cure for the memory of a lady lost than wild, unadulterated debauchery.

And Harclay was sure to find that at White's.

He rarely visited the establishment anymore, having fleeced half its members at the tables while stealing the other half's wives, daughters, and favored courtesans. It was a point of pride, actually, that he scared these fashionable men speechless.

Only now he didn't care about wagers or courtesans. He came for White's astonishing array of cognacs, and for those cognacs alone. It soothed him to be in the company of other men, besides, the cigar smoke swirling about him in a comfortable haze of familiarity.

Harclay took a seat toward the back of the club, as far away as he could get from the infamous bay window at the front of the house. He wished to remain anonymous tonight; his hope was that he'd drink himself into a stupor and wake three days later in the comfort of his own bed, or perhaps in hell.

Poor as a pauper, rejected by the woman he loved, and entirely clueless as to how to find that blasted diamond, Harclay was starting to think hell the more attractive prospect.

The waiters came and went, setting before him an array of etched decanters. And slowly, with great patience, he began to make his way through each of them.

Still he was haunted by the memory of Violet's face, her laugh. Still he could not gather his wits long enough to form a plan or even decide on a first step. Raid all the pawnshops between here and Cheapside? Sidle up to the regent, ask if he'd heard anything about a fifty-carat diamond?

Hopeless, hopeless, nothing short of *hopeless*.

Life was beginning to appear bleak indeed.

Harclay sank farther into the butter-soft leather of his wingback chair, his despair deepening, his mood black. By now he'd drunk enough cognac to fell the Russian army, but Harclay felt no different from how he'd felt two hours before. Either he was on the verge of death or his pain was still besting the liquor.

It was at that moment, when Harclay thought he might indeed be dead, that an enormously fat man collapsed into the chair behind him, nearly catapulting the earl from his. A second, equally fat man sat beside the first.

The back of Harclay's chair faced the back of the first fat man's, so that the backs of their heads nearly touched. The man wore a white powdered wig, the intricately curled, heavily perfumed kind that had been fashionable when crazy King George hadn't been so crazy—in other words, sometime last century.

Harclay was about to turn around, face snarled into a rebuke, when the fat man began to speak.

He spoke in low, languid French, his voice nasal and high, as if he were used to speaking down to company.

"You little rat," he said to the fat man beside him. "How dare you make me wait! A king waits for no man, not even his brother. I passed an hour at cards, which you know I'm not very good at, and everyone looked at me as if I had crossed eyes."

Harclay's ears perked up at the mention of "king."

The second man sniffed. " 'Not very good' is an understatement, dear brother. What is it the English say? Oh, yes. 'Piss-poor.' Ha-ha!"

If Harclay weren't so intrigued, he would've rolled his eyes. Frenchmen were a peculiar breed. These two gentlemen were very peculiar indeed, for Harclay knew them to be the exiled Louis XVIII and his degenerate younger brother the Comte d'Artois, scions of the house of Bourbon.

Those French aristocrats lucky enough to escape *madame guillotine* lived in exile across Europe—in the Low Countries, Russia, Naples, Edinburgh. But because of the political threat the king and his brother posed, and the great debts they seemed to rack up wherever they went, these two corpulent princes had been denied asylum time and time again.

Until, of course, King George III had offered them a cushy welcome in England some four years past. The prince regent continued to support the exiled Bourbons, and the English had watched King Louis XVIII grow from fat to positively corpulent off the generous grants bestowed upon him by Prinny.

For a time Harclay had pitied the exiled king. Poor man had no country to call his own and had lost countless loved ones to a bloody revolution. Surely he deserved to live with all the dignity and respect accorded to him by virtue of his exalted position.

But then White's had extended membership to the French king and the profligate Artois, and Harclay's opinion of them took a sharp turn for the worse. For one thing, the brothers drained all the best liquors from the cellar; for another, they never paid their debts and owed Harclay a rather mountainous sum. Never mind the fact that the Bourbon brothers were rude, overly perfumed, and utter, complete imbeciles.

And now they were seated behind Harclay, crying out at each other in very loud whispers. Harclay slithered back into his seat and snapped open a paper, holding it to his nose while he eavesdropped.

"Let's get on with it," Artois said, snapping at a waiter—probably for more food. "You are wasting my night, and I've somewhere to be. What are you doing in London, anyway? You never leave that little farm of yours up in Buckinghamshire. Has someone died?"

Harclay sensed the king eyeing the room before he burrowed closer to his brother.

"No, you idiot, no one has died," the king replied. "I've come to solicit your aid."

Artois scoffed, taking a long, noisy swig from his snifter. "*My* aid? Last time we spoke, you told me I wasn't worthy to clean your chamber pot. And now you ask for my aid?"

"Trust me," the king growled, "I wouldn't involve you if I didn't have to."

"Well?"

The king's voice dropped lower. "It's a miracle, surely, but

I believe I've managed to locate *le bleu de France*. Just as we suspected, it's been in London all along."

Harclay's heart erupted to a stop. *The French Blue*. The king was speaking of Hope's diamond!

The earl wasn't the only one excited by the news. Artois choked on his brandy, and Harclay heard the waiter pounding his back until the coughing fit passed.

"A miracle indeed, that Napoléon hasn't gotten to it first," Artois replied. "But how are you going to pay for it? Despite your proclamations—the missing jewels *do* belong to the family, yes—these English, they have no decorum. Whoever has the diamond is ransoming it for a hefty sum, surely."

"That's where you come in," the king said. "Your agent. Have him secure a loan. Thirty thousand, no less."

"Thirty thousand! But I don't have access to so large a sum!"

"Listen," the king hissed. "I would do it myself, but no one will lend me any more money. Besides, the war is going against Napoléon. It will only be a year, maybe two, before the English defeat him. And then we shall be restored. What sort of king shall I be without jewels? If you ever inherit the throne you will be glad to have them, too. What is thirty thousand when our royal dignity is at stake?"

Smacking his lips, Artois was silent some moments.

Harclay thought he might jump out of his skin. What luck to have stumbled upon these two miscreants! It made perfect sense the self-proclaimed King of France would be searching for the stolen crown jewels. Napoléon would be furious if he discovered Louis XVIII had gotten to the French Blue before he did. Not only was it a point of pride; it was yet another blow to the diminutive emperor's floundering campaign to claim the world as his own.

"All right," Artois said at last. "I will try to secure the loan. But I want to be with you when you claim the diamond. Who has it? And how did you find it?"

"That crook of a jeweler, Monsieur Eliason. He knows I've been searching for the lost jewels. When he was approached by a 'friend' "—here the king held up a hand—"and no, he would not tell me who that friend was—when he was approached by this man with the diamond, Eliason came to me straightaway."

"A crook indeed. Sold me an emerald a few years ago that turned out to be naught but paste! How do we know he isn't tricking us? I do not trust that man."

The king sighed, annoyed by his brother's surprisingly intelligent line of questioning. "It is *le bleu*, brother; I can feel it in my bones. The diamond was, and always has been, ours by right. And now it shall be ours once again."

"Yes, yes," Artois said and took another pull of his brandy. "Enough with the speeches. You are not on the throne yet. To secure the loan I shall require at least a week. Such a sum is not easy to come by. We may have to ask the Italians."

"Heavens, let us hope not," the king replied, patting his forehead with a lace-edged kerchief. "We have a few days, no more. Eliason is threatening to sell the jewel from under us. Says he has other interested parties."

Harclay very nearly scoffed. *Several* other interested parties, in fact: Mr. Hope, himself, Lady Violet, Mr. Lake, and doubtless the prince regent. That profligate buffoon wouldn't allow such a treasure to slip through his fat fingers.

Artois finished his brandy and belched so loudly half the club looked up from their games and papers and drinks in dismay.

"Very well," he said. "Give me a few days, then. When shall we meet?"

"No later than five days hence. I shall come to you, and together we will meet Eliason."

Artois nodded his agreement. He stood and Harclay felt the heat of his gaze on the back of his head. After a moment the sensation passed, and Artois was gone.

The king called for his wheelchair—gout had felled him yet again this year—and snapped at the waiter for a roast goose to be brought up to his private room.

Harclay had no doubt King Louis would eat the entire goose in a single sitting. And would probably order another.

Feeling suddenly alive with energy and purpose, Harclay set down the paper and slipped out of the club, mind racing.

The earl burst through his front door and began speaking before Avery so much as reached for his coat.

"Avery, what do you know about the exiled French king?

Surely you've an acquaintance, or perhaps an acquaintance of an acquaintance, who has served in his house or knows someone who has."

"Perhaps," Avery replied steadily, taking his master's hat and gloves. "What would you like to know?"

Harclay scratched his chin. It was late, and very dark—well past three o'clock—and yet Avery appeared as pressed and perfectly turned out as he had been that morning.

"Anything," Harclay replied, practically panting with excitement. "Everything. I'm going to need your help on this one, Avery, and I don't know anyone with connections like yours."

Avery bowed, failing to suppress the grin of satisfaction that tightened on his lips. "Very well. I shall see what I can dig up. Discreetly, of course."

Harclay pounded him on the back in gratitude. "Thank you, Avery; your efforts shall not go unrewarded."

"They shall if you die from lack of rest," the butler replied. "Best to sleep while you are able, my lord."

"No sleep for me, Avery. Not with the chase begun anew!"

Thirty

The next day

The warm evening sun that slanted into the library did nothing to alleviate Violet's overwhelming anxiety. Despite her body's plea for sleep, she had spent the previous night awake. Her mind racing, she'd stared at the ceiling until she'd practically gone cross-eyed.

This was bad. Though she'd always considered herself something of a rebel, without a care for society or what it thought of her, even this was outside her expertise. A missing diamond, a lovesick rake, and now—

She couldn't bring herself to even *think* the words.

Never mind the fact that whenever she closed her eyes she saw William, his dark, flashing eyes and handsome face and enormous, hardened hands. Her entire being ached with the desire to feel those hands on her again.

How she missed him every moment of every interminable day. She *missed him*.

Missed him so terribly she could not sleep. Each night her loneliness grew and grew until it suffocated her.

The earl kept his promise; he did not come for her after she refused him.

This is the last time I'll stand before you and ask you to be my wife, he'd said. *I shan't ask again.*

And so, after a night spent in the prison of her bedchamber, then another, and another, Violet had bribed the surgeon's men to assist her down to the first-floor library. She lay stiffly on an overstuffed chaise, a stack of correspondence spread out on her lap in the hopes it would distract her from William's glaring absence.

There were the usual letters, notes from friends, and invitations to balls, breakfasts, garden parties. Mr. Hope's card appeared again and again; apparently he had been over several times in the past few weeks to call on Cousin Sophia. As had that other beau of hers, the one with the castle; the Marquess of Worth of Wormswood or whatever his name was.

And then there were bills—so many bills it made Violet's stomach hurt just to think of them. One by one, the family's creditors were cutting them off. With the income from Violet's shares of Hope & Co. dwindling on account of the missing diamond, she could no longer pay off their debts. The milliner, the grocer, and now the fishmonger were refusing to extend Lord Rutledge further credit until his bills were paid. By now, Violet owed the grocer hundreds of pounds alone.

It was enough to drive a lady to drink.

There was a letter from Violet's solicitor, full of warnings and high-handed advice. He cautioned that, if Violet did not come up with the money in the next week, she would likely have to sell the family's London townhome to pay its debts. She'd already mortgaged the family seat in Essex and quietly sold off their carriages and horseflesh. There was little left to sell, the silver and the jewelry having been pawned long since.

If this house were to be sold, Violet and her family would have nowhere to go.

With a sigh of defeat, Violet gathered the letters in a neat pile and tossed them onto a nearby table. Carefully she creaked to her feet, wincing as pain sliced through her side.

It felt surprisingly good to take her first few steps in as many weeks. Her legs felt wobbly and unsure, but as she made her way toward the windows her steps grew steady. She stopped before an open window, the warm summer breeze tickling the loose hair at her temples.

Behind her, she heard the door creak open. Violet breathed a sigh of relief; she was due for another dose of laudanum, thank heaven, for the pain in her ribs had grown steadily through the morning hours.

"Fitzhugh, is that you? Praise God, it feels as if I'm being stabbed in the side—"

The words died on her tongue as she turned her head.

For standing in the threshold, his dark hair burnished bronze by the light of the sun, was William, Earl of Harclay.

At first she thought he was a ghost, conjured by her delirium; but then he took a step toward her, and another step, his skin glimmering in the light.

He did not disappear.

He was *real*.

Her heart turned over in her chest.

Yes, he'd shot her; yes, he'd stolen the French Blue and in so doing jeopardized her fortune.

But that did nothing to dull her visceral reaction to the mere sight of him. His scent, that heady, delicious scent, filled the room as he stalked toward her.

Violet froze, steeling herself against the onslaught. Her mouth felt suddenly dry and her thoughts—well, they scattered to unknown corners of her mind, leaving her mute and defenseless.

Isn't it just like him, she thought ruefully, to take captive my entire being just by *walking into the room.*

"Good morning, Lord Harclay," she said, turning to the window. She could not bear to meet his gaze.

Violet sensed the earl drawing up behind her, his chest nearly touching her back. She felt his breath on the nape of her neck; he was very close.

"Hello, Violet," he said softly. "How are you feeling?"

She swallowed. "Much better, thank you. The pain is still beastly, especially at night. But it is getting better."

Suddenly she felt his lips brush her ear. "You shouldn't be on your feet yet. Come, let me help you to the sofa."

Violet shook her head. "I'm tired. Tired of sitting."

"Very well," he replied.

Silence settled between them. Violet's throat swelled with tears. She had so much to say; so much, and nothing at all. For she had already refused him—twice—and she knew he was no fool. William would not ask a third time. Her chance to be with him, to become a family with him, had come and gone.

"I've missed you," he said at last. "But you made it very clear that you did not wish to see me again. I can't say that I blame you."

"William, I—" she began but stopped when her eyes flooded with tears.

He took a step closer. His body brushed against hers and for a moment she allowed herself to relax against him, her eyes fluttering shut with pleasure, with relief, at the feel of his solid flesh against her own.

Behind her, Harclay sighed. He wrapped his arms around her, carefully, as if she were made of porcelain. His elbows rested against her hips; his hands on her low belly, as if he *knew*. Knew that beneath the layers of her gown and chemise and skin, a small piece of him grew.

Longing washed over her. She placed her palms over the backs of his hands. For a moment she allowed herself to pretend that they were a family, a happy family. How wonderful it felt to be wrapped in his arms. She felt safe, loved, protected.

This is what every woman should feel, she thought. *This kind of love, unconditional and overwhelming. This is how everyone imagines it should be. How everyone hopes it will be.*

And then William was kissing her lightly on the back of her neck, and she knew she should push him away, tell him that he wasn't making it any easier for her to forget him. But she couldn't find the words, the strength, and so she melted against him, pressing into his lips as they trailed across her shoulder to her collarbone and jaw.

"God, Violet, I've missed you," he murmured.

"I know," Violet whispered. "I know."

One of her hands snaked up to circle the side of his neck, pulling their faces closer. At last their lips met and Violet moaned into his mouth. His kiss became messy and urgent and deep, and together they gasped for air, and for each other.

Slowly his hands wound from her hips to her belly, his

fingers carefully trailing ribbons of fire across her flesh. When he came to her ribs his touch became featherlight, lingering a moment over the outline of the bandages that pressed through her morning gown.

Violet kissed him harder, her body pounding with desire, with pain. She clawed at him, pulling him closer, and his hands wandered up, up, until they covered her breasts.

Before she could protest, he gathered her bosom in his fingers and prodded the soft flesh there with his fingers, running his thumbs over the hardened points of her nipples.

A stream of fiery pain sliced through her at his touch, and she cried out, shocked by this new and unwelcome sensation.

William immediately held up his hands and pulled away, his eyes clouded with concern. "My God, Violet, have I hurt you? Is it your side?"

"No," she panted, blinking back tears. "No, it's not my side."

He ran both hands through his hair. "I am very sorry, Violet; you know I never meant—I would never intentionally hurt you. Dear God, I'm an idiot. I beg your forgiveness—"

"Please, William, that's enough. It's not your fault."

"I just—I just can't seem to control myself around you."

"It's not your fault," Violet repeated and turned back to the window so that he might not see her biting the inside of her cheek to keep from crying.

"Violet." He stepped closer, placing his hands on either side of her neck. With his thumb he traced small, patient circles on her skin. "If it wasn't your side, what was it? Your—er, bosom, I do so hope it wasn't bruised in the accident."

"No," she replied. "It was not bruised in the accident."

"Then what is it?"

When she did not reply, he asked again. "Violet, what is it? You're not telling me something. I can feel it."

She turned to face him, her eyes latching on to his. For a moment she wished to tell him everything, the secret she'd been hiding, the regret that plagued her.

But then she remembered herself, the pain in her side bringing her back to the present. She still suffered from a serious wound; the diamond was still missing; Harclay was still out of reach.

Violet squared her shoulders. "I assume you did not call merely to kiss me."

William surveyed her through narrowed eyes. "No," he said, his voice edged with something akin to anger. "I did not. Don't worry, darling, I haven't come to propose again, if that's what you're thinking. I gave you my word. No more talk of marriage."

"Good," she said, a familiar heavy blackness snaking its way around her heart, making it difficult to breathe. "What did you come to discuss, then?"

He turned toward the room and motioned to a pair of settees. "Let us sit first, shall we? Your legs are shaking. I can see them through your gown."

Horrified, Violet looked down. Surely enough, her skirts were trembling; she hadn't felt her knees knocking together until this very moment. How easily she forgot herself while in this man's arms. Her knees, the pain, their past, her condition—in their moment of shared passion she'd forgotten them all.

"All right," she replied. She took a step—or tried to, anyway—sucked in a breath.

William caught her by the arms, holding her steady in his warm grasp.

"The surgeon said you'd be well enough in a few days," William said. "You should heed his words. What if I hadn't been there to catch you? You'd have broken your other ribs, that's what."

He led Violet to the settee, and propped several pillows beneath her shoulders so that she might be comfortable.

She was breathing heavily, that single step having nearly exhausted her. Perhaps William was right about listening to the surgeon. Violet had never been one to follow directions, but then again, she'd also never been shot in the ribs.

"Thank you," she said. "I may have overestimated myself."

William took a seat across from her with a little sigh, curling back a stray lock of dark hair with his fingers. "It's difficult to stay still for so long," he said. "A few years ago I fell from my horse and broke my leg. After being confined to my bed for a week, I couldn't take it another moment. I got up, got on my horse, and proceeded to fall off yet again, only to break the other leg. That time, I stayed put."

"That sounds just like you," Violet said, a smile rising unbidden to her lips.

"Our blood runs hot, yours and mine."

"Yes. Yes, it does."

For a moment William gazed at her, a silly grin on his face. She grew warm under the scrutiny of his flashing eyes and looked away.

"I have come to share what I hope you will consider happy news," he said at last. "About Hope's diamond."

Violet's ears perked up. "The French Blue! Have you found it yet? Sitting still has been difficult enough, but knowing the diamond remains missing makes it almost unbearable. Please tell me you have it, or you know where it is!"

"I've a good idea, yes," he replied. "It's still in London, if that's what you're worried about."

"Thank God! It's kept me awake these past nights, wondering where it could be. Paris, Rome, Moscow? What a great stroke of luck! Is it the acrobats?"

William shook his head. "We're through with those filthy little fellows, though I'm afraid we've traded them for quite a motley cast of characters."

"I wouldn't expect anything less," Violet said, laughing. "It seems we capture the strangest creatures in our net, wouldn't you agree?"

"Better strange creatures than dull debutantes or half-witted earls," William replied with a smile. "Myself excepted, of course."

"I wouldn't be so sure."

"I knew you'd say that."

Together they laughed, and when they were done a beat passed between them as Violet struggled—and failed—to tear her eyes from his glorious, delicious, wonderfully scented person.

"Why are you telling me this?" she quietly asked. "You forget we chase after one another, the cat and the mouse. Those two do not chase together, not without one devouring the other."

"I would happily allow you to devour me, Violet, if it meant easing the pain I have caused you. I'm telling you because I want you to have the French Blue. Once it is in our possession, it shall belong to you and you alone. What you do with it shall be your decision. I don't believe I'll ever forget the way it looked around your neck, the way it reflected the blue of your eyes. What I would give to see that lovely picture again, Violet—I'd give anything. Everything I have, I'd give it."

Violet swallowed hard and sat up on the sofa.

"You said you had a good idea about where the diamond might be. I think it best we act quickly. Though it may yet be in London, no telling when it might disappear again, and this time for good."

Harclay told her about his stroke of luck at White's. He told her about the enormously fat king Louis XVIII and his brother, the Comte d'Artois, and their plans to secure a loan of thirty thousand pounds and meet the day after tomorrow, so that together they might buy the French Blue from a certain Mr. Eliason.

"That is where we come in," William continued, face alight once again with the prospect of a new chase before him. "I had Avery do a little digging on my behalf—you'd never know it from his demeanor, but the man knows half of London—"

"What did he find?" Violet blurted out. "Is the king a bastard? No, an impostor! The possibilities are endless, just *endless*!"

William cleared his throat. "Well, Avery didn't find much on the king or his brother. Aside from the usual royal follies, of course—eating, a peculiar interest in tiny dogs, that sort of thing."

"Oh," Violet said, deflated. "I always believed royals would choose far more intriguing sorts of sin. Especially the French."

"But"—William held up a finger—"Avery did uncover one interesting tidbit about King Louis. It seems he has a taste for unsavory women."

Violet drew back in surprise. "But the man's big as a cow and can hardly walk! How is he supposed to 'do the deed,' as they say?"

"He doesn't. That's the key. Apparently he just likes to watch."

"Well, that *is* intriguing," Violet replied. "I assume you mean *watch* as in—"

"Yes," William said quickly. "The king prefers to watch the courtesans pleasuring each other."

Violet brought a finger to her lips. "Hm," she said. "I would've never guessed."

"It's common enough," William replied, "especially considering your average peer's diet and drinking habits. Many cannot 'do the deed' themselves, as you say, so they prefer to watch others do it."

"But what has that got to do with the diamond? How will this information about the king help us?"

Harclay leaned even closer, rubbing his hands together with glee. "I've got a plan. And I think you're going to like it. We've got a week, maybe less, to find the French Blue."

Thirty-one

———— ❖ ————

The Ear of Harclay's Residence, Brook Street
Later that evening

The plan—rather ingenious, in Harclay's humble opinion—consisted of the following: assuming she was well enough, Violet and he would lure King Louis to Harclay's townhome under the pretense it was a "Palace of Pleasure." Once they had the king in their possession, they would make him lead them first to his brother, Artois, and then to Eliason, the shadowy jewel merchant claiming to have the French Blue.

Harclay had yet to iron out the details—like how, exactly, they would pry the jewel from King Louis' sausagelike fingers—but it was at the very least better than the plans offered by his fellow jewel hunters.

"It's too dangerous," Mr. Hope said. "What if this Eliason character is setting us up? Why don't we try to find him first and leave that ridiculous man who calls himself king alone?"

"We should just torture Louis," Caroline said calmly, stirring sugar into her tea. "It won't be difficult. We'll just starve him for a day or so. I guarantee he'll tell us everything we need to know."

Harclay rolled his eyes and tugged a hand through his hair. "No one is torturing the *King of France*, Caroline. Especially not you."

They were seated in the earl's drawing room, set to rights thanks to the scrupulous efforts of his staff. If it weren't for the prospect of a very dangerous, very exciting chase ahead, Harclay would've engaged in fisticuffs with Mr. Hope. Had it *really* been necessary to ransack the earl's house, just to prove Hope's point?

"I, for one, like Lord Harclay's plan," Violet said, glancing at him from across the room. "With King Louis at our side, and the thirty thousand Artois brings to the table, I believe we've got as good a chance as any."

Standing by the fire, Mr. Lake placed his saucer and cup on the mantel and crossed his arms over his enormous chest. "I'll help with your plan, Harclay, if you swear you'll hand over Hope's diamond to us. It doesn't belong to you. Never did. I'll need your assurance that you won't be pulling the wool over our eyes. I'll be watching your every step, every movement."

Harclay bowed his head. "I can't say that I blame you, Lake. You have my word as a gentleman; I've no interest in keeping the French Blue myself."

Cousin Sophia cleared her throat. "Then why are you helping us find it?"

Harclay glanced at Violet. She was trying very hard not to blush.

"Because I owe a very dear friend a favor," he replied quietly.

The stain on Violet's cheeks flared. He couldn't help but notice how pale she appeared. Not twenty minutes before, she'd excused herself for a lengthy bout in one of his newly installed water closets. The surgeon had privately assured Harclay that Violet's wounds were healing nicely and that her color would return in a matter of weeks. But the earl knew better; something was amiss, something she was hiding from him.

"Very well." Mr. Hope clapped his hands together. "Where

do we begin? I've a decent collection of costumes and plenty of props. Tell me, Harclay, exactly how far do you want to take this little 'Palace of Pleasure' ruse? I have a . . . a *friend* who might be of assistance."

One week later

The following evening was warm and potent, the kind that hummed with possibility. Harclay and his parade of castmates—Hope, Sophia, Mr. Lake, and Caroline, Auntie George, and even Violet's father, Lord Rutledge—enjoyed an early dinner, then continued to transform Harclay's house from a tastefully appointed earl's residence to a glittering, luscious house of ill repute.

Mr. Hope transported props by the wagonload: enormous marble statues of suggestive nudes, swaths of red satin bedclothes, costumes and jewelry, and even a fat yellow snake he brought back from the jungles of Africa.

"You are quite the collector," Harclay said to him earlier that day, as together they watched the wagons being unloaded. "Do you ever *use* this stuff?"

Hope grinned, a small, lascivious thing. "If the occasion calls for it, yes. Lady Sophia especially prefers the bedclothes—"

"Thank you." Harclay clapped him on the back. "Thank you for your help, Hope. We couldn't do this without you."

The banker glanced sideways at him. "After our ploy is played through, Harclay, and the diamond is once again in my possession—I'd like us to be friends again, if only for Sophia's sake, and for Lady Violet."

"I'd like that very much," Harclay replied slowly. "You know I never meant to hurt you or your business, Hope. I hold you in the highest esteem; why else do you think I keep all my accounts with you? You've a brilliant mind for business, and it is my sincerest wish that our relationship is a long and fruitful one."

Mr. Hope sighed, chewing thoughtfully on his cigar. "I know you can't help yourself, Harclay; I saw that wildness in you the moment we met. Just do me a favor and steal other people's diamonds from now on, would you?"

"No more stealing for me," Harclay replied with a laugh. "At least for the time being. After all this, I've discovered there's nothing more thrilling than a night spent in the company of a clever woman and a table with strong legs."

Hope raised his brow. "A table, eh? That's for beginners. Try a desk. Or before a fire, right on the floor. Add some port and a little medieval art, and you've got a thrill indeed."

Harclay didn't know whether he should laugh or blush, or both.

"You and Lady Sophia," he replied at last. "Are you —"

"No." Hope's expression darkened. "We are not."

Harclay rolled back on his heels. "Well, then. Sorry to hear that, old chap."

"But you and Lady Violet . . . I see you've fallen. Fallen quite hard, by the look of things."

The earl glanced back to the house; the earthy scent of Hope's cigar was strong in his nostrils. "I'm sorry about all this, Hope," he said after a beat. "We'll get the diamond back, I swear it."

Hope rolled the cigar between his thumb and forefinger. He brought it to his lips one last time before tossing it to the ground, stamping out the ashes with the heel of his boot.

He turned and made for the house. Harclay followed a few steps behind.

Hours later, as Harclay's valet put the finishing touches on his master's exquisitely knotted cravat, the earl recalled Hope's words.

I see you've fallen, fallen quite hard.

He was right. Harclay had stupidly, thoroughly, irrevocably fallen in love with Violet. And fool that he was, he'd managed to make a right bloody mess of it by stealing the diamond and leading her in circles, all for his own enjoyment. He did not blame her for twice refusing his proposal of marriage; and yet his heart ached at the realization that she would never be his.

These dark thoughts had no place in tonight's plan. And so the earl pushed them from his mind and instead focused on the evening ahead. At least he would have Violet at his side

for one more night. After that—he would cross that proverbial bridge when the time came.

The valet ran a stiff horsehair brush over the tailored
shoulders of Harclay's blue velvet jacket and stepped back.

"Bang up to the knocker, you are, my lord," he said, eyes
gleaming with pride. "Must say, it pleases me you're finally
wearing one of the patterned waistcoats I selected. Fits like a
second skin."

Harclay surveyed his reflection in the full-length mirror.
He smoothed his palms over the garishly adorned waistcoat—
a thousand embroidered sheep were mewling merrily across
his belly—and smiled. It was just the sort of thing a dandy
might don to visit his favorite paramour.

"Thank you, Knox," he said. "It's perfect. Shall you require
any further instruction on the role you're to play tonight? I
know it is a most unusual request."

Mr. Knox clicked his heels together and straightened his
back. "I shall take my role as chambermaid quite seriously,
my lord, you have my word."

"Remember, you must wait for my signal before you bind
the king's hands."

"Of course," he replied and, in a rare show of emotion,
clapped his hands and nearly leapt into the air. "Oh, my lord, the
staff and I are *so* honored to be a part of your deception. Such
excitement is a rare treat indeed, seeing as things are usually
so very quiet around the house."

Harclay's smile tightened. He swallowed, looking away so
that Mr. Knox might not see the regret flashing in his eyes. He
knew what the valet was getting at: a house full of family, of
children and grandparents and women, was a far happier
place to live than one occupied by a debauched bachelor. For
the first time in his life, the earl agreed with Mr. Knox's
sentiment.

But it was too late for Harclay, too late, and they had a
whorehouse to build besides.

"Let us enjoy it, then, while the excitement lasts," Harclay
said.

With one last glance in the mirror, he turned and nearly
knocked headfirst into Violet.

"Good God, woman, since when have *you* learned to step so softly?" he said.

And when his eyes raked hungrily over the length of her, he said again: "Good God!"

Violet fastened the last button on her jacket and straightened, greeting his incredulous gaze with a wide smile. "Don't you just *love* it? I wish I could wear breeches every evening! So comfortable, though I'm afraid they are not cut to flatter the feminine figure."

She whirled in a little circle before him, the long tails of her jacket rustling against his legs. She was dressed in the garb of a gentleman, complete with top hat and cane. Harclay swallowed, his eyes lingering on the shapely lines of her legs, clearly visible through the tight-fitting material of her breeches. Her long hair was tucked carefully into the hat, which was a smidge too large and sat low on her forehead. Good thing, for hers was far too pretty a face to ever be mistaken for a man's.

He gritted his teeth against the familiar rush of heat in his groin.

"Take it off," he growled. "I'll have Caroline accompany me to The Glossy."

"Take it off?" she said, smile falling. "But it's perfect! And don't think for a moment I'd let you have all the fun. I'm *going* to this rather glamorous-sounding house of ill repute, whether you escort me or not."

Harclay ran his finger along the edge of her sleeve, eliciting from her a small gasp of pleasure. *Ah,* he thought. *So neither of us is immune to the desire that simmers between us still.*

"It's too . . ." He gestured with his hands. "It's too *much.*"

"Too much?" she replied. "Mr. Hope said there's no such thing. And for once, I agree with him."

Digging a hand through his hair, Harclay sighed in defeat. "All right. But we'd better pray every dandy in that 'house of ill repute,' as you so endearingly call it, is dumb with drink. Despite your costume, I doubt anyone in their right mind would mistake you for a man."

Violet glanced in the mirror, turning this way and that. "That's a compliment, I suppose. But it doesn't serve our current purpose very well."

"No, it doesn't," Harclay replied sharply. Each time she turned, his eyes seemed to land on her perfectly pert bottom, the breeches accentuating the delicate curve of each cheek.

Without willing it, a groan escaped his lips.

"Are you unwell?" Violet said, turning to him with wide, innocent eyes.

He swiveled on his heel so that she might not be witness to his embarrassing condition. "Er, as well as can be expected. Come, let's go over the plan with our cast one last time."

The drawing room—now transformed into Aphrodite's Temple of Love—crackled with excitement as Harclay detailed the intricate steps of the plan from his perch before the fire.

"And when Lady Violet and I return from The Glossy with the king in tow, that's your cue, Lord Rutledge, to lead him into this room. Sophia, you'll offer Louis some refreshment from a tray—make sure he chooses the cognac laced with laudanum; I've marked it clearly—and Hope will then appear, weaving a tale of Greek goddesses and the like."

"And then I come in!" Caroline exclaimed, clapping her hands. "That's right, isn't it? Violet and I come to the temple steps—"

"Yes," Harclay interrupted, before Caroline made everyone choke on their wine, "you and Violet come to the steps. You'll dance, twirl your togas, and the like. When the laudanum starts to take effect, Mr. Lake, Mr. Knox, and Avery will discreetly bind his hands. Together we'll haul him to the carriage. Oh, Lady Georgiana, you remembered your wheelchair, did you not?"

Auntie George beamed. "I did indeed, Lord Harclay."

"Excellent, most excellent," Harclay replied with a smile and patted her gently on the shoulder.

"What about the king's feet? Shouldn't we bind those, too?" Lake asked.

"He's too fat to escape, really," Violet replied. "More than anything, binding his hands serves to scare him."

"Lady Violet is correct," Harclay said, clasping his hands behind his back. "Once we have the king in our possession,

we'll have him take us to Artois. We'll get the money and
seek out Mr. Eliason, the jewel merchant, wherever the three
of them have arranged to meet. And then the diamond will be
ours. Hope's, I mean. Simple enough, no?"

The earl couldn't keep the triumph from his voice. He was
awfully proud of his plan, no use denying it. And though he
would never say so aloud, he was proudest of the part of the
plan where he and Lady Violet were at last together and alone.

The room erupted into eager chatter as everyone rose to put
the finishing touches on Harclay's Palace of Pleasure. From
across the room, the earl caught Violet's eyes. She stood behind
a chair, her coat glimmering in the temple-like light of gilded
Persian torchères Hope had purchased for his "Emperor's
Hareem"-themed fete two years before. Her blue-gray eyes
were alive, her color high. For a moment she smiled at him, the
kind of smile that twisted his insides into a happy knot.

It was all he could do not to stalk across the room and
press his mouth to hers.

Instead he grinned, a foolish, lopsided thing that bared his
heart to her as plainly as a spoken declaration.

She looked away, drawn into conversation by her aunt.
Harclay cleared his throat and pulled inordinately hard at the
sleeves of his jacket.

The clock on the mantel chimed the hour: ten o'clock.

It was time to go.

Violet sauntered to his side—the way her hips moved in
those breeches, my *God*!—while the others turned and looked
at them expectantly.

"Godspeed," Mr. Hope said. "And good luck."

Harclay nodded his thanks.

Not that we'll need it, he thought smugly as he escorted
Violet from the room. *After all our plotting, all our hard
work, what could possibly go wrong?*

Thirty-two

Butterflies—and not the good kind—fluttered in Violet's belly as the Earl of Harclay's carriage drew to a stop before The Glossy, a discreet house wedged between two grossly large mansions in a shadowy square off St. James's Street. Its staid entrance loomed in the darkness. The gas lamps on either side of the front door flickered menacingly, two beady eyes of fire staring out into the night.

A now-familiar rush of unsavory sensation flooded her mouth, and for a moment Violet feared she would lose her dinner on the impeccably brushed carpet of William's carriage.

Perhaps her earlier bravado had been premature.

The earl must have sensed her distress, for he took her hand in his and squeezed it gently.

"I will be by your side the entire evening," he said. "You've nothing to fear. Remember we are in our element! A cunning deception, a trap well set, a thrilling chase. You are exceptional at this sort of thing. Keep faith in yourself, Violet. Besides, Hope assures me the madame of this establishment—they call her *La Reinette*, the Little Queen—is a dear friend of his."

"Of course she is."

The carriage door swung open, and Violet followed William

out onto the street. Violet pulled the hat lower over her eyes, and together they made not for the front door but for a small alley that ran along the side of the house.

As if he'd done this a hundred times, William ducked into a hedgerow at the bottom of the alley, pulling Violet in after him. After a terrifying moment of wading through the darkness, they emerged onto a well-lit courtyard at the back of The Glossy. At the far end of the courtyard, an enormous vine of wisteria hung like a hairy brow over a squat, if elegantly paneled, door.

A handsome, impeccably groomed young man opened the door before William even raised his cane to knock.

"Good evening, my lords," the man said, proffering an elegant bow. "Welcome to The Glossy. We've been expecting you. Please, do come inside."

Violet followed William over the threshold. She was at once inundated by a heady mix of potent scents—cigar smoke, sweat, perfume. Tucking her chin into the shadow of her hat, she discreetly surveyed her surroundings. It was far more elegant than she had imagined such an establishment would be, even a fancy one hidden in plain sight in Mayfair. Gleaming carved panels lined the walls, and enormous crystal chandeliers glittered off polished marble floors. The quiet sanctity of a museum, or perhaps a palace, permeated the space, punctured every so often by the tinkle of female voices in a distant room. The air was cool and calm, the light low, inviting.

Violet looked down at her jacket, her top boots, and her breeches. The butterflies suddenly disappeared, replaced by a heady excitement. Heavens, she was parading through a *whorehouse*, dressed as a *courtesan* in the guise of a *man*. If this wasn't fun—well, Violet didn't know what was.

And because fun seemed to be in such short supply these days, she resolved herself to enjoy every minute of this frivolity, this chase, this thrilling episode. She had Lord Harclay at her side, and a white gauzy toga beneath her jacket. She would never be here, playing out this ridiculous plot, again.

Diamond and bullet wound and bills be damned. Pushing her fear aside, Violet would be as brash and clever as she desired tonight. For now, at this moment, she had nothing and everything to lose.

The host led them up a curving stair and paused before a door at the end of a long hallway.

"I'll bring him up when he arrives," he said. "This is the king's favorite room. Shouldn't be too long now."

Harclay tucked a guinea into the man's lapel. "Thank you."

The earl opened the door and ushered Violet inside the room. It was a large and well-appointed chamber, decorated in varying shades of pink and coral. There was an enormous canopied bed tucked into a dim corner, while sensually shaped chaise lounges and a trio of chairs occupied the center of the room. The light was low, inviting.

Violet's gaze strayed to the bed in the corner; her cheeks burned. It made her think of Harclay's bed, the caress of the bedclothes at her back as he moved over her, ardently.

William met her eyes, a small, knowing smile on his lips.

A heartbeat of silence passed between them, then another, another, another still.

At last Violet swallowed.

"Well," she said, glancing about the room, "we should probably make ourselves comfortable."

Violet walked toward an oversized chair marred by an enormous, telltale imprint of the king's enormous royal arse.

"This is the king's room, all right," William said. "It's shocking the man hasn't exploded by now. They say he once ate *twenty-two* beef pies in a single sitting."

Violet sank into the chair, feeling like a child at play on a forbidden sofa. "Imagine witnessing that. I don't think I could ever eat another pie. Heavens, William, however are we going to *drug* a man this size? I doubt there's enough laudanum in all the world to fell a man as fat as the king."

"I told Hope to measure out a lethal dose," William said grimly, falling onto the sofa across from her chair. "Lethal for you and me; but for the king, it will likely just serve to make him a tad sleepy. Though I can't say I've ever drugged a man his size before. It's a bit of a guessing game, you see."

Violet cocked an eyebrow. "You've drugged other men?"

"Dozens," Harclay replied, his tone teasing. "Of course I haven't—well, except myself. But that hardly counts. Why, my sweet, innocent darling, do you ask? Have *you* drugged other men?"

"Yes." Violet grinned. "But only two, and those cads deserved it."

His arm stretched over the back of the sofa, the earl surveyed her with amused eyes. She wondered what he was thinking. Were his thoughts, like her own, a riot of excitement and fear, confusion and heat?

Beneath his scrutiny, Violet grew warm in all the wrong places. The familiar tug of sensation between her legs; her nipples rushing to hard, eager points; a certain breathless tingle coursing through her limbs.

As if he were aware of the desire taking captive her body, William slowly began to lean toward her, eyes never leaving hers. His arm fell from the back of the sofa and rose to caress her face. On her skin his breath felt warm; his lips hovered above hers.

"Violet," he said hoarsely.

"Yes," she replied. It was a question, a command, a plea—all those things, in a single, breathless word.

William leaned in for the kiss, *yes, yes,* and just as his lips brushed hers, there was a clatter behind them.

Pulling away from his caress, Violet leapt to her feet. She tried not to wince at the sudden, searing pain in her side.

William rose to stand beside her. The door swung open, revealing King Louis XVIII's horrified face.

Leaning heavily on his cane, the king cried, "What the devil is this?"

Harclay swept the hat from his head and bowed deeply. Violet also bowed but did not remove her hat. "Your Majesty! What an unexpected pleasure! It appears we've had a bit of a mix-up with our rooms. That butler, bless him, is new to The Glossy and doesn't quite know his way around yet. He must have mistaken your private room for my own. My sincerest apologies, Majesty."

Violet bit back a smile. William was good—*very* good—at playing this game.

The king surveyed the two of them for some moments. Beneath his feet the floor groaned ominously.

"Are we acquainted, my lord?" the king said at last. "Your face, it is familiar."

William rose and smiled broadly. "Indeed, I have had the

pleasure of gazing upon your royal countenance for some time now, at White's. I joined back in '03; I believe you've been with us since '09?"

The king's round face brightened. It seemed even royalty was not immune to William's handsome charm.

"Why, yes, it was April of '09," Louis replied. "An astonishing memory you've got, good man."

"Indeed, I remember it well. Such an honor it has been, to count you as a fellow member," William said and bowed again. "William Townshend, Earl of Harclay, at your service, Majesty. We've gambled a great deal together."

"Ah, yes, Lord Harclay," the king said, a conspiratorial smile on his lips. "I remember you. They say you've bedded half the women in England; even in France I know they speak of you. The ladies of my court are quite enthralled by your"—here the king's eyes flicked to the front of William's breeches—"your *bravado*, as they say."

"The ladies of your court, they are so lovely, and far too generous," Harclay said, ignoring the evil look Violet shot him.

A short silence filled the room. William brought his hat to his chest, as if he were making to leave.

"Best be on our way, then," he said. "Again, my sincerest apologies for this terrible mix-up. I will see to it that butler does not make this mistake again, Majesty."

He had Violet by the arm, and was about to tug her toward the door, when the king took a labored step into the room and spoke.

"Wait," he said, gesturing to Violet with his cane, "who are you?"

Excitement pulsed through her at his words. William had done his part; now it was her turn, her chance to win over the king. She swallowed her fear and, raising her chin defiantly, seductively, she looked into his eyes.

"Who, this?" William said innocently, gesturing to her. "Nothing more than a good friend, Majesty."

Sliding her fingers along the brim of her hat, Violet lifted it from her head and tossed it carelessly across the room. Her hair fell in dark waves about her shoulders and breast; she shimmied her head, just for good measure, and the waves of her hair trembled suggestively around her face.

The king shut the door, quickly, with his cane. He swallowed, eyes wide as saucers.

This, she thought, *is going to be fun.*

"A good friend indeed," he replied breathlessly. "What else can she do?"

Violet directed her most sensual smile at him. "I can do many things, Your Majesty," she purred, swaying her hips as she made her way toward him.

Slowly, with great care, she removed one arm from her jacket, then the other; the garment fell with a delicious *swoop* to the floor. Pausing before the king, Violet began to unbutton her waistcoat, one button at a time.

The king licked his lips, staring. "I do believe I'll sit," he said, holding out his hand. "Harclay, if you would be so kind."

William helped the king onto the chair, his enormous behind settling nicely into its own imprint on the cushion.

"Go easy," William hissed into Violet's ear as he straightened, "or you'll give the man an apoplectic attack."

She shrugged out of the waistcoat and, dangling it from her first finger, allowed it to fall to the floor.

"Oh, yes," the king said, transfixed. "Oh, yes, keep going!"

Violet giggled and tossed her hair in his face. She listened to his sharp intake of breath with no little satisfaction.

From the scowl on William's face, she could tell she was playing her part as a courtesan with aplomb. Whether or not that was a good thing, she had to admit it was quite a rush to take a man wholly captive with her body alone. The king had begun to perspire, dabbing his forehead with a handkerchief. Violet's smile deepened, and she tore off her cravat and shirt with a suggestive growl.

The king's color rose from pink to red to purple in the space of a single heartbeat.

Violet stepped out of her breeches and stood before King Louis, her eyes never leaving his. She wore naught but a single layer of shimmery gauze, artfully draped so as to display her curves to their full advantage.

Beside her, William swallowed, hard. Her smile deepened yet again.

"Might I introduce," he said, clearing his throat when his

voice came out high and tight, "might I introduce Aphrodite, the goddess of love and pleasure."

"My God, Harclay," the king breathed. "Wherever did you find her?"

"Ah, Majesty, a gentleman does not kiss and tell."

"But!" the king sputtered. "But you must tell *me*! She is exquisite, positively *exquisite*! A beauty the likes of which I haven't seen in ages. Is she one of *La Reinette*'s girls? I haven't seen her before. Come, share your secret with me, Lord Harclay, and I promise to tell no one."

William sucked a breath in through his teeth. "I don't know, Majesty. It's nothing personal, you see—"

"I'll give you anything. Name your price—just tell me where I might seek out this lovely goddess at play with all her nymphs!"

William met Violet's eyes; his flashed with triumph, and something else—she recognized that look, a simmering gaze of pain and lust and heat.

For she felt all those things herself.

"Anything?" William said, turning his attention to Louis.

"Yes, anything, anything at all," the king said, gnawing on his bottom lip as his gaze raked the length of Violet's body.

"You must come with us," Harclay replied. "To Aphrodite's Temple of Love."

The king's flabby face screwed up in confusion. "But why can't I just have her here? The Glossy is the finest palace of pleasure in all of London."

Harclay threw back his head and laughed. "You think *this* is the finest London has to offer?"

"What?" The king shifted uncomfortably. "Is it not?"

"Ah, my dear, *dear* majesty, how I pity you." Harclay placed his hand on the back of Louis's chair and leaned down, lowering his voice. "*La Reinette* reserves Aphrodite's Temple of Love for only her best, her most loyal, clients. She has deemed you worthy of the honor."

The king's narrowed eyes shot from Harclay to Violet and back again. Violet returned his gaze steadily, willing her wildly beating heart to be still.

"You know precious little of our great city, Your Majesty.

Allow me to show you the best London has to offer, for the best is what you deserve. There are other goddesses, lovely, like this one." Harclay nodded at Violet. "Goddesses who are most eager to make your acquaintance at Aphrodite's Temple."

Louis surveyed Violet dispassionately, the tiny curve of his frown lost in the fleshy folds of his drooping jowels.

"Very well," the king said at last. Then, with a wave of his shaggy brows: "I am most eager to know what pleasures there await us mere mortals. Though we must make haste, for I've—er—I've an appointment later this evening."

Thirty-three

———— ✦ ————

"Welcome," Violet purred as they made their way to the front door of William's house, "to the Palace of Pleasure, where your every desire shall be fulfilled."

With Harclay's help, the king ascended the last step, panting as if His Majesty had pulled the horses, and not the other way around.

"Ah," the king wheezed. "I do so hope it was worth the trip."

Harclay stretched his back. Dear Louis was fatter, and heavier, even than he looked. "You shall not be disappointed, Majesty. We take our pleasure most seriously at Aphrodite's Temple of Love," the earl replied.

Violet flashed her eyes at the king. "*Very* seriously."

Harclay gritted his teeth against the frustration that flooded his every limb. It was enough that he'd had to watch her strip nearly naked without touching her; but to have another man ogling her, swallowing her whole with his beady, doglike eyes—it had taken every ounce of self-control not to drive his fist into the king's fat face.

Violet played the part of a courtesan well—*too* well, in Harclay's opinion. Not that he'd been surprised by her brash display. She had a lovely shape, and lovelier face, and she knew how to use both to her advantage. That she was clever and confident made her all the more alluring. She made a wonderful partner in crime, and if he weren't so consumed by his desire for her, he'd be enjoying himself quite thoroughly.

But the idea that she was not *his*, that he could never put his hands on her again, drove him absolutely, positively wild.

The near-transparent toga that peeked through the collar of her jacket did nothing to help matters, either.

She rapped twice on the door. As they waited, the king craned his neck to look inside the windows. Though the view was partially obscured by Hope's swaths of red satin, the seductive twinkling of the Persian torches was visible.

The king licked his lips and, turning back to the earl, waved his eyebrows suggestively.

It was all Harclay could do not to roll his eyes.

A moment later, the door cracked open and Lord Rutledge's face appeared. With a barely contained grin, he eagerly swung open the door and ushered them inside.

"Good evening!" he said in a baritone so deep and so loud it made Harclay jump.

Violet placed a steadying hand on his shoulder. "Yes, good evening, Mr. Smith," she said in a quiet voice. "I have as guests the Earl of Harclay and a special friend of his, visiting the Palace of Pleasure for the very first time. We must see to his every comfort, ears included."

True to form, her father ignored the hint and continued to speak in his circuslike baritone.

"Please, gentlemen, follow me. I shall show you to Aphrodite's Temple of Love."

By now, King Louis was panting with excitement. Harclay followed him down the hall—nearly unrecognizable, what with the strange wallpaper and clay pots Mr. Hope had installed—before they came to a halt before the double doors of the drawing room.

With her back to the doors, Violet bowed low. The jacket slipped from her shoulder, pulling the sleeve of her toga with it; Harclay reached out and set the gauze to rights. For half a heartbeat, his fingers grazed the pale skin of her rounded shoulder. She looked up at him, blue eyes wide and naked; between them the air crackled with want.

But just as quickly as she disappeared, the peerless courtesan returned. She ducked out of Harclay's grasp and directed a burning smile at the king.

"Gentlemen," she said, "welcome to my temple. Tonight you shall be treated as kings of all the gods."

Harclay's gaze slid to her bosom. Both of her breasts appeared eager to escape the confines of her toga at any moment. And if Harclay was staring in the hope that such an escape would indeed occur, so was the king.

Balling his fists at his sides—it wouldn't do to bloody the King of France, not with Hope's diamond, and Violet's future, at stake—Harclay swallowed his rage and managed a small, tight smile.

"That's quite enough, Aphrodite." He nodded toward the doors. "Let's get on with it."

"Very well, my lord," she replied tartly, and with a dramatic flourish she ushered the men into her temple.

Harclay very nearly laughed aloud when his eyes fell upon the drawing room. Hope had completely transformed the place into something out of an opera. Swags of red velvet, red satin, and red gauze covered the ceiling and walls. The carpets were strewn with sweet-smelling rose petals, and a virtual forest of candles and Persian torches winked from every available surface.

A stage of sorts occupied the center of the room. It was built to resemble a Greek temple, complete with carved Doric columns and wooden blocks painted to look like marble. At the wings of the stage, a handful of Harclay's handmaids strummed fake lyres and leapt awkwardly about, bearing their pale legs through white cotton togas. A harpist plucked a rather vile tune from some unseen corner.

If there was ever a time Harclay needed a drink, this would be it.

"Please, gentlemen, do sit," Violet said. They followed her to a pair of overstuffed chairs upholstered in—what else?—red satin. Harclay grimly noted that the king's chair was three times the size of his own.

With a smile and a suggestive twirl of her toga, Violet excused herself and disappeared behind the stage. On cue, Lady Sophia then emerged in toga and sandals, her long brown hair loose about her shoulders.

Harclay blinked, and blinked again, not believing his eyes. It was as if he were seeing Violet's cousin for the first time. Gone were the missish ringlets, the frightened, lost expression; in their place bloomed a beautiful, glowing goddess, tall and proud and captivating.

The king, too, gawked, and only remembered to close his mouth when she leaned over him and placed a snifter of brandy in his hand, another in Harclay's.

"For your refreshment," she murmured.

The king swallowed audibly. "Thank you," he replied, still staring.

Sophia drew a single finger across the length of the king's pudgy chest and waited for him to start draining his brandy. When he did not, she settled on his lap and laced her arm about his shoulders.

"Might I offer you anything else?"

The king blinked, as if emerging from a spell. "I should like to see you dance. With the other ladies."

Sophia met Harclay's gaze over the king's head. She smiled slyly at him, a knowing, self-satisfied thing; and before he could stop her, Sophia drew back her hand and slapped the king soundly across the face.

The king's face froze into a mask of utter shock. Harclay would've burst into laughter had Sophia not just seriously jeopardized their *entire* plan. What the devil was the girl doing?

Grasping the king's jowls in her hand, Sophia turned his face toward her. "I am no lady, sir, but a *goddess* of love and beauty. You shall address me as such."

And, apparently for good measure, she slapped him again.

For several long, excruciating moments, the king sat in stunned silence. Harclay hardly dared to look at the man; he waited for Louis to start shouting obscenities, to cry for help, to pour his laudanum-infused brandy down Sophia's toga.

Harclay took a healthy swig of his own. It burned its way down his throat; at once he felt it melt into his veins. He wondered which of his brandies Mr. Hope had selected for tonight. It was good. Very good.

Taking a deep breath, Harclay looked to the king. To the

earl's very great relief, Louis' face broke into a sinister smile as he crooked a finger beneath Sophia's chin.

"As you wish, *goddess*," he mewled.

"That's more like it," Sophia purred. "Now drink up, gentlemen. We've quite the heavenly show for you tonight."

As she stood, the king returned the favor and swatted her bottom. Harclay swallowed the impulse to swat the king, and none too gently.

He took another long, glorious pull of brandy and leaned over to watch Louis do the same.

"Enjoying yourself so far, Majesty?"

The king nodded vigorously. "Why have I not heard of this Palace of Pleasure before? The women—goddesses, I mean!—are beautiful and lively; the brandy is very good. Well worth the trip, good man, thank you."

"The Palace of Pleasure is a well-kept secret among *La Reinette* and a very select group of gentlemen like myself," Harclay replied. "You must understand that we do not like to share our women."

"Of course! With girls who look like *that*, I hardly blame you."

The earl's smile deepened as he watched the king down the last of his brandy.

Now all they had to do was wait for the laudanum to take effect.

The harp swirled to a rather hair-raising crescendo, and Mr. Hope burst onto the stage. Harclay choked on his brandy and was forced to spit it back into his glass. Hope was dressed as a triumphantly muscular Achilles, a brass breastplate (complete with erect, etched nipples) hanging from the leather straps at his shoulders; a toga was slung artfully over his right arm.

He banged on his shield once, twice, and stared down at his audience of two in stony silence.

"In the ancient times," he began gravely, waving his shield at the room, "goddesses of great power lived at the top of Mount Olympus. They were beautiful, nubile, and wise. But to mortal men, they were a danger, a temptation that could not be resisted!"

Harclay couldn't help it; he let out a giggle, which he tried to disguise as a hiccup. Somewhere in the back of his mind he knew Hope's speech wasn't even all that funny; but he couldn't control the laughter that bubbled to his lips.

He managed a glance at the king. As he spun his head the room rolled ominously onto its side before righting itself again. He blinked, dizzy.

He wondered vaguely what in *hell* was *that*; but at that moment Violet appeared, her gauzy toga glittering in the stage lights.

Harclay's mouth went dry. She was beautiful. So beautiful it brought tears to his eyes, which he wiped sloppily away with his sleeve.

He hadn't realized he'd said the words aloud—"Dear God, save me"—until the king leaned over and patted him on the arm.

"All in good time, Lord Harclay," he said. "And tonight there is no God. Only god*dess*."

The earl blinked, trying to focus on the stage. Caroline had joined Violet on Mount Olympus and was leaping about the stage about as elegantly as he'd expected she would.

At first, Violet focused her gaze solely on King Louis, her lips curled into an alluring grin. She was an accomplished dancer, with hips that moved in time to the music. With a flood of longing he remembered their waltz together in Hope's ballroom and how light she'd felt in his arms.

He felt suddenly light himself, as if he were floating on a cloud. The sensation made him at once giddy and nauseated. And when Violet at last directed her gaze at him, he thought he might explode with desire and gratitude and brandy.

What in the world *was* that stuff? He looked down at his near-empty glass, only to discover that he could no longer *see* anything.

Panic spread its wings in his chest. He blinked furiously, to no avail; his thoughts had gone oddly mute, and the sensation of falling—down the stairs, off a cliff, from a ladder—overwhelmed him.

He tried to open his mouth but no sound came out. His chest felt tight, and it became difficult to breathe. Blindly he groped the glass in his hand, his fingers sliding over its cool surface until they came to rest on the telltale jagged chip at its base.

Oh, God, he thought, *my God, I've just drunk the king's laudanum, haven't I?*

And then the falling became too much for him to bear, and he closed his eyes.

Thirty-four

——— ✦ ———

Violet noticed something was amiss the moment she pranced onto the stage. First William laughed, trying (and failing) to pass it off as a hiccup; then she caught him staring at her with tears in his eyes.

Though she had brought the poor man to tears more times than she cared to count, Violet knew the Earl of Harclay was a proud man. He was not one to weep easily; certainly not in Aphrodite's Temple of Love, of all places.

He began mumbling to himself, and even the king reached over to calm him. When at last she met his eyes, they were clouded with confusion. By the time she noticed his panic, it was too late. Eyes fluttering shut, his chin fell to his chest and he tumbled forward off the chair.

"William!" Violet leapt from the stage. She caught him just in time, before he fell face-first to the ground. Her ribs throbbed with white-hot pain as she righted him, calling out his name.

He was out cold. His face had taken on a bluish pallor; he was hardly breathing, a small wheezing sound escaping his pale lips every few seconds.

Mr. Lake, Avery, and Mr. Hope appeared at her side.

"What's happened?" Hope said. "Good God, is he dead?"

"I don't believe so," Violet replied through gritted teeth. "Help me lay him out."

Together Lake and Hope lifted the earl from his chair and laid him flat on the floor; Avery tucked a red satin pillow beneath his head. As he did so, he very nearly stepped on Harclay's empty snifter.

"My God," Avery whispered, holding the snifter up to the light, "we've poisoned him!" His voice rose in horror. "He drank *the king's brandy*!"

"My brandy?" the king said, holding up his own drink. "But I've got mine right here."

Violet snatched the snifter out of his hand. She felt its base for the telltale chip. That was how cousin Sophia was supposed to tell the king's drugged brandy apart from Harclay's: a small chip on the base of the snifter signified its lethal contents.

And there it was, a small chip in the glass, same as the one on the bottom of Harclay's snifter. Sophia had accidentally given William the brandy dosed with laudanum.

Swallowing the bile that rose in her throat, Violet turned to Avery. He was as white as a sheet.

"A doctor," she managed. "We need a doctor!"

"Wait," Mr. Lake commanded, falling to his knees beside Violet. "He won't live long enough to see a doctor. We need to purge his body, and quickly. Avery, bring water, salt, and whatever mustard you have in the house—ground seeds will work—and hopefully we can keep him awake long enough to swallow it."

Avery broke into a run and disappeared from the room; Violet began to shake William, willing her panic to remain at bay. Fear, hot and wild, pulsed through her; tears blurred her vision as her hands worked feverishly to bring him back to life.

King Louis leaned over in his chair. "Excuse me, goddess, I hate to interrupt, but what about the dancing—"

"Shut your mouth, you silly man," Violet snapped. "Would someone tie him up already? Gag him, too, if you please."

The king drew back. "Now, the tying up I wouldn't mind, but the gagging—"

For a moment Violet looked up at him, daggers in her eyes.

"You, *Majesty*, are just as birdbrained as they said you'd be. You're being kidnapped, you fool! And you're going to lead us to the French Blue, so that we might take back what belongs to us."

"The French Blue?" he barked, his face growing red. "It belongs to *me*, *salope*, to *my family*!—"

Before he could finish, Mr. Hope calmly stuffed a sock into his mouth and, together with the valet, Mr. Knox, went to work at the king's hands with a piece of twine.

Satisfied, Violet turned back to William. She tapped the palms of her hands softly against his cheeks. His skin felt cold and wet.

"William," she called, more forcefully, "William, please, open your eyes, William."

Mr. Lake rubbed his hands, his arms. "He's still alive," he said. "Barely."

As they worked, Violet prayed for him. Prayed that he would make it out of this alive, that he would keep breathing long enough for them to help him, that he'd be able to swallow the water, that she would not have to say good-bye to him.

Not tonight, not ever.

"Damn you," she whispered, caressing his face in her hands. "Damn you, William, how many times have we almost lost each other? We are alive, aren't we? What's one more time? *One more time?*"

His eyes flew open, round and wide, as if she'd startled him from sleep.

"William?" she cried.

Avery appeared at her side then, a glass of murky liquid in his hand. He looked to Mr. Lake.

"What you asked for—salt, mustard seed, and water. Are you sure this will work?"

"Sometimes it works," Lake replied. "Sometimes it doesn't. Here, pass it to me."

"No," Violet interrupted, taking the glass from Avery's outstretched hand. "I'll do it."

She turned to William, imploring him with her eyes. "You've got to drink this, William, do you hear me? Drink it all, and quickly."

He blinked, once. Violet took it as a reply of affirmation. Guiding his head into her lap, Violet brought the cup to his lips and tilted it back.

He drank slowly at first; he sputtered. When he'd drunk half the glass, his head grew heavy against her legs and his eyes fluttered shut.

"William!" Violet said, shaking him. "Wake up; there's still more to go—"

Sophia, who up until this moment had stood over them, elbowed Mr. Hope aside and came to crouch beside Violet.

"Allow me," she said. Drawing back, she delivered a ringing *slap* to the side of his face.

William's eyes flew open again and landed on Sophia. Before he lost consciousness, Violet tipped the glass to his lips. He managed to finish most of the emetic.

"William," Violet said, "can you hear me?"

He turned his gaze to her. She was surprised to see a small smile playing at the corners of his lips.

And then, without ceremony, he turned his head and vomited on her lap.

Though she nearly vomited herself at the sight, Violet bent down and kissed William's sweaty forehead, heart thrumming with joy.

"I'm sorry for ruining your toga," he said, blinking. His dark eyes appeared lucid, wide, like a child's.

"That's all right," Violet replied. "I lost my dinner on your shoes at Hope's ball, remember? I suppose the score is settlēd—for now."

"Of course I remember," he said quietly. "You looked so beautiful."

Mr. Lake bent over him and held two fingers to his neck. "How do you feel? I'm afraid we mixed up the brandy glasses and ended up poisoning you instead of *le roi*."

"I'm so very sorry," Sophia said feelingly. "I don't know how it happened—"

Pushing himself upright, William waved away her words. "Think nothing of it, Sophia. Just promise me you'll never again raise your hand to another man—you seem to enjoy it a tad too much. Bloody hurt, too."

Sophia smiled. "I promise."

William held out his hands. "Lake, Avery, help me to my feet. We've still got work to do."

"Work?" Avery nearly yelped. "My lord, you very nearly *died*!"

William rose, wobbling a bit as he took his first steps. "Nonsense. We are too close to the diamond to give up now. Avery, bring round the hack—the king here is going to lead us to the French Blue."

"Are you sure you're all right?" Violet asked.

He looked at her and smiled. "Of course I'm not all right. But you know me well enough by now to understand that I can't resist the chase, even when I'm half-dead."

He continued to wobble, and halfway across the room he lost his footing. Mr. Lake caught him before he fell.

"Someone tell Auntie George," Violet said, dashing to his side, "we're going to need that wheelchair now."

I t took all six of them—Lake, Avery, Hope, Caroline, Sophia, and Violet—to force King Louis out of the Palace of Pleasure. At last Mr. Lake drew his pistol and threatened to shoot the fat royal if he didn't move.

Even then, the king kicked and screamed his way to the carriage. Harclay was waiting inside the unmarked hack, having been helped up the ladder by Lord Rutledge and Auntie George. Though he felt better with each passing moment, the laudanum's lethal effects still lingered in his body. Avery had brewed him a pot of strong coffee, which helped somewhat; but the fact that Harclay could hardly walk concerned him. What use would he be in capturing the diamond?

Leave it to me, he thought glumly, to be poisoned in the midst of my own plot.

The hack groaned in protest as King Louis clambered into the seat across from Harclay's. Good thing the earl had thought to request an extra team of horses; otherwise it would take them ages to get to Artois, and then to the French Blue.

Harclay's heart leapt when Violet climbed into the seat beside him, dressed in a fresh gown and pelisse. Wordlessly he took her hand and squeezed it. She did not meet his eyes, but he saw her cheeks flush a happy shade of pink.

Mr. Lake stood at the open door, his enormous frame blocking out the night. "D'you need my help?" he asked, nodding to indicate Louis.

The king's eyes were wide with fear, his ridiculous wig stuck to the rivers of sweat that coursed down his face.

"I think we can manage, thank you," Harclay replied. "Keep an eye out, Lake, and follow our lead."

Mr. Lake bowed and closed the door. Together with the other players in Harclay's plot, he would follow in a second hack behind Harclay's.

Not letting go of Violet's hand—the earl would hold it as long as she would allow him the pleasure—he reached across with his free arm and pulled the gag from the king's mouth.

At once a string of sordid French curses left Louis' lips. Harclay waited patiently for the swearing to end and, when it did some minutes later, drew a pistol from his waistcoat and pointed it at the king.

"Take us to Artois," he said.

"Go to hell, you bastard. You tried to *poison* me!"

It could've been the laudanum dulling Harclay's reflexes, but in the blink of an eye Violet managed to snatch the gun from his hand. She held it against the king's forehead and pulled back the safety.

"You may think the earl sympathetic to your cause," she said, "but I can tell from the look in your eyes you know I am not. Where is Artois? Where were you supposed to meet him tonight? When?"

Together Harclay and the king swallowed. Violet was downright terrifying with a pistol in her hand.

It thrilled the earl to no end.

"Midnight," the king mumbled. "Near the bridge—Swan Lane. We are to meet there and ride together to meet Eliason."

"And where are you meeting Eliason?"

For a moment the king did not reply, surveying Violet through narrowed eyes.

She shoved the pistol against his head. "Where," she repeated through gritted teeth, "are you meeting Eliason?"

"London Docks," he said at last. "Eliason keeps a ship there."

Violet turned to meet Harclay's eyes. The London Docks, east of the City, in Wapping, were an enormous area and a dangerous place besides, especially at night. King Louis could easily be setting a trap; he could be leading them astray in the hopes that he would lose them in the maze of warehouses and wharves.

It was entirely possible. But what choice did they have? They would have to trust the king, whether or not they believed him. They'd come too far, and had too much to lose, to turn back now.

Harclay pounded the roof with his cane. "Corner of Church and King," he called to the driver. "And make haste!"

Thirty-five

The hack creaked to a stop. Around them the darkness was almost complete; the ancient bulk of London Bridge hovered in the distance.

Harclay's every sense was alive, straining in the dark for a clue, a sign, anything that would lead them to Artois.

He reached across the hack and drew the musty curtains closed.

"When your brother arrives," he said to the king, "you will open the curtain—slowly—and motion him inside."

"He won't step foot inside this heap," the king sniffed.

Violet waved the pistol. "Yes. Yes, he will."

Harclay was glad for the darkness, for he could not suppress the smile of pride that rose to his lips, the longing and love in his eyes as he looked upon Violet's dim outline. There was no hiding from his feelings for her, not anymore.

He wanted to reach out and touch her, let the warmth of her skin lend life to his own.

But she was not his to touch. She sat by his side not as a lover, his betrothed, but as a partner in crime. She sat beside him so that they might reclaim the diamond and restore to her the fortune she had worked so hard to protect.

They waited, and waited, and waited longer still. Harclay dug his pocket watch out of his waistcoat and checked the time.

Ten past twelve.

"As you well know, my brother is something of a—how do you English say it?" the king said, searching for the word. "Ah, yes, a loose fish. He is always late, running from the club, or his mistresses."

And so they waited some more.

At last, when Harclay had begun to pinch his legs to keep himself awake, the sound of an approaching carriage broke the silence.

It grew louder until it suddenly stopped. Harclay peeked through the curtain and smiled when he saw an enormous carriage—Artois' carriage, it had to be—making its way back down the street, away from them. A lone figure waited in the shadows of the lane.

Harclay nodded at the king. "Open the curtain," he said. "Motion for him to come in."

With a sigh of annoyance, the king did as he was bidden. Harclay heard the sound of a carriage door opening and closing and then a small tapping on their own door.

Violet pressed the gun to Louis' head. "No false moves," she whispered.

The king swung the door open. Artois stood on the street, the smells of liquor and cigar smoke wafting off him like a poisonous fog.

"Louis, is that you?" Artois said, hiccuping. "Louis, dear God, what sort of coach is this? Reeks of common folk."

"Have you got the money?" Louis replied.

Artois patted his breast, weaving a bit on his feet. "Indeed I do. But how I do know you won't take it for yourself?" He ducked his head into the hack. "Wait a moment, who is that—"

An ominous one-two click sounded behind Artois. Mr. Lake's looming figure appeared in the lane, a gun in each hand.

"Get in the carriage," he growled to Artois. "Make a sound and I'll kill you."

Eyes as round as saucers, Artois held up his hands. "What the devil is this?"

Grasping the *comte* by his cravat, Mr. Lake shoved his bulbous person into the hack and slammed the door unceremoniously behind him.

Lying spread-eagled on the floor, Artois was too stunned to speak.

"I'm afraid, brother dearest, we've got company," the king said grimly.

Violet aimed her pistol at Artois. "Give me the note."

The *comte*'s tremulous gaze darted from the king to Violet and back again.

"Give her the note, Artois," the king said, voice rising with impatience.

With shaking hands, Artois managed to pull the folded note from his jacket. He handed it to Violet.

She held it up to what little light streamed through the curtains.

"How much is it for?" Harclay asked, straining to take a look.

"Thirty thousand," Violet said, folding the note before handing it to him. "Looks genuine enough to me."

Harclay slipped the note into his waistcoat pocket and banged the roof of the hack, calling for the London Docks. They creaked slowly into motion; with both the king and his brother inside, the hack probably weighed more than a house.

While the hackneys were hired, the coachmen were not; they were Harclay's men. He prayed they knew their way around the East End, where they were headed. It would not do to be lost in so squalid a place as Wapping.

"Who are you?" Artois spat out, looking up from the floor at Harclay. "And what do you want?"

Harclay smiled and leaned forward. "The French Blue, of course," he said. "And you're going to help us get it."

William's strength was fading. Violet could tell by the way he winced with every jolt and shove of the hack as they rode toward the Docklands.

Her own wounds had begun to pulse as the nervous, thrilling excitement of the evening wore off. Praise God she had not torn her stitches during the whole "Palace of Pleasure" episode, but she had certainly bruised her ribs anew as she brought William back to life.

The Comte d'Artois' stench did not help matters; more than once she thought she might empty her stomach all over the hack. Though after everything they'd experienced in the last handful of hours, what was one more horror, one more embarrassing, foul-smelling incident?

Her heart raced faster and faster the closer they came to the docks; the anticipation was unbearable. She had a bad feeling about what lay ahead. They were going to one of the most dangerous areas of the city, a thirty-*thousand*-pound note in their hands, to seek out a shadowy figure they'd heard about but never met. What if this Eliason fellow proved to be no better than a thief himself, or worse, a murderer?

She fell back against the seat, trying to still the shaking that had started in her hands and was now spreading up her arms. The gun felt cold and heavy in her lap.

As if reading her thoughts, Harclay reached over and took the pistol. For a moment his hand lingered, his fingers brushing against hers. She took a deep breath and allowed herself to melt into his touch.

"Soon," he said. "Soon."

Soon we will have what we came for.

Violet smelled the river before she saw it. A hint of water and salt, overwhelmed by the odors of fish and unwashed men and sewage.

She swallowed audibly. She was *definitely* going to be sick.

William laid his hand on her knee.

"I'm all right," she said. She turned away from him so that he might not see the nausea written so clearly on her face; but with his hands on her she did feel a rush of faith, of fortitude, to face whatever came next.

The hack pulled to a stop. Violet squared her shoulders.

Mr. Lake opened the door and helped Violet and William to the ground. While Avery, Lake, William, and Mr. Hope pried the king and his brother from the hack, Violet walked to the edge of the water and quietly lost her dinner.

There was a tap on her shoulder. "Violet," William murmured, tucking a stray curl behind her ear, "that's the second time I've seen you sick in as many days. I want to know the secret you've been keeping from me. You don't have to tell me tonight, but whatever is happening, I know it's got something to do with me. I'll have the truth, if only so I might help you to feel better. Here."

He pressed a flask into her hand.

The thought of brandy made her gag. "No, thank you, I'd rather not—"

"It's water. Wash out your mouth."

Violet did as he bid her; the water felt clean on her lips.

"Thank you." She tried to pass him the flask, but he held it against her breast.

"You keep it."

Tucking the flask into her stays, she took a breath and managed to smile. William clasped her arm in the crook of his own and led her back to the waiting hackneys. King Louis and Artois were leaning against a hack, catching their breath after the exertion of climbing out of it.

Mr. Lake and Mr. Hope stood off to the side, pistols in hand, with Caroline and Sophia.

William approached the two royals. "You know where this man Eliason keeps his ship?"

Neither Artois nor the king answered. Harclay stepped forward, waving the thirty-thousand-pound note before them.

"I've already got your money. Don't make me take your manhood, too. Do you *know* where this man *Eliason* keeps his ship?"

"Oui," Artois sniffed.

"And you will lead us to him?"

Before Artois could answer, the king stepped forward and motioned to their small crowd. "Yes. But we cannot take all of you. Eliason is a greedy man but he is not stupid. If he sees so many coming, he will turn up his tail and run."

Artois nodded. "Yes, he will run. We will only take two."

Mr. Hope shook his head. "It's a trap, Harclay. If these two won't lead us to Eliason, then we'll find him ourselves."

Violet looked over her shoulder at the vast, darkly glittering pit of the docks. A few tiny lanterns punctured the night, but otherwise the blackness was complete. There was no sound, save for the quiet lapping of the Thames, the slow, weary creaking of the ships. Somewhere a horse whinnied; in the distance, she could hear the muted cacophony of a tavern.

Unless William was indeed the cutthroat pirate she imagined, they would never be able to navigate the docks, much less locate a *single* man on a *single* ship.

"No," Violet said, stepping in. "Lord Harclay and I will go with the king."

Everyone erupted in protest. Mr. Lake warned that William may collapse again; Caroline noted that Violet did not look very well herself; Avery wrung his hands; and Mr. Hope growled that he did not trust Harclay with the diamond, not for a bloody moment.

"You have my word, Hope," Violet said, looking Hope steadily in the eye, "I will return the French Blue to you."

Hope's gaze slid to the earl. "You must understand why I question your loyalty, Lady Violet," he said, eyes flicking to William.

"I do." She nodded. "But you've got to trust me. Trust us. Lord Harclay's the one who started all this—let us, together, finish it. Mr. Lake is too big, too obvious. He's liable to scare Eliason witless. And you, Mr. Hope."

Violet looked past his shoulder, at Sophia. "You have other matters to attend to."

A beat of silence passed as Hope considered Violet's proposal.

"Very well," he said at last, Sophia's hand on his arm. "But make no mistake, Lady Violet. If you're not back here in half an hour with my diamond in hand, I'll search for you myself and have you both thrown in jail. Do I make myself clear?"

William rolled his eyes. "Set your watch, Hope: we shall be back before the stroke of one with your precious diamond. You forget I was the one who fooled you all and stole the French Blue out from under your noses; and I will be the one to get it back again."

Violet could not suppress the smile that bloomed alongside the pride in her chest. William had been poisoned and smacked silly by Sophia, but he was still up to his old tricks. And she had no doubt he *would* find the diamond.

Then all would be well in the world and she could go back to her family and her fortune and her life.

A life without William.

Violet pushed the thought from her head. There would be plenty of time to think of that later; she had William at her side and the French Blue within her grasp, and she was going to enjoy the thrill of the chase one last time.

"Let's be off, then," William said, cocking the pistol and aiming it at the king. "Ready, Majesty?"

King Louis and the Comte d'Artois exchanged glances. They pushed off the hack and drew to their feet. Artois accepted the lantern Avery proffered, having stripped it from the coach; and then, together with Louis and Artois and William, Violet descended into the darkness.

"Remember what you promised me!" Hope called after them.

Artois led them along the edge of the docks. Weathered storehouses lined the lane to their left; to their right, a thirty-foot drop into the River Thames. A thousand ships, and then a thousand more, creaked quietly on its surface. Ropes snapped and rubbed against the plank docks below; sails crackled in the breeze.

Pausing before a stuccoed arch, Artois held up the lantern to a small wooden sign that swung from a beam overhead. It read: LONDON DOCK, EST. 1805.

Before them loomed a tall wooden door, bolted to the arch with an enormous iron lock.

Artois turned to them. "I don't have the key," he said, shrugging innocently. "I suppose we shall have to turn back."

William held up the gun. "Don't make me strip you to your skivvies, Artois. Take out the key and unlock the door."

"You heard him," the king said, dabbing the sweat from his forehead. "He doesn't have the damned key. Now let's go!"

William jammed the pistol against the *comte*'s chest. "Get the key or I'll shoot. I will, *Majesty*. Best not test me."

Violet watched as Artois glanced at his brother. Almost imperceptibly Artois nodded; then he turned back to William and smiled smugly.

"I do not have the key to open this door. Go ahead, shoot

me. Eliason will hear the shot and scurry off, and the diamond will be gone forever. Take us back to the carriages and bring us home. I demand it. Enough of these stupid games. I am tired and hungry!"

Violet's heart rose to her throat. What the devil were they to do now? Artois was right. If the diamond merchant—never mind the guardsmen—heard the shot, they would be done for, all they'd come for lost.

William, however, appeared to harbor no such reservations. In the space of a single heartbeat, William swung round his outstretched arm, aiming the pistol at the lock. Unlatching the safety, he gritted his teeth and pulled the trigger.

Violet had just enough time to cover her ears with her hands. She fell back from the tremendous sound of the report and the bullet tearing its way through the lock. Both the king and his brother jumped, eyes and mouths agape; William caught Louis just before he fell over the edge and into the water.

The lock buckled; the door swung open.

"Now," William panted, nodding at the door, "take us to Eliason."

This time, the royals did not protest.

Artois led them down an ominously rickety stair onto a wide quay. Triple-masted ships bobbed on either side of the dock; in the shadows they appeared enormous and sinister, alive with the motion of the Thames.

"Stay close," Artois murmured, holding up the lantern. "No doubt every thief and murderer in this godforsaken place heard that racket you made."

In the darkness, Violet saw William smile. "My intention exactly," he said. "Now they know to leave us the hell alone."

He took her hand and held her back a pace or two, allowing Artois and the king to walk ahead of them.

"What is it?" Violet whispered. "Are you all right?"

His hand felt clammy, cold; his palm was covered in sweat.

"Yes," he said. Her heart shot to her throat; the strain in his voice implied otherwise. "I can see it in your eyes: you're afraid. But we will do this. Stay by me, and follow my lead."

Yes, she replied silently, *I'm afraid for* you.

But she merely nodded, looping his arm through hers for support. At first he did not lean on her; but the farther they walked, the more he leaned on her, until she was supporting almost all his weight. Her side ached; pain stabbed through her with each step.

Luckily enough, Artois and his brother the king set a very slow pace—really, it was a miracle their bellies hadn't swallowed whole their legs yet—and Violet was able to keep up.

"A few more steps," Violet whispered to William. "Just a few more, one foot in front of the other."

He was breathing in hard, short wheezes. Violet pulled and pulled, her legs burning with the effort. For once she wished Harclay weren't so tall nor so broad; it felt as if he weighed as much as a horse.

Just when Violet thought she might collapse, the Comte d'Artois suddenly stopped and held up the lantern to a low, sleek vessel. On its wide bow, the ship's name was scribbled in slanting, elegant script: *Diamond in the Rough*.

Violet would have laughed if she weren't on the verge of tears. After all this—kidnapping a king, the costumes and the Palace of Pleasure and the poison—she could have found the shadowy Mr. Eliason herself.

"Stand up if you can," Violet whispered to William. "It won't do for these men to see you like this."

William did as he was told. In the yellowy light of the ship's lanterns, Violet saw the color drain from his face. He was in pain. A lot of it.

Silently she took the gun from his hand and tucked it into the waist of his breeches.

Artois motioned for them to follow him around the ship's stern. Violet stayed close to William, her heart pounding as they rounded the darkened corner.

"Vous êtes en retard," a voice, gravelly and low, sounded from the blackness. You are late.

The king sniffed. *"Mieux vaut tard que jamais."* Better late than never.

Artois held high his lantern, and the man to whom the voice belonged suddenly appeared.

Together Violet and William drew back. The man was quite literally a giant, nearly seven feet tall and as wide as a horse.

As if he weren't enough to scare one witless, a second,

identically giant man emerged from the darkness at the first man's side.

Violet nearly choked.

Giants. *Twin* giants.

And they were staring her down with a wicked gleam in four identical eyes.

"No funny business," the second giant said in heavily accented English. "Give me your weapons, yes?"

When no one made so much as a move, the first man stepped forward. Without ceremony he reached into William's coat and pulled out the pistol. Violet's heart dropped.

"Fool, we heard the shot," the giant continued. "Do you have any others?"

William stood very still and held up his hands. "No, no other guns. Just the one."

The giants searched him for good measure; they searched the king and Artois, too. When they turned to Violet, William stepped in front of her.

"Lay a hand on her," he growled, "and I'll kill you both with my bare hands, *comprenez-vous*?"

For a moment the giants looked at William, amused by his bravado.

"All right," the first one said. "Come. Mr. Eliason waits for you."

Violet followed the giants' enormous shadows, each a night unto itself, up a narrow gangplank. With each step her ribs pulsed, white-hot pain.

They clambered onto the deck, the king and Artois leaning against the ship's balustrade to catch their breath. The *Diamond in the Rough* was an old but well-kept vessel, the deck was scrubbed clean, and the ship just barely bobbed beneath their feet in time to the wavelets on the river. At the bow was an open space, occupied by coils of thick rope and several barrels. A cabin occupied the stern, accessed by a squat, rickety door. Its glass windows blinked with candlelight from inside.

"Remember," the giant said as he led them toward the door, "no funny business, or this."

He made a twisting motion with both hands, followed by a violent crack over his knee.

The giant gently knocked on the door.

"Come in!" a voice called.

The giant opened the door and stepped aside.

King Louis was the first to enter the room, followed by Artois, then William and Violet.

Violet ducked as she crossed the threshold. It was a small, low-ceilinged room that stank of tobacco and salt water. A large table, covered with boxes of all shapes and sizes, occupied most of the space; several tiny, unmatched chairs took up the rest.

Behind the desk, a spritely man with a shock of orange hair leapt to his feet and bowed before the king.

"Ah, yes," the man said, a wide smile on his wide lips, "Majesty, what a pleasure to see you again. I see you brought with you some friends?"

"Eliason," the king replied, voice edged with disdain. "A pleasure, as always. Those goons you employ, they were rather rough with us."

"Ah, yes," Eliason repeated. He gestured to the boxes on the table. "A necessary precaution, I'm afraid, what with all my precious cargo."

The king sighed, rubbing his eyes. "As for my friends—it's a bit of a story, one I do not have time for. So let us get to business. Show me the diamond. The French Blue—you know the one."

Eliason rubbed his tiny, square hands together. "Ah, yes," he said. "But first the money."

The king and Artois turned to William. Pulling the note from his waistcoat pocket, he wedged between the royals' rotund bellies to place it on the table before Eliason.

"And you are?" Eliason said, eyes raking William from head to toe.

"It doesn't matter who I am," William replied steadily. "We've given you the money. Hand over the diamond."

The jewel merchant pursed his lips, his eyes never leaving William. "I procured the French Blue for the King of France, and the King of France alone. My clientele, you see, is quite a select group."

William placed his hands on either edge of the table and leaned forward.

"I won't ask again, Mr. Eliason," he growled. "You have your money. Thirty thousand, good as gold. Now *show us the diamond*."

His pale eyes dancing, Eliason grinned, a slimy, sour grin that lent him the look of a snake.

Fear shot through Violet. She didn't like this man, not one bit; whatever William was doing, it irked Eliason. And Eliason, despite his size and strange hair, seemed the kind of man one did *not* desire to irk.

A beat of silence. Then another.

"Very well," the jewel merchant said.

Tugging open a drawer, Eliason pulled out a small, empty tray lined in red leather. He placed it on the desk. He turned to the wall behind the desk where a shabby, if graphic, painting of a mermaid hung in a gilt frame. Eliason carefully lifted the painting off the wall, revealing a small black square—a safe-box!—that glimmered in the light of the candles. A clever contraption surely; but not quite as cleverly concealed.

She watched with bated breath as Eliason removed his watch from his pocket. A tiny gold key dangled from the watch chain; Eliason inserted it into the safe-box keyhole. He turned the key, slowly, and the safe-box door swung open.

Violet strained to see inside the safe, but the merchant's cloud of carrot-colored hair blocked her view.

Closing the door and locking it back up with the key, he turned to face his audience.

His grin had deepened to a sinister smile. In his hands he clutched a velvet pouch. He slowly, very slowly, opened it with his short, squat fingers, his eyes all the while never leaving William's.

Beneath the desk, Violet touched her foot to his. The creases of tension along Harclay's mouth and eyes receded; her pulse slowed its frantic pace; *perhaps,* she thought, *perhaps we will make it through this alive after all.*

She felt the pull of the French Blue before she saw it, that strange, magnetic energy that caused the hairs at the back of her neck to prickle; though it did little to lessen the shock of seeing the jewel, actually *seeing* it, when Eliason pulled it from its pouch and laid it carefully on the tray before him.

Hope's diamond glinted and flashed in the low light of the

room. It appeared inky blue, a shiny dark blot upon the red leather; a stain that lured each of them to rise to their toes, draw closer.

For a breathless moment, everyone stared in stupefied wonder. It was a jewel worthy of a king, an emperor;

It sparkled, sending shards of such brilliant light across the cabin. The stone glittered green, then violet, then blue and green again; for a moment it even flashed red, transforming into a succulent, seductive clot of bloodred flame.

The diamond, it was casting a spell on them; Violet sensed it in every fiber of her being: a certain chill tingle at the base of her neck.

Artois licked his lips; the king let out a low moan; but William—he was smiling, color rising to his cheeks.

She saw the light return to his eyes, the vital intelligence so essential to his being at last restored.

The William, Earl of Harclay, she knew and loved was back. His blood ran hot; his hands itched for action; his thoughts turned in a whirlwind of plots, plans, deceits.

But Violet hardly had half a heartbeat to revel in his return.

For at that moment there was a tremendous shatter that shook the ship whole.

The door crashed open. Avery tore into the room in a cloud of smoke and ash.

"It's done," he panted. "Everyone off the ship—she's burning!"

William turned to Violet, who was mute with shock, and grinned.

"I told you Avery's got a strong back."

Thirty-six

The poison was having its way with him, but Harclay's heart leapt nonetheless at the sight of Avery crashing through Eliason's door.

Quick as lightning Harclay turned for Eliason, who appeared as if he'd just had his head lopped off; his face was frozen, a mask of terrified surprise.

Mustering what little strength was left in his limbs, Harclay gritted his teeth and leapt for the French Blue. His muscles screamed with pain, blood thundering through his veins, and still he pushed, and pushed some more.

He landed hard against the desk, sending everything on its surface flying—including the French Blue. It darted across the desk and into the dark puddle of the floor.

"You bloody fools!" Eliason shouted. He fell to his hands and knees and desperately scavenged about the ground, growling curses all the while.

Harclay followed suit, launching himself onto the floor. He ran his hands over the floorboards, invisible in the dim light of the cabin; nothing, nothing, save crumbs, dirt, and the boxes that fell from the table.

Above him, Harclay saw the Comte d'Artois make a dash

for the thirty-thousand-pound note—it, too, had fallen to the floor—only to tip over onto his belly. With a little cry he began rolling about along with the ship's undulations.

Harclay would've laughed if he'd had the breath to do so. Instead he turned back to the ground and began his search anew for the diamond.

His heart was pounding a steady beat inside his chest, and then—then it hiccuped, and took a moment to begin beating again. Harclay closed his eyes; the laudanum was having its way with him.

He opened his eyes and glanced about the cabin for Violet. She was cowering in a corner, hands grasping the wall behind her for support. He knew that look: she was about to be sick again.

"Violet," he called out, his voice hardly more than a whisper. "Violet, darling, please—"

Before he could finish, Eliason's giants trampled through the door behind Avery. The butler put up a good fight, but the giants pushed him aside as if he weighed no more than a feather, and then they bore down on Harclay, twin pairs of eyes blazing with dark intent.

He tried to scurry away, tried to stand. But again his heart hiccuped and his breath fell short, and he landed heavily on the ground.

This was bad. Very, *very* bad.

The giants reached for him. Their fists felt as heavy and sharp as battle-axes as they pummeled him, jabbing, pulling, tearing at his flesh. They lifted him from the ground and tossed him across the cabin.

He landed hard against the wall. The pain was so overwhelming that for a moment his vision dimmed. When he came to, he tasted blood in his mouth and felt it dripping down his face.

"Kill them!" Eliason was shouting. "Kill them all! Then help me find that blasted diamond before we're all burned alive!"

An enormous, ominous groan shuddered through the ship. There was a great cracking sound, and a blast of heat shot through the open door. The *Diamond in the Rough* listed sharply to the side; everything, and everyone, slid across the floor.

Avery had done a thorough job of torching the ship—perhaps a bit *too* thorough, as it seemed they had only mere minutes before she sank with the lot of them—and the French Blue—on board. With the munitions supplied by Mr. Lake—Lord knew how the man had managed to scrounge up such heavy cannon—it came as no surprise.

Still, that meant Harclay would have to act quickly. No matter the twin giants or his hiccuping heart or the missing diamond, he had a handful of minutes, no more, to grab Hope's gem and escape safely with Violet and Avery in tow.

Again the ship lurched violently to the side. Smoke billowed through the door into the cabin. Harclay choked, the air suddenly dense, pungent, and opaque. The king screamed, a high-pitched thing; Artois rolled on his belly, grasping fruitlessly at the air; Violet—his pulse quickened—where was she?—he couldn't see her.

Behind him, the giants managed to scramble to their feet. He felt a violent tug at his back, and they resumed their attack on him. One of them pulled him upright and held him steady while the other delivered a ringing blow to his belly, and another and another and another.

The giant holding him suddenly cried out, releasing his grip. The other giant's eyes went wide.

As if on cue, Violet appeared at Harclay's side. In her hand she held his silver flask and was wielding it as one would a sword. With a force he would not have thought her capable of, she brought down the butt of the flask on one giant's head, then whirled around to slam it into the other's cheek.

Both giants fell back, weakened from the smoke, and clutched their heads. Violet did not stop. She pounded them again and again, the flask a metallic whirl in her hand as she bloodied Eliason's men.

At last, Violet managed to beat the giants through the door and out onto the burning deck. Satisfied, she turned back to Harclay and cradled his face in her hands.

"You look terrible," she said to him, eyes wet with tears. "Come, let me help you. We've got to get off this ship—"

Harclay held fast—well, as fast as his wobbly legs allowed. "No," he replied softly, wrapping his hands around her elbows. She was shaking, but hot to the touch and alive with exertion.

"No, Violet, I'm not leaving without Hope's diamond. We've come too far—it's too important to you, your family— I owe this to you—"

"We've got to go," she said, looking him in the eye. "Remember what you said to me: *none of this matters, has any meaning whatsoever to me, if you are gone.*"

Harclay smiled; even through the pain and the blood, he smiled. "You've got a good memory, Violet."

"Even one so callous as I," Violet replied, grinning, "could never forget so good a line. Come, we've got to go!"

He shook his head. "*You* must go, Violet, you must go now. I'll be right behind you, I swear it. I've just got to find the diamond."

But before Violet could reply, Eliason emerged from the haze and dashed by her, grazing her with his elbow. With all her strength, Violet pushed against him, throwing him against the wall.

In the midst of the smoke and the fire, Harclay caught a peculiar dark sparkle emerge from Eliason's hands and soar through the air. Whatever it was, it soared through the air and landed somewhere very close to the earl's feet.

His heart leapt, then sputtered.

The diamond.

It was the French Blue. *At his feet.*

He heard a fleshy *clap* and turned to see Eliason grabbing at Violet, pummeling her face and arms with his tiny hands. She cried out, trying to fight back, but for so little a man he was strong, and he was fast.

Wrath, rage, fury like he'd never known before rushed through Harclay and took captive his body. His limbs snapped into action as if guided by an unseen force; *one, two, three*, his fists found purchase in Eliason's cheek, jaw, temple.

One, two, three: belly, chest, shoulder.

When it was over, and Eliason slid to the ground a bloody, blubbering mess, Harclay turned to Violet and pulled her against him.

"Are you all right?" he asked, smearing her face with blood

as he ran his thumb across her cheek. "My God, Violet, I'll
kill him—"

"Don't," she said. Her voice shook as she spoke, but she
straightened, squaring her shoulders. "William, let's *go*."

A great, gurgling rush of water roared through the door. It
pooled around his feet and sopped the hem of Violet's dress.

By now the smoke was so thick Harclay was unable to see
much at all. Somewhere in the haze he heard Eliason moaning and the king and Artois choking as they rolled about the
floor. Harclay's own lungs felt as if they were stuffed with
cotton; his eyes and nose and mouth burned and blood trick-
led down the back of his throat.

He had a handful of minutes, maybe less, before the smoke
finished him off.

Nothing like waiting until the last minute, he thought
wryly.

"Go," he said, holding Violet very close so that he might
look into her eyes. "Go now."

"I won't leave you—"

"Go!" he said. Without waiting for a reply, he gently
pushed her to the door. The water was now up to his knees.
"Can you swim?"

"Not really," she replied, pausing.

He cursed under his breath. "If you go now, Violet, you'll
be able to jump from the ship onto the dock. Go, do it now!"

And he pushed her again, this time out the door. The
smoke clouded the distance between them.

And then she was gone.

With her went his strength. The pain returned with a searing
vengeance. His eyes watered and burned and he could barely
see. The water against his legs was cold and foul smelling.

He didn't have much time.

Gritting his teeth, he turned back to the cabin. All but the
very back was underwater. Somehow the king and Artois had
risen to their feet and were now clasping each other by the
elbows, moaning and cursing as they splashed toward the door.

Through the smoke, the king glared at Harclay, his fat fingers scrambling to save what was left of the wig on his head.

"You scum! You bastard!" he cried, waving the wig at the
earl. "Look, my favorite wig is *ruined*!"

"Never mind your bloody wig," Artois grumbled. "What about my life? The note for thirty thousand, it's gone! Poof! Just like that. What if it floats down the river and some fisherman picks it up? The Italians, they will have my head!"

He turned to Harclay, eyes blazing with hate. "We ought to beat him, brother, right here, right now, for what he's done to us."

The king slapped the wig back onto his bald head and turned on Harclay. Together the royals tottered toward Harclay, waving their polished canes menacingly.

Harclay would've laughed if it weren't for the weak numbness spreading through his limbs. Any other day he could outrun and outsmart these egg-shaped idiots without breaking a sweat. But today he was afraid.

The earl fell to his hands and knees, the water seeping into his breeches and coat. Frantically he felt about the floor for the diamond. Eliason had dropped it *right here*—or was it over there, by the table?—it was impossible to tell . . .

King Louis and Artois were very close now. Artois reached out and with his cane swatted Harclay on the arm.

He scooted away from them, running his palms over the submerged floorboards. Nothing; he couldn't see or feel anything, save the slowing beat of his heart.

He looked up and through the fog saw Eliason's giants rising behind the king and Artois. Panic flooded his every sense. How in hell had they survived Violet's attack? With a bit of luck he could outwit the royals; but together with the giants— it was too much.

Pain radiated up his right arm; it gave out.

Harclay's left arm managed to hold him aloft for half a heartbeat before it, too, gave out.

He fell with an unceremonious splash into the water, face-first.

The water was so cold that Harclay almost didn't feel his nose pound against something sharp and hard.

Again he tasted blood. But something else, too: something akin to excitement, relief, a thrill that shot up the length of his spine.

With what little strength he had left, he grabbed for his nose but found instead a small, hard object with razor-fine edges.

He knew without looking that it was the French Blue.

The diamond.

Hope's diamond.

Harclay fell back on his haunches and pulled the jewel from the water. Even in the haze, it glittered seductively, flashing blue, red, purple. For a moment he stared at it in disbelief.

The diamond felt heavy in his hand, and cold. As if under a spell, he was hard-pressed to stop staring. There were few things in this world more beautiful, more alluring, than this jewel.

Very few things.

In fact, the only one more beautiful was Lady Violet Rutledge.

Harclay blinked, one last pulse of strength rushing through him at the thought of her. He had to get out of here, and quick, so that he might yet salvage her family, her future, her fortune.

He tucked Hope's diamond into his jacket. With no little effort he managed to rise to his feet. As soon as he was upright, however, he came face-to-face with King Louis and Artois; at his back, he sensed the giants approaching. They grabbed his arms and twisted them behind his back.

Helpless against the onslaught, Harclay bit his lip against the ringing blows the royals delivered to his person. Bastards were stronger than they looked; their canes felt as if they were made of steel.

As if four against one weren't enough, Eliason suddenly emerged from the smoke. His eyes were bloodshot and crazed.

Pushing aside the royals, he shouted, "Where is the bloody diamond, you scum, where is it?"

When Harclay did not reply, Eliason drew back his fist and flung it into Harclay's cheek.

He saw stars, and then he was falling, falling, and landed hard on his knees. Even then he struggled to remain upright, but at last he twisted and fell on his back into the water.

Eliason was holding him under. Harclay's lungs burned with the desire for air. He waited and prayed for a reprieve, but none came. Eliason's grip on him was firm, and without air, he hadn't the strength to fight back.

This is it, he thought wildly. *So this is how it all shall end.*

His eyes flew open underwater, one last look at the world. The water burned his eyes, but he resisted the impulse to close them.

For, to Harclay's great surprise, and even greater relief, his gaze met that of Avery.

Last the earl had seen him was sprawled on the ground, blood dripping down his face on account of the giants' ministrations.

Avery winked at him, his hair fluttering wildly about his head in the water, and waved something white—paper, it was a piece of paper—before his face.

Harclay winked back, just before his vision dimmed. The burning in his lungs became unbearable; he felt as if his entire body might explode.

There was a great rush of pain from his toes to the very top of his head.

And then there was nothing.

Thirty-seven

———— ✦ ————

London, Mayfair
Two weeks later

It was the Rutledge family's last night in the London house they had called home for five generations. There were too many bills that had to be paid, too many debts to settle. And so Violet had been forced to sell the home in which she and her father, and his father before him, had been born.

There were trunks and crates everywhere. Standing at the back door, the family's solicitor scribbled furiously in his ledger as each crate was carried out. Nearly everything, save their clothes and personal effects, was being sold. Even then, Violet knew they would be hard-pressed to settle all their debts.

"Well," the solicitor said, slamming shut his ledger, "I believe my work is finished here. I shall be back in the morning to make the final arrangements."

Violet stared blankly at the deepening darkness, arms crossed about her ever-increasing bosom. If only William could see her now; pleasurer that he was, he'd probably enjoy her changing body, the widening curves, the new, aching sensations. And in his hands—God have mercy—such spots would be plied and teased and pleasured to their full effect.

Swallowing the moon that rose in her throat, she pushed the thought aside. No more thinking of William. He was gone, to heaven or hell or India, she did not know. But he was gone nonetheless; it had been two weeks now since that hellish night on board the *Diamond in the Rough*, when she'd seen him last. No one had heard from the earl or seen him. His house was dark, and when Violet called, no one answered the door.

Harclay had disappeared.

It made Violet ache to no end.

She squared her shoulders. No matter her aching; she had other things to think about, matters to tend to. And such matters would not wait.

"Thank you, Mr. Riley," she replied, still staring out the open door. "We shall be leaving for Essex in the morning. Please do be early."

Mr. Riley bowed curtly. "If there is anything else—"

"No, thank you. You may go."

He turned to leave, but at the last moment he hesitated.

Violet turned her gaze to him. "Yes?"

Clutching his ledger in his hands, he said, "I'm awfully sorry about all this, my lady. You understand I did everything in my power to keep you here."

A beat passed between them. Violet managed a small smile. "Of course."

Bowing a second time, Mr. Riley offered a sympathetic smile. He turned and left.

Violet uncrossed her arms and closed the door. Behind her, the kitchens were oddly quiet. Cook, and Cook alone, was preparing their last dinner, a simple meal of cold bacon, bread, and butter. The lonely sound of a single knife, slicing a single loaf of bread, was enough to break Violet's heart.

Above stairs, everyone gathered at the table in silence. There were no footmen left to serve them, so Violet sat beside her father and helped him cut his bacon and butter his bread.

Halfway through the meal, Auntie George began to weep. Her weeping grew steadily noisier, so noisy that Sophia, too, started to cry.

Violet very nearly rolled her eyes. If the thought of brandy did not make her retch, she would've raided her father's liquor cabinet on the spot. It was enough to keep her own emotions in check; but witnessing her family's heartbreak made her feel exhausted and utterly defeated.

And still she could hardly think of anything but William. Yes, her world was crumbling all about her, but *within* her another battle raged. She tried to forget him, to accept that he was either dead or a cad who'd run away with the diamond, her fortune, her heart.

But day and night he stayed with her. He followed her through the motions of her day, from breakfast to tea and back into her bed at night. She hardly spoke or ate; his memory, it seemed, was enough to sustain her. But when across the pillow she reached for him, imagining the feel of his shirt in her fingers, the tears came heavy, hot.

He was gone, he was gone, *gone*, and there was nothing she could do to bring him back.

The regret she felt was suffocating. Only when he'd left, disappeared, died, did she allow herself to embrace her love for him. It swallowed her whole, eviscerated her.

But it was too late. The earl was not coming back. She would never have the chance to apologize, to beg him to take her back, to say *yes, yes, darling, I will be yours today and all the days after that.*

The shock of losing him kept the truth at bay—that she'd never again feel the thump of his heart as he pressed his chest to hers, that she'd never have the chance to curse at him one last time, the chance to witness the lust that sparked in his eyes.

She would have to face that truth someday.

Today, however, was most certainly *not* that day.

Later that evening, as Violet made her way up the wide stair for perhaps the last time, she paused, clenching the polished rail as if for life itself. Her side hurt, and her never-ending nausea was particularly virulent this evening. She stood very still, listening to the sounds of the house. The creak of the floorboards in Sophia's chamber; the soft ticking of the clock in the hall downstairs; a clacking carriage passing outside the front door.

And then—a muffled *clap*.

An unfamiliar sound.

Heart pounding, Violet crept across the landing to her chamber door. She pressed her ear against the wood, listening.

Nothing.

Slowly she turned the knob and pushed the door open.

The room was dark, save for a single candle on the table beside her bed. Its flame danced in a warm gust of air that blew in through the open windows.

The open windows.

Earlier that day, Violet had closed them against the evil smells rising from the lane below. Fitzhugh was ill, and she'd returned to her chamber after helping Violet dress that morning; the other servants had been dismissed a week since.

No one could have opened the windows.

Except an intruder.

Violet's heart leapt in her chest. There was only one man she knew daring enough to climb three stories and through her window.

With, of course, the aid of a strong back.

She turned back to the room, breathless.

"William?" she whispered, choking on her tears. "Is that you?"

Silence.

Violet took another step into the chamber, closing the door behind her. She reached for the candle and held it aloft as she swept across the room. She looked under the bed, peeked inside her wardrobe. She ducked her head out the window and looked both ways down the street.

Nothing. No one.

William was not there.

She fell heavily onto the bed, wiping away her tears with the heel of her hand. Placing the candle back onto the table, she collapsed against her pillow in anticipation of a good, long cry.

A *crunch* sounded beneath the weight of her head. Bolting upright, Violet reached behind her and found a packet of thick paper placed carefully on the center of her pillow.

William.

His scent rose from the paper as surely as if he were in the room himself.

A familiar endearment, written in familiar script, was scrawled across its surface.

Darling.

For a moment Violet thought she might be sick all over the bedclothes.

She cracked the Earl of Harclay's wax seal and tore open the envelope. A small card fell into her lap, followed by a folded sheet of wrinkled paper.

Violet opened the card and in a single breath read the note aloud.

This should cover the two thousand I owe you. Yours always, W.

She glanced at the folded sheet in her lap. The paper appeared worse for the wear, wrinkled with water stains and marred by muddy blotches.

Taking the sheet in her hands, she carefully unfolded it. Its edges were frayed; she winced as she accidentally tore off a corner with a fingernail.

She held her fingers to her mouth and cried. And cried. And cried. So many tears, she could hardly breathe in the tiny beats between them.

Violet held in her hands the thirty-thousand-pound note the Comte d'Artois had procured to buy back the French Blue. Like all flimsies, the note bore the name of the issuing bank— in this case, an Italian house based in Florence—but made no mention of to whom, exactly, the note belonged.

The note, and the accompanying fortune, belonged to whomever possessed it.

And now it belonged to Violet. For now, at least. How like William, the blackguard, to believe stealing thirty thousand pounds from French royalty fell under the same romantic notion as stealing a priceless diamond. She'd have to give it back; Violet was many things—drinker, cheater, adventurer (albeit one prone to injury)—but she was not a thief. As much as it pained her, she would return the money to that rascal Artois.

Eventually, that was.

Surely he wouldn't miss a thousand or two, perhaps in exchange for her goodwill. Just enough to pay off her creditors, keep the house, repair the family vehicle . . .

It was, after all, only money.

* * *

The next morning Fitzhugh ran breathless into the break-fast room.

"What is it?" Violet asked with alarm, dropping her tea-cup with a clatter. "Is something amiss?"

Fitzhugh merely shook her head and handed Violet an enormous packet inscribed with the finest calligraphy. "For-give me, my lady, but this just arrived. Thought you'd like to see it straightaway."

For a moment Violet stared at it, pulse racing. "Did you see who delivered it?"

Fitzhugh again shook her head. "Some strange fellow, bruises all over his face and his arm in a sling. Stooped over, too, as if it pained him to stand straight. Very polite, though."

Violet could not suppress the smile that rose to her lips. Poor Avery.

"Well?" Cousin Sophia said. "Open it!"

With trembling hands Violet opened the packet.

"It's an invitation," she said, furrowing her brow as she read it.

To His Grace the Duke of Sommer
and all the ladies of his house,
His Lordship the Earl of Harclay
requests your presence
At a Masquerade Ball
This evening, at half past eight o'clock.
A prize shall be awarded
To the jewel who shines brightest.

Violet met her cousin's eyes across the table.

"Well?" Sophia said, voice high with anticipation.

"We're going to need Mr. Hope's help. Mr. Lake's, too—come, Sophia, we haven't much time!"

Night fell lightly upon the city, the slow dimming of a lovely summer day. The weather was fine and warm; stars blinked awake one by one across a bluebell sky.

Perhaps it was the prospect of seeing William, after presuming him dead, gone forever these past weeks; perhaps she was relieved to finally end this chase, in the hope of beginning another; or maybe it was a revived hope that William had recovered the French Blue, so they might return it to Hope and share in the success of his bank.

Whatever it was, Violet felt magic in the air around her. The breeze wove a spell; she could feel it coming to life just beneath her skin. She stood before the open window in her bedchamber, the summer air tickling stray wisps of hair about her temples as she waited for the night to begin and the magic to unravel.

At last it was time. Cousin Sophia came to her door, all smiles and glimmering gauze. Violet had convinced her that they should wear the same nymph costumes they'd donned for Hope's ball.

"Otherwise, he might not recognize me," Violet had said, pressing her domino mask to her face.

"Oh, for heaven's sake," Sophia replied with a roll of her eyes. "Lord Harclay would recognize you anywhere, dressed in anything. The man's got eyes for only you."

Violet climbed the familiar steps of Harclay's town house arm in arm with her father. She leaned heavily against him, glad of the support he offered her; she trembled with anticipation as they crossed the threshold.

A thousand questions swirled in her head with every beat of her heart. Was William really alive? Where had he gone? Was he hurt, was he still reeling from the accidental poisoning, and, God *damn* him, why hadn't he written sooner? The diamond—had he managed to rescue it from Eliason's clutches? Or was it gone, lost forever to the River Thames?

If he was indeed alive, and he did indeed show his face tonight, Violet didn't know how she'd react. Part of her longed to kiss him wildly, to have her way with him right there in public; the other part itched to slap him soundly and turn her bare shoulders to him, torturing him with the knowledge that he could've had her shoulders, and all her other bare parts, if he'd only behaved.

Together with Cousin Sophia, Auntie George, and her father, Violet was escorted inside by a masked footman she did not recognize. It was not yet nine o'clock and the crush was immense. Every member of *le bon ton*, it seemed, had turned out at the earl's last-minute invitation, and in extravagantly inappropriate costumes. Every guest wore a mask and a mischievous grin; apparently Violet wasn't the only one who enjoyed the anonymity of a masked ball, the titillating possibilities it presented.

The house blazed with light and life; it was impossible to imagine that just days prior it lay empty, its dark windows gaping at passersby. That familiar scent—William's scent—invaded her every sense. For a moment she closed her eyes and allowed relief to wash over her at the mere presence of the house, of *him*, around and in and above her. For two weeks now she'd believed she'd never step foot in this house again. Now that she was here, she was not about to pass the precious time doing anything other than relishing the fact that he was alive. And he might yet be hers again.

Just over her shoulder a man cleared his throat. Holding the domino mask to her face, Violet whirled about. Her eyes fell on a somberly dressed man stooping uncomfortably before her. His right arm was tucked into a sling; with his left he held aloft a silver tray, on which rested a small, square note.

"Avery!" She gasped in disbelief, heart dropping to her knees. "Are you—does it—might I—oh, heavens."

"Indeed," he said with a grin. He lifted the tray. "My lady, this is for you."

Violet eyed Avery as she took the note in her hands. "Thank you."

Before she could ask him how he'd found her, or who'd sent the note, he disappeared into the crowd.

Assured that no one was watching, Violet excused herself from her father and slipped into a dimly lit alcove toward the back of the house.

Her gloved fingers were clumsy and slow, but she managed to tear open the letter nonetheless. She unfolded it quickly, in her haste dropping it not once but twice to the floor.

Her heart pounded ruthlessly as she read it.

The waltz. Save it for me.
When I see you dressed like that, I am indeed an expert
in wood.

Yours, W.

Violet raised her eyes and looked about the alcove and
adjacent gallery, hoping to find William there, waiting for her
with a sly smile and a coupe of champagne.

She found nothing but a whirl of masks and laughter, people milling clumsily about. Desire perfumed the air; she was
drowning in her own, set ablaze by the three blunt sentences
she read over and over again.

Violet had to find him. Never mind that waltz; she couldn't
wait that long. Tucking the note inside her stays—good *God*,
it was tight in there, tighter than the day before—she slipped
from the alcove and lost herself in the search for William.

Thirty-eight

———— ✦ ————

"There you are!" Mr. Hope exclaimed, pulling back his mask. "We thought you'd abandoned us, Lady Violet."

Violet bit her lip to keep from swearing. She had hoped to avoid her fellow plotters, her impatience rabid and wild to at last put her hands on William and feel his on her own body.

"I would never," she replied wryly. She looked past Hope's broad, rounded shoulders into the cavernous ballroom. She'd never seen so many people; how was she ever going to find William?

Her heart sank.

"Our plot is still in play, yes?" Hope said, raising a brow.

Violet sighed. "I gave you my word, Mr. Hope. If Wil—if Lord Harclay does not hand over the diamond tonight, we'll have him arrested. But he's here; I know he's here. And if he's got the French Blue, he'll give it to us."

"I wish I shared your unwavering faith in Lord Harclay," he replied. "I do hope you're right, Lady Violet. This business has gone on long enough."

"I couldn't agree with you more. Now if you'll excuse me, Mr. Hope, I was just on my way—yes, on my way to the retiring room. I'm feeling a bit flushed."

With a nod of her head, Violet scurried into the ballroom. The dancing had already begun. A string quartet filled the space with loud, boisterous music, and dancers thundered across the crowded floor, clapping and twirling in time to the beat.

She did not recognize a single face, each hidden behind a mask. He'd done it on purpose, that *cad*; William had intentionally hosted a masquerade ball so that he could watch her, see her, without allowing her the same courtesy.

Stamping her foot in frustration, Violet accepted a glass of punch from a footman and pretended to sip it as she pushed her way through the ballroom. Behind curtains and fans, couples engaged in explicit games of seduction; a few women fainted, taking care to keep on their masks as they did so; old men ogled said women freely.

All this, and yet no sign of William. She felt his presence everywhere, in the music and the sweet-smelling punch and the scent of the air. But he was nowhere to be found.

Just as her eyes were beginning to well with tears of disappointment, she sensed a peculiar prickling at the back of her neck. In her chest her heart skipped a beat.

Violet *knew* that sensation—the feeling that someone was watching her, his gaze boring through the layers of her skin and setting fire to her blood.

It was William.

She whirled around, pulling the mask from her face.

Frantically she searched the crowd around her, looking for his dark eyes, his dark hair, that dark smile.

Nothing, save a sea of masked faces, gleaming silks, mouths wide with laughter.

She blinked, straining her eyes. Was she missing something? He couldn't have gone far; he was close, very close, she felt it—

"The next dance," a voice, low, rumbling, whispered in her ear, "is a waltz."

A shiver shot up her spine at the feel of his lips against her skin. Her eyes fluttered shut.

When she opened them, he was gone.

Struggling to catch her breath, Violet pushed her way toward the dancing in the center of the ballroom.

The music swelled to a rousing climax and ended abruptly two beats later. The room erupted in the spirited clatter of polite clapping and drunken shouts for *more! more!*

Ducking onto the dance floor, Violet looked about for a sign, any sign at all, that William was here, and that he indeed intended to dance a waltz with her.

For a moment the ballroom filled with the conversation of a thousand guests. And then, to gasps of shock and delight, the leading lady and master of the dance together announced a waltz. A stunned silence descended upon the crowd.

Violet swallowed, heart pounding so loudly in her ears it was a miracle no one else heard it.

The dancers began to pair off, two by two. In the flurry of coupling, Violet turned this way and that, standing like a fool by her lonesome in search of a beau who might never come.

The room spun about her, a whirl of color and light and sound. Where was he? Had he run, leaving her stranded for everyone to see?

Her lips burned. She'd never longed for anything like she longed for his mouth against hers.

A note was played, and then another. Violet turned and turned, eyes raking the crush about her. She'd know those shoulders, that tapered waist, anywhere, even here, surrounded by hundreds, thousands of bodies.

Panic pulsed through her. *William wasn't there.*

The music bloomed to life, heady and hypnotic. Around her the dancers began to move. Men with their straight backs and splayed fingers; ladies, their skirts whispering, their bosoms pressed ever so slightly against their partners' chests.

If only William knew how willingly, how *thoroughly*, she'd press her bosom to his chest—would he come for her then?

Ignoring the stares of the dancers that spun around her, Violet continued to search for him.

Out of the ether a warm, callused hand slid around her own. The hand pulled her around, and around again, and then Violet was facing a tall gentleman wearing a black leather mask. His eyes flashed; his shape—it was so perfectly formed, angles and slopes and sinew, it made her heart skip a beat.

It was *him*.

The breath left her body as he tugged her to him, enveloping her with a single arm. His hand slid to the small of her back, fingers digging into her stays.

She couldn't speak. Neither did he.

William pulled her against him and pulled again, their bodies gasping for each other, insatiable. His hands on her were firm and brooked no resistance.

Fire sliced through her, white-hot desire that made her limbs feel drunk with need.

He took a step; she followed. They began their dance, her eyes never leaving him as they worked their way, *one-two-three*, through the steps.

She felt the fire seeping back into her spirit as he looked at her, a small smile playing at his lips. He was alive. He was here.

He was *hers*.

For a moment, at least.

Violet had so much to say, but for now she was content to stare, swallow him with her eyes.

He appeared healthy, and happy. His face was bright with color and bore no trace of the poison or the episode on board the *Diamond in the Rough*.

She didn't realize she'd been holding her breath since the dance began until it ended. She exhaled long and hard as the music ground to a stop around them. William loosened his grip on her—*no!* she wished to cry, *keep holding me*—and stepped away, bowing.

Violet blinked.

When she opened her eyes he was gone, disappeared as if he were never there at all.

"William?" she whispered, turning, and turning—

There was a small breeze at her back and then a strange, cold weight against her chest. She caught William's scent just before she looked down at her bosom.

The French Blue winked from between her breasts. It hung from the very same collar of white diamonds Hope had lent her that fateful night some weeks ago.

Polished and gleaming, it bore no trace of its long, bloody journey to this very spot, this very moment. In the light of the chandeliers it appeared more blue-black than gray; its facets winked purple and red and nearly blinded her with their brilliance.

She swallowed the nausea that rose in her mouth.

William, Earl of Harclay, had at last returned the French Blue.

"But how—?" she said, throat thick with tears. She brought her fingers to the diamond, as if to assure herself that it was real, that the jewel that once belonged to the *kings* of *France* was now hanging from her neck.

How the devil had Harclay managed it?

Again she looked up and searched for him. By now guests had begun to stare, forming a circle around Violet. Behind their masks they whispered, pointing to the enormous diamond that glittered from her bosom.

William was nowhere to be found.

The bastard had *left*, escaped into the anonymity of the night.

Heart pounding, she tried to think. He couldn't have gone very far. If she found him, she might catch him before he was gone forever.

And she had a good idea where he'd gone.

Gathering her skirts in her hands, she plunged into the crush, shouldering a passage through the sea of bodies. It wasn't easy—a woman spilled her punch down the back of Violet's dress, and a trio of gentlemen as fat as bears refused to move until she stomped their bejeweled feet—but at last she made her way out of the ballroom and into the gallery.

Moving as fast as her legs would carry her, Violet pushed past the crowd to the back of the house. A footman carrying a tray of champagne coupes was just emerging from a door at the end of the gallery. Violet flew past him, ducking through the door just before it closed.

In her haste, she nearly fell down the narrow servants' stairs. The smells of the kitchen grew stronger as she descended into the bowels of the house: roast chicken, butter, the yeasty tang of freshly baked bread.

Violet ran headfirst into a handmaid, causing the poor girl to cry out and drop the mop and pail she was carrying.

"Oh! Oh, dear, I'm sorry," Violet said, helping the girl

collect her instruments from the floor. "You'll have to forgive me; I'm in a bit of a rush—"

Without looking back, Violet darted into the kitchen.

Though the cavernous space bustled with activity, her eyes fell on the large plank table in the center of the room.

The cook, a small, round woman with white hair, looked up from her cake. Her face creased into a smile.

"And where do you think you're going?" she said to Violet, her pastry bag of icing poised in midair.

"I—I'm looking for—"

The cook nodded toward the back door. "He's thataway, my lady. Just missed 'im, you did. You'd best hurry!"

Violet didn't want to ask how the cook knew she was looking for William—had the woman heard them that night on the table?—and instead thanked her and leapt into the narrow servants' hall.

Running, running, her lungs burning with the effort, Violet turned a corner. At the end of the hall she saw a man slip through the back door, his coattails nearly catching between the door and frame before they disappeared altogether.

"William!" Violet panted. "Wait, please wait!"

She reached for the door and yanked it open, the warm night air rushing to meet her as she tripped into the drive.

"William?" she called. She looked right, looked left.

The drive was crowded with carriages of every shape and size, horses chuffing at one another in annoyance. Twenty paces ahead, the shouts and laughter of drivers, groomsmen, and hired hands sounded from the stables.

Out of the corner of her eye, Violet caught William's dark figure slipping around the side of the house. She bolted after him, gravel flying from the heels of her slippers.

Breathlessly she rounded the corner, reaching out with her hands as if to catch him by those elusive coattails.

All she managed to snatch were two fistfuls of thorny rosebushes.

Cursing, she pulled back her hands and sucked gently on her sliced fingertips.

"Damn you, William, where did you go?" she cried out to the night, stomping her foot.

This side of the house was deserted, save for the coaches

that lined the drive. It was quiet here and very dark. Even though it was warm outside, she shivered, and for the first time wondered at her foolishness. She had Hope's diamond around her neck and all the world at her feet. What was she doing here, alone in the dark, searching for a man who *clearly* didn't want to be found?

Tears welled uninvited in her eyes. She wiped them away with the backs of her hands, willing her heart to harden, her feet to move back toward the house and the masquerade. Mr. Hope, Sophia, all the others would be waiting for her; they would not wait forever.

She looked into the night one last time. Disappointment pulsed through her.

He was gone.

William, that rogue, that delicious, conniving wonder of a man, was gone.

Violet turned and began to trudge toward the house. Just a heartbeat or two before, her legs were as wings; now they felt heavy as lead. She didn't want to go back; didn't want to face whatever came next. Not without *him*.

A strange creaking noise sounded behind her, followed by the unmistakable clatter of a team of horses trotting down the drive.

Taken entirely off guard, Violet spun around, nearly losing her footing in the process.

Out of the darkness emerged an enormous carriage, lac-quered in a familiar shade of blue. Though the horses hadn't slowed their pace, the carriage door swung open.

Two arms appeared from inside the carriage, followed by a familiar face hidden behind a black leather mask.

Before she knew what the masked man was about, he reached for her and in one strong, steady movement whirled her up and into the vehicle.

Violet tumbled to the floor of the coach in an ungainly mess of skirts, stockings, and slippers. As if she hadn't cursed enough that day, she cursed one last time for good measure. Though her dress was up over her ears, and she could hardly see, she heard pleasant, rumbling laughter beside her.

"You!" Violet gasped, trying in vain to calm the sea of gauze. "You, how dare you! I demand you unhand me—"

And then his mouth was on hers, pulling, biting, caressing, a savage assault that left her breathless. She knew those lips and the smell of that skin.

It was William.

He hooked his hands under her arms and hauled her onto the seat beside him. The kiss knocked her backward and he fell onto her, the feel of his weight against her delicious. She held his face in her hands and inhaled him with her every sense.

At last he pulled back. She opened her eyes and met his, gleaming dark in the light of the carriage lanterns. Taking the mask in her fingers, she pulled it from his face and blinked, and blinked again, just to be sure he wasn't a dream, a trick of her imagination.

William bent his neck, kissing the tender skin of her throat. She let out a little breath and he kissed her again and again and again.

"You," he said between kisses, "had me"—another kiss— "worried, darling."

"I had *you* worried? Good heavens, William"—her eyes fluttered shut as his lips grazed a particularly sensitive stretch of skin—"I believed you *dead*, drowned in the Thames!"

"Oh, come, Violet, surely you think me worthy of a better, more thrilling end than that?"

She would've smacked the smug smile from his face if she weren't so happy to have him in her arms. "How did you manage it?"

William shrugged, as if it were the most natural thing in the world to have escaped from a burning ship, two giants, a pair of imbecile Frenchmen, and a bloodthirsty jewel merchant— and with Hope's diamond in hand, no less.

"I admit I cannot take credit for my dashing escape," he said. "Avery not only managed to get me off the *Diamond in the Rough*; by some miracle he saved King Louis and the *comte*, too."

"A strong back indeed," Violet said, shaking her head in disbelief.

William hoisted himself onto his elbows and fingered Hope's diamond. "And all for this little thing," he said. "You should keep it, Violet. I've always believed it belonged to you; it's a perfect match for those lovely eyes of yours."

Violet looked down at the diamond and sighed. "I don't think so. It's caused enough trouble already, and besides, it's a bit much, even for me."

William's smile deepened. "Ready for our next adventure, then?"

Violet looked away, her throat suddenly tight. "*Our* next adventure?"

His hand slipped to her swollen breast. A current of understanding passed between them. Violet's heart began to pound as the smile slowly faded from his lips.

"Why didn't you tell me?" he said, voice low, soft.

She smiled weakly. "You were dead, remember?"

"Fair point," he conceded. His hand traveled from her breast to her belly. "Even after all the excitement of these past weeks, I do believe *this* next adventure shall be quite a thrill."

Her pounding heart grew wings and took flight. Mute with tears, she nodded her agreement.

"We couldn't have timed the birth of our baby any better if we tried," he said, his smile returning. "February, if I'm not mistaken? She—or he—will be born in the very same room I was, at my country seat in Oxfordshire. If, of course, you'll make me the happiest man in all England and become my wife." He thumbed her chin and tilted her eyes toward his. "Violet, I've wanted you from the day we met. And I shall want you all my days, 'til the very last one. Please, please say yes, darling."

He took her left hand and slid something on her fourth finger that flashed and glinted in the half-light of the carriage. "Your mother's ring," he explained. "The one you lost along with Hope's diamond, remember?"

"Of course I remember," Violet whispered. "I thought I'd lost it forever."

William shook his head. "I had a few diamonds—smaller than Hope's, I'm afraid—added to it. Thought it would make a lovely wedding ring for you."

Happiness, joy, love like she'd never known warmed her through and through and through again as she held the ring before her.

And I shall want you all my days.

So much happiness that she could not speak, and instead buried her face in William's chest and wept noisily.

"Yes," she managed at last, pressing her mouth to his. "Yes!"

He squeezed her tight against him, kissing her lips, her head, her shoulders and neck and belly. She laughed and cried and he laughed, too, laughed until they collapsed against each other in a breathless tumble.

When they had at last caught their breath, William sat up and pulled Violet up next to him. Only then did she realize the carriage was moving, and had been moving all along.

"Kidnapping me, are you?" she asked, tucking back a stray lock of hair from his forehead.

His eyes gleamed with mischief. "Our scandalous affair is deserving of an equally scandalous ending, don't you agree?"

Violet bit her lip, grinning. "I was never one to be married, much less in a proper ceremony at St. George's."

"Ah, Violet, we may not be proper, but we are properly matched," William said, pressing a kiss onto her cheek. "To Gretna Green, then!"

"First, to Hope's; I think you've kept him waiting long enough, don't you? We'll deposit the diamond so he might come home from your ball to a *very* pleasant surprise. It's early enough that the happy news might even make tomorrow's headlines. *Then* to Gretna Green; and, afterward, a lifetime of bliss, and perhaps"—she wagged her brows suggestively—"a bit of pleasure, too."

William's lips roamed down her cheek onto her throat. "A bit?" he murmured against her skin. "No, we'll have a lifetime of bliss *and* pleasure. Surely you haven't forgotten I enjoy pleasuring above all things."

Violet gasped as his teeth nicked her earlobe. "No," she panted, smiling. "How could I ever forget?"

Historical Note

The French Blue vanished from historical record following its theft in Paris from the Royal Warehouse in autumn 1792. It reappeared some two decades later in 1812 London, in association with French émigré and jeweler John Françillon; in his papers, Françillon described an enormous, and enormously unique, blue diamond that was at the time in possession of another jeweler (you may recognize his name from the last pages of this book!)—Daniel Eliason.

The diamond disappeared again, mysteriously, for another two decades. It is posited Eliason sold it to the Prince Regent, famous for his extravagance; that Prinny's long-suffering, eccentric wife, Princess Caroline, owned the stone for a time; that Napoleon lusted, rather ardently, after the French Blue as part of his scheme to restore the Crown Jewels of France.

The jewel resurfaced in 1839, when it was recorded as being part of Henry Philip Hope's impressive collection of gems. The Hope who appears in this book, however (and who, it just so happens, is the intrepid hero of the next!), is *Thomas* Hope, Henry's elder brother.

So why not Henry? For starters, I found Thomas a more compelling historical figure; as you'll learn in book two, he was an intriguing, well-traveled member of London society, and an author in his own right.

I'd like to imagine that, as heirs to the immense Hope & Company banking empire and expatriates marooned together in London, Thomas and his brother Henry worked together to build their collections—art, books, *jewels*. Perhaps they even comingled their possessions; in *Hope: Adventures of a Diamond*, Marian Fowler suggests that Thomas's wife wore the French Blue to a ball in 1824.

Thomas was well connected in royal circles and would likely be among the first to know when such a unique stone came up for sale. While no written records exist, it's possible Thomas was involved in the purchase, and perhaps at some point even the ownership, of the stone—after all, Thomas's sons would go on to inherit it.

The theft of the French Blue by a daring—and daringly handsome—earl, however, is entirely the product of my imagination (well, my agent's, too, but that's neither here nor there.)

It is true King Louis XVIII and his brother, the Comte d'Artois, lived in exile in London following the Revolution. They would return to France in 1814 during the Bourbon Restoration. That they frequented White's—and had a penchant for nubile women—is, as far as my research tells me, purely fiction.

For more on the Hope Diamond, check out Richard Kurin's excellent *Hope Diamond: The Legendary History of a Cursed Gem* and Ms. Fowler's *Hope: Adventures of a Diamond*, both of which proved indispensable to my research for this book.

Turn the page for a preview of the next book in
Jessica Peterson's Hope Diamond Trilogy

The Millionaire Rogue

Coming from Berkley Sensation in January 2015

Prologue

THE FRENCH BLUE:
A HISTORY OF THE WORLD'S GREATEST DIAMOND

Volume 1

By Thomas Hope

Across lands dry and rivers wide, through centuries of bloodshed and the downfall of great kingdoms, the French Blue's siren call has, like forbidden fruit, proven irresistible to royal and common man alike.

It all began in that mythic land across the great sea: India. Nearly three hundred years ago, a blue-gray diamond the size of a snuffbox was mined from the bowels of the earth. The great Shah Jahan, an emperor the likes of which the world had never seen, made an offering of the jewel to the goddess Sita; he commissioned a great statue of his goddess, the diamond glittering from the center of her forehead as her all-seeing third eye.

It was during this time that a Frenchman by the name of

Jean-Baptiste Tavernier traveled to the court of Shah Jahan. Being French, Tavernier was by nature dirty, wily, a born thief, and, of course, a libertine. Goading the Shah with false gifts and flattery, Tavernier gained his trust, and the love of his court.

It is impossible to know what, exactly, happened next; but it is widely assumed that, just as the Shah pressed Tavernier to his breast as brother and friend, Tavernier betrayed him. Some accounts even posit that the Frenchman slit his host's throat; others, that Tavernier poisoned him and half his glorious court.

The goddess Sita was witness to the violence, and when Tavernier pried the jewel from her forehead with a dagger thieved from Shah Jahan's still-warm body, Sita cursed the Frenchman, and all those who would come to own the diamond after him.

Sewn into the forearm of a slave girl, the diamond was brought to Europe, where Tavernier sold it to Louis XIV for the princely sum of two hundred thousand *livres*. The Sun King recut the jewel to improve its luster, and wore it slung about his royal breast on a blue ribbon. As part of the crown jewels of France, the diamond would be henceforth known as the French Blue.

Alas, the jewel that bewitched the Frenchman and the king with its beauty would also bring doom upon their heads; Sita would see her curse satisfied. Tavernier, living out his last days exiled in the wilds of Russia, was torn limb from limb by a pack of wild dogs, and buried in an unmarked grave.

Neither were the kings of France immune to Sita's curse. It was on a bitterly cold day in January when the last king, Louis XVI, lost his crown, his fortune, and his head before a crowd of angry Parisians.

And yet Sita's thirst for vengeance is not yet satisfied. The French Blue, along with most of the crown jewels, was thieved in late 1791 from the Garde Mueble, a royal warehouse on the outskirts of Paris. No one knows who stole it or where it might be hidden away; in a Bavarian duke's treasure chest, perhaps, or the dirty pocket of a serving wench in Calais. The diamond could be anywhere.

While the trail grows cold, Sita's thirst burns hot. The

French Blue is far too glorious a gem to remain hidden forever. Only when it is again brought into the light; only when it is claimed by whoever is brave, or perhaps daft, enough to claim it; only *then* will Sita's lust for blood be satisfied, and her curse at last fulfilled.

One

Resisting the impulse to leap from his chair, fists raised, with a great *Huzzah!*, Mr. Thomas Hope thrust the quill into its holder beside the inkwell. He gathered the pages scattered across his desk and settled in to read the history.

The gray afternoon light was fading, and he drew the oil lamp closer so that he might read his masterwork without having to squint. For a masterwork it was, surely; how could it not be, after all the years Hope dreamed of the diamond, researched its origins and the fantastic claims behind its curse?

But as his eyes traveled the length of each sentence, it became abundantly clear that Hope's history was no masterwork. Indeed, it was something else altogether.

Dear God, it was *awful*. Dramatic to the extreme, like an opera, but without the painted prima donna to compensate for its lack of narrative savvy. *The size of a snuffbox*. Whence had come *that* rubbish?

Tossing the pages onto the desk, Hope tugged a hand

through his tangle of errant curls. He was reading too much of that brooding, wicked man Lord Byron, and it was starting to take its toll on his pen.

He didn't have time for such frivolity besides. Hope had a goodly bit of work waiting for him back at the bank, and an even larger bit—a barrel, actually—of cognac to drink this evening.

Literary aspirations all but shot to hell, Hope was about to crumple the pages into his fists when a strange noise, sounding suspiciously like muffled laughter, broke out over his shoulder.

His blood rushed cold. Not one of his men, the butler or steward or a cashier from the bank. He was not expecting any visitors, and the hour for social calls had long passed.

Hope glanced across the gleaming expanse of his desk. His eyes landed on a silver letter opener, winking from its place beside the inkwell. Then there was the pistol in the top right drawer, of course, and the Ottoman *kinjon* in its box on the shelf; and his fists, he couldn't very well discount *those* weapons—

He swallowed, hard. Those days were behind him. The time for violence and subterfuge had passed. Hope was a respectable man of business now, like his father, and his father before him.

Respectable men of business did *not* greet visitors with a sock to the eye or a bejeweled dagger thrust at their throats.

At least not in England.

Removing his spectacles one ear at a time, he carefully placed them beside the pages on his desk. For a moment he closed his eyes, pulse racing.

Hope spun about in his chair. The breath left his body when his gaze fell on the hulking figure that loomed half a step behind him.

"Oh, God." Hope gaped. "Not you. Not now."

Smirking in that familiar way of his—one side of his mouth kicked up saucily, provokingly—Mr. Henry Beaton Lake reached past Hope and lifted the history from his desk.

" 'Forbidden fruit'?" Lake wheezed. "Oh, God, indeed! That's bad, old man, very bad indeed. I advise you to leave alliteration to the feebleminded, poets and the like. And the curse!"

Here Mr. Lake whooped with laughter, going so far as to bend over and slap his knee with great jollity. "Brilliant, I say, brilliant! Reading your little history I'd almost venture you believed it. Heavens, what a good laugh you've given me, and how in the gloom of these past months I've needed it!"

Hope snatched the pages from Mr. Lake's pawlike hand and stuffed them into a drawer. "It's a work in progress," he growled. "I wasn't expecting to share it, not yet. What in the hell are you doing here, and in daylight? Someone could have seen you."

Lake turned and leaned the backs of his enormous thighs against the desk. He crossed his ankles, then his arms, and looked down at Hope. "Anxious as always, old friend. You haven't changed a bit—well, except for those clothes. You look like a peacock."

Hope watched as Lake's penetrating gaze lingered a moment on Hope's crisply knotted cravat, his simple but exquisitely cut kerseymere waistcoat, and the onyx-studded watch peeking from his pocket.

"And you, Lake, look like a pirate out of *Robinson Crusoe*. What of it?" Hope took in Lake's broad shoulders, the corded muscles in his neck. He wore the black patch over his eye as some men wore a well-cut dinner jacket: with pride and a sort of impudent, knowing smile, confident any female in the vicinity would find him a little dangerous, wholly debonair, and far too tempting to resist.

"Thank you for the compliment." Lake's smile broadened. "And you needn't worry about being seen associating with the likes of me. I used the alley, and came in through the drawing room window."

"Of course you did. Still up to your old tricks, then?"

"King and country, Hope." Mr. Lake sighed, the laughter fading from his face. "Boney didn't stop when you and I parted ways. Someone needed to stay and fight."

Hope looked away, blinking back the sting of Lake's words. A beat of uncomfortable silence settled between them.

At last Lake pushed to his feet and made his way to the sideboard.

Hope watched the man limp across the room, his right leg remaining stiff at the knee. For a moment, sadness and regret pressed heavy into his chest. Too many memories, memories that Hope did not care to revisit.

Mr. Lake held up an etched decanter. "Mind if I pour us a finger or three?"

"I do indeed mind, very much," Hope replied.

But as he expected, Lake paid him no heed. His guest busied himself at the sideboard, and a moment later returned with a generous pour of brandy in each of two bulbous snifters.

"I've too many engagements this evening to begin with brandy, and at so early an hour," Hope said, but even as the words left his mouth he found himself reaching for the snifter Lake had set before him. Something about the man's stone-set gaze made Hope feel as if he'd need a drink, and then some, after Mr. Lake revealed what he'd come for.

Hope watched Lake lower himself with a wince into the high-backed chair on the other side of the desk. He took a long pull of brandy and, after he felt the familiar fire relax his limbs, asked, "How's the leg?"

Lake finished his own pull before replying. "Good, bad, it's all the same. Scares off the right people, attracts all the wrong ones. I rather prefer it that way."

Hope scoffed, grinning wistfully at his brandy. "And you. You haven't changed, either. Not a bit."

Again, charged silence stretched across the desk. Hope gulped his liquor. Lake did the same.

"The outcome of the war in Spain shall be decided in the coming weeks." Lake's voice was low. He did not meet Hope's gaze. "Wellington marches for Madrid. When the battle comes, it shall turn the tide of our fortunes there. For better or worse, I cannot say. That wastrel Frenchman Marmont, damn him, has the luck of the devil. The lives of thousands, tens of thousands, of British soldiers hang in the balance. My men—good men, smart men—they will die. Men like you."

"I was never one of your men, Lake. I was a refugee in need of aid and asylum. You gave me what I needed, and in return I gave you the same." Hope looked down at his glass. "I was never one of your men."

Lake's one pale eye snapped upward. "Yes, you were. You still are."

Hope tried not to flinch as he waited for what he knew came next.

"We need you," Lake said. "Your country needs you. To turn the tide in our favor."

Ah, so there it was. Hope knew he should run and hide, for those very words spelled the death of hundreds of England's finest men.

But with his earnest eye—the one eye the field surgeon managed to save, after the accident—Lake pinned Mr. Hope to his chair.

"I would help if I could." Hope splayed his palms on the desk. "But it's the same as it was ten years ago. I was born to count, Lake, not to spy. My father was banker to the great houses of Europe, and his father before that. After I fled the Continent, I dreamed of restoring Hope and Company to its former glory. And now I've done that. I'm a respectable man of business—"

"Man of business, yes, but the respectable bit is questionable."

Hope chewed the inside of his lip to keep from rolling his eyes. "Regardless, I've a lot at stake. People depend on me, lots of people. Clients, employees. I can't risk the livelihood of thousands of families—never mind my own, my brothers, bless their black souls—by engaging in your sort of intrigue. It's bad business. I've worked long and hard to build my reputation. I won't see that work undone, and millions lost along the way."

Hope sipped his brandy, then swirled it in its glass. "But you knew I would say all that. So, Lake. Tell me why you are here."

Lake drained his glass and smacked his lips. "I'm here because of that diamond you write so very *ardently* about."

"The French Blue?" Hope eyed his visitor. "Quite the coincidence, that you should appear out of the ether just as I am finishing my history."

"I thought together we might begin a new chapter of your lovely little history," Lake said. "And you know as well as I do it's no coincidence. You've heard the rumors, same as me. You're going to buy the diamond from her, aren't you?"

Hope looked down at his hands. Damn him, how did Lake

know everything? He assumed the existence of the French
Blue in England was a well-kept secret. The Princess of
Wales made sure of that, seeing as she likely came into possession of the diamond through illegal, perhaps even treason-
ous, means.

But Hope had assumed wrong. He should have known better, especially when it came to Henry Beaton Lake, privateer-
cum-spy extraordinaire. The man sniffed out secrets as a
bloodhound would a fox: instinctively, confidently, his every
sense alive with the hunt.

"Perhaps." Hope swept back a pair of errant curls with his
fingers. "I admit I am looking to expand my collection. And
diamonds—jewels—they are good investments. In the last
decade alone—"

"Psh!" Lake threw back his head. "You're buying it for a
woman, aren't you?"

This time Hope did not hold back rolling his eyes. "I avoid
attachments to women for the very same reasons I avoid the
likes of you. Much as I admire the female sex."

"You did a great deal more than admire said sex when we
were in France."

"That was almost ten years ago, and hardly signifies."

Lake leveled his gaze with Hope's. "The distractions of
women aside. You are attempting to buy the French Blue
from Princess Caroline. I'm asking you to buy it for me. For
England."

Hope choked on his brandy. Before he could protest, Lake
pushed onward.

"We've tried to buy the stone from the princess, but she is
holding it hostage from her husband, the prince, and, by
extension, our operation. Relations between them are worse
than ever. I'm shocked, frankly, that they haven't yet tried to
poison each other."

"Would that we were so lucky as to be delivered from that
nincompoop they have the nerve to call regent."

Lake waved away his words. "I'll pretend I didn't hear
that. If we manage to obtain the French Blue, we could very
well change the course of the war. For years now old Boney's
been on the hunt for the missing Crown Jewels of France. We
have reason to believe he'd trade valuable concessions for the

largest and most notorious of those jewels. In exchange for the French Blue, that blackhearted little toad might hand over prisoners, a Spanish city or two. We could very well save hundreds, if not thousands, of lives, and in a single stroke."

Hope let out a long, hot breath. "You're shameless, Lake. Absolutely shameless. I refuse to be cowed into thinking I'm a selfish bastard for wanting to protect the interests of those who depend on me for their livelihoods, and their fortunes. I care for the thousands of lives you'll save, I do, but—"

"But." Lake held up his finger. "You *are* a selfish bastard, then."

Hope grit his teeth, balling his palms into fists. "I've too much at stake," he repeated. "Princess Caroline has been a client of Hope and Company for years. She is more dangerous than she appears, and wily besides. I'm sunk if she uncovers the plot. I won't do it."

For a long moment Lake looked at Hope, his one pale eye unblinking. He shifted in his chair and winced, sucking in a breath as he slowly rested his weight on the bad leg.

The leg that had saved Hope from becoming a cripple, or a corpse, himself.

"Not even for me, old friend?" Lake's face was tensed with pain, and glowing red.

Hope shook his head. "Shameless." He laughed, a mirthless sound. "How do you know I'm worthy of the task? I am not the nimble shadow I once was. These days, a daring evening is a few too many fingers of liquor and a long, deep sleep—alone, sadly—in my bed."

All traces of pain disappeared from Lake's face as he grinned. "You are not as handsome as you once were, I'll give you that. But I wouldn't have asked you if I didn't believe you were a capable partner in crime. We shall work together, of course."

"Of course." Hope sighed in defeat. "So. What's the play?"

Lake leaned forward, resting his forearms on his knees, and rubbed his palms together with a look of fiendish glee. "Those engagements you have—cancel them. We make our move tonight."

"She is a rebel, a rule-breaker,
and above all, a romantic."
—Lisa Kleypas

FROM

SHERRY THOMAS

Author of *Private Arrangements*

Beguiling the Beauty

When the Duke of Lexington meets the mysterious
Baroness von Seidlitz-Hardenberg on a transatlantic
liner, he is fascinated. She's exactly what he's been
searching for—a beautiful woman who interests and
entices him. He falls hard and fast—and soon proposes
marriage.

And then she disappears without a trace . . .

For in reality, the "baroness" is Venetia Easterbrook—
a proper young widow who had her own vengeful reasons for instigating an affair with the duke. But the
plan has backfired. Venetia has fallen in love with the
man she despised—and there's no telling what might
happen when she is finally unmasked . . .

M1056T0212

Enter the rich world of
historical romance
with Berkley Books . . .

Madeline Hunter

Jennifer Ashley

Joanna Bourne

Lynn Kurland

Jodi Thomas

Anne Gracie

Love is timeless.

berkleyjoveauthors.com